Sarranda's Heart
A Love Story of Place

Also By Celia H. Miles

Novels
A Thyme For Love
Mattie's Girl: An Appalachian Childhood
ThymeTable Mill
Sarranda
Journey to Stenness

Short Stories
On a Slant: A Collection of Stories
Islands One and All: Stories and Otherwise

Anthologies Co-Edited with Nancy Dillingham
Christmas Presence
Clothes Lines
Women's Spaces Women's Places

College Textbook Co-Authored with Sally Lordeon
Writing Technical Reports: Basics and Beyond

Sarranda's Heart

A Love Story of Place

Celia H. Miles

Stone Ivy Press

Sarranda's Heart: A Love Story of Place

In this work of fiction, real counties and towns in North Carolina are named, but Greene's Valley is real only in imagination. Governor Zebulon Vance and the Garrett family are the only real persons; all others are imaginary. The existence of a Universalist Chapel in Haywood County I transferred to Jackson County; I am indebted to Phyllis Inman Barnett's *At the Foot of Cold Mountain: Sunburst and the Universalists at Inman's Chapel* for a sense of this group's beliefs.

Mill photos by the author.

Cover art by Carol Branton Morrow. Pastel.
www.carolmorrowstudio.com

Printed in the USA
Stone Ivy Press

ISBN 978-0-9834717-1-4

Order from
STONE IVY PRESS
828-277-6910
www.celiamiles.com

Dedicated to SPOOM—the Society for the Preservation of Old Mills—and all its members whose interest in and care for old mills helps to keep them from disappearing from the American landscape.

As Lila was fond of saying, I thank my lucky stars for the following:

My Monday morning critique group—Nancy Sales Cash, Cynthia Drew, Holly Simms, and Peg Steiner. Their encouraging words, smart suggestions, and corrections have been invaluable all along the way.

Joe Rhinehart who gave me a good sense of early Webster.

And especially, Louis for always believing I'd get it done and for his fact-checking and acute editing eyes.

A Musing

Ruth amid the alien corn. An unlikely visitor in a strange land. My bemused thoughts were overwrought, I told myself. I stood in a fine room with far greater comforts than the cabin I had once called home. I was no Biblical Ruth, no subject worthy of Keats' melancholy ode, and I was not on some distant shore but in my own homeland, tenuous though that connection had seemed less than two decades earlier. Two days' journey by rail from North Carolina's piedmont city to a Massachusetts town, from familiar to fairly novel surroundings, did not constitute sufficient grounds for self-pity. I was made of sterner stuff. Yes, I had given up an easeful and secure position, and I shook my head to banish any regrets about leaving comfort for uncertainty. Boys from the North had marched south to preserve the Union—or destroy it, depending on one's sympathies.

Now I, a southern mountain woman, was in the North preparing to return home as a soldier of a different sort, an emissary sent to serve my people, not to shoot the enemy. I could not turn back now.

PART ONE

CHAPTER ONE

My train journey north had been without incident. Adelaide Bell and I read or gazed out the window, speaking little. It was only my second time on a train and I was content to watch the landscape, marveling at our speed and the accompanying steam and noise. After many hours, soot, smoke, repetitive sound, and sleeplessness drained me of energy. If Adelaide was pensive I didn't notice. On the second day, however, she turned to me and revealed that I was to lodge not with her but in Mrs. Harrison's more commodious home.

"A telegram came just before we left Charlotte," she said. "I learned that my sister's daughter and her two children will be at my house, possibly for some time. Her husband is being treated at our General Hospital. She feels she must be near him and she could not leave their young children with anyone where they live."

Her face showed genuine contrition. "You will like Mariah, I'm sure. You'll have more privacy for study and less noise."

"I'm sorry for your niece's difficulties," I said. "How old are the children?"

"Four and six, Adam and Abby. My niece, Lucinda, thinks highly of John and Abigail Adams." She rubbed the bridge of her nose. "I suspect I will visit Mariah quite often. I am not accustomed to small children, nor, indeed, to having much company." She glanced quickly at me. "I didn't mean I didn't want you, Sarranda. You're a quiet woman."

I knew that Adelaide had lost her fiancé to the flu. He had served in the Massachusetts 3rd Regiment and suffered a chest wound in Sheridan's Shenandoah

Valley campaign. Posted to Fort Leavenworth, he was assigned a desk job fit, she said, "for a soldier with damaged lungs." Soon, he was discharged for medical reasons. I sensed she blamed the military for sending him home in a weakened condition. She had not married following his death and she still wore mourning black.

I would have felt more at home with her than a new acquaintance, but I assured her I understood.

"You'll serve a higher cause," Miss Adelaide Bell had told me some weeks earlier. And so I believed. Now I surveyed the room in Mariah Harrison's home on Andrews Street in Bramford, Massachusetts. It was finely detailed, every cushion placed with an eye for symmetry, each picture hung and the heavy curtains swept back at just the right level, each crocheted doily centered by an appropriately chosen vase, box, or ornament. My hostess clearly liked everything neatly displayed. In a small frame, even the delicate woven heart, of gray-white hair probably belonging to Mariah's dead mother, was dust free. Glancing upward, I wondered if the dust particles, had there been any along the window sills, were lined up precisely. The room looked so ordered, so arranged that I hesitated to move my reticule from where Mariah had set it on the high, four-poster bed.

Stepping into the glimmer of weak light filtering through the lace curtains, I was overcome with a sense of resentment, surely partly the result of travel weariness. Sweeping the bag to the floor I fell upon the bed in a most unarranged posture. It seemed my life was being directed and arranged and I was merely a pawn in it. For several moments as if I'd been flung there by some careless arm, I lay like a girl abandoned by a lover, distraught by loss.

Breathe, I told myself, breathe. Remember why you are here. I loosened my buttons, closed my eyes, and let my common sense take over. "I am the master of my fate. I am the captain of my soul." That's what Mrs. Whitney's brother quoted to me one day. Naturally I went straight to the small room that served as the library and looked up the poem. The sentiment had struck me as noble and still did even though right now I did not feel very much in control. "I thank whatever powers there be for my unconquerable soul," I muttered, invoking Henley's "Invictus." Put out a bit with myself and breathing more easily, I reached over the side of the bed to pick up my bag and groaned. My stiff joints reminded me I was no young girl who had been flung by fate anywhere. My head reminded me that, though my present situation had been arranged, I had agreed to it—with a compliance I could not deny.

I sat upright and said to the room, "I am in the right place."

I splashed tepid water on my face from the basin a young girl brought to the room. "I'm Lila," she said, with a decidedly Irish lilt. "Miss Mariah says can you join her in half hour, please." We smiled as tentative friends might do, and she bobbed a curtsey as she closed the door.

When Mariah had escorted me upstairs she softly and honestly said, "You must be tired." Pushing my hair back, I agreed with her assessment. My gray eyes were dull, no sign of the sparkle that had been rekindled during my years as companion and friend to Alice Whitney in Charlotte. I soothed the tiny lines at the corners unconsciously. At least, I smiled into the mirror, my hair is mostly black and I have all my teeth.

Having been persuaded by Adelaide that I could do some good and knowing I needed a purpose for my remaining years, I was here to learn how to minister to the needy and uneducated in my native mountains. Now the ladies' circle waited downstairs.

"Ah, Sarranda, dear, do come in," Mariah said. I hesitated in the doorway, taking in the comfort of the drawing room, the aroma of ginger cookies and black tea. Three other ladies looked at me with curiosity and courtesy. Mariah at once came to take my arm. "You are most welcome. I've told our committee a bit about you. I hope you had a rest after your long journey. Adelaide will be here shortly." She guided me to a chair that completed the circle.

"Adelaide needs her rest," one of the women said. "And she must see to her home after her absence in the South." The others appraised me openly and introduced themselves.

Hertha Settler, who had spoken, looked to be the eldest member of the circle. Her white hair was coiled neatly at her nape and her silk dress appeared slightly worn. Her sharp eyes peered over tiny spectacles and her hands clutched a sheaf of papers. "We're delighted to have someone of your," she paused as if wanting to choose precisely the right word to describe me, an outsider, "your background and knowledge of the environs we seek to serve."

Smoothing my somewhat rumpled travel dress, I felt like an awkward schoolgirl. I remembered being interrogated in our log school house by the stern circuit rider preacher for whose visit the schoolmaster had required us to learn the books of the Bible and pertinent other details that might be asked of us. I had stammered after the first ten books, lost my way entirely after Samuel, and sat down in disgrace. I had memorized all the books in the Old Testament but in the glare of Preacher Hawkton, I faltered like a sinner called to account. It had been shameful then, but recalling now the schoolmaster's wink brought a small smile to my lips. Let Hertha assume it meant my acceptance of her acceptance of me. I murmured, "Thank you. I'm sure I have much to learn."

Georgina Allison, stout and assertive, reached for a cup of tea that Mariah was pouring. She wore a dress of calico, beautifully stitched, with a row of buttons straining against her bosom. Something in her demeanor told me that she and Miss Settler would be at loggerheads, but their differences would be quietly ladylike. "And you'll have much to teach us. We want to help, to send women to your part of the country, but we think we must proceed with some caution."

"The land lies waste," Hertha said. "Caution must go hand in hand with haste."

I nodded and said nothing. Did they mean caution because of the unsettled state of the population so soon after this "Reconstruction" time, the possibility of violence against more outsiders invading, however benevolent their purpose? Or did she imply a cautionary approach in terms of the kind of and amount of assistance provided?

"Women are best suited for the work we intend to do." Laura Abbot offered her hand in a spontaneous gesture. "Men incline toward converting souls and starting churches." I set my cup of tea aside and we exchanged handshakes. Her fingers were smooth, her nails well-burnished, but her grip was strong. A determined woman. I liked her immediately. "Our goal should be instructing children, opening schools, preparing the young."

"Please, more tea? Try these cakes." Mariah passed a plate of delicate shortbreads around. I took two and saw her smile with approval. "We are a small group," she said, "part of a larger circle of women. And two ladies could not be here this afternoon. You will meet them another time. Meanwhile, we want so much to help—"

Hertha said, "We have much to decide."

"Not necessarily this afternoon, Hertha," Georgina said. "All in good time."

I was already noting a certain caution in the dialogue. These ladies were surely more kindhearted than some of the magazine writers who pointed out the dire need for education and improvement in a remote and lonesome land, what one writer called, "a strange land of peculiar people." They were not likely to venture the word "defeated" in reference to the South or use words such as "benighted, poverty, ignorance, or debased" about the region they intended to uplift. They were being careful of their guest's sensibilities. I would be the same toward theirs.

"I feel somewhat a pilgrim," I confessed. "Miss Bell told the literary club and the church's women's group in Charlotte of what you hope to accomplish, but exactly how women are to affect any major change, after such devastation, I cannot imagine."

"Women carry the lamp of culture," stated Hertha. "We can light the way with education, education offered in a spiritual context. Already we have sent three young women to Kentucky and—"

"And none have remained. Two returned here before the year was out," interrupted Laura. She turned to me. "One returned to care for her ailing parents. Another, to our surprise, married a farmer down there, and they set out for Texas. Apparently the third was of such delicate sensibilities that she could not endure the harshness of the living conditions."

Hertha almost snorted. "Melanie Foster was a mistake. I told you so. She is as strong as a young filly. Her heart was not in the work and she never so much as washed a dish while there. Heavens, she lived in a boarding house the entire time. She went to escape the embarrassment of a failed engagement and returned a martyr." She set her cup down with authority.

Mariah opened her mouth to intervene but I said, "Neither poor health nor an engagement will impede me, and certainly not youth." With a smile I indicated my healthy body, stiff joints aside. "The lamp of culture, however, is somewhat metaphorical." I knew I was treading on dangerous ground, but my use of what my sons would call "hi-falutin'" language was deliberate.

Hertha didn't immediately find words to respond and silence hung in the air.

"Sarranda," said Laura, "we know relatively little about the, shall I say, the nature of your people." She waved an apologetic hand. "And what we know is quite naturally brought to us by our missionaries in the field and by writers who have ventured into the southern mountains."

"Ah yes, *Harper's* and *Scribner's* and the like have published several articles." Although I had read the magazines, I was unprepared to comment further on their descriptions.

"We hope you can enlighten us and help us forge a means to aid, to elevate, if you will, the people whom the war damaged," Georgina said.

"The spiritual condition—" Hertha said. "We cannot forget the church's moral obligation to offer more than food and raiment."

"The level of need is extreme," Georgina said. "Children are hungry."

"Education, it seems to me, to us, is all-important," said Mariah. "We must center our efforts on the poor children."

"You know," I inserted, "my own education did not extend very far. Schooling was not always available outside towns or large settlements. I am not certified to teach."

"We know you married very young," Hertha said.

Ah, yes, I thought, and that was education in itself. Before I could answer, Laura said, "Certainly you are both well-read and articulate, Sarranda."

My eyes gleamed. "I can even do sums." I pretended to count on my fingers and was rewarded with a titter of laughter.

Laura mimicked my actions. "As can I." She picked up another cookie and held up her fingers. "Three is my limit.

Hertha looked aside, refusing to enter into any frivolity. For the next few minutes the conversation swirled around me: the need for schools, doctors, teachers, ministers, community leadership. The women of the North, I gathered, were bound and determined to create a new world, a world which they would assist in birthing, a world they, for the most part, could not join or participate in but to which they could be instrumental in sending select, chosen bearers of good will, financial assistance, and "culture." They kept coming back to that word.

The conversation reminded me of Grandda's hens clucking as they came running for the kernels of corn he threw out. My head began to swim and their words blurred. I had eaten little on the train, and after Adelaide mentioned a brother—a brother I dared not question her about for fear of arousing her suspicions—of what I wasn't sure—I ate even less. I sipped more tea and nibbled another shortbread.

Into the maelstrom of female voices, stepped Adelaide Bell. Her firm, "Good afternoon, ladies," immediately lifted my spirits. I sat straighter. She drew up a chair and placed her gloved hand on my arm.

"I hope you are faring well among these lionesses, Sarranda. They can be fierce at times." She smiled at each in turn. "All in a good cause, but let's not overwhelm our guest on her first day here." At once Mariah asked about Adelaide's journey and how she found her house and her niece upon her return. The discussion turned to details of home and hearth.

In only a few minutes, Adelaide stood and said, "I must excuse myself, ladies. Duties at home...forgive me for arriving late and for rushing away."

The conversation did not return to the Circle's mission. The women spoke of domestic problems close at hand, difficulties with their gardener or their housekeeper, and then of immigration in general. About this topic I could contribute nothing, so I listened. From their rapid speech, I caught snatches of commentary about the onslaught of those less desirable, Irish working girls filling the streets with their healthy cheeks and cheeky attitudes, about the apparent need for factory girls, railroad workers, street cleaners, and about the difficulties of working with these newcomers.

Hertha Settler feared that the country was being overrun by what she called the sheer physicality of numbers. "We can hardly walk in our own streets without being bumped into," she lamented. "And our town has nothing like the hordes in Boston." Alternately described as hard workers and criminal, these newcomers apparently brought no "breeding" or culture to their new country, only need and, one woman lowered her voice, disease.

I excused myself, went to the kitchen, dampened a cloth in cool water, and held it to my forehead. Even though the women were not discussing my part of the country or me, a surge of anger flushed my face. Their attitudes seemed remarkably at odds with their mission work. *I must stop thinking of it as "their" work. It must now be my work because I am committed to it. I cannot announce that I'm returning to the comfort of Mrs. Whitney's home. She would take me in, comfort me, assist me however she could if I were in need, but I'm not sure she would countenance what she would see as a perverse attitude.*

To stay out of sight in the kitchen would be cowardly or seem insulting. I returned to sit primly with cooled cheeks. In time, with ladylike handshakes, Mariah ushered the women out, promising "an entire day tomorrow after Sarranda has rested."

On my first night in the New England familiar to me through the works of Hawthorne and Melville and Thoreau and Emerson, a full moon brightened the sky. The grandfather clock downstairs chimed the two o'clock hour. From the window seat, I gazed out on the neat street, with wide lawns, some stone walls, a white picket fence farther down on the corner. The same moon rose over my mountains; yet here it seemed too bright, a sharp orb piercing the firmament. I knew of Maria Mitchell's studies in astronomy and could, in a limited manner, look upon the moon scientifically. Tonight, however, its cold remove reflected my own sensibilities. Unlike my earlier glaze of anger at the ladies' conversation, I now felt as distant from them as the moon from the earth. This distance, I told myself, would have to be breached if I were to succeed.

Perhaps I should consider this evening as part of my training—in learning to listen, to absorb the attitudes of the women's group, to keep quiet. Knowing little of the immigrant situation I had been loathe to comment. Something in the women's tone was disparaging, something superior in the inflection upon certain words such as "breeding" and "culture."

Did they feel the same about the very people they were sending mission workers to?

Thus upon retiring I had tossed about like a child with the croup, my head a muddle of *shoulds* and *whys* and *wherefores* until I left my bed and sat at the window. I thought of Mrs. Whitney who believed in me, who believed in these women's work, who told me I needed a challenge. She reminded me that I was too young to settle into comfortable knitting and sewing routines.

"Young?" My thimble had poised above the shift I was hemming.

"Compared to me," she returned equably. "Admit it, Sarranda, you pace through this house, read late into the night, have become bored with our outings. You miss your mountains."

"I can't go back there." I conjured up lonesome widowhood in my—now my son's—cabin. He would have to turn out the family he'd rented it to. Family honor would demand he do so but the honor would be grudging. My beloved grandda's mill was in the hands of outsiders. Yankees had taken it over for debts my relative couldn't pay. "I can't return to Greene's Valley," I said. "My cousins wouldn't take me in, not now. They'd find me citified, uppity. My soft hands and neat dress would offend."

Before I became too self-pitying, she said, "You'll find your place. It isn't here now. It may or may not be with Adelaide's work."

She twirled her tiny glasses, a habit that had broken more than one pair. "You may join the westward trek. Many are heading for the western plains, my banker tells me. It's new territory and requires women of endurance."

"And youth."

"Ah, Sarranda, living with me has made you old beyond your years."

"In truth, Alice, I feel younger than when I left the Valley five years ago. I was worn down to a nubbin then." I glanced at my smooth hands. "Still, I'll not see forty again."

"And I'll not see sixty-five," she returned. We had sat silent, contemplating our futures.

It was too soon to have doubts about my training to return to the mountains to help others, especially women. How could I doubt the importance and the necessity of giving, somehow, women a firmer grasp of their lives? How could I wonder about the need that existed after the destruction of the war? I'd seen it, suffered it, survived it only (or so I believed) by leaving. I was, I knew, one of the lucky women. I could read and write sufficiently to gain a place in the home of a benevolent lady of some means. I had traded my scrub board for a side board, my brooms for books. People back in Greene's Valley would think I had every reason—except the desertion of my sons—to live in gratitude. I fell asleep telling myself I could be useful. But my last waking moments had nothing to do with being useful. I remembered my lavender-scented night with the stranger.

The days that followed gave me little opportunity to reflect. Life ran at a fast pace around me. I seemed too often to be standing still while people bustled by or I lagged a step or two behind. My waking hours were filled with visits to tenement houses, to elegant homes, to shops and churches, meetings, teas, and luncheons. It was late summer and Miss Bell wanted me prepared to return to North Carolina's mountains before the winter set in. The leisurely pace of Charlotte was no more; we hurried in ladylike steps or rushed in carriages through the streets, always on time though we might be slightly breathless. I would soon be on my way south, dressed in serviceable woolens and muslins, with a trunk of books and the backing of Miss Bell's circle, backed in turn by other churches and social clubs.

Hardly had my mind fixed on one thing before another was introduced and trotted by. One presentation by a Reverend John Stokes left me reeling. He told of his travels through central Kentucky: the low income of the people, the skimpy school days, the number of churches, elections held, elections disrupted. He told of one college forced to close because the state outlawed its teaching colored and white students within so many feet of each other. Although he had been in the state less than a month, his conclusion was clear. Help was desperately needed. His demeanor and gestures demanded action, even violent action if necessary, to bring Kentucky into line "with truly Christian principles." His facts rolled on, indisputable. I winced but could not refute his descriptions—women barefoot in the frost and snow of November, hungry children in threadbare clothing, men lying in doorways, churches unable to meet the needs of their own congregations, understandably unwilling to send aid beyond their church's sway.

Unemployed men sleeping in doorways—I saw that in Bramford, as well. The day after Reverend Stokes' lecture, Adelaide came for me unexpectedly, and we ventured some distance beyond Mariah's neat neighborhood. Rather quickly well-kept houses with picket fences were replaced by small hovels, streets by dirt paths. Dogs and cats, even a goat, lurked or scurried from the sound of the horse's hooves. Ragged boys ran behind trees and shacks.

"Where are we going?" I asked as the buggy skirted a clump of children.

"My brother's school." She looked grim. "You see that our town is not perfect, Sarranda. Most of the ladies refuse to come down this way. I want you to see what we face here, as well."

Her brother's school? The brother she had mentioned on the train? Possibly my lavender-night man? I brushed my hair from my face. My chest tightened and I drew a deep breath. She pulled on the reins before a one-story wooden building next to a charred carcass of a larger structure. In this warehouse area, other buildings were scattered beyond, some upright and others falling into disrepair. This shack did not appear to be a school.

No one appeared as Adelaide picked her way through debris to the door. "Let's see if he's in." She rattled the knob. A worried frown marred her face. "I fear he's lost his way again."

From around the corner, a boy appeared, long-haired and thin. The left side of his face was swollen and his closed eye was black. His other eye was alert and, aside from the discoloration, his face was clean. "He's in the back, Miss."

"Sick?"

"Yes'm." He stared at us and then at his feet, rubbed one foot against his shin. "He said we're to come back after the whistle blows."

"Noon," Adelaide translated. "The rope-making factory further down the street."

She opened a bag. "Please give him this sweater." To me she said, "My niece's husband's. He will never wear it again." She thrust it in the boy's hands. "And you'll find some cookies for you and your sisters." She handed him a coin. "Will you bring him coffee before the children come for lessons?"

The boy nodded. "I saved him a piece of bread from Mr. Stanton's bakery," he said. "But he ain't gonna eat it."

"Coffee, plenty of it," she said, "and you eat the bread." She explained, "Mr. Stanton gives his week-old loaves to Carly for the children. Joey collects." She looked at his face, touched her own eye. "Your father?"

He shuffled his bare feet. "Don't hurt much now. Wisht he was like Mr. Carlyle, just sleep it off."

"Drink affects men differently," she said. "You would let me know if—if Carly changes?"

The boy looked uncertain. "Like a lamb, he is, when he wakes up."

"But if ever he becomes violent, you'd let me know?"

"I'd think on it, Miss. But he's awful good to us."

"We'll be going, Joey. Come, Sarranda. He would not want to be seen now."

"Snoring, he is," Joey suddenly confided. "Sound asleep, but he's shouting before."

"And your pa? Your sisters?"

"Pa set out toward the railroad around sun-up. He'll not be back 'fore dark. I'll round us up for Mr. Carlyle after the whistle blows."

As we drove away, Joey settled himself into the sunlight at the side of the building. Adelaide said, "No one can keep these children in regular school. Truant officers have given up. At least they come for Carly's lessons."

"My brother is named Joe," I said. "He has a school of sorts in the tidewater of Virginia. He fought for the North."

"Oh." She gripped the reins. "Carly didn't fight. He wanted to. He tried to sign up when he turned eighteen, but his asthma's bad and his eyesight, too."

So this brother had not been wounded while in the South. He was not *my* brother.

"Carly ran away, determined to do what he could. He saw the awful battle at Gettysburg...helped with the wounded, until one of our friends, a Colonel Morris, recognized him. Thank goodness he wasn't shot, but he'd had a fit of some kind or maybe a really bad asthma attack. Colonel Morris sent him home, told him he had to help with the wagons of wounded being returned. He never got over the slaughter he saw and has nightmares even now. That's when he takes to the bottle." She sighed. "Usually he's all right for a few weeks afterwards. He reads to the children, teaches them to write."

I turned toward Adelaide, wishing to say something that would help but her face had closed down. She shook her head slightly as if to warn me from any comment that might smack of pity. I touched her arm lightly but did not let my fingers linger. Her hands clenched the reins tightly and she concentrated on getting the buggy through a smelly, rough street. Then it seemed she willed her hands to relax, her shoulders to ease. I ventured a small, "All families have their troubles."

Useless words but they broke the silence. "Yes," she said, adding with a touch of bitterness, "Carly's troubles are just so public. I am glad that our mother didn't live to see it. She cared a great deal about her neighbors' opinions."

"Mothers do."

"I try not to but I, too, care. I'm sure the circle will know of Carly's lapse and find comforting words for me." At that moment I felt close to Adelaide. She was not a complete paragon of virtue. She was capable of a bit of bitterness, a nip of irony.

"And do none of them have their own family troubles?" I said. "If not, then blessed are they, indeed. Or blind."

Adelaide glanced at me and a small smile erased some of her grimness. "Blind, indeed. The families of most of the ladies you've met are beyond reproach. I mean that quite literally. They are decent, respectable, civic minded. And if they have problems...well, their troubles have sometimes been," she hesitated, "sent out West to explore new lands or sent away for help."

"Sent away where?"

Adelaide directed our horse into a quiet residential street and admired the late-blooming flowers before answering. "Well, sent to the March-Bach Institution, for example. It's a home for those whose behavior or, uh, attitude might not, indeed, does not always suit their families."

I craned my neck to admire the dahlias of purple and gold.

"A word, Sarranda. It's best to let your new friends tell you what they want you to know about their family situations. We Yankees are notoriously close-mouthed."

"Of course," I said. "I will ask nothing of their families." I doubted I would ever consider asking personal questions of them. They, however, apparently did not have the same reservation about questioning me: they now knew I had two brothers, one having served the Union, the other wielding his sword for the South; both now living outside our mountains and both married. I did not see the need to enlighten them about Joe's highly unusual living conditions. They knew my baby boy had died very young and the two others were grown, that Larsen had left to seek his fortune as had my father decades before, that Fredrick farmed successfully considerable mountain acreage. I let them assume his new family had blood ties. They did not need to know that Fredrick had chosen to become their "adopted" son, expecting to inherit more property than my pitiful acreage.

I pointed to late roses on a perfect lawn.

The next day Mariah had errands to do, Adelaide was keeping her niece's children, and the various committees weren't meeting. As I sat down to my boiled egg and brown bread, Mariah gave the young girl who served my breakfast instructions about the laundry and adjusted her hat pins.

"The day is cool, Sarranda. You may like a walk or you might review the materials and commentaries we've been studying. The day is yours."

With a smile she was gone. I felt at loose ends and at the same time quite free. Since leaving Charlotte I had not been alone very much except at night. Then I fell into an exhausted sleep or lay awake pondering my situation, anticipating leaving Bramford and returning to my mountains, dreading what I might face and welcoming it as a challenge. If anyone ever was of a "mixed mind," I was.

"Lila, where are you from?" I asked the girl who removed my plate and refilled my tea cup with a careful awkwardness. It was the second time I'd seen her. Her reddish-brown hair was neatly capped though a tendril had escaped, and her hazel eyes sparkled. Freckles sprinkled her fair skin. She was the picture of health. "Are you new to Mrs. Harrison's household?"

"Oh, yes, Miss. I've not been here two months, have I? My aunt worked here for a long time and took sick with the pleurisy, didn't she? She was training me, but I went home to look after her right after you came. Then there was her wake and service."

I murmured my sympathies. Her aunt had lived to be sixty-eight and was, so Lila said, "ready to leave this world o' trouble."

She eyed the room, looking for something to do. "This is from Miss Mariah's grandfather's China trip," she said. She moved a large vase very slightly before answering my question. "We're from down the shore, a long day's buggy ride from here. My mam and da's from across the water. Galway born they was, but I was born in Flecton, on the ocean."

"You can't get home often, if your family's so far away. Are you lonely, then?"

"That I am, sometimes, but Miss Mariah, she lets me take two evenings each week to go to the Women's Institute. I have mates there. We're learning about history and doing figures and learning our tables."

"Then you don't expect to do this sort of work all your life?"

Lila drew back a bit. When she spoke again, her tone was guarded. "It's fortunate I am to have this good house and a good mistress."

"I didn't mean to pry, Lila. I'm simply curious." I changed the subject. "I'm from North Carolina. Have you studied anything of its history?"

"It was one of them rebel states that caused all the war and troubles." She grinned. "You have a nice slow voice, don't you?"

"You mean I have a southern drawl," I said with a smile. She almost giggled.

"Yes, Miss. We're not studying much about the big war. More the beginning of the country. George Washington and Thomas Jefferson. The Constitution."

I nodded and sipped my tea. She went on, "Is it always warm down where you lived? Would I like your state, do you think?"

"Where I lived, it can get very cold," I answered the first and easiest question and thought before answering the second. "Like my state? Maybe not now, Lila. Times are bad there. Too many of our men were killed in the war and now too many...too many men have come down from the North to buy up or somehow take property, one way or another. To speculate."

"Specu, speculate?"

"When a country is defeated and thus weakened, certain greedy people tend to make the most of that situation," I said. "They may get rich but others are left in poverty, without the means to help themselves. So it has always been, I suppose." I repeated, "Times are bad in my mountains and in most of the South."

"Did you have slaves, Miss?"

"Not at all. The mountains are not suited to large farms or plantations, though a few families did have a few slaves. Even my grandfather. Well, a colored man, Rankin, but he was like family. He wasn't a slave, at all."

Her eyes grew wide. "Like family? Molly Ann, my friend at the Institute, told me about a book her mistress was reading. Uncle Somebody's House, wasn't it? She said the coloreds was treated like animals and hunted down in the snow and whipped, that's what her mistress said."

"*Uncle Tom's Cabin*," I supplied. I had not read Harriet Beecher Stowe's novel. Some of Mrs. Whitney's friends had dismissed it as radical and she had been disinclined to have me read it to her. Thus I could not be sure of its portrayal of slavery, only sure of my attitude toward Rankin. Until I journeyed to Charlotte I had not seen another person of color. So far, I had seen very few in Bramford.

Lila nodded. "That's it, and they was treated awful."

I could see that she didn't believe my statement about Rankin. Perhaps, in time, I could tell her that Rankin was present at the birth of my second son and that he had gone to live with my brother in his wife's community. He had sensed it was time to leave, as I had a few years later.

Lila curtsied. "The parlor needs a dusting," she said. "Miss Mariah don't like no dust around here." She wielded the duster in a warlike manner. Later as I stitched serviceable flannel undergarments, I pondered our exchange. *They was treated awful.* Most surely, though I had no experience of it. But war treated everybody awful. Many men and boys had not returned from the battlefields, leaving families bereft. Some returned, damaged in body and soul.

It was time for some who had, of necessity, forsaken their devastated coves and valleys to return. I was one of those. I could do something. I was glad I'd spoken to Lila. I could see my way more clearly now.

CHAPTER TWO

For days discussions and disagreements about the church's role in the southern mountains and about my part in the ladies' endeavor to assist the people eddied, stalled, and flowed around me. I realized that in her enthusiasm Adelaide had appeared certain of the policies and procedures of the group when away from it. Up close, however, differences of opinion were many.

In the evenings, while sewing or reading reports of mission workers, I thought of exactly how I might be of most help. I was to do *something*, yet an indefinite quality pervaded many of the meetings, a rambling indicating either a lack of understanding of the area to be served or an uncertainty about expectations—or both. I heard a great many words without a corresponding show of power. I was reminded of a waterwheel turning without sufficient water force to keep the mill stones grinding, its potential lost at the source. A great deal of water flowed through the sluice and raceway, but without a certain amount of directed force behind it, nothing happened. Certainly I didn't have all the information others had and none of their resources. But more and more I grew impatient to move forward. I could not sit and listen or sit and sew much longer, even in these comfortable surroundings. When I left, I had to have a direction.

At today's meeting, several circles that met each month for edification and refreshments came together. Circles seemed an apt term; there was much circling back to points already made, not much forward movement. Mariah's circle was in charge and

Hertha and Laura, among others, spoke of their endeavors and expectations, about possibilities and, naturally, impossibilities. My head was spinning like a toy top. I squirmed in my hard chair. Rather than simmer like a covered pot about to boil over on a hot cook stove, I resolved to speak. During a moment of silence, I clutched the back of the chair before me and rose.

"Ladies, may I speak?" My legs felt like melted butter but I straightened my back and hoped my voice was stronger than my legs. I cleared my throat. They turned as one toward me and politely inclined their heads. I had been introduced earlier and thanked them for what they were doing. I was committed now to speaking, whether or not my legs and voice cooperated.

"Ladies, it appears that other societies are sending teachers and are having some success in remote communities. Dedicated men and women have worked long and hard to see that schools are started. You have named some of them today. Your own circles have sent young women as school mistresses. The church is doing much, as all of you know." Heads nodded in agreement.

I recounted three or four stories that their lecturers had talked of. I started with the founding of Scotia Seminary for Negro girls in Cabarrus County. Begun in 1870 or thereabouts through the Presbyterian Church, it was close to Charlotte, but I had never heard of it until Adelaide Bell told us of the tireless work of the Reverend Luke Dorland. From other ministers and educators we had learned of the hardships facing the Bear Ridge Mission in Kentucky, of the settlement school in southwest Virginia, and of two small schools for freedmen in northern Alabama, floundering but determined to continue, according to a cousin of a worker there. The women listened, undoubtedly wondering what I could offer beyond the churches' efforts.

"I believe in education, of course, and in the children who ultimately will lead their communities. Perhaps, though, we have forgotten the families.

Especially the women. The women themselves need some means of feeding those children, of putting shoes on their feet, of keeping them warm." My voice broke. I remembered my own little boy, whose hand-me-down shoes I'd given to a returning soldier when he told me he hoped to find his own child alive whereas little Joe, he said, "for sure was dying." The soldier had given me a piece of dried apple to moisten in warm water so that my Joe might not die hungry. In spite of the years and my resolve, the tears in my eyes must have shown in the dim light of the church hall. I saw Mariah dab at her eyes and Hertha avert hers, perhaps in embarrassment.

"Please understand—some families are too proud to send their children to school, if there is a school, if their clothes are in rags and their feet are bare and their stomachs rumble with hunger. Those who have returned from the South would surely bear testimony to that pride." I squared my shoulders. "When I go to North Carolina, let me help the mothers help their families. Many men were lost or incapacitated, in body or spirit. It's difficult for women to farm as they should to produce more than food for their own use if, indeed, they have sufficient acreage to farm. Agriculture is unpredictable. They need an income that is not based on land."

A slight buzz broke out among my listeners. Most of these women did not work and had never worked outside their homes. Even if they had hired help, they considered their families, their church, and community responsibilities their work. Their fathers and husbands were merchants, bankers, educators, clergymen. Some, though, had daughters who, with or without parental approval, went for teacher education. Teaching was a respectable occupation, if one had to or chose to work outside the home. Other work was less acceptable. In fact, one woman had, with pride, told me she had forbidden her youngest daughter from even thinking of studying medicine or becoming a nurse. Medicine, she declared, was a profession "unfit for young ladies." Her daughter had thought to follow Clara Barton's lead. The woman had ended with: "It was a rebellious phase she was going through. Now she's married and cries at the sight of blood if a child cuts its finger." She stared at me with narrowed eyes and distaste.

For several moments I waited in the silence. "I have not thought of exactly how my work might be accomplished," I said. Actually I suspected they would want to work through the details of finance, territory, and whatever else necessary. I would not wish to usurp that authority.

"But I can sew, weave, make baskets, do needlepoint—work that most women either know or have a natural talent for."

I thought of the bed clothing under which my grandda slept, the intricate design and the colors that resulted from walnut hulls or onion peels. My mother, however, had not taught me more than to sew rough. The quilts I made were for warmth, not beauty. And I had learned to weave not at our fireside but under the tutelage of a woman paid to teach me. But I was speaking for women who needed help and who could certainly learn, as I had, given the time and materials.

"Many would not consider what they do, and what their mothers and grandmothers did, a talent. It was a necessity. Beauty was simply a by-product of a skill learned at the fireside, at their mother's knee."

My weak trembles over, I took a deep breath and continued. "For some years, they have been—they have been without the means to weave, to sew..." I didn't want to say the sheep had been killed, the looms burned for firewood, the plants and herbs used for making dyes trampled, overgrown, neglected.

"With direction, wouldn't fine basketry, fine needlework, expert weaving find a market?" I looked directly at the woman who had forbidden her daughter to study medicine. "Would you purchase a handmade coverlet if you knew you were helping to feed a family?"

When she nodded as did a few others, I went on. "Especially here in your area where already those womanly arts, I'm told, are being lost, I believe there is a market." I could only hope that my generalization hit home and, for some, at any rate, it did.

"My Amanda loves fine stitchery," exclaimed a woman, "but she can't sew a stitch, in spite of my attempts to teach her!"

"I cherish the coverlets my grandmother left me," another said. "But I simply can't make one. And who has the time? I'd prefer to purchase them."

"And now we're seeing so much that is not handmade, but put together in a factory, useable but hardly something we'd want to leave to our children and grandchildren," decreed a woman. For a few moments, the women spoke to each other, decrying the quality of some manufactured goods, muttering about the nature of the factory workers, the horrors they'd heard of the garment district in New York City.

Above their modulated voices, a young woman, began to recite in a loud voice: "Stitch! Stitch! Stitch! In poverty, hunger, and dirt, / And still with a voice of dolorous pitch / She sang the 'Song of the Shirt.' Work! Work!—"

"Oh come, Susanna," Hertha interrupted.

The young woman uttered a final defiant, "Stitch!"

Some listeners muttered to each other, and the rumble grew, a litany of irritation: "We have to have clothes to wear! That poem's about England's sewing girls, not here. She's always disrupting ...Spoiled she is. What is the point, Susanna?" Some women looked sympathetic or uncomfortable, and others obviously annoyed.

Realizing that I had not sat down or relinquished the floor, Hertha raised her voice. "Ladies, our manners are deplorable." She glanced at and then averted her eyes from the sullen young woman who had recited. "Some more than others. Mrs. Boylett has given us much to think about. It has been a rigorous morning. Shall we adjourn for refreshments in the parsonage? Mrs. Ackers?"

The minister's wife's satin swished as she came to her feet and thanked those who had provided tea and pastries. "I believe the girls have everything ready. Mr. Ackers will be there greet you."

Earlier, Mariah had told me, "Each circle provides food. Lila is helping out today. The girls consider it a privilege to serve. The refreshments will be bountiful and the Reverend Mr. Ackers will partake bountifully, in keeping with his rather long-winded grace."

Mariah stood up and spoke, "Afterwards, in our smaller circles, we will think on and give prayerful attention to what you've said, Sarranda. Thank you." She took my arm in a protective gesture and we drifted toward the door.

"What was that poem?" I asked. "The girl, Susanna, looked as if she wanted to cry, but she was angry, too. I'd like to meet her."

"Thomas Hood wrote it, over thirty years ago."

At that moment, Laura joined us. "Susanna has left already," she said. "Poor Hertha. She is embarrassed once again."

Laura touched my shoulder. "Don't expect all of these ladies to warm to your idea," she whispered. "They can be like sheep one moment, all grazing in the same direction, and the next they're like the ponies roaming the western range, each going a different way, scattering everywhere."

I chuckled. "But surely, each headed toward the same goal, water or food."

"In this case, first food," she returned. "And strong black tea."

They steered me to a table, announcing that since I was a special guest, they would bring refreshments to me.

"I will look up that poem," I said, under my breath. And I would like to get to know Susanna. Hertha's niece. The poem had touched me—as had her courage in breaking into the meeting. I didn't mind being interrupted. The women had listened but partly it was my southern accent that captured their attention. In the smaller gatherings when I spoke, a silence sometimes fell on the group even when I was speaking to only one individual. No one smirked or snickered, though I noticed a smile or two when a "y'all" slipped out. In fact, I listened to them with the same intentness. If I felt as if I were at a racetrack, trying to comprehend the sentences that sped from their mouths, they likely saw me as a steed reined in, slowed down to a wastefully slow pace. Sometimes a woman consciously governed her rapid speech, but, no matter that I might have wanted to, I could not seem to speed up my words.

I looked around at the women, all intent on doing good works and I admit to a pang of resistance to their goodness. Though they had lost loved ones and suffered deprivations during the war, they had not *been there.* They were comfortable in their convictions and certain that what they did was in line with God's purpose—whatever they did. These women, pleasant and well-meaning, saw me as a means to an end, a small factor in improving the lot of the less fortunate. Yet would anything I or other workers could do suffice? Was I—and the other women and men who went to help their fellow citizens—a sort of salve to their consciences? Did that matter as long as something was done? And was it my place to ascribe motives beyond the acknowledged one of assisting those in need? "As Jesus would expect of us," Hertha said more than once. Perhaps it was just as well that they viewed the problems and the solutions from afar. Perhaps they couldn't see the problems in their own backyards—as Carly Bell saw them, as his sister acknowledged them.

The swath of destruction across a defeated countryside went much deeper than the visible ruination: the destroyed vineyards in the piedmont, the scorched tobacco and corn fields, the trampled gardens, the burned barns and mills—all, in good time, could return to normal. The damage done to bodies was also visible in amputations, scars, weakened lungs. That our spirits, our attitudes had been forever affected was less visible, yet deep-seated. A terrible anger and desire for vengeance was shown by the actions of the hooded men in the KKK. No rational person could justify their fiery crosses, their beatings and lynchings; yet they happened and, so I understood, went mostly unpunished by the courts. Legislators were reluctant to enforce policies pushed by carpetbaggers. Mrs. Whitney's friends spoke of the 1869 law that provided for separate schools for the races. North Carolina's leaders had stalled because the school system was administered by a carpetbagger from the North and his assistant, both advocates of educating white and Negro children in "mixed" schools. Thus little had been done.

I smiled halfheartedly as Laura placed a plate of sandwiches and sweets before me. "You're going to need all the strength of sugar and eggs," she said and popped two cookies into her mouth. "Why the long face, Sarranda? I thought you made a good speech."

"I was thinking that I have learned much about the political and social situation up here." I sighed. "Perhaps I was too comfortable in Charlotte. Of course, it was the men who were most aware of the violence that occurred after the war. The soldiers did not talk much about the war itself, at least not to the women, and not even much about what was happening in our own back yards or counties." Much easier, I realized, to talk of crops and money, English novels and the philosophies of Emerson and Thoreau.

"The same up here," Laura agreed. "They likely didn't want to disturb the womenfolk."

"Or," I said, "maybe they didn't want to disturb themselves."

Adelaide Bell disappeared from my life, at least temporarily. I might not see her before journeying south, Mariah told me, and then Adelaide rushed into the parlor, breathless and apologetic.

"Oh, Sarranda, I am so sorry. I must return to Concord with Lucinda and her children and her husband. He is much, much worse." She took my hands. Her fingers were icy. "He demands that the hospital dismiss him. Sometimes he's quite irrational but he knows he's dying. He wants to be in his own home. His parents, though frail, can help us care for him."

"Is there nothing to be done?" I asked. "Here or in his hometown? He is young, perhaps...."

"No. The doctors say it's really only days, not weeks. Douglas looks ghastly already. Lucinda says he frightens the children." Her reddened eyes revealed she had been weeping. "I must, of course, go with them. Lucinda is near collapse. She needs my help. He wishes to die surrounded by neighbors and family." She attempted a smile. "I've become quite adept at caring for the children."

When she turned toward me with a look beseeching understanding, I said, "Of course, you must go. I understand."

"I feel as though I'm abandoning you, especially now, now that there is some confusion about what you may be doing when you leave next month."

"Three weeks," Mariah said, returning with a teapot. "We've travel arrangements for three weeks, though I suppose that could change." She rang a little bell to summon Lila. "We can change the date if necessary. Right now, dear Adelaide, you need tea. Or a small sherry?"

"No sherry, thank you. Tea is fine. I am in a tizzy. Everything is happening so fast. We leave in two days' time."

"I'm quite comfortable here with Mariah."

"No, Sarranda. That's the other thing." She wrung her hands. "Would you consider staying at my home for a time? I have repairmen coming. The work must be finished before cold weather. Someone has to be there. Oh, dear! It's all so difficult."

"Stay in your home?"

"It's a good walk from here," Mariah said. "Thank you, Lila. Just set the tray here, please."

"The walk I wouldn't mind," I said. "I am eating too well and walking too little these days. But to stay—to take responsibility for workmen?"

"Begging your pardon." Lila bobbed a small curtsey. "Miss Mariah, I know one of them who'll be doing your chimley. He's a friend of me da's, up here for the season."

I smiled at Lila. It had been years since I'd heard "chimley," and it felt comforting.

"Why, Lila, that's good," Mariah said. She and Adelaide exchanged speculative glances.

Before I knew it, they arranged that Lila would accompany me to Adelaide's house and keep me company until I left Bramford. After lunch and a visit to an ailing church member, the three of us walked over to Adelaide's home, some twenty-five minutes through the leaf-strewn streets. She had become almost cheerful at the quick resolution to her problem; apparently she had no fears about leaving her home in the care of Lila and me.

In a short time, Lila adopted me, perhaps thinking me an elderly aunt. She served me simple meals from Adelaide's ample pantry and even turned down my bed the first night and slipped a warming pan under the covers. It was clear we needed to talk. At our second breakfast, I asked her to sit at the table with me. She hesitated and wiped at some silverware. When she realized that I waited, she barely perched on the edge of her chair. I stood, poured a cup of coffee, and placed it before her. Her eyes widened and I knew she intended a protest. I held up my hand and returned to my toast.

"Lila, we must stop this servant-mistress business," I said in the tone I'd used with my boys when they were acting like young colts. "I do not wish to be your 'lady,' so to speak. I'd like us to be equals and share in the tasks around the house."

"Oh, no, Mrs. Boylett," she exclaimed. "I can't do that. 'Tain't what I'm paid to do. Why, Miss Mariah'd have me job for that, she would, and Miss Bell wouldn't like it, either."

"Miss Bell is not here to know, nor is Mrs. Harrison. I am uncomfortable being in charge of this large house, and to have you treating me as its owner makes me even more uncomfortable."

"Oh, I don't mean to do that." She gave me a direct look. "Miss Mariah's teaching me how to behave in a fine home and around her lady friends. What would she say if you and me become friends?" She placed her cup carefully on the table. "I have to have this job, don't I? I daren't go home in disgrace."

"I promise you won't lose your place here. But I've tried to get up early and make my own breakfast only to find you have the stove stoked and the bread cut. I intend to make my own bed and find you've done it." I rolled my eyes. "I know you're young enough to be my daughter—"

"I'm nineteen, fair on the way to being a spinster."

"Old enough to be my daughter and unlikely to be a spinster," I said. "I would like you to be able to speak freely to me and I to you."

At her skeptical glance I went on, "Let me tell you a bit about myself, Lila. Is that all right with you?"

She nodded.

"I was born poor, lost my husband in a prison camp, lost a child to the cold and hunger in 1864. I have two sons, older than you. One chose to stay in the mountains, living with an older couple more well-to-do than I would ever be. The other went out west."

She leaned toward me, listening intently.

"To survive I took a place as a lady's companion and there I stayed, until Miss Bell came along. I was treated more like a sister than an employee, but Miss Bell offered a chance to do more than be comfortable the rest of my life. The work of the Bramford ladies, their sending mission workers to the mountains seemed a challenge."

"They say everybody down there is always feuding and fighting." At my slight frown, Lila said, "You was born poor?"

"In a log cabin." I covered her hand in mine. "Lila, in time I think we will be friends. For now, let's at least be equals."

She ducked her head. "Equals is something I ain't never been."

"We can start now. I'll wash up these dishes and you can dry and put them away." I smiled at her and my heart warmed when she smiled back. "And while at it, we can practice being equal. Shall I mop or sweep?"

"I can't let you do that, Miss. Neither one." She sounded genuinely horrified.

"Will you call me Sarranda? I'm no Miss. I don't feel like a Mrs. and Madam is too formal. Back home I'd be Ma'am. I'm named for my two grandmothers. I'd like you to call me my name."

I plunged my hands into soapy water. "Please." I flicked a bit of sudsy water toward her, feeling younger, freer than I had in the past weeks.

Lila giggled. "Yes. Sarranda. I will call you that. You can sweep, and I will mop."

What a fine morning we had of it, doing chores easily, humming a bit. Lila told me about her family: parents from west Ireland, escaping the famine and grateful but hardly living beyond the hard fist of the creditors month by month. The men and boys lived by the fishing seasons, either going out in the boats or working in the fishing industry ashore; the women went into service, as had her aunt and Lila in her footsteps, or took in washing and ironing while taking care of their homes and "babies, more babies." A flash of guilt crossed her face as she uttered those words. After a few minutes of swishing a duster around the bookshelves she said, not looking at me but at the absolutely dust-free shelves, "Me, I'm thinking I don't want babies. Mam lost the last two. She's not well and me da, he, he sometimes hits her. She cries all the time."

I wanted to hug her as my Charlotte acquaintances hugged their young friends who needed an understanding shoulder. But it was too soon for that; she rushed toward the kitchen, exclaiming, "Mercy, I forgot to stir up the cookies for Miss Hertha. I'll have them ready for you. Everything's clean as a pin now."

"Thank you, Lila." I paused in the doorway. "Would you like to walk with me? The day is fine for sitting in the garden or you might visit with her girl."

Pleasure flooded her face. "'Tis Molly's day off, but I will go with you." I heard her clanging pans as I went upstairs to change.

I had never visited Hertha and wasn't looking forward to it, but she had sent a boy around to invite me and, without a reason or another social engagement, I could not refuse. I hoped to learn more about her niece Susanna, without appearing nosy, of course. I had found "The Song of the Shirt" at the public library and copied it out, careful to blot the tear that fell onto the book's page as I did so. I could quote most of it though I certainly had no intention of doing so this afternoon.

CHAPTER THREE

Lila didn't seem inclined to chatter as we walked to Hertha's and neither did I. She had donned a coat too long in the sleeves and fraying at its hemline and had scrubbed her face so it glowed almost fiercely. Of course, I, too, had changed for visiting; my dress was neither flashy nor dour—a dark green worsted with cuffed sleeves and a tatted collar. I did not wish to be regarded as some poor cousin come calling and I held my head high, enjoying the brisk wind along the pleasant streets. Every time Lila dropped a few steps behind me I slowed and waited and without words conveyed that we were, at least on this walk, equals. A young man driving a wagon of potatoes and turnips doffed his cap to her with a, "Hiya, Irish lass." She blushed and after a quick glance looked straight ahead. Whether she was interested in his attention or angry at his greeting I couldn't tell.

In a few moments she volunteered, "He's Mr. Moynihan's driver. He waits outside the Institute to talk to us."

"A young man with a job..." I deliberately let my words to trail off. He looked a healthy lad, but I was not the one to admire or condemn his interest or character.

"I don't have eyes for him," Lila said. "Now Molly, she could take an interest. He's a regular down at Sammy's but just a pint or two, so they say."

"Here's where we turn into Miss Settles' street." Her directions had been concise. "Hers will be the fifth house with the iron railings out front."

"'Tis a grand street, indeed, is it not?" Lila ran her hand across the iron scrolls of the fence at the third house.

"It is." At Hertha's house, built, I'd been told, by her grandfather, we stopped, to catch our breath.

Adjusting my bonnet, I noted that the yard was immaculate but that one shutter hung loose on its hinge.

"I'll just go around to the back, Miss...I mean Sarranda. I hear the cook's on the stingy side, but mayhap she'll have some cake and tea." I detected a sly humor when she said, "Enjoy your visit."

Hertha greeted me with a reserved, punctilious cordiality. The tea was laid out in a side parlor where a small coal fire burned. She served me herself, saying, "It's my girl's day off." The pumpkin bread was somewhat lacking in both quantity and taste, but that suited me. I had been eating too well too often and my thin frame had taken on curves and softness. Pouring, she complained, "The tea's the best one can find now in the shops. Before the war the tea was superior to anything now available."

"It's full-bodied," I murmured and she frowned as if I'd seriously disagreed with her assessment. That frown forecast the conversation that followed.

"I have tried to understand your comments at the meeting about our southern missions," she began, "and I'm somewhat troubled in my mind, Mrs. Boylett."

She was the only lady of the circle who did not call me my given name. I set my cup down. "How have I troubled you, Miss Settles?"

"You are undoubtedly an exception," she said, "but having read a great deal about your mountains, I must question your view, rather, your assumption, that the first duty of our mission should be to aid the women." She held up a hand. "Surely men, there as here, control the business and commerce. Women have little or no voice in anything outside the home. I believe, as the Bible says, the wife must be the helpmate. By her behavior and her words, a wife instructs her children in virtue and her husband in morality. I believe in educating the children—and here I don't hesitate to say, both boys and girls. Girls must know how to read and write, to keep household accounts."

Before I could respond she went on. "I myself have enjoyed the pleasures of a good schooling and I have read much about that isolated and strange area called Appalachia. Have you read Miss Woolson's recent piece in *Harper's Magazine*? She has visited Asheville and writes becomingly of it."

"I have not read it." I had seen western North Carolina's largest town only once, but I did not tell her that. She had me at a disadvantage and she seemed to know it.

"She and others describe the appalling, albeit somewhat romanticized, circumstances under which the populace lives. I believe the church is crucial, the church and the schools it fosters. That is our first line of defense against an illiterate and degenerate people. I fail to see that encouraging women to compete, to engage in commerce will raise the level of—" she paused but only briefly. "—of culture and prevent the further deterioration of morals."

"Degenerate? The deterioration of morals?" I was glad I had put the cup down or my fingers might have broken its thin handle. "When has that happened? Do you mean the whole issue of slavery? Or do you refer perhaps to the onslaught of men from the North who prey on a defeated land?" I clenched my hands to prevent their trembling. My face was surely mottled with anger, but in the dim parlor it wouldn't show.

"Perhaps I chose my words poorly," she said. The stern set of her mouth didn't indicate she believed what she was saying. "Forgive me if I offended, but you yourself have been out of those mountains, removed from the circumstances that promote a certain decline—"

"Miss Settles, I was under the impression that the mission to the mountains was to improve conditions under which people now live, conditions I think not brought on by any connection to morality." I struggled to maintain my composure, to keep my voice modulated. My stomach felt as if I'd been kicked by a mule. Had I been deceived all along in what I was to be doing? Was I to improve a degenerate people? Prevent a moral decline? Did the other women feel as this wretch of a woman did?

"Do you deny, my dear Mrs. Boylett, the drunkenness that is rampant, the violence that is commonplace? It makes the printed page, after all. It cannot be ignored by God-fearing persons, nor can it long be tolerated." She met my eyes with a hard stare. "My own brother's sons have journeyed to the backwoods of Tennessee. They are improving the lot of the natives, quarrying stone for factories that their connections here in our state will build."

"And did they pay a fair price for the land they're working? Did they pay any price at all?" I sucked in my breath and throttled my anger, aware of the power Miss Settles might have, surely would have, over my life in the weeks ahead. She might even derail or terminate my "mission." Uncertain of exactly what the circle's next step would be, I knew that this stout viper could delay or destroy the hopes of the circle, the hopes that lay with me. I was aware of a pang in my ribcage. "Many have gone to the southern states purposefully to reap the gains from a burned-over land," I said. "Your brother's sons may not be of that ilk, but undoubtedly they and others profit from the weakened government, from the imposed—"

One hand came up to her chest and with the other she pushed the delicate plate from her, sending it skittering across the small table. It stopped at the edge as if on command.

"The South must pay the price for its rebellion," she said. "As it inflicted a moral evil on its Negro people, it is now paying. The church, not the governors or legislators, must take the lead in benevolence, in guidance, in raising the standards of civility."

"The church is engaged in gathering converts," I said, "so I read, so I'm told. The church's concern is for the souls of its members." Aware I was teetering on the edge of propriety, I plunged ahead. "At the meeting, I was thinking of people's earthly needs, not their souls. Should people be fed and clothed based on their coming into a church, however good the church? I want to see women become capable of feeding themselves, not be forever in the position of begging for alms, for needing charity."

Hertha's tightened lips told me the battle lines were drawn and retreat was impossible. So be it. My dander was up. I sounded on the offensive and touchy, but I felt as if I'd been surprised-flogged by a wet hen. In short, my feelings were hurt. I was *now* well-fed, dressed well enough, had shoes on my feet, combs in my hair, but *then* would always be a part of me, hidden by outward trimmings. My heart sank, but I stiffened my spine.

"Careful, Mrs. Boylett. You're close to blasphemy. Our church's work is not to offer sustenance depending on one's becoming affiliated with our faith. That affiliation is quite naturally a by-product. Lost souls come to see a way to the Lord through the church. The church family grows and the church takes care of its own."

I stared at her. How could I refute those words? The churches of the North had indeed started schools, built or rebuilt churches, offered succor when it was sorely needed. I leaned back, trounced in this skirmish. But retreat though I might, sitting as it were in the enemy's camp and liable to further ambush, I would not accept that Hertha Settles' way was the only way or the best way to accomplish what the ladies' missions meant to do.

I lowered my eyes. "We obviously disagree on how to move forward," I said.

"You have introduced a path I am not prepared to follow," she stated. "And I can't believe the other ladies will either. I have some influence there. Perhaps your experience with the church, a church, has colored your view, has cast a pall of disillusionment over your eyes. Do you not understand the value of what our church is doing in your mountains and elsewhere, improving the lot of children?"

Her bosom almost shook with pride or fury. I wondered if she referred to the thousands of city children sent westward on "Orphan Trains" to provide a better living for them—and to provide labor for farmers along the route. I dared not question for fear of another lecture on her views of assisting the poor.

"I do understand it," I said. "I know schools have been established and no one can doubt that they are educating the children for a better life. But I cannot accept that the church is the only way." I shifted in my chair. For my sake, I should terminate my visit before I was dismissed like an ignorant or unruly child. I stood up. "An honest exchange of views is preferable, is it not, to proceeding with an unclear or uncertain program?"

"Indeed." Hertha pushed herself to her feet and rang a bell, summoning Lila for our walk back to Miss Bell's home. "Our next meetings will show us the way, I have no doubt."

She meant that she fully expected her views to prevail. Perhaps they would. Our farewells were civil, if not overly cordial. I extended my hand and she graciously took it. She appraised me as if she'd hired me as her washerwoman, but was uncertain as to the wisdom of it.

I managed to walk with ladylike steps to the front gate where Lila waited. Down the street and out of Hertha's sight, my ladylike stroll turned into a stalking gait. I even huffed a bit. Lila hurried to keep up. After a few minutes she could no longer contain her curiosity.

"Did you have a good tea?" She skipped ahead, turned, walking backward, and faced me. "That one's not someone I'd like to have tea with, she isn't. And the cook didn't offer me more'n a cup of tea and yesterday's brown bread."

I didn't speak.

"And just a smidgen of butter for it. The jam pot was empty, wasn't it?"

Just how much I wanted to confide in Lila I wasn't sure. Yet, I felt close to her, and I couldn't simmer and stew without letting off some steam. Strangely, I felt stronger and more confident now that I had spoken so rashly to Hertha. I realized I had been holding back, drifting in the current of the ladies' circle. Now I had to think of hard realities. Was my goal in returning to my valley compatible with theirs? Could it become so? Had I been too easily recruited simply because I needed a change from continued years of ease with Mrs. Whitney? Had I joined up, so to speak, for the wrong reason? I had to think about my course. I had cut my ties with Alice Whitney, though if I were cast out like a demon from the fold, she would certainly help me find another suitable place. I would, however, go that route only under dire circumstances. I owed Adelaide and the other women some loyalty; I should at least hear, refute, or accept whatever plans they made. Or—did I dare—I had to leave the comfort of the circle and venture out independently. I had to think. Meanwhile, Lila waited.

"A most interesting tea." I exaggerated my drawl.

"Whatever you talked of, it huffed and puffed you up, Miss—I mean Sarranda, if ye don't mind me saying it."

"I have some thinking to do," I admitted. An ugly outburst of spleen might have been justified, but I said no more and Lila didn't press me. The leaves swirling in the street suited my mood, and a brisk walk brought us to the quiet of Adelaide's kitchen where Lila prepared a supper of roast chicken. After our repast, she labored through a study booklet, moving her lips as her fingers traced its lines, and I read haphazardly in the books on Adelaide's shelves, not being able to put my mind on any one subject, though I looked for the magazine Hertha mentioned. Finally, almost simultaneously we sighed and slumped, then gave a little laugh at ourselves.

"I'll put the kettle on," Lila said. "There's fresh apple cake with brown sugar, but I burned it a bit, didn't I?"

"A big piece for me, please. I must get beyond this grump I'm in."

Ten minutes later, she returned with our tea. "Tell me about your home," she said. "I've only lived in Flecton and here. I can't imagine tall mountains with snakes and such. I remember our teacher read us a poem about snakes and tigers. Have you ever seen a tiger?" Frowning as if trying to remember, Lila pushed her finger into her cheek. "Crouching tigers and hateful snakes, it was." She smiled. "Have you seen a tiger down there?"

I searched my memory, even as I answered. "No, Lila, I've never seen a tiger and the South has no tigers. Tigers are far away on another continent. I've seen a bobcat or two, and some snakes."

"Oh." She smoothed the momentary disappointment from her face. Bobcats must have seemed mild and domestic compared to crouching tigers. Ah, I remembered the poem, with its "crouching tigers."

"I think the poem your teacher read is about a village deserted in England, when most of the people had to leave to live in the city or leave the country during a terrible time. I'll find the poem and we'll read it again." I sipped my tea. "Meanwhile, I'll tell you a bit about my mountain home, though I warn you—no tigers but rattlesnakes and copperheads aplenty."

Like Goldsmith's villagers, I had left, deserted my valley for the city. And weren't many others, younger than I mostly, fleeing to the plains and prairies of the West? As I talked of growing up, marrying, surviving the war, Lila's expression saddened. I realized that my tone unconsciously revealed homesickness for my mountains. I was fortunate to have had the option of leaving—leaving or lingering to be forced into servitude, either marriage or kinship. Mrs. Whitney and I had spoken about my situation, but this was the first time I spoke from a deeper place, from my heart, not my head, and spoke to an equal, for so I deemed Lila. She was a younger me, in a different state, from a different family, but young and untried, seeking a better life.

Tears formed in my eyes.

Lila started to reach for my hand but quickly drew back. I smiled, aware that she "knew her place" and could not yet assume a friendship based on equality. "B'gorry, Miss," she said. "You've had a time of it, you have."

"And another time to come." I admitted, "I'm less certain now of what I should be doing when I return to my state."

"Oh, you must go, Miss," she said. "But I'll miss you, I will."

"I will go, Lila." I studied my fingers. "But with what support and even with what enthusiasm, I don't know."

I stood up, partly to shake off the aura of melancholy in the room. "I'll find the poem by Goldsmith. He's a fellow countryman of yours. I'm sure there's a copy somewhere on the shelves."

CHAPTER FOUR

In the subdued night noises, the soft padding and meowing of a cat in the garden, the clopping of a lone horse in the street, the rustle of a bird alighting in the tall tree beyond my window, I lay wide awake. Aware of every sound, aware of my ankles slightly sore from walking, alert to the creaks of the house when the wind gusted, I tossed and remembered. The window was open an inch or so, for I liked the chill of the outside air as I lay submerged under the covers in Adelaide's guest room.

In this comfort and ease, how could my thoughts not return to my one night of unexpected, but invited bodily delight? In my cabin, with my husband in the army, my boys at Grandda's, when night riders might come calling and burning, looting and scaring, I had entertained a stranger. Wounded, cold, tired, a stranger I could not assume was on our side, one, my rational mind knew was not. A stranger traveling through the mountains, beset by a saber or knife slash.

I could blush even now, these years later, recalling that I had rubbed lavender on my neck and bosom. I had cleaned and dressed his wound, and had taken the man to my bed. The ecstasy he had brought me to—I looked through the billowing lacy curtains. No stars shone tonight, but on that night the stars had exploded and my body with them. I had married very young and had, I suppose, the typical youthful appetite for sex, an appetite diminished by the births of three boys, the hard work and fears during and following the war years. Not until that night did I realize what I had missed—the caresses, a burning gentleness, the need that went beyond physical, the hunger that being close to death might instill and the oneness that being close to death might bring. I awoke a different woman.

I chose not to marry again—when later I had two opportunities—for survival or convenience. A woman might yearn for such a lover, for this lover, but have no expectation of ever seeing him again. Even as I traced the indented feather pillow and then held it to my face in the morning light, I enclosed the night in a velvet memory, like a diamond hidden from public view, from my own view—too beautiful to be on display, too private to be talked of.

And yet, Adelaide had casually mentioned a brother, a brother wounded in the arm, a brother...No, I yanked the covers from me and went to the window, opened it wide and breathed in the cool air. It was inane to even consider. Many men had been wounded. Many men had lain with women they didn't know and would not see again. It was a wartime night, and I knew one or two babies born of such encounters. Then why did I wonder? Why, enfolded in memory's velvet, did the night gleam with a mute dimness? Why did I hope? Was my concealed yearning even hope? Looking at the deserted street, I realized that I might not recognize my bed-stranger, having seen him only by moonlight, a flickering small fire, not by lantern or daylight. Prudence, shame, or duty had sent him away before I awakened to a cold bed, a cold cabin, cold ashes. What he wore was not a proper uniform, but that was not unusual. Though he served his country, his country was not, at that time, my country.

Such were my nighttime dreams, not my daytime thoughts. I was smart enough to know to some extent I had created the night. So I told myself and so I must believe. With one last shiver, I slammed the window shut on my wandering memory.

The following afternoon, after a light luncheon, I put my mind on my sewing, determined to think neither of Hertha's tea nor my nighttime memories. The coat I was mending hung heavy and cumbersome across my knees. I forced my fingers along the hemline to keep them from wandering with my thoughts right out of the room. A vague anger hovered over me like a thunderhead over the Tuckasegee.

The door knocker sounded repeatedly, small thunder claps, interrupting my mulling over the last circle meeting. Where was Lila? The fire blazed before me. The room was warm, and my face grew hot as I recalled the arguments ("civil disagreements," Laura called them) that ran through the meeting. Another clang of the door knocker reminded me that Lila had rushed off to meet a friend who had sent a boy around with a message to meet her at Paxton Circle at three. We had cleaned the kitchen cabinets and I sat with my stocking feet on the footstool. What fool was calling in this rain? Most likely, a vendor with autumn vegetables. They all seemed to know that Adelaide wouldn't turn them away even if she only bought an onion or a parsnip.

Stabbing my needle into the thick wool, I jabbed the fleshy part of my index finger hard. By the time I was in the foyer, a red blob of blood had popped up. I sucked my finger with irritation and impatience as the knocker thumped again. I flung open the door. The man had turned toward the street where a wagon was obscured by sheets of rain. From a brown felt hat pulled low over his face, water dripped onto the stoop. A sodden cloak and scarf obscured his lower face and throat. I did not envy anyone hawking vegetables on such a miserable day.

"Uh, Good afternoon." He appeared surprised. "Where's your mistress?"

My mistress, indeed. He mistook me for a housekeeper, not the lady of the house. Granted, my disheveled state made that a reasonable assumption. I was at a disadvantage, discomfited about the blood swelling again on my afflicted finger. Surely no lady would bleed so much from so small a jab. My handkerchief was in my sewing basket. I hardly wanted to wipe the blood on my clean apron. I put my finger to my lips again and muttered, "She's out, away—"

It wasn't prudent, Lila had said, to tell the whole world that Miss Bell was away for days or weeks. Yet, the man must be desperate to subject himself to such a cold rain to sell a few vegetables. "What do you have today? A pumpkin, perhaps?"

He stepped back, a scowl on his lips. "No vegetables today. A message for your mistress." He dug under his cloak and slipped a white handkerchief from some pocket. "Use this." He thrust it toward me.

"No, no." I instinctively extended my hand for a written message. Instead I took the handkerchief and wrapped it around my finger. I peered toward the wagon. "No pumpkins?" My vision of warm pumpkin pie disappeared. Absorbed in my bandaging, I sensed a cool stare but I couldn't see his upper face.

"Thank you," I said. "If you call around next week, I'll return your handkerchief to you. I'm not usually so careless."

"No need. Give your mistress this message. Her brother Carly was set upon by a gang of toughs. He's being cared for by Dr. Arthmore in Central Street." He turned and was halfway down the steps when he must have heard my gasp. Carly!

"Is he badly hurt?" I called. Something clutched at my heart. It seemed to stop for a moment.

"He'll live, with some broken ribs and without some teeth." He stepped up into the wagon and directed his words to the horse. "Where the hell is she this time?"

I stared at my wrapped finger. The messenger was ill-mannered in speech, yet well-mannered enough to provide a handkerchief. A handkerchief of fine linen. The wagon pulled away with such a jerk I expected to see apples and turnips flying into the street from under the canvas. Carly hurt? I must write to Adelaide. But I would go at once to Dr. Arthmore's to see about him. I knew that Central Avenue had, in earlier years, been a main thoroughfare in town but the town had grown away from it; now it was considered an undesirable neighborhood, commerce encroaching on the few old homes along it. I could certainly find the doctor but I should wait for Lila to return. It was close to dusk, and I preferred not to walk alone in unfamiliar streets. I rinsed the handkerchief in cold water and wondered where my courage had gone. Gone with my youth? Left behind in Greene's Valley?

Annoyed that I had paid so much attention to a prick of my finger when an important message was being delivered, I looked around. I was growing more impatient and irritable each day. My Charlotte years had been a kind of plateau, it dawned on me, a learning place, a place of finding another existence, one of the intellect, of books and conversation, one that developed my mind and softened my rough self, the self predicated on surviving. Now I needed to go home. Home to the mountains. Life here was too easy even with the verbal skirmishes going on. I stormed around the house, straightening items already straight and lining up books already lined up. With relief I heard Lila open the back door. Her face was flushed and her hair wet. She offered no explanation of her meeting and, preoccupied as I was, I asked her no questions.

I heated chowder for a quick supper and told Lila of the visitor's message. She had met Carly and was instantly sympathetic. "O' course, I'll go with you," she said. "We can take our bumbershoots and no street bully will dare come near us." She flourished an imaginary weapon.

We found our way to Central Avenue where Lila stopped an older man to ask directions. He pointed us a few hundred feet to a dark, shuttered house. As we approached, I read the sign: Dr. Artemis Arthmore. Clinic. Lila's mouth gaped. She looked furtive and apprehensive.

"Do you know this place?" I eyed the house with some reservation. Clumps of wet leaves littered the walkway and dead plants in pots sat on the wide porch. It looked uncared for or unlived in. "Is this the doctor's office, I wonder, or does he live here?"

As we stood at the porch steps, I asked Lila, "What's wrong?"

"I know, I know a girl who's been here." Lila averted her eyes. "The sign wasn't here when me and Anna come with her."

"Well, it must be clean and...acceptable," I said, "or Carly wouldn't have been brought here."

At our knock, we were admitted by a woman of about my age. Her eyes were tired and lines ravaged her face. She kept us standing in the small entryway longer than I deemed polite. She squinted at Lila who stooped to remove specks of mud from her boots. I said, "We're here to see about Mr. Carly Bell."

Before she could ask I said, "No, we are not related. His sister is out of town and her home has been entrusted to my care. I wish to write to her at once about her brother's condition." I extended my hand, a gesture that surprised her. She barely touched my gloved fingers.

"The doctor is out. This way, please." The interior smelled of bleach and soap yet it struck me as needing a complete airing out. Odors did not so much hang in the hall as seem to escape in spite of soap and water. We passed closed doors from which no sounds issued and arrived at the back of the house. I saw a pot of water and a huge pot of soup simmering on the stove. If little attention had been paid to cleanliness, at least the doctor's patients would be fed.

Lila sniffed. "Vegetables and beef," she said.

The woman peered into a nearby room and stood aside. "He is sleeping, poor man. Please do not overtire him." She assumed, rightly so, that I would wish to awaken him, to be sure of his condition.

"Please, Miss, uh, Sarranda," Lila stayed in the doorway, "Mayhap I can help in the kitchen?" I nodded. She had seen the unwashed dishes and unswept floor.

Tiptoeing to the bedside, I looked down at Adelaide's brother. His eyelids flickered as if he knew someone was there. The left side of his face was blue-black, in sharp contrast to his paleness; one eye was swollen shut. A bloody ooze had crusted around it. He hadn't been shaved and his lips were dry. A shudder ran through him and he opened his right eye and groaned. I poured a small amount of water in a glass and held it to his chapped lips. He sipped with a grimace, looked puzzled.

"I'm Sarranda Boylett." I replaced the glass on the table. "Your sister brought me to your school one day." He closed his eye as if in thought. I went on, "You were indisposed. We haven't met."

"Who...?"

"I'm staying at Adelaide's," I interrupted. "She returned to Concord with Lucinda and Douglas and the children. I must write and tell her your condition. We had a message that you were here." I pulled up the one straight chair. He pointed toward the water and I again held the glass as he sipped. His other hand, I saw, was bandaged; some blood had soaked through but was dried.

"Pardon me for not sitting up," he said, as he moved slightly. His head fell back on the pillow. "Can't talk much either."

"Is your jaw broken? How long have you been here? Who did this to you?" I stopped, realizing his face had slackened. "I really must let your sister know your situation, Mr. Bell. I can't stay long."

He nodded slightly. By asking questions that could be answered yes or no, I ascertained that he had been at Dr. Arthmore's since Thursday, two days. A gang of men or boys had attacked him as he was returning from a temperance meeting. The boy Joey had found him and had run for the doctor. Though bruised, his arms and legs weren't broken but a few ribs were. He had a pumpknot and headache, a damaged hand and eye. He pointed to his mouth, when I asked about his jaw. "Teeth knocked out," he said. "I'll live."

The woman came to the door. "The doc prescribed morphine for pain," she said. "I'll be right back." Her frown told me I should conclude the visit. His expression told me he was hurting more than he wanted to show.

I stood up. "I will return when I can." I moistened a handkerchief and carefully wiped at his swollen eye. Warm compresses would help. But I didn't think the nurse would welcome my staying to minister to him.

"Not a pretty sight, am I?" He tried to smile. "Thank you."

Lila trailed behind the woman who returned with the medicine. She gave him pills and water and dismissed us with, "He'll sleep now."

From the doorway, I looked down the dark hallway. There wasn't the hustle bustle of what I envisioned as a clinic. No other person was around, no noises; in fact, no doctor. Lila was at the front door before I bestirred myself. It would be helpful to see the doctor and ascertain how long Carly would be kept in the clinic, but that would have to wait for another visit.

I had a hard time keeping up with Lila's brisk steps. She kept her head down, perhaps because a sharp wind had risen. I was breathing heavily when we entered Adelaide's front hall and sloughed off our coats. City living must be slowing me down. I told myself to take at least two walks each day, regardless of the weather. I couldn't return to the mountains with the stamina of a city slicker.

"I will write to Adelaide at once," I said. "Shall we take tea later? Perhaps a boiled egg for our supper."

Lila disappeared toward the kitchen. I sat at the dining room table, not comfortable with using Adelaide's desk. My letter was short. I described receiving the message, her brother's condition and all that I knew of why he was there. Unsatisfactory, surely, but my information was limited. I closed with, "I will visit again and write tomorrow. Rest assured he is likely to be released soon. Your friend, Sarranda."

When Lila brought tea, it promised to be a quiet affair. She cast longing glances at her book one moment, the doorway the next, as if anxious to escape any conversation about visiting Carly. After a few minutes I said, "I need more information for Adelaide. Perhaps you could ask at the Institute to see if anyone knows about the attack? Your friend who called to you the other day, Mr. Moynihan's driver, he may have heard something."

She halted her hand, in the act of salting her egg. I went on, "I have yet another meeting tomorrow, but I shouldn't think the women will know of Mr. Bell's injury. And, of course, I will say nothing yet." I wrinkled my brow. "Strange. It was not robbery, I think." There would have been little or no money on Carly's person. A jealous lover or husband? Resentment that Carly taught neighborhood children? He had been beaten but his injuries were not serious enough to assume anyone intended to kill him. Had the police been informed? Lila was my best bet to find out anything. Since she had not answered, I said, "I'm not asking you to spy on your friends, Lila. Perhaps one of them knows the boy Joey. However, if you are not comfortable asking, you must do as you see fit." I pushed my clean plate aside.

"I'll ask, Miss, but I won't find out much, will I?" She picked up our plates, returned them to the kitchen, and brought more hot tea. At once she sought her book.

To set her at ease, I picked up the poetry collection from Adelaide's library and reread Goldsmith's "The Deserted Village." My first introduction to poetry was my grandfather's volume of Mr.Wordsworth's poems. I had struggled through them at first and grew to love them, wanting to see the natural world as the poet did—in rainbows and daffodils and frolicking lambs and hares on meadows green. My grandda had smiled when I asked what a hare was. "A big rabbit, just a big rabbit," he said. Long before he died and the book became mine, I could quote many of the verses by heart.

Goldsmith's poem struck me as somber and his attitude as both nostalgic and realistic. His melancholy matched my own as I read of the villagers who abandoned their home place, read of the poor girl arriving in the city slums with nothing to offer but her body and youth. How fortunate I was to have escaped such a fate. I had to smile faintly. Charlotte, like London town, had its seedy streets where I might have eked out a living somehow, if not selling my beyond-youthful body. I gave my head a shake. I must remain as positive as possible. Thinking backward seldom helped. I said, "Shall I read the poem we talked of earlier?"

"Yes, please. I'd like that, Miss Sarranda."

"Am I ever going to persuade you to call me simply Sarranda?" My grin mocked the firmness of my tone.

"Sarranda, yes, I forget, I do." She sat upright, like a schoolgirl, her hands in her lap. I pushed a footstool toward her and settled a pillow at my back.

Lila placed the old woolen shawl Adelaide had given her on the footstool before putting her feet on it, careful that the soles of her boots stuck out beyond the cloth. I was undoubtedly undoing all her mistresses had taught her about sitting properly in someone's home.

I admit I liked reading aloud. Oh, not to Mrs. Whitney's well-educated friends, as I was occasionally expected to do in book discussions. With them I felt embarrassed when I stumbled over words and mispronounced some. But with her alone, and now with Lila, I gave myself to the rhythm and cadence of the poem. Finishing the passage that begins, "Ill fares the land, to hastening ills a prey, / Where wealth accumulates, and men decay" and ending, "Those far departing seek a kinder shore, / Where rural wealth and manners are no more," I glanced up to see tears in Lila's eyes. She swiped at them with her sleeve. The words moved me, as well, and we sat silent for some time.

"Far departing—that's what we done, me da and mam, I mean," Lila said.

"For a kinder shore," I said. "As did I for a northern shore."

"It's a sad poem. I wonder if me da would call it a kinder shore. I guess so. We don't go hungry." She mustered a smile. "There's always fish."

"There's pie in the kitchen," I returned. "Let me finish, though. The poem goes on and on, and," I warned, "it doesn't get happier—except in memory."

When I closed the volume with a flourish, Lila's eyes were red and she had retrieved a handkerchief from a pocket. "You do read good, just like a professor," she said. "Better than our Institute teacher." She hesitated. "Could I see the book?"

I marked the poem with a slip of paper and held it out to her. "The poem was written over a hundred years ago. Goldsmith left Ireland, as your parents did, only he went to London." I was beginning to sound like a teacher.

"Leaving is hard," Lila observed, with a sniff and a sneeze.

"Necessary, at times," I said. "And returning? I wonder how easy that is."

"I won't ever go to Ireland and me parents neither." She laid the book aside. "We've had a sad enough day of it, we have. I'll bring the pie."

Time and past time for me to look forward, not backward. Goldsmith realized there was no returning to the idyllic village of his youth or his imagination, and I could not return to the security of my grandda's knee or his mill. That security was born of childhood ignorance and nurtured in memory. Soon the war brought awareness of the precariousness of life in my remote valley and destroyed any illusion of safety.

The following day Lila's cold kept us home in the morning. She apologized for not being able to go find out about the attack on Carly. I brushed her words aside. "He's in good hands for now," I said. "I can't have you risking your health." I soothed her hot forehead with a cool towel. "What would I do without you?"

However, at mid-afternoon I felt obligated to attend the circle meeting; I went but my mind was elsewhere. Hertha summed up of our tea-time discussion, putting her points forward with vigor, and dismissing my concerns. Even when one or the other woman glanced my way, I felt no need to defend my attitude or to refute hers. When Hertha stopped talking and a few questions were raised and dealt with, the group fell silent. The silence brought me out of my reverie, just as Hertha said, "Mrs. Boylett appears to have left us, ladies. Or perhaps," she twisted her formidable frame toward me, "you have come to see the truth of my position."

Any answer I made would have been waspish and unladylike, but before I could respond, she said, "If so, my dear, I accept your apology for your forwardness at my home."

The women stirred, uncomfortable with this outright offensive remark. "Oh, Hertha," Laura murmured. "Unworthy of you."

"Miss Settles and I clearly have our differences and I thus find myself in a difficult position." I waited long enough for Hertha and the others to realize I wasn't apologizing. Then I drew a deep breath. "I am in Bramford at your invitation. I certainly subscribe to the need for assistance to the southern states, the southern mountains, specifically. I want to return to help." I looked at each one except Hertha, finding in their faces a mix of sympathy and confusion. "I intend to return."

I did not wish to invite a further haranguing from Hertha nor to elicit outbursts of questions and comments that might offend her. We would never be friends, but I had no desire to be her enemy, public or private. I stood up and spoke in a quiet, forthright manner. "It might be best to discuss the matter without my being present. You may conclude you cannot support my efforts, knowing, as you have been told," I nodded toward Hertha, "and as you heard a few days ago, that my emphasis would be economic, not, uh, denominational. I am a practical woman rather than...a religious one. I would wish to help women support themselves and their families, with or without the church's help. If my attitude conflicts too much with what you see as your mission, then—then." I stopped, hoping I had not created an entire enemy camp. I raised my palms and turned toward the door.

Among protestations that they would look further into the matter, that they must consult higher ups, that they believed in me but, among their words and handshakes, I donned my cloak and pulled on my gloves. Laura walked with me to the door.

"You're brave, Sarranda, to face up to Hertha. I won't say more than that the church—"

"The church is your foundation, I know." I took her hand. "You must do what you feel is right. I have not behaved as you expected. For that, I am sorry, but I suppose I was not fully aware of what I agreed to when I stepped on that train."

"It seemed so simple," she agreed. "I don't like conflict. Adelaide will sort us out."

"Yes. I hope she returns soon."

As I trudged through the leaf-littered street, my thoughts swirled with the wind. Was I a traitor to my friend? Would my Charlotte acquaintances think me an ungrateful friend to Adelaide, even an unworthy Christian? Wet oak leaves came to rest on my bonnet and I brushed them off absently. I had attended Alice Whitney's church, had came to appreciate the formality and rituals of the Episcopalian worship services, certainly a far cry from the spontaneous nature of the "amen corner" and the lengthy exhortations at my Baptist church. I found the service easeful rather than agitating. However the outward manifestations of faith varied, it seemed to me that, within the congregations, the goodness of most and the hypocrisy and sins of some were no more or no less evident in each. Somewhere along the way, I had accepted that faith and good works were highly individual matters, not to be understood in either motivation or consequences. Although it might not serve as such in my current circumstances, that belief I found comforting.

CHAPTER FIVE

In the days following my "comeuppance speech," as I later heard Hertha had called it, I attended to the workmen who repaired Adelaide's chimney, fed them a hot mid-day meal, dressed the cuts on their hands, and provided tea in the afternoons. All with Lila's competent help. It was surprisingly easy to keep my mind occupied with the daily chores around Adelaide's home. I heard nothing from the ladies' circle. But Laura stopped when she saw me on the lawn. She was on her way to another meeting and couldn't stay to visit. What she left unsaid indicated that the circle was eddying around the issue with nothing decided.

When I determined to see Carly, I sensed that Lila did not want to accompany me, and, indeed, it was a fruitless journey. The door of the clinic was closed, the shades drawn, and no one answered my knocking. An old woman hobbled by and told me, "Gone and closed up." When I asked if she knew about the patients or where I might inquire about them, she shook her head. "The doc comes and goes," she said. "Nobody can keep up with him, and good riddance." I hailed a man driving a wagon and went to Carly's address. There I found a similar situation—a locked door and no one around, not even the boy Joey.

The man in the wagon waited, impatient to be off yet not wanting to leave me there alone. "Will you return me to Andrews Street?" I asked. I fished in my small handbag for some coins.

"Old Lucifer's gitting tired," he said. He slapped the horse's flank, gave me a hand up, and turned the wagon toward a better part of town. I could only assume Carly was well enough to leave the clinic and to find solace elsewhere. To that effect, not overly worried, I wrote to his sister that evening.

On the third day, one of the Irish workers brought Lila news from a friend of her mother. As I came from the kitchen, I saw he spoke reluctantly and kept his eyes on his feet. Lila rushed by me. At my insistence, he repeated the news: her mother's miscarriage during another of her father's raging drunks. "A sot, he is," he muttered.

Another quickly said, "When the drink's not on him, he's a good man."

Lila retreated to her room off the kitchen and stayed there for hours. When darkness fell, thinking she must be famished, I knocked on her door. "Hot bean and bacon soup and warm buttered bread."

"Come in, Miss, Sarranda." I heard her rise from the squeaky cot and water splash in the basin. After a few moments, I entered and placed the food on the bedside table.

"Adelaide sent word that she will be home by week's end," I told her. Then I went to her and hugged her hard. "You must not blame yourself, Lila, for being here, not with your mother."

The girl's face crumpled, but she attacked the food with the hunger of youth. I went out to carry back two mugs of strong coffee. Tea in porcelain cups didn't seem the right beverage at this time. She finished the soup and put the last of the bread in her mouth. "How did you know? How did you know I feel that way? I should be home with her. I could have—"

"What could you have done, Lila?" I asked quietly. "What would you have done?"

"I don't know. Oh, Sarranda, when he's drinking Da's the meanest man. He hits all of us, 'cept now me brothers run away, Timmie scoots out the door, sometimes he sleeps under a tub behind the house, he's just turned ten, and Jimmy, James he wants us to call him now, he tried to stop our da a few times, got his nose broke, he sneaks to the pub, the bar, he's starting to drink. I could have tried to stop Da's fists."

She ran out of breath and two tears rolled down her face. I put the coffee mug in her hands. "He has struck you?"

"Beat me black and blue, last time. That's when Mam made me come up here, to her cousins. But I could have—"

"Listen to me, Lila," I took a sip of the coffee, so hot it strangled me and I coughed. "Look at me. Would your mother welcome you if you went home to stay?" I made my voice harsh. "Would she want you there, to see her misery? To see her knocked about the next time? Would she?"

"No, no. She packed me bag and put me on the wagon when I left." Lila warmed her hands on the mug. She said fiercely, "She's proud, she is. She won't go out of the house after... afterwards. She thinks the neighbors don't know." She managed a small, bitter laugh. "She thinks they don't know."

"Of course they know. Wasn't it a neighbor who sent the message?"

"And a neighbor already arranged for Mary Sue, she's only eleven, to live with people on a farm outside Chatham town. The neighbor worried about her. Me mam knowed it but she halfway fought against letting her go."

I nodded. "She let her go to protect her and she put you on the wagon to protect you, Lila."

We sipped our coffee. I wondered about the safety of the young Timmie, already smart enough to get out of his father's reach, and about Lila's mother. What could she do, a woman without resources? Neighbors could help only so much, sympathize privately and pretend all was well publicly. Aware as I was of the battle going on in her mind and heart, I could not decide for Lila. And she could not decide for her mother, not even if she returned to the home. Short of murder, I shocked myself with this thought, what could two women do against the fists of a drinking man? Lila glanced at me once, twice, but I said nothing.

"I know you're right, Sarranda. If I'd go back, Da'd take me wages, whatever wages I had, and he'd not likely change, would he?"

"Not likely, Lila. Until, until—" Until he damaged or killed his wife or child and the law had to be called. Possibly Lila was thinking the same thing.

"I won't go back," she said. "But mayhap I can send a bit of money to Mam, and maybe that shawl Miss Adelaide give me."

"The men will finish here in two days. You could send it then, if you trust the man who told you."

"I do, well, I have to, don't I?" She reflected for a moment. "I'll tell Mr. Jeremy as well, so he'll see she gets what I send."

"Smart girl. Now, can you sleep or would you like to read in the parlor?"

"I don't feel like pretty poetry, Miss, Sarranda. I'll sleep after I clean up the kitchen."

My protests didn't prevent her from jumping up, washing the dishes, and going at the kitchen with mop and broom. She pushed me gently toward the library and an hour later announced, "Now I'll sleep, won't I?" She picked up the shawl from the settee, folded it and said, "Goodnight, Miss."

Years and years ago, angry at finding my brother Joe sitting by the creek, his chin cupped in his hand, I asked what in the world he had been doing while I worked in the hot cornfield alone. He'd looked up, surprised to see anyone there. "I've thought and thought and thought some more," he said, brushing twigs from his pants. "Hard work, sister, thinking."

I remember thinking *not as hard as hoeing corn all day*.

That evening, I thought and thought and thought some more. And went to bed exhausted.

The next afternoon Adelaide returned to sort us out. When she stepped down from the carriage, I could not read her face, beyond a pale weariness. I took her cloak. "We can have tea immediately unless you wish to rest."

"Thank you, dear Sarranda. Strong tea would be most welcome. I managed to rest on the train, but train tea? Well, I prefer our blend." She smiled. "I'll wash up and join you in a few minutes." She glanced around the foyer, the sparkling chandelier, the polished steps. "It's good to be home."

Her recital over tea was straightforward, as if the hours on the train had swept all emotion away. Douglas died two days after getting home, perhaps weakened by the trip. "He whispered at the end, 'Home. I'm going home.' At least," Adelaide said, "so the minister heard. He may have whispered he was glad to be home. Either way, he died in his own bed, with his wife by his side." What Adelaide's niece and her children might do in the next months was not settled; the house was a burden the widow could not afford. For now, Douglas's brother and his wife were there but that arrangement was temporary.

"A bad time for her," I murmured, "and for you."

Adelaide talked in a preoccupied way of the funeral, the details attached to any death, the kindness of neighbors and family, the uncertainty of the future. When she did not mention Carly, I asked if she had received my letters. She nodded and thanked me for writing.

"I understand he is in the care of our old family physician who has moved several miles out of town. He's recovering and does not know who set upon him or why, so, of course, he won't press charges. I'll go and see him later this week." She sipped her tea and gazed around the room. "Everything here is so pleasant," she said. "No smell of sickness or death. It is a large house, is it not," she said, "for one woman alone?"

"A very comfortable home."

"Sarranda, Laura met me at the station. She told me of the, ah, meetings and of the situation, if I may call it that, in which you—I should say we—find ourselves. Be assured I will not forsake you." She touched my hand lightly and stood up. "I shall do some visiting tomorrow. For now I'll say no more."

"I don't want you worrying about me," I said. "My time here has been most constructive." She glanced at me sharply but seemed disinclined to continue the conversation. "I am glad your brother is in good care. It can't be easy for you—you must rest. Pray do not fret about me."

She made no promise about that and we said our goodnights. Lila soon came in from her Institute evening and I told her the news as we immersed our hands in dishwater.

"Poor lady," Lila said. "I hope she won't mind me sending Mam the shawl."

"I think she'd be happy about that," I said. "And your mother will know you love her even if you can't be with her. She'll know it each time she covers her shoulders with the shawl."

Adelaide was gone all the next day. Having cleaned the house so thoroughly during her absence, Lila and I set to clearing the lawn and back garden. Even though my back and shoulders began to ache by mid-afternoon, I enjoyed picking up the fallen branches, raking leaves, and tidying up the garden. Physical activity outdoors in the cool, dry air offered a pleasant change from discussions and the clinking of teacups.

While resting in the wicker chair I dreamed of Grandda's old mill. I loved that mill as never I loved a cabin home or a city home. I hoped it was kept in good condition by whoever owned it now. I wished to see it and yet feared to find it falling into ruin. I told myself the mill was a childhood escape. It could have nothing to do with my return to the mountains—as return I would. My meager savings could hardly support me beyond a few months unless I returned, a supplicant, to my son or, heaven forbid, my cousins. I could surely find work as a domestic in Webster or even New Webster, keeping house, caring for someone with more money than family. That thought was hateful to me, but it was a possibility.

That evening Adelaide dropped onto the settee with a weary glance at the papers on her desk, and I took the opportunity to ask, "Shall I be returning to Mariah's home," I waited a moment, "until something is decided?"

"Oh no, Sarranda. You must stay here. Lila, however, will return to Mariah's the day after tomorrow. I know you'll miss her company, especially since I am obligated to be away much of the day." I was quick to assure her I understood and we spoke no more of it. When I brought her warm milk she was frowning at some article in her hands and I retreated to my room. Of course, I felt the burden I had imposed on her. Just when she must think of her niece's family, she had an obstinate woman on her hands rather than a willing missionary, and she had to explain that she must have misjudged me, she who prided herself on being a good judge of character.

A smothering of guilt pressed on me. *Did she or the other ladies think I was abusing their hospitality? Did they find my recalcitrant attitude beyond the bounds of proper behavior? Was I an ungrateful wretch who deserved to be put on a train and sent away without further ado? My thoughts tumbled and twisted but did not unwind in a new direction. I am sorry* I breathed in a whisper. But I said aloud to the darkness, "I cannot be Hertha's sort of mission worker. I cannot."

After our hurried breakfast the next morning Adelaide spent most of the day away. She did not ask me to accompany her to meetings. I determined to get out of this limbo into which I had placed myself.

However, Adelaide's face when she came in that evening revealed that something had been decided. We sat down and I listened.

The ladies' circles, who truly wished to aid the mountain people, could not in their official roles sponsor my journey. The ministers and congregations from whom they drew their own validation and who must ultimately supply support, both moral and financial, had apparently heard of my outburst. Their doubts were sufficient to withdraw, for the time being, at any rate, their backing.

Her report did not surprise me. After a few moments, I said, "They do not doubt my character?" I wondered how much damage Hertha could have done had she wished, and perhaps she had.

"Not at all, Sarranda." A smile flitted across Adelaide's face. "If anything, I've heard of your 'strong character.' Now, all is not bad news. That the churches and congregations cannot provide support is somewhat understandable. What did your mother and mine say? He who pays the piper calls the tune?"

"And every path has its puddles. But it was my grandfather who said it."

Adelaide's eyes sparkled behind her spectacles and I took heart.

"Several women believed strongly in what you advocated and were not shy about speaking up. They could not prevail, however, in the face of the church's dictums."

Looking into her face, I realized that she herself must be torn in both directions. I took her hand. "Tell me everything, dear friend. I am no callow youth."

"Quite simply," she said, "some like-believers have raised a sum of money, enough to take you back to North Carolina and keep you there, with great frugality on your part, for several months, perhaps a year." She went on with details I was too stunned to take in.

My smile interrupted her recital, and we clasped hands. "It will take a few days to get everything in order, to write to one or two persons we think will help you," she said. "This, I admit, is uncharted territory for us, working outside the church. Of course, we will give you names of any friends who will welcome you."

"You have not deserted me." I took a deep breath. "I have some small reserves of cash," I said. "I can make a start. I have thought of what I might accomplish and how."

"It will not be easy. You must know that, Sarranda. A lone woman venturing into a defeated and ravaged land, without the arm, the roof—" She drew a hand across her forehead. "I'm mixing my thoughts. Without the clear umbrella of the church—"

We laughed at her incoherence. "Parasols keep the rain off, true," I said. "But the puddles are still there."

"And just what, southern woman, do you mean by that?"

"I don't know. I suspect I'll get my feet muddy along the way, but I won't starve." I felt ridiculously happy. "This calls for tea and cake."

"Bring the sherry, please." With an exaggerated moan, she fell back on the cushions. She unbuttoned her shoes and placed her feet on the footstool. She must have dreaded telling me that her church leaders had been less than benevolent. But I didn't mind; surely I was better suited to be under the umbrella of women who believed in me enough to raise money rather than to rely on the coffers of the church.

With our sips of sherry, Adelaide became more specific. "It was Hertha's niece who spoke up strongly in your defense—she of the 'Song of the Shirt' recitation. She will give you particulars about a small chapel deep, I'm told, in your county. She somehow knows a young cousin of the minister. An unusual ministry, she says. Perhaps to your liking."

Soon Adelaide's eyes drooped and she announced she must retire. I sat for some time thinking before realizing that I wasn't thinking at all. I was feeling a bit nostalgic already for the comforts I would soon leave and at the same time seeing in my mind's eye the vast layers of the Balsams and the Great Smoky Mountains.

The next morning, Adelaide forgave Lila once more for sending the old shawl to her mother. The girl had apparently never received such a gift and she needed Adelaide's thrice-spoken assurance that she had done the right thing. I walked the despondent Lila to the door, knowing she had enjoyed the freedom of being beyond her orderly mistress's eyes. Even as we said goodbye, an idea was forming in my head, an idea I could not yet allow to become a full-fledged hope.

"I will certainly see you, Lila, before I leave. It's an easy enough walk over to Mariah's. Give her this basket of my pumpkin torts." I put the egg basket in her hands. "They're the one thing I can bake."

"Besides cornbread," Lila said. I had introduced her to my version of what I only halfway jokingly called, "the delicacy of the mountains."

Adelaide came to the kitchen door and presented a wrapped bundle to Lila. "For you, lass. It's the shawl I wore to the funeral."

Lila clutched the bundle to her chest and thanked Adelaide, blinking back tears. Black would keep Lila as warm as a pretty green to match her eyes would, even highlight her youth. She smiled as we again bade each other farewell.

In the kitchen, Adelaide looked down at her somber dress. "I've worn black long enough. Today I am going to my dressmaker. Navy blue, do you think, Sarranda? Or perhaps lilac or rose?"

"Rose," I said. "Dark rose, if you must."

Adelaide sat down and I put coffee before her. "Will you visit Hertha's niece this afternoon? It promises to be a fair day." I saw the beginning of a worried frown on her face.

"Indeed, I shall. What is it, Adelaide? Was the battle with Hertha and her forces so tiring for you?"

"A series of skirmishes," she said. "I was so sure you were the perfect candidate for our mission that perhaps I am downcast now. That I freely admit, Sarranda."

She sipped her coffee. Her mood seemed to lighten. "Far better that we know now, is it not?" She went on, "I have battled with my own conscience as much as with the views expressed at the various meetings. I believe firmly and strongly in our church's commitment and will continue to foster that commitment, but surely with more understanding of the overall battlefield, to continue the comparison. I'm steeped in the theology of my church, the church I grew up in. I support you, believe in you, but I also must stand with our synod and our leaders."

"Of course. I should have thought more deeply about my own reasons—"

"I feel I have made a friend in you, Sarranda. That alone justifies my travel to Charlotte. Now, say no more." She rubbed the bridge of her nose. "I shall have enough here to keep me busy."

"I'm glad you will abandon your mourning dress. I should like to see you turn the heads of the men of this town."

Her smile hinted at the girl she had once been. "I hardly aspire to that," she said. We both knew that men in the North and South were at a premium, at least undamaged, physically or emotionally, men of our age. "Carly may come to stay with me. He may be ready to seek treatment for his difficulty, but if that fails, I would like him near me."

"That is good. I hope he will continue to reach out to the community where we visited." I thought of young Joey, a boy who needed firm and sensitive guidance, as all children did. Without it, in another year or two he would spend his evenings in the tavern, emulating the men who frequented them.

As if reading my thoughts, Adelaide said, "The young boy we met there, remember him? He kept asking questions until he learned where Carly had been taken and he walked all the way to Dr. Cannon's home, miles beyond the town limits."

I replenished our coffee cups. "Joey has great perseverance, then. I remember his bare feet."

"Dr. Cannon has offered him a small room in his home, for now. He might take him on as a sort of apprentice. He hasn't told Joey, waiting to see how trustworthy he proves. And I assume he will need his father's approval. Carly will see that the proper papers are signed, if that should be the case."

Her grin told me that Carly might not be adverse to supplying drink in return for a signature or an X from Joey's father. I nodded when she said, "Sometimes we must work our Lord's miracles in our own way."

"You will not be alone, then, when I leave."

"The household will grow quite a bit. Lucinda and her children will likely come live with me. Douglas's family will shoulder some of the medical expenses and possibly help with the children's education in time. She faces being turned out of their home, possibly before Christmas." Again she removed her spectacles and rubbed her nose. "Carly will be a help with the children, I think. We hope. He will have to share the boy's room. Unless he wishes the room Lila slept in." She glanced toward the tiny room off the kitchen.

"Will it be difficult to accommodate yourself to the addition of four relations in your home?" I gestured toward her comfortable surroundings. "It is good of you."

"This was our parents' home. I must share it. How can I not? My brother and niece will be good company for me in my old age."

"Old age, indeed." I lifted my cup in a mock toast. "Here's to rose-colored dresses."

CHAPTER SIX

"Speaking of my brother," Adelaide stood and moved toward the door, "he says he brought the message about Carly. He said a woman with a bloody finger answered the door."

Surprised, I glanced at my hand as did she. With a barely suppressed chuckle, she went to the foyer. Choosing her hat for the day, she called, "I'm off to the dressmaker's."

My fingers loosened on the cup. I recalled myself in time to catch it before it fell to the table. Her brother. The man at the door in the rain, his hat pulled low, his collar high. I had seen him and didn't know him. *It couldn't have been my stranger. I would have known, wouldn't I? I would have sensed something about him.*

Foolish woman, I admonished myself. After so many years, why should my body or my heart have recognized the stranger in my cabin in those war years? A sense of desolation swept over me. I would be gone from New England before I ever knew if Adelaide's brother was my "lavender night" man. *I will stay, I could live here, I could wait, wait for an introduction*. No. I could not. This town, this state was not mine and never could be. And if I had not recognized my stranger-lover, neither had he recognized me. But then I had probably been no more than a woman handy on a dark night, lonely, willing, needy, perhaps one of many he had bedded as he traveled on whatever his assigned duty. Should we meet and be introduced formally, why should he remember? Or if reminded, care? Or if care, risk embarrassment by saying anything. On that rainy day, my attention centered on his message and a pricked finger. I stared at my finger as if it were the culprit.

The door had closed behind Adelaide for many minutes before I shook my head to clear it of regrets and hopes. First a few chores and then I would visit Hertha's niece. I anticipated a pleasant time with this apparently rebellious woman who dared quote poetry uninvited at public meetings. Yet, at the wash basin, rinsing the cups, I glared again at my finger. *Why had I not somehow seen beyond the man's clothing to his face, to his very essence?* A shiver ran through me. Then, my hands on the table top, I spoke firmly to myself, words my mother so often said to my brothers and me at the slightest misbehavior: *You know better than that. You ought to know better. You're old enough to know better.*

When Jim was only seven, he had chopped off a bit of Joe's trusting finger as he held a stick of stove wood on the stump, and Jim's hatchet fell. At our young ages, we should have known better. Jim knew the hatchet was newly sharpened, Joe even then knew his brother was capable of meanness, and I watched as the slice of Joe's little finger fell and blood gushed.

And, decades later, I ought to know better. If, I vowed, I ever came face to face with my stranger, I would know how to behave. If I had not erased him from my memory, I need demonstrate no outward knowledge of his kindness, his lips, his body. I was old enough to know better—neither an innocent girl-child nor a needy, lonely wife. The war had shown me the cruelties of man and nature. I knew not to expect too much of either.

Still, as I turned from the window where sunlight now brightened the room, a small hope remained unhardened. I ignored it.

The brisk walk down the main street and across the commons left me invigorated. In twenty minutes I stopped in front of Susanna's home, or rather the home of her father, Hertha's brother. He was widowed and Susanna, his youngest daughter, lived at home. When one woman had said Susanna "kept house for him," another woman rolled her eyes. I wasn't sure how to interpret that unspoken comment. But I was unprepared for the chaos that met my eye the moment I saw beyond the rotund, red-faced and bald man who opened the door.

He peered over half-moon glasses and stuck out his hand. "You must be the southern lady Susanna's told me about. Come in, come in." I shook his hand and announced my name.

"I hope your daughter is here," I said. "I wasn't sure of the exact day I'd come calling."

With a wave of his hand he ushered me into the parlor. "Pay no mind to this mess," he boomed. "I don't." He pushed a cat, some books, two cups, and a bonnet from one end of the settee and indicated I should sit there. "Scat, cat," he said and the calico unwound itself, stretched and disappeared under the curtains at the window. "Susanna!" He looked up the staircase. "Your southern belle is here."

The untidy room looked somewhat like the room to which Mrs. Whitney and her friends brought what she called "jumble" for the next church's sale. I had been amazed at the sheer quantity of goods, clothing, household items that could be discarded or, in their case, put to good use raising money. Here, three coats were strewn on chairs, and the pegs near the front door were laden with cloaks, hats, scarves, and gloves. However, a draft from the back of the house freshened the air and cooled the room. I removed my gloves.

"I was a sea captain," Susanna's father announced. "On board, everything had its proper place, never enough room for anything." His eyes sparkled. "Hardly enough for me in that confined and confounded cabin."

I began to understand the joy he might feel in simply throwing anything anywhere, not worrying about ship shape. However, I almost itched to arrange the books, straighten up the side tables, and dust the lampshade.

"Mary couldn't bear it," he said, looking around. "The place was neater then. But Susanna—she lets it be." This house was definitely not "kept."

"Father has a woman who comes in once a month." Susanna bounded down the final two steps. "Last Thursday it was neater. Sometimes it stays that way for the whole afternoon. I'm glad to see you, Mrs. Boylett." She gave my hand a hearty shake.

"I'll leave you two alone." Mr. Settles heaved himself from the chair. "Come on, cat, let's go sit in the garden." He looked toward the window where a tail curled from beneath the curtains. "There's hot cross buns in the kitchen, daughter. A pleasure to meet you, Mrs. Boylett."

"They smell wonderful, Susanna." I stood and followed her down a hallway cluttered with boots, brushes, and copies of magazines.

"No credit to me. Poppa's the baker," she said. "Mother wouldn't let him near her stove before she died. 'A woman's place,' she'd tell him. Now he bakes though he can't fry an egg or boil one either." Her laugh was infectious. She hardly resembled the sulky girl-woman at the meeting. "Sit here," she told me.

The polished table gleamed, free of food except for a basket of fragrant rolls covered with a white cloth. From a sideboard, she took two starched napkins and two plates and placed them before us. After pouring strong coffee, she pushed cream toward me, along with a mold of butter. In companionable silence we buttered the rolls.

"Heavenly," I said after the first bite. "Your father could hire out at any bakery."

"Now, my mountain-woman friend, what shall we discuss? I know a bit about you—what all the women know—and that you'll be going back to your state soon. With a little help from some women here." She bit into her hot cross bun with a sudden fierceness.

"Of you I know only that you read poetry," I said. "I think we could be friends, and for that reason I'll be sorry to leave Bramford."

"Have you felt at home here?" This girl was nothing if not direct.

"Welcome, yes. At home, no." I sipped the coffee and sighed my appreciation. "Perhaps I wouldn't feel at home anyplace except the mountains," I said. "They call to me, whether I go with a plan or simply go back, a beggar-woman, as you might say. Could you be 'at home' anywhere else? Am I hopelessly provincial? I don't fit in here. I doubt I ever would even if—"

"If?"

"Even if by some unlikely chance, a marriage opportunity should come my way." The words simply popped out of my mouth. What was I thinking? To no other woman in Bramford had I uttered a word about my single state, my widowed status. It was a subject I hadn't thought about. True, I'd thought about the stranger, but not of marriage.

Susanna's openness brought my thoughts out into the open. "Don't misconstrue my words, please." I touched her hand lightly. "Marriage is not an option for me. I turned down a most pleasant man in Charlotte and sent another most unpleasant one packing before that. And," I smiled, "they were natives of my state. No. I will make my own way."

"Sink or swim—alone?" Susanna said. "I believe you."

"I'm old enough to be your mother, Susanna, but you have a lifetime ahead. Is there a young man in your future?" I gazed at her earnest young face; intelligent and forthright she certainly was. I doubted she would keep house for her father forever. She must be no older than twenty-two or three. Unless she turned into an eccentric, indeed, until she did so, society would expect her to marry. Her aunt Hertha would be a chief prod.

"May I tell you a secret, Mrs. Boy—"

"Sarranda, please."

"Sarranda." At my encouraging nod, she rushed on. "Poppa has agreed that I am to go to England in two years' time. When I come into a small trust, my mother's legacy. If I still wish it—and I will, I know I will."

"How exciting! To study? Where?"

"To London where Poppa has sea captain friends. One family has promised to take me in—to study with their daughters or go about in society." Her eyes sparkled. "Oh, I have read so much about England. I want to see it for myself. Then I'll know what I want to do. Poppa says I should have more definite goals. If I should leave now, he says, I'd be setting sail without a compass, without even knowing my direction, except away." I saw a trace of the sulky girl about her lips. Perhaps she felt as confined in her hometown as her father had in a ship's cabin.

"Yes, I can see his reasoning," I said. "Are you so unhappy here?"

"I want to see more and do more than 'tis allowed me here." Her voice lowered. "All the women who knew Mother and who would like to befriend Poppa, all the older ones," she threw an apologetic glance at me, "want me married and out of the house."

I laughed. "They see you as a threat? A barrier to the heart and hearth of a healthy widower? Yes, I can believe that."

"You're a strong woman and a determined one. I admire the way you spoke up at that meeting and your wish to help your people. The South is a place, a concept even, that I cannot truly grasp. I even wish I had an inclination to travel there, to open my mind, but honestly, my way is east. Did you know I was born on Poppa's ship, as it was sailing from Southampton?" She grinned. "On the one and only sea journey my mother ever went on. She hated sea journeys after that—and who can blame her? I was supposed to be born in England, not on choppy seas. I tease Poppa that they should have thrown me overboard, to make my way back to England." She chose another bun. "It's easy to talk to you, Sarranda. But let's talk about you."

"I almost wish I were your age," I said. "Younger than you, I was married and the mother of two boys, a third on the way." I stopped. It was not the time for me to remember those hard years "In some ways," I said, "going home will be like crossing the ocean. I cannot be sure of what I will meet or how I will proceed. But I must go. Women need so much there now. The war is over but the land has not recovered, nor the spirit of those who lost so much."

Susanna nodded in sympathy, but how could she understand the two girls who had come to the mill one day at the end of the war? They were hardly into puberty, wasp-thin, eager, gratefully accepting the attentions any man who could provide adequate food, a roof, safety—necessities in a land scorched, homes destroyed and men damaged and dangerous, war weary and soul-stripped. I did not speak of them.

I needed to learn what I could of Susanna's friend's ministry in the North Carolina Mountains.

"Tell me about this unusual church you know of. I understand it is in my county but I know naught of it."

"And I know only from correspondence from the minister's young cousin, Lannette Blanchard. She visited relatives in Boston last year, and Poppa and I met her at a concert. She is now in Rhode Island. Her constitution is poor. I think she suffered much deprivation, even hunger, during the war. Her aunts sent her to a private sanatorium somewhere near the sea."

"I am sorry," I said. "Does she expect to return home?"

"It seems unlikely. Her letters come irregularly and sometimes I see a smudge as if a tear had been dried on the paper. But I do not discern any homesickness such as you have, Sarranda."

"She may have endured such harsh times that she has no desire to return to the mountains," I said. "I can understand. Almost."

"She says her cousin was much changed by his war experiences. He was wounded and imprisoned for many months. During that time, a Union guard engaged him in conversation about God and the nature of religion." She stared at her coffee.

"I am on uncertain ground, Sarranda, when it comes to theology. You must understand—and even forgive me—if I offend without meaning to. Poppa and I attend the Congregational church but he encourages me to read and to question, as I could not do when my mother lived. Anyway, Lannette's cousin found the Universalist belief to his liking and after he returned home, he became a minister in the faith. He has some following among the people there. A good and noble man, so he seems."

"Universalist?" I was unacquainted with such a church. "How does it differ, I wonder, from other churches?"

"I can only say that it seems more," she hesitated, "more all-embracing. Lannette said he believes and she would like to—those are her words—that all people will be saved. No one will burn in hell's flames. Goodness will win over evil..." Her voice trailed off. She pushed the buns away and gave me a speculative look.

"It is indeed different," I said. "No hell?"

"But a heaven for all, I think he believes." Susanna squirmed in her chair. "Would that we all could believe that sentiment." She smiled. "What would my aunt Hertha make of that!"

"And what do the people in his settlement think of it? Tell me anything else you know of this minister."

"I know very little more. He preaches. He has has built a church. The family lives far from a town." She frowned trying to remember. "I've asked Lannette to write to him about you but have not had a reply. I hope she is not ill."

"We have been given a few names of persons to meet. It will be good to have a minister in my county to contact," I said. "Universalist? Universalism? There must be tracts from which I can learn about it."

"Just don't ask my aunt." Susanna grinned. "Let's sit more comfortably in the other room."

We chatted for another hour. I think Susanna needed a woman's ear, a woman who was not judgmental about her dreams and her poetry. She confessed that her poetic outburst resulted partly from irritation with her aunt who, she said, perceived the world "with the blinders of old Jem Ackers' nags." I deemed it wise to listen, rather than say anything about her aunt. She was impetuous enough that at another time she might inadvertently repeat my comments. I did, however, nod in agreement.

. When her father's footsteps sounded on the stairway, I rose to take my leave. He peered around the door, sea-blue eyes twinkling. "I see the maid hasn't started our evening meal. What's a papa to do?"

"He's funning, Sarranda." Susanna directed a broad smile at him. "We eat late and light." She pointed to his stomach. "Regardless of how it looks."

"I wish you well, Susanna," I said. "I believe you'll make your dreams a reality." I left their home, pleased with Susanna's acquaintance and curious about this unfamiliar religion.

Walking back to Adelaide's I slowed my pace and mused about what I might find at the Reverend Julius Blanchard's church. A minister preaching a religion with no hell? To be honest I had some time since forsaken the idea of a hell full of flames and suffering. It lacked the reality for me that apparently had been instilled in others. I heard the word routinely in the church services back in Greene's Valley but whether the preacher had shouted warnings or pronounced threats, a concept of hell had not adhered to my thinking. If a man said, "May his soul rot in hell" or a woman said, "He'll roast in hell for doing what he done," they may have meant it literally, but I took the words for sheer emotion. Even when a stony-eyed blacksmith declared that "the bastards that come through and burnt the Masons' farmhouse and set them little children a-flaming will taste the fires of hell in the next life," I cringed at the vision of the farmhouse flames, not the flames in the "depths of hell in the hot bowels of the earth."

I remembered words spoken in the heat of revival meetings, words condemning and damning. If those who heard them truly believed them, the Reverend Blanchard would have a difficult time swaying them to a belief in the goodness of all men and the existence of a heaven without its counterpart. It took a brave or devout believer to espouse such a view in the years following the time many deemed a hell on earth. I looked forward to seeing such a man. My grandda, Baptist though he was, might have liked him. And Rankin, removed for a better life with my brother Joe and his Negro wife, and now dead, might have said "amen" to his preaching.

I am no minister, I told myself. I can accept help from any and all who believe in helping those who help themselves. Wasn't that scripture? God helps those who help themselves? I wouldn't discuss this Universalism with Adelaide. She was sure of her faith and her church. If she had doubts, in youth or now, she was not one to convey them to her friends, or so I judged.

At Adelaide's I entered through the front door, of course, but the draft in the hall told me the back door was ajar. I hurried to see who might be in the kitchen and found Lila, looking as forlorn as I'd ever seen her.

"What's the matter, my dear?" I wanted to hug her as a sister or mother might but feared she'd burst into tears at a sympathetic touch. "Is there bad news of your family?" Tossing my cape aside, I found two glasses and poured cider. "Here, drink this." I sat beside her and pushed the cider toward her hand.

"It's me da," she said. "He's gone. To sea, they say. Mam wants me home with her. She sent word by one of the chimley workers."

Her eyes were dark as if too many unshed tears had dimmed their hazel brightness. "And, and, I'm of marrying age. She wants to see me provided for and there's a neighbor who's—"

"Willing?" I finished. She blinked. I took a large gulp of the cider, and, as if seeing it for the first time, she did also. "She wouldn't force you to marry this man, would she?"

"No." Lila wiped at her eyes. "But I can't let her starve or go to the poor house, can I? I can't forsake my mam."

The light-heartedness with which I'd left Susanna's had been swept a world away, as had thoughts of an afterlife. Enough troubles in this one.

"I'm sorry, Miss, I mean Sarranda. I had to tell someone. The girls at the Institute say I don't have many choices. And, maybe he's a good man." Lila attempted a smile. "I couldn't talk to Miss Mariah, so I came here." She looked around the kitchen. "I been sitting here thinking, and I 'spect I'll go home. The boys have been sent to work at a farm way out from town. Better that, than be sent to the city workhouse or to the trains. James will take care of Timmie. Mam needs me."

"There must be some way other than a marriage of necessity," I said. "Come, I'll put the kettle on. Surely there's a sweet in the cupboard." I was not in the least hungry but Lila needed the comfort of tea and cake. "Have you eaten?"

"Not since breakfast. I been out walking the streets." She bit her lip. "I went to Mr. Carly's place but it's closed up."

"He's away now, recovering. I believe he will be moving in here soon."

"Oh." She stood and took the kettle from me.

As I went toward the stairs, I wondered if I imagined a disappointed look in her eyes. "I'll join you in a few minutes."

Although I couldn't offer Lila much advice in the next hour or so, I listened and even drew a smile or two from her. About my visit with Susanna I told her simply that we'd had a most pleasant afternoon. Susanna's plight was hardly as dire as Lila's. As long as the Captain didn't foist a stepmother on her, and he seemed in no hurry to do that, she would find herself in England as her heart desired. As dusk turned to darkness, Lila said, "Thank you for listening," and gathered her shawl. "Miss Mariah worries if I walk in the streets after dark. My mind's a bit easier now."

When I heard Adelaide's carriage, I was comfortable on the dark green haircloth sofa and had rehearsed what I intended to say. My thoughts had turned and crisscrossed themselves in several directions before, as if untangling a skein of yarn, a solution presented itself.

Moments after Adelaide divested herself of cloak and hat, a storm descended. I hurried to close windows and light lamps. Adelaide picked up a book from the marble-topped table, glanced at me, and replaced the book. "Something is on your mind, Sarranda." She frowned. "Has Hertha called? Have the ladies reconsidered their offer?" She looked more closely at me, "No, your face tells me it must not be bad news."

I sat straight-backed as a Harvard student. In a few sentences, I outlined my proposition and she agreed so wholeheartedly that I clasped her hands in delight. In short, two women needed help—Lila and her mother. I proposed that Lila accompany me south, promising, "Her presence will incur no extra expense. I will see to that." I further proposed that Adelaide consider having Lila's mother come to live with her, as housekeeper and cook.

Adelaide's face shone with warmth. "Yes," she said. "We will need help with the household, with the children." She leaned back. "How clever of you, Sarranda. Now, it only wants their agreeing."

"I am optimistic," I said. "I would like to go at once and tell Lila—rain or no. She was utterly disconsolate when she left here."

"Pray contain your enthusiasm, friend. It will do you no good to get wet and perhaps catch your death from the cold. Even my large umbrella would not protect you. Tomorrow we will send for her and see." Adelaide was ever practical, but her next words were teasing. "Perhaps she will have decided to marry this man who is willing."

"It would be a solution," I agreed. "But Lila has an independent spirit, I find."

"A kindred spirit, yes."

"And we are great conspirators, are we not?"

Lila came within an hour of being sent for and, though clean, her frock had hardly seen the hot side of an iron. With her thin shoulders wrapped in Adelaide's shawl, her fingers fidgeting with the fringes, she looked as if she had not slept at all.

"No, ma'am," she answered when asked if the boy had come for her too early. "Seven's not so early for me. I had Miss Mariah's breakfast laid out. She sent me straightaway." Lila stood straight but her voice quivered a little. "It's not that I've done something amiss, is it? Miss Mariah worried that p'haps I've offended."

"Nothing of the sort, dear child." Adelaide guided Lila to a chair. "Here, drink this." I handed her hot coffee, knowing that Mariah only offered tea.

When Adelaide nodded to me, I spoke. "Lila, we have discussed your situation and your mother's and we believe the both of you can help the both of us."

She took two gulps of the hot liquid, shivered and cupped her hands before her. "Help? How? Oh, you know I'd do anything but I can't leave me mam alone." Tears threatened and she grasped the cup again.

I hastened to put her out of her misery. "Could you leave your mother in a good house, doing good work? And would you go with me to North Carolina?" There I'd said it, as plain as I could.

Lila's coffee sloshed onto the table. She quickly moved to wipe it up, but Adelaide motioned her to stay seated, murmuring, "I'll get it."

Lila exclaimed, "Oh, I could go with you, yes, Miss, yes, Sarranda. I could leave this town—" Lila's eyes glowed, but a flicker of doubt and then another crossed her face. "I could leave. But me mam? What do you mean?" She looked at each of us in turn.

Adelaide answered. "I need someone here to help when Lucinda and her children come to live with me. Children are tiring for one unaccustomed to their liveliness. And, my brother will also move in."

"Oh, Miss Bell," Lila's look conveyed both sympathy and understanding. "That they can, children, I mean. And Mr. Carly? Your brother—" She floundered and dropped her eyes.

"Adelaide knows that your sister and brothers are no longer living at home and that your father has sailed." The man had abandoned his family in a cowardly fashion, but "sailed" seemed a kinder term. I poured more coffee for Lila and filled a cup for me, giving her time to absorb our words. "I would be more comfortable traveling with a companion," I said, realizing just how true that was. "And certainly Miss Bell will require household help."

"Only that small room," Adelaide gestured, "is available. Would it be satisfactory for your mother?"

"Mam's not never had her own room, with nobody in it," Lila said. "And it's warm and the roof don't leak." She spoke with the authority of one who knew her family's circumstances. "Me young sister is well looked after. Mam don't worry about her. I think she would be happy to come here, especially if sometimes she might see my brothers at the farm."

Adelaide started to speak, but Lila went on. "They're a sight better off where they are. They sleep in the barn in the summer and in the attic in the winter. They get three meals every day. Johnny seen a boy who said they're working hard but sleeping sound, with 'no drinking and disputing and disturbing' around. Timmie might get to go to school after the crops are in." Her face flamed with embarrassment. "Oh, I beg pardon. I'm chattering away."

Adelaide took her hand. "We can arrange visits, I'm sure. About going with Sarranda—it may be a hard and even treacherous journey."

"Yes," I said. "We'd have to watch our pennies and we don't know exactly what we'll be doing—"

"But helping people?" Lila said. "And I'll be a great help to you. I swear it."

"A promise will do." Adelaide chuckled. "I don't hold with swearing."

My heart lightened as we sat around the table, talking of cloaks to be mended, shoes to be resoled, arrangements to be made, notes to be written, tickets, our mission, my hopes, Lila's expectations. I would miss the company of Adelaide and Mariah, who combined formality with friendliness, and I would keep in touch with Susanna. Laura and some of the other women I respected and liked, as acquaintances rather than friends. Hertha I would not miss at all. I was warm, comfortable, accepted in this home, but it was not mine. My home I had to find again.

Handyman Harkey carried messages back and forth between Adelaide and Lila's mother. I saw Adelaide slip him some money to assist Lila's mother, who, it turned out, was recovering from a broken wrist. Luckily, it was her left wrist and healing nicely. She could travel to Bramford within two weeks. Adelaide's skillful questioning had revealed that Lila's father had thrown his wife against a wall, resulting in the break and in his precipitous sailing to avoid possible arrest. The neighbors, tired of the family's woes, and against Lila's mother's protests, had threatened to call the authorities.

"They'd have done but nothing, Miz Bell," Harkey said, "but it put the fear into the man, and a ship sailing that night needed a hand in the hauling. Good riddance to him."

Lila flew into tears of rage at her father and then, surprisingly, spread her hands in resignation. "Me mam, she never could stand up to him, but she's strong in ever other way. Married at fourteen she was. She's but thirty-eight." She managed a smile. "Living without me pap will be a blessing. I'm sorry I won't see her before we go, but she'd not want me to know what he done, did, to her."

Before I could ask, she said, "No. I ain't marrying. I'm going traveling."

CHAPTER SEVEN

Flushing with excitement, Adelaide announced the next day, "Sarranda, air out your best gown. We are invited to the home of Anson and Juliet Beckley this very night. How I could have lost the invitation, I will never know. Juliet saw me today and was highly perturbed that I had not replied. Oh dear, it must have been misplaced in all the furor of my leaving and returning. Oh never mind." She bustled about. "It's a small party, perhaps thirty or so guests, for an informal concert at their home. Her cousin is visiting from Boston, and Juliet said we may expect an announcement. She emphasized *may expect*. At any rate," she finished, "it will be an interesting evening."

I turned my head this way and that as Adelaide fluttered around the room like a pent-up butterfly. "Please, calm yourself," I said. We went into her bedroom, the first time I'd seen it, and she pushed gowns aside in the wardrobe, muttering as she shifted the garments.

"Will my dark navy do," I finally asked, "with my Nottingham lace?" It was my one "smart" gown. "Are you sure I'm invited? We have not met."

"Oh yes, I told her we would come together. Your blue will do nicely," she said, "and I have some gloves for you." Almost dramatically, she held out two gowns. "But which of these for me?"

She'd chosen a becoming black silk and a taffeta of deep rose, so dark it was almost a burgundy, the gown just the day before delivered from her dressmaker. We both knew which gown most suited her, but she was accustomed to wearing black. I assumed a pondering look, fingers to my mouth. She held the rose before her, a lovely gown with puffed sleeves and tiny pearl buttons.

"Yes" I said. "A perfect choice. You must wear it."

"People may think poorly of me."

"Not so," I assured her. "Or only those who envy you."

"Then I shall wear it, with my black hooded cape. I will ask a friend to come do up my hair," she said. "Unless you would like to try your hand at it."

"Not I." My own hair I could twist into an acceptable coiffure of coils but beyond that I was hopeless. I sometimes wished for the pigtails of my childhood.

The grandeur of the Beckley home awed me; it sat far back from the stately avenue lined with elm trees, a quiet street in the best part of town. Tonight the street was only slightly disturbed by the occasional snorts and pawing of the horses at the heads of various carriages. The attendant drivers sat silent or spoke quietly in twos and threes. They doffed their caps as we descended from the hired buggy that would return for us in three hours. "Three hours at any party is my limit, I fear," Adelaide confided. I hoped I was up to that amount of time. However, on each side of the home were elaborate gardens and a luxuriant rose garden adorned its front. I could escape to the gardens if I became uncomfortable in the elegant company. With that thought I walked into a social setting that no home thus far in Adelaide's town had prepared me for.

In two large rooms settees and chairs had been pushed against the walls to allow the crowd to circulate around tables, each centered with a mass of autumn flowers, in becoming shades of autumn orange, deep yellow, dark green. The tables were piled with sweets, cheeses, fruits, and sandwiches. Shining silver and crisp linen napkins beside stacks of fine china beckoned the guests. At two tables liquids shimmered in large, cut glass punch bowls and at a smaller one a silver coffee urn sent aromatic fumes circulating. The chandeliers glowed with dozens of gas lights. The evening was reasonably cool but the French windows were open. A bit overwhelmed at this splendor, I welcomed the fresh air.

At the grand piano, a young woman sat, running her fingers over the keys and her eyes over the men surrounding her. She and the other younger women sparkled with gems, competing with the chandelier's glow. Surely those rings and necklaces could not be real. One ring would feed and clothe a boy like Joey, his whole family even, for months. A few women held wine glasses or cups of punch. "It's a mild rum punch with origins in the Caribbean, from when the Beckley grandfather owned pineapple plantations there," Adelaide whispered. She handed me a cup. "It's mostly fruit juice."

"What are the men drinking?"

"They've likely found a flask or two in the library." She waved toward the hall.

Though I responded politely and correctly to Juliet Beckley's greeting, the scene rendered me almost speechless. I wore no jewels, and my dress was respectable enough, if not in any way daring or memorable. As Adelaide steered us around the room, introducing me, chatting of this and that, I saw that the eyes of several women followed her circuit. They certainly noticed her gown and her quite elaborate hairstyle. I was sure that tomorrow's talk would be of her giving up her mourning dress and speculation about why or whom.

The woman who had now left the piano literally sparkled, in a dress of light blue bedecked with hundreds of tiny beads. It was the loveliest gown in the room and she knew it. Her voice was both high and breathy, and when she laughed heads turned to her. She was encircled with admirers so that Adelaide and I hesitated in our moving through the room and looked in admiration. I marveled at her poise and at the long curls of auburn that decorated her neck. Someone said, "A Worth gown, is it not?" but the words meant nothing to me. Adelaide certainly was not frowning but I sensed a small disapproval.

Without appearing to do so, her eyes explored the room as if searching for a face not there.

"Are you expecting someone?" I asked.

"I thought perhaps Colonel Morris might be here." She sighed. "I wonder if the announcement, the *may be* announcement, has to do with with Juliet's cousin and him? Or perhaps, with my brother—"

A jovial man with great mutton chops, already red-faced from social exertion or spirits, clapped Adelaide on the shoulder. After a cursory nod he guided her to the punch bowl. I had not caught his name. Was he her Colonel Morris? His demeanor did not strike me as being compatible with the serious woman I knew. The room swirled with color, punctuated with black. Most women, my age and older, wore black with offsets of cream and soft color touches. A reminder that the war had taken husbands and sons. I recognized two women; they nodded but made no effort to leave their conversations to join me. Everyone appeared confident, sure of his and her place in this gathering. If they didn't know each other, kinship and business connected them. Their families were not newcomers; no carpetbaggers here.

I wondered if, smoldering beneath their cordiality and their pleasant words to me, lingered resentment—an anger against a rebellious group of states that had cost them dearly in sons and husbands, fathers and cousins, brothers and friends. Even the winners in war lose. I breathed deeply, remembering those opportunists who had hurried south to rape or reap, to certainly profit from defeat. I hoped I did not meet anyone who spoke of finding in the South a wealth of financial prospects or anyone who spoke truly or not of those who fell prey to or aided their ventures. Did they see me as an ignorant, slow-talking and thus slow- thinking or no-thinking woman? Standing alone surrounded by chatting people, I drew myself up into an attitude of indifference, even insolence.

Adelaide turned and moved to disengage herself from her companion, but he laid a restraining hand on her arm and leaned toward her, starting another conversation. It would be awhile before she could leave him. Juliet's cousin had cornered a tall gentleman and was leaning immodestly close to him. Even as he bent to hear her, he looked toward Adelaide with something of amusement in his expression. Perhaps he was her Colonel Morris. Juliet's cousin touched his cheek with an intimacy that surely any man would understand and most would welcome.

Knowing my thoughts were unworthy of me, I relaxed my facial muscles, moved toward a less-crowded wall, and studied two landscapes. After several moments I sensed that I was the object of scrutiny; someone was watching me intently. I did not want to turn to confront the rudeness. I swept my eyes swiftly around the room and, without pausing, saw a man studying me, a wine glass now covering part of his face. It was the man with whom Juliet's cousin had been flirting. Ungentlemanly as his staring was, I was glad he had separated himself from her, if only temporarily.

As Adelaide moved toward the man, I turned and slipped through the crush of bodies to the outside. The cool air held a hint of rain and a small rumble of thunder sounded in the distance. A downpour would be welcome; it would dampen my inner anger as I walked on the brick garden path edged with clumps of hydrangeas. My anger lay heavy and uncomfortable in the pit of my stomach. Those appraising eyes had unsettled me.

I stepped down into the garden, near a small pond with a fountain bubbling in its center. There was a faint scent of late roses and another scent I could not name. Jasmine? A bit like mountain honeysuckle. Lanterns had been placed throughout to guide guests' footsteps along the path. A few minutes of strolling, stopping to admire clumps of asters, various shrubs and more hydrangeas, soothed my spirit. I was ashamed of myself. These people were Adelaide's friends; she had made me welcome. It was I who judged them, not the other way. They did not know me and, thus, whatever they may have thought was inconsequential to me. They would remember me only as the mountain woman who had caused some consternation among the ladies' circles. I turned at the sound of footsteps.

Adelaide had found me, and she seemed somewhat agitated.

"There you are, Sarranda! Why did you leave? The concert has begun. The young man is studying in New York and has family here." She looked around. "Let us sit. This bench is clean enough."

All the wrought-iron benches had undoubtedly been scrubbed before the party. I obediently sat beside her. "I don't think anyone will miss us," she said. "Oh, Sarranda, I confess I feared that the cousin intended to announce an engagement. I simply must stop calling her 'the cousin.' Her name is Josephine Emma."

"Why fearful? Do you know her so well?"

"Not at all, but what an immodest woman she is."

"Then?"

"Have I not told you...oh, everything has been so rushed lately, so much to consider. I feel completely beside myself. Did I not tell you my brother would be here tonight? Not Carly," she said quickly when I gasped. "Not Carly, he is hardly ready for a party such as this—all those strong spirits in Mr. Beckley's library. Carly—"

"Your brother?"

"Yes. My brother Addison. He came to the door with the message. You remember?"

Of course I remembered a man at the door. A vendor. He was here?

"I feared that the cousin Josephine had ensnared him. They were once considered a suitable match. That was before the war, before she—"

"He's here?"

"Yes, Sarranda, what's wrong? You are pale. Josephine intimated they were to be engaged, but he was called into service and essentially disappeared for several years. She meanwhile went to France and, oh,

I'm gossiping. It isn't fair to her and most of what has been said is surely untrue. However she has recently returned, this time from Ireland, this time a widow she says. Wearing blue! And this time with a small child. Did you not see her with him? Not the child, I mean—"

"Adelaide," I said as sternly as I could with my heart beating so rapidly, "I do not know your brother. Addison. He did not introduce himself that day. I only took the message."

She brushed at her hair, now in some disarray.

"Carlyle," I said, to distract me and calm her, "Addison. Your mother read the English essayists?"

"Yes. She loved the eighteenth century writers. She named her sons Johnson, Addison, Carly. Those were her favorite essayists in that order. Though I believe Addison was our mother's favorite son." She chuckled. "Thankfully she didn't read Defoe or I'd be Moll."

"Or Richardson and you'd be Pamela."

"She didn't read novels," Adelaide admitted. "And, to be fair, each brother has a grandfather's name attached. Johnson Francis, Addison Ellis, Carlyle Wilton."

We both realized we were skirting the reason she had come to find me.

"Is your brother," I could not call him Addison, "is he the cousin's suitor? I saw her flirting with someone. Will they announce their engagement tonight? As Mrs. Beckley thought?"

"I don't know, Sarranda. I looked around for you but Manley Gilmer detained me. Then Addison also disappeared." She let out a long breath. "He's good at that. I thought he might be here, in the garden. Parties bore him, and he's been known to leave without a courteous goodnight." An exasperated elongated sigh. "Brothers."

"Yes," I said, thinking of my own very different brothers.

"I must find the powder room and repair this hair," Adelaide said. "I'll slip up the stairs while the pianist is playing and come back here. We can then say our goodnights."

I sat as stone, an idle mill stone. The aroma of roses wafted by in a slight breeze and I smelled lavender, just a smidgen or I dreamed it. I closed my eyes, willing the scent to stay, knowing surely at this month and in this garden it couldn't be. Perhaps I dozed, though I had barely sipped from the punch, its fruity taste not to my liking.

A cough startled me. "Pardon, madam," a cultured voice came from the shadows. I sat straighter and straightened my gown, not totally alert.

"Forgive my staring earlier—inside, but you remind me of someone. Have we perhaps met?"

I knew the voice. *My stranger-lover of years before, the soldier or spy for whom I'd rubbed lavender on my neck and arms.* My heart thumped in my chest. I knew who he was and what we had done. Giving and receiving pleasure unchecked by thought or consequence. My cheeks burned and I blessed the darkness. I had imagined how I would react upon meeting him, if ever I did, rehearsed a polite introduction in a drawing room, me self-assured, in stylish dress. He would sweep his eyes over me with the recognition of...of what? My foolish girlish thoughts had not involved a dark garden.

"Madam?" He did not step closer, and I wondered how much he could see of me, in the small clearing, no lantern nearby. I saw only a dark form and the toes of polished boots. But the voice, I knew the voice, edged now with impatience.

"We have not been properly introduced," I said. "Who are you?" It was my lover but was he Adelaide's brother? At that moment I hoped not. What would she think of me should he have revealed our encounter? But no gentleman would have spoken of it. Nor of the possible, nay, likely other nights with other women. Soldiers did not discuss war experiences with a sister. The returning soldiers I'd met did not talk of the realities of war, though some surely lied and boasted or embellished their exploits.

Most buried those bad times or made light of them—in polite company, at any rate.

Silence flooded over me as the roar of rushing water from a spring freshet drowns everything in its way. My ears roared with the silence. I wanted to see his face. I feared to see his face. My eyes darted toward the house. Within two days, I would be out of this state, out of this town. Did I want to risk possible ridicule by giving this man my name? Could I risk his recognizing me as bedmate and nothing more? Indeed, he might be the bespoken of that cousin. She had touched him with an air of expectancy if not proprietorship. The thought of his belonging to another woman might have loosened my tongue, but when I opened my mouth no words came. I shook myself. Wanting to flee, I dared not stand; my legs would not hold me up.

"Then, madam, I bid you goodnight. I'm sorry to have intruded." His form became shadow and my hand went to my bosom. A fool—that's what I was. A fearful fool, like an old horse spooked at a squirrel or possum in its path. Stuck. Immovable. A frightened old mare that even a flick of a whip would not stir she was ready.

His footsteps receded; the danger was gone. I breathed again and braced myself to stand. I would not return to the bright lights of the drawing room. Adelaide could bid our hostess goodnight. At that moment I despised the party and despised myself for protecting my heart. I might never see him again, but he was the stranger.

Inside I had seen his dark hair streaked with silver at his temples. His eyes I had not seen, bound as they had been by the cousin. His body. I knew that body, not attired in immaculate evening wear, but wounded, lean flesh smelling of blood and war. An ache of wanting coursed through me. I was a foolish old mare but not yet dead to feeling.

Deception, pure and simple, flat-out deception. I bent over, my head in my hands, my elbows on my knees. I heard Adelaide's soft, "Sarranda. Sarranda, what is it?"

Within minutes she led me back to the buggy, helped me inside, and went to tell the Beckleys of my sudden indisposition. Unfortunately, once a lie is begun it must be followed through, an excellent reason for not starting one. In the buggy, I drooped and on her arm I went up the stairs of her home, assuring her I could undress and fall into bed. She appeared after a decent interval with pennyroyal tea and dry crusts to aid my roiling stomach.

"Stay, if you will," I said. Not that I intended to tell her I wasn't sick, for in truth I was ill, upset with my behavior. I wanted to know—something of the stranger.

"Is he engaged, your brother?" Had I asked her that question earlier? Was I repeating myself?

She gave a small snort and settled herself in a chair near my bedside. "Not a bit of it. The scoundrel. He disappeared, as is his wont, and the cousin said nothing, nor did Juliet. There was no announcement. I am bound to think it was mere hope on Josephine's part." Adelaide tossed her long, now loose, hair. "He is a handsome one and by most women's standards surely a catch. Me, I prefer a more settled type."

"Colonel Morris?" I ventured.

"You will persist, won't you, Sarranda? I will miss you and," she paused, "even be a bit jealous of your intrepid self heading into the mountains."

"They are my mountains," I reminded her. "Not the wilds of the Amazon."

"Surely changed since you left," she said. "As have you."

"Have I?" As I said it, I could not doubt her assessment. I was not the same woman who had left her beloved Greene's Valley and its mill. Neither, however, was I a New Englander with Adelaide's confidence of her place in society.

I returned to my questioning. "The colonel was not at the party?"

"I was told he had business elsewhere. His family has commercial interests across the state. He must give some attention to them, since it seems his older brother is, shall we say, sometimes indifferent to the demands of the mills."

"Mills?"

"Cotton mills. Great buildings set on the rivers upstate. I am not, Sarranda, his major interest."

"But," I ventured with a sly smile, "you could be his *colonel* interest—if you continue to wear color and put your hair up as tonight."

She laughed. "I believe you are feeling better already! Is it worth it, you think? The dress, the hair, the bother?"

"Only you know that," I said. "I am no great expert on what women will do or men expect."

"You may very well face the same question, my friend," she responded. This was the first time we had spoken directly, as women in regard to men, and I both welcomed it and feared I might give myself away. Deception by omission is difficult, perhaps more difficult than lying. What could come of facing my memory of years past? Of revealing that memory? Was I a rational coward? A cowardly rationalist? I could flog myself with my unseemly behavior or I could face the reality: a past is past and in no way could it be recreated in its original intensity. Memory is safe, even sacred, if sealed; and beware the prince or the troll who would unseal it, lest what leaps out is nothing like the original.

"Sarranda," Adelaide's voice came as if from some distance, "are you feeling faint again? Here, drink some water. You look dazed." Her concern caused me to focus on her face.

"I am feeling tired, drained," I said. That was no lie, if not the whole truth. "But, dear Adelaide, while I hope and rejoice to hear that your colonel returns from family business soon—and to you—such is not my hope for myself." I sipped from the glass she held out to me. "One husband was enough for me."

"And if not a husband?" Her blunt question was so unlike her that I set the glass down with a thump.

"A lover, you mean?"

"Would you take a lover if marriage were not an option?"

"It has been done through time forever." I hesitated. She waited and I stumbled on. "Would I? Circumstances might prove it the one alternative..."

"Circumstances such as?" Adelaide looked down at her hands, her face in shadow. She was not letting the subject go. Perhaps Colonel Morris had intimated it was a route he preferred. I pulled myself up on the pillow to allow myself some time.

"In my life I know of some such circumstances. After the war, as men returned to find women alone, there were couplings without the benefit of law or the church's blessing, but as far as I know they were long lasting." I shifted on the pillow, not entirely comfortable with my answer. "Survival and, ah, mutual need sometimes do make for," I searched for a word, "for ties that bind."

"Ah, ties—"

"Even before the war, one of Grandda's friends sired two different families within a half-day's horseback ride from each other," I said. Grandda's mouth had twisted in a smile I didn't understand then and wasn't sure I did now. "Each woman, one married to him, the other not, knew of the other though I was told they did not meet until the man died. Eighteen children stood at his graveside and three others lived in the Oklahoma territory, too far away to come for his funeral."

Adelaide nodded, not appearing shocked.

"However, the wife's last child was indeed her last at the risk of her life. And the man wanted a big family." I continued, "It did not end happily, though. The legitimate children inherited all the property, and its big barn burned mysteriously one night. The second woman's oldest boy was seen in the neighborhood, but the culprit was not discovered."

When she said nothing, I went on. "Money and property can be a problem in families, marriage or no."

"Financial considerations aside..." she mused. Then she blurted, "It is rumored that Franklin, Colonel

Morris, took an Indian as wife some years ago when he served in the territories. Some say he cannot bear to ask, cannot presume, to ask a proper lady to marry. That is a rumor. I do not attest to its truth and I daren't ask him."

"I am sorry not to have met him," I said. "But I am sure he is not the only lonely man to succumb to," I mumbled, "to his body's needs. If he did indeed marry, doesn't that speak well of his, well, his upbringing? That he would want to do the right thing?"

"You are right, Sarranda. I am glad we can talk this way." I sensed a smile in her voice when she said, "It would likely not happen if we both weren't aware you'd be leaving soon."

"And the room is dark enough," I said, "to hide our expressions."

"My women friends do not talk of such matters. Gossip, yes."

"I am not one to advise in these matters, coward that I am." *As tonight I so amply demonstrated.* "I mean, might you not lead the conversation in this direction at some comfortable point?" I paused. "Over a small sherry, you might judge from his face and words what is true."

"Perhaps I shall. I have known love, though not in the, uh, Biblical sense. I should not like to go to my grave knowing only the love of nieces and nephews."

"It would be a waste, Adelaide," I said. "You have so much to give." I sat up straighter, turned so I looked into her eyes. "Promise me you will—"

"No, I cannot promise. I cannot be sure that I could push the moment to a conclusion. Franklin is dear to me, though he does not seem to know it. I would not want to lose his friendship and gain nothing beyond."

I wondered if she could accept the colonel's liaison with a woman not of his social standing, if it were true. Seeing her open countenance I believe she would meet the woman with courtesy and understanding. But accepting the man's part in the attachment might be more difficult. And what might she say if the woman were I and the man her brother?

As if sensing my downcast spirit, she said, "Do not be disheartened, Sarranda. I shall be fine, whatever may happen."

"And so shall I," I whispered. "So shall I."

Perhaps embarrassed at revealing her private concerns, she stood and bent to take my hand. "I shall think of you as a sister, Sarranda."

PART TWO

CHAPTER EIGHT

Two days later Adelaide, Laura, Susanna, and Mariah bade farewell to Lila and me at the train station. Our goodbyes were formal. Who would guess that Adelaide and I had ever spoken of men and our attitudes about them? A hurting part of me wanted to stay in Bramford just a bit longer, long enough to—*Stop this.* I turned to receive hugs and smiles from our friends.

Lila and I had bundled up warmly. Captain Settles cautioned us that there were often delays and the cars might be cold. He sent us each a small round muff for our hands. We carried a basket and a large reticule of foodstuffs, enough to last us to our destination. We wanted neither to spend our money nor to brave the dining car. In the brisk wind, Laura whispered, "Goodbye. Keep a "stiff upper lip." I think we were ready for the train's departure, so we could unstiffen our lips and let our faces lapse into comfort.

With some relief I settled into my seat and removed hat and muff. We waved and the train pulled away with great chugging and steaming. A pensive Lila stared out the window for the first twenty minutes without a word. She had not seen her mother, who was not yet able to travel.

Adelaide had told her, "Don't be troubled about your mother. I am sure we shall get along fine."

Lila nodded. "Harkey says she's not sorry to be leaving Flecton. It's only hurtful memories she has there."

To me she said, "It's not like a sea voyage, is it now? Not like there'll be storms or pirates or such," and she had set about washing, ironing, packing with a determined expression. I heard her humming and singing some words of "An Irish Lullaby" as she folded her meager belongings. Her "Tooraloora...hush, now don't you cry... Tooraloora...that's an Irish lullaby" and even "Oft in dream, I wander to my home again..." lightened my heart. Oft in dreams I had wandered to my home again.

We were soon in the countryside. Seeing the pastures and fields, brown and stubbly, brought a smile to my face. I was glad to leave city streets, lawns, houses lined up, glad to see cream-colored cows, horses, some goats in pastures—all looking content and placid. My happiness must have shown in my face, for several passengers spoke as they passed to and fro. Soon, however, I buried my nose in a tract about the Universalist faith. I wanted to know about the Reverend Blanchard's sect, and I needed to occupy my thoughts, not linger in the land of what-might-have-been. I would leave my stranger—and I would henceforth call him *the* stranger—behind, relegated to what-was-and-is-forever-over. I would do it, even if I had to memorize the pamphlet in my hands.

At the foot of Old Fort Mountain, we had a few minutes while the train took on water before tackling the next steep grade. A small depot was under construction and the site did not invite wandering around. Only Lila and I stepped down to breathe fresh air and stretch our legs. While the stationmaster carried the mail bag away, Lila strolled toward the building, stepping carefully to avoid barrels and tools.

Paying no attention to the men grouped in the scant shade of the new roof's overhang, I stood at the edge of the platform, soaking in the fall foliage, the oaks' deep burgundy, the poplars' yellow, clinging to the trees on the hills across the track. My mountains. Behind me, a commotion erupted—loud male voices, a scuffling sound, a snarl, a slap, and a sharp Yankee-Irish, "See how you like that!"

Lila's voice! I turned around in a heartbeat. One fellow held her wrist and she strained to get away. A barefoot boy, barely bearded, held his hand to his cheek, seemingly struck dumb.

He dropped his hand. "Hold on to her, Charlie. No little spitfire of a gal is gonna hit me and get away with it."

He stepped toward her, his arm raised. As I rushed to her aid, another man growled, "Leave her be, Paul David. Ye asked for it."

The boy jerked his head toward the speaker but he grabbed at Lila. She had pulled as far away as she could get from the one called Charlie who, though he looked sheepish, apparently dared not release her. She kicked at his shin. He laughed and looked for direction at Paul David, who in turn stared angrily at the man who had spoken.

"Don't be telling me what to do, old man," he snarled. He yanked at his overalls pocket for a weapon, I assumed. For a moment, we stood frozen. All except the "old man" of perhaps forty who slipped a hunting knife from somewhere. It flashed in the sunlight. The arc through the air and the thud when the knife hit the ground seemed simultaneous. It quivered less than two inches from the boy's dirty toes.

"Step back," the man ordered the immobile boy who stared at the knife close to his feet. Another boy jerked him sideways. The man stepped forward and with a grunt pulled the knife free and wiped it on his pants.

"Is it worth it to you, Paulie? You've seen what I can do with this. Keep your hands out in plain sight 'til these two ladies get back on the train." Charlie dropped Lila's wrist and stepped back. But as he did, Lila's boot connected with his shin. He swore and would have fallen to the ground had he not stumbled into Paul David. Someone laughed and the others sniggered. The man with the knife stood impassive.

"Lila," I yelled. "Stop it. Get on the train." I took her hand and we quick-stepped to the tracks.

Safely at the steps to the rail car, I turned to the boys, silent and staring. One spit a stream of tobacco juice in our general direction. Lila stuck out her tongue at him. They looked foolish and young. The man held the gleaming knife casually as if he meant merely to clean his fingernails.

"Thank you," I said to him. "Thank you and—" with all the dignity I could muster I pushed Lila ahead of me and boarded the train, "—and good day." The man touched his hat with the tip of the knife slightly in acknowledgment.

Settled in our seats we removed our hats. I fully intended to chastise Lila, for antagonizing the group and for kicking the boy. Instead I smiled at the silliness of sticking out her tongue. However, now that her safety was assured, Lila seemed shaken. She took out her handkerchief and wiped her hand; her wrist would show some bruising. Instead of berating her, I patted her shoulder.

She burst out, "I didn't do nothing to them, I didn't! I think that Paul'd been drinking and him so young. I smelled it. He come, he came right up to me and stuck his face in mine and called me a right pretty little bitch. And, when I said to him to shut his mouth, he said right back, 'Hey, boys, here's a little Yankee bitch. Bet she's never been kissed.'"

She blew her nose and wiped at her eyes; we looked out the window as the train chugged from the station. The group stood as they had when we stepped off the train, listless, waiting, idling, their amusement gone. Our rescuer leaned against the station wall, no knife in sight.

"They need to be working," I said. "Too much time on their hands. And they likely resent two 'fancy women' with nothing better to do than ride around on a train—without a man for protection."

Lila half-giggled. She took the apple I offered and, sounding very much like Adelaide a few days earlier, said, "Men."

I hoped this stop so close to my mountains didn't bode ill for the rest of our journey. I understood the behavior at the depot; we had seen similar scenes in Bramford: male and idle, no work they could find or would stoop to, farms or other means of livelihood gone or in the hands of others. I said, "The boys, had they not been surrounded by buddies, might have been eager to meet such a feisty Yankee girl."

Lila sighed. "He was right. I ain't never been kissed proper."

Adelaide had arranged for a Miss Fairfield to meet us at the Asheville Railway station. It was a bustling place; its noise and great number of people hurrying could awe any visitor. But I was back in the mountains, not to be intimidated. We left the train as if we were sure of what our next steps would be.

A well-dressed woman was weaving her way through the wagoners, porters, and passengers collecting trunks, crates, and large leather cases. She raised her parasol to indicate she saw us. Just before she reached us, Lila whispered, "I don't understand a word I hear."

"I'm sure you'll understand Miss Fairfield," I assured her. "It's the hubbub."

Slightly breathless, our contact announced, "I'm Claudia Jane Fairfield. Welcome to Asheville." She beckoned a young boy to her side and instructed him to find our bags. Lila followed him to point them out.

"You must be weary from your journey," Miss Fairfield said. She turned toward the boy struggling with our bags. Lila had managed to wrest one from him so he tilted only slightly from their weight. At Miss Fairfield's raised hand, another boy appeared and took a valise from the over-laden lad and Lila's bag.

"It's good, it is, to be on firm ground," Lila said. We followed Miss Fairfield to a row of wagons and carriages. An elderly Negro jumped down assist us into the fringed buggy. Once the luggage was stowed, we set off at a slow pace. I had time to take in the route, the river, and the hotels near the station before we were climbing above the river bottom.

"You'll be staying with my aunt and me in Victoria," Miss Fairfield said. "There's a fine view of the valley and the mountains to the west where—"

The carriage struck a rough spot that jarred our teeth.

"—where we will be heading as soon as we can arrange transport," I finished her sentence. "Miss Fairfield, have you perhaps received a letter from Mrs. Whitney?"

"Indeed. It awaits you." She smiled. "I didn't think you could ride and read at the same time. Please call me Claudia." She clutched her hat as Jebb steered the horse around a pile of household furnishings. "Miss Fairfield is reserved for my aunt. A maiden lady of some distinction in our township."

"The railway had not come this far west when I was last here," I said. "I had to take the train from Morganton."

"With much danger and loss of lives, the tracks were laid and the tunnels built to bring the train over the mountain." The horse shied when the train's engineer gave a blast of its whistle. "We're not really accustomed to it yet." She raised her voice but it held a teasing quality. "Right, Jebb?"

"Right, Miss. Me or this hoss, here."

I sniffed, struck by a sudden sharp memory of Grandda. When I drew another deep breath, Claudia said, "Tobacco. We have warehouses and a factory has started up. You get used to it."

Indeed with a breeze, the tobacco scent wafted in another direction.

Claudia went on. "The railway has brought more businesses. Why, we have a new hotel and a fine public library. My aunt is on the Asheville Library Association." She pointed out businesses and streets along the way. I marveled at the busy-ness of this place; even with the occasional team of oxen plodding along, it was a sight to behold. "And now," Claudia continued, "tourists have found us and we're called 'The Land of the Sky.'"

"'Land of the Sky,'" Lila repeated. Lila said. If not for the smoke and cinders from the engine's boilers, she would have had her head out the train window ever since we saw the mountains rising near Old Fort. The depot episode had not dampened her fascination with the forested landscape and the twisting and winding upward grade. We expected the tunnels, but she gasped each time and put her head down in the darkness. During the last tunnel, which was almost two thousand feet long, I might have heard a murmured prayer. "That's beautiful."

"It is," I agreed.

"I'll write me mam," Lila said, "and tell her to call Flecton 'The Land of the Sea.'"

Claudia and I looked at her with a bit of amusement and, on my part, more than a bit of gratitude that I had brought Lila with me. Youthful eyes see the world differently, I thought. She'll be good for me.

We turned into the side drive of what I would have called a grand home had I not seen several of similar size in Charlotte and in Bramford. Certainly the building of native stone was imposing with a hip roof and interior chimneys. Mrs. Whitney had called a house similar in construction Gothic Revival, reserved more often for churchly buildings; it looked both comfortable and slightly foreign to my eyes. Seeing its tin roof, I exclaimed, "I hope it rains while we are here. I do like the sound of rain on a tin roof."

Lila's grin reminded me that she wasn't the only one who voiced her enthusiasms. "Oh, so do I," Claudia said. "We hope you will be with us a few days, Mrs. Boylett." At her questioning look I realized how tenuous our plans were. "And surely we'll have a good rain for you, right, Jebb?"

"More'n likely, ma'am, 'cording to my Jessie." He handed down our bags. Lila leapt to the ground and held out her hand. I took it gratefully. We'd been in motion so long my legs were wobbly. She turned to Claudia and did the same.

"Why, thank you, Lila," Claudia said. "You are a blessing, I can see that."

I was glad she didn't say "a blessing to us old folk;" at that moment, with wobbly legs and a stiff back, I would have agreed.

"You'll have time to bathe and change before meeting my aunt," Claudia said. "I sent her out visiting our ailing cousin." She chuckled. "Aunt can be like a steam engine itself sometimes."

Within minutes we were in our separate rooms on the second floor; each had a large basin with towels and soap neatly laid out. Though the windows were open, a faint odor of a room long unused lingered. The high bed with its crazy quilt spread across the bottom and its fluffy pillows looked most inviting. An herbal sachet had been tucked under one pillow. As she left us, Claudia said, "My aunt's name is Modene Maline Missouri, but she doesn't like any of them, and only a few close friends dare call her Modene. She will return before six. Please rest in your rooms or come down to the parlor."

Drowsily I awoke to hear voices below; the aunt had appeared and so must we. I knocked on Lila's door and heard a groggy, "Is it time?"

I stretched, straightened my clothing, and ran my hands over my hair. Looking into the ornate wall mirror I told myself to be careful of my words with this "steam engine" woman. Surely not another Hertha. The particulars of getting to Jackson County might depend on the impression Lila and I made.

Miss Fairfield was a mighty fortress of a woman, ample-bosomed, full-skirted, and of florid complexion. Up close I saw that an excess of powder did not entirely conceal the ruddiness of her skin. However, she stood on tiny, booted feet that seemed incapable of holding her up. She extended a small hand to me and a nod to Lila. I knew I'd have no invitation to call her by her triple name.

"Sit," she announced. "We will have a small sherry before dinner. It settles my nerves, does it not, Claudia? I ordered lemonade for your, uh, for young Lila." I introduced Lila as my friend and travel companion, but Claudia's aunt undoubtedly viewed her as servant-girl. If Lila noticed the hesitation, she did not let on. Miss Fairfield sank at once into a great chair. "Visiting the elderly and ailing is our duty, of course, but quite exhausting in this late autumn heat." From the table beside her chair, she picked up a fan and waved it before her face.

"Your home is beautiful." I gazed with appreciation at the highly polished chair railing and grandfather clock. The heavy velvet window coverings had been pulled back to allow the late afternoon sun to lighten the room.

"Thank you." She gestured toward the window. "Claudia Jane, please close the drapes. The room could be cooler." She waited until her niece had done her bidding. "Fairfield House was built by my late brother's wife's family. Claudia Jane was my brother's only child. He died at Gettysburg and her dear mother soon after. The war also took his wife's father and brothers." She fanned more vigorously. "Thus the home came to Claudia Jane—and to me."

Claudia said, "The family is dying out. Our cousins have long abandoned the mountains and us. I will not marry." She spoke with a firmness that surprised me.

Miss Fairfield sighed as if obligated to reveal at least a modicum of background. "I fear Claudia Jane has seen her friends marry poorly and suffer accordingly. It has not been easy since the war." She looked up as an elderly woman carried a silver tray toward us. "We will speak of it no more," she said. "We must hear of our visitors' lives and expectations." She indicated a small table. "Here, Jessie. Dinner?"

"In half an hour, Miss Fairfield. The chicken's 'bout done." She walked stiffly from the room. My mother had walked with the same arthritic care.

"Arthritis is slowing her down," Claudia said. "Chances are we'll have rain tomorrow."

Miss Fairfield handed tiny glasses to her niece and me, lemonade to Lila. "True. We can almost forecast rain by Jessie's walk these days."

Claudia sipped her sherry. "Jessie and Jebb have been with us since the war. They showed up one day from out Leicester way, freed and nowhere to go, and have been with us ever since. We can pay them only a token wage, but they have a small cabin beyond the garden and eat from our kitchen usually."

Before dinner Miss Fairfield extracted from Lila and me information enough to satisfy her curiosity and to deem us, I assumed, worthy of introductions to her friends and acquaintances. About why I left my home, I said, "It was leave or marry again for all the wrong reasons and definitely the wrong man."

Claudia's face darkened; then, seeming to remember her role as hostess, she smiled at me as if in approval.

"Marriage is not for everyone," her aunt declared. She glanced at the grandfather clock just seconds before it chimed the hour. "Let us go in."

My mouth watered when Jessie opened the door from the kitchen. The Fairfields' home was elegant, but the aromas bespoke plain food well seasoned: a platter of fried chicken, fried squash, a basket of light biscuits, and green beans cooked the way Mama and I had learned to cook them—hours and hours with streaked meat. There was a beautiful mold of butter for the blackberry jam and biscuits. Lila tucked into seconds on everything, and I wasn't shy with my helpings. We finished with fried apple pie and hot coffee. Lila looked to see how I dealt with the pie, an individual semi-circle of browned dough filled with dried apples. I used my fork although when growing up we'd eaten the pies with our hands. From the kitchen, Jessie surely heard the compliments Lila and I paid her cooking, and we asked our hostesses to tell her how much we enjoyed our southern meal. Lila said, "I've never had such a meal, Miss Fairfield. Thank you so much."

"We will sit in the parlor," Miss Fairfield said.

Our appetites had curtailed conversation during our repast, but with somewhat regular interruptions from her aunt, Claudia gave us bits of information about Asheville and the surrounding area. Even before what she called "The Southern War for Independence" and her aunt deemed "The War on the South," the town attracted summer visitors from the hot and steamy lowlands of South Carolina and Georgia, especially after the Buncombe Turnpike opened. "That was in the late 1820s," said Miss Fairfield. "I was just a girl."

And now, with a few private schools and its sanitarium for tubercular patients and its warm springs ("And Warm Springs Hotel," inserted Miss Fairfield) some miles away and with the railway, visitors were buying land and building fine homes. "Some of them evidently intend to stay for more than the season," sniffed Claudia's aunt.

"They are providing much needed jobs," Claudia said. "Many former slaves and small farmers have come to Asheville in need of work. We are growing in population quickly—"

"And with that torrent of out-of-work men, some dragging their poor families, comes a wave of crime. We daren't go out without a proper escort after twilight," Miss Fairfield said.

"It's not that bad, Aunt. Of course, we don't go out at night without Jebb or a driver. But no doubt we will soon have Main Street macadamized and even lighted."

Lila's eyes were wide, but we both knew proper women did not venture far from home without companions in populated areas. "We will not be in a town this big, will we, Sarranda?"

"We have surpassed twenty-five hundred," Claudia said.

"Yes," her aunt said. "Our former governor, Zeb Vance, was born in this county, and he is a wonder. Now he's in the Senate in Washington and newly remarried. He's sure to bring more prosperity to our state and to our part of it." She said with certainty: "We are poised to grow."

I had read of Senator Vance, always described as a mountain man, and I hoped she was right. Turning, I answered Lila's question. "No. All of Jackson County may have a smaller population than Asheville's, but we will likely be traveling unescorted. We'll be careful, whatever the case."

"I'm not scared," Lila said. I deemed it wise not to mention the encounter at the railway depot at the foot of the mountain.

When our conversation dwindled, it was clear that tonight we would not talk of our purpose, and that suited me. I needed to be refreshed by sleep uninterrupted by the snorts, chugs, whistles of the train. Its rolling motion and clackety-clack sounds were not conducive to restful slumber.

"Sleep well, ladies," Claudia said. She smiled at Lila's expression at being so designated. I took her arm and steered her toward the stairs.

"Thank you both for your hospitality," I said. "We are in need of a good bed in a stationary place."

A quick wash of my face and unbraiding of my hair and I was in my nightclothes, but not before I heard across the hall Lila's soft snores.

We spent three nights in Fairfield House and were extended much courtesy and hospitality; Miss Fairfield and Claudia seemed to be on intimate terms or speaking acquaintance with almost everyone in Victoria Township and many in the wider Asheville area. Jebb drove us around the town, up a very rocky Patton Avenue and down South Main where we admired the new Swannanoa Hotel, rising four floors of handsome brick and boasting, Claudia lowered her voice, "An inside toilet, so they say."

Such grand structures in my part of the state impressed me, and Lila positively gawked at times. Once she whispered, "I thought we'd be surrounded by red Indians, with not a parlor anywhere." She grinned. "And when will I be old enough for a glass of sherry, ma'am?"

"Don't be uppity," I retorted, "just because you're not washing pots and pans!"

Mrs. Whitney's letter, read before breakfast, prepared me somewhat for the town's vitality. In her spidery hand, she wrote: *Asheville has a great future, my brother says. 'A sleeping giant' he calls it, to be awakened by tobacco money and the influx of financiers ready to invest in tourism. He sometimes himself longs for the beauty and coolness of the mountains.* She went on to describe her busy life, her grandchildren, her wishes for my success, and finished with: *Remember me to Maude. And remember, dear Sarranda, should circumstances ever warrant it, you have a home here. I miss your reading and your spirit.* She gave me the name of sisters in Webster who would assist us if possible and a far-distant Asheville cousin.

We met Mrs. Jones-Abley, the far-distant cousin, the next afternoon. She was a no-nonsense woman whom even Miss Fairfield allowed to control the conversation. "Tobacco and tourists will not greatly assist the people you come to serve, Mrs. Boylett," she announced.

"I must agree," I said. "Though—"

"The church has made great inroads in some areas, though not, if my information is correct, in your county. We must support its efforts with our giving and our prayers."

"Of course, but—" Another Hertha Settles, I thought.

"The Reverend Dorland Bell's school for Negro girls in Concord may be to the well and good. Our church supports his cause. Here in Asheville, though, I believe our first duty is to our white citizens and their children. It is through education and the church that the poor will be lifted up."

"It is difficult to refute that, of course." I did not wish to pursue any discussion of the merits of Negro or white children's education. "However, in my county the churches are Baptist and Methodist, not Presbyterian, for the most part—"

Mrs. Jones-Abley picked up a small dog begging for her attention, patted it, and sent on its way, and started to speak, but Miss Fairfield said, "That is only because our Presbyterian seminaries are not turning out sufficient numbers—"

"And those who are ordained do not necessarily wish to venture into this so-called ignorant and benighted land." I kept my voice neutral. I had read the church papers and I knew what I said was true, if not the whole truth.

"And why should they?" retorted Mrs. Jones-Abley. "My own great-nephew has recently completed his studies at Lane Seminary in Cincinnati and will be seeking a call to a parish in a few months and then ordination."

"But not before he goes to Europe," Miss Fairfield interrupted.

"I cannot advise him to come here. He might be suited to Asheville, perhaps, were there an opening but not—" Mrs. Jones-Abley waved toward the window, "not to the western counties."

"Cities such as this are certainly to be admired, as are those on his 'grand tour,'" I said, my feathers ruffled. I'd read about wealthy young men's grand tours of the continent, but I had no desire to investigate the cities the railway had taken us through "However, my heart lies in the mountains, not in city streets."

Already I was feeling beset by the city, hemmed in or, at least, less free. Perhaps it was Mrs. Jones-Abley's tone, her dismissive words, her neck so unbending, her chin so high that put me on the defensive when I knew I should be careful with my words.

Claudia Jane defused the growing tension with a gentle chuckle. "It's a choice, is it, for you, Mrs. Boylett, city streets or cow paths?"

"Given that choice, I know which I'd choose," I said, "but some don't have that choice. I'm mindful of that."

Lila laid her hand lightly on my arm.

"My cousin Alice spoke highly of you." Mrs. Jones-Abley's eyes swept over me. "She said you are well-read and that you can do what you set your mind to. The question is, Mrs. Boylett, what have you set your mind to?"

The blunt assault left me floundering for a few moments. Wits gathered or not, I plunged in. "It's a question I've struggled with, as you may know, if Miss Bell has written to you. I had some unformed intention of returning, with the assistance of her women's circles, to help somehow. To—if not heal—soothe the scars I know are here. Healing and soothing, though, must be accompanied by accomplishment, not by charity alone."

Their expressions didn't encourage me to continue in such a general vein. I was stumbling, like a schoolgirl given a thirteen-syllable word to spell. Still, mindful of Lila's watchful eyes, I swallowed hard, took a sip of water, and forged ahead. "My people, the people to the west, lost everything down to the last nubbin," I said. "They need a way to work, to work their own land if that's possible, a way to buy seed corn, and more, they need a way to survive bad crops, dry spells and flooding. I speak of the women, especially, who feed their children first and eat the scraps, the women who have to scratch every potato from its hill, save every grain of salt, dare not spill the milk, who cry when the calf dies, and who help bury it. The men work at what they can find to do, but many of the young who went to war came back old men. They came back welcomed but lost. You've seen them around town, surely."

Claudia nodded. "Some came back ruined in more than body."

At her aunt's disapproving look, Claudia retreated. "Yes, with all that's happening in Asheville now, much of it is not us, not our kind."

"Be grateful, girl," Mrs. Jones-Abley said. "Somebody has some fire—and some funds. And you can't fault our governor. He's doing all he can."

"That I know." Claudia looked ready to weep. "But, but, look at us, some of us. We're barely holding on."

"Enough, Claudia Jane," declared her aunt. "You're overwrought. Go, please, and fetch us some coffee. I am developing a headache."

Lila picked at her fingernails. Claudia paused at the doorway. "Would you like to help, Lila?"

When they left the room, I vowed to hold my tongue and keep a close rein on my feelings. These women were not enemies; they had not caused the war. I had to be better prepared to discuss my position. Much as I had thought of what I wanted to do and how to do it as we steamed southward, I had not yet a firm plan in my head. I wanted to go, as quickly as possible, to Greene's Valley. But I did not want to leave animosity behind me.

After Mrs. Jones-Abley stirred thick cream into her coffee, she said to me, "You are not in sympathy with our church's views? I sense some reluctance to support our tenet of education as the route or the means of relieving the poverty and the backwardness of parts of the region." She drew herself up and went on, "The poverty not only of body but the poverty of spirit."

"What do you mean, precisely?" asked Miss Fairfield, apparently taking offense. "I have not noted what I assume you refer to as a spiritual lack among our acquaintances."

A hornet's nest had been disturbed in this somber room. In a moment stinging comments would follow.

Lila glanced at me, put her hand to her forehead and then to her mouth. "Your pardon, Ma'am," she gasped, looking toward our hostess. "I fear the lunch did not agree with me. I feel..."

She leaned toward Claudia, seated next to her. "I feel faint."

I had never known Lila to have any but a strong stomach, had teased her on the train about eating like a young filly at the haystack.

Miss Fairfield paused, her cup halfway to her lips, and took charge. "We must get this young girl back to our home. She is pale, indeed."

Claudia assisted Lila, who swayed a bit as she held onto her arm, and we said our goodbyes. I pressed a cold towel against Lila's forehead. Occasionally she appeared to stifle a gag and almost retch.

We spoke very little as Jebb drove the old horse toward Fairfield House. Miss Fairfield directed, "Careful, Jebb. Careful."

"It's his only way," murmured Claudia.

Alighting from the buggy, Miss Fairfield muttered, "Grand tour, indeed." Her nose was out of joint. She peered at Lila. "And you, away from that company and young as you are, you are sure to feel better soon."

I could have sworn I saw a twinkle in her eye, quickly hidden. I liked her at that moment.

Although Lila allowed Claudia to help her to her bed, remove her boots, and bathe her face, her recovery seemed remarkably swift. When we were alone, I said, "Now you must, *must* lie here at least until dinner and then, Lila, you will take only broth and cold chicken." I looked as stern as my restored good humor permitted. "That is your punishment."

"Punishment?" Her cheeks glowed. "Are you not grateful, Miss, uh, Sarranda?"

"Indeed, I am." I fluffed her pillow. "I vow that even Jebb saw through that ruse and has told Jessie! We shall leave here with a reputation for mendacity. But I bet Jessie sends you a sweet." I grinned and gave the pillow a hearty blow.

"That parlor was smothering me," she said. "Truly. But I'm better now."

"Better or not, you must stay here through the dinner hour. Shall I bring you some castor oil? Epson salts? Surely there is something medicinal about?"

We smiled, and I wondered if the Fairfields weren't doing the same. Downstairs I assured them that Lila wanted nothing, that she seemed to have no fever and that she was resting.

During our quiet evening meal, not one of us intimated that Lila was anything but ill. She suffered, I implied, from her monthlies, and both women were solicitous but not unduly concerned. "She has been overexcited," I said. "Young as she is, the trip may have taxed her—or thinking of our next journey."

Afterwards, avoiding any theological discussion, we talked of books and foods, and the evening ended with Claudia playing, to my surprise, Stephen Foster tunes for us in the parlor. Jessie had attended to Lila; she whispered that she'd left the door open so Miss Lila could hear the piano. I retired early. On the next day we would meet a woman who was actually *doing* something, a woman intrigued by the weaving and basketry skills she had seen among a few mountain women and who set about attempting to establish centers for teaching others those skills.

Mrs. Jones-Abley had told us that the woman was unmarried, a graduate of a northern college, sponsored not by a church but by her sorority. I hoped to learn much from her. Too soon I must embark on a destination with clear goals, but those goals, like indefinite wind-driven clouds, swirled in my head. My sleep was fitful.

CHAPTER NINE

Miss Fairfield greeted Miss Leatherwood with a kiss to the cheek and declared, "Antonia has given the better part of the past five years to our mountain women and, indeed, is admired among them. Though," she turned to me, "she will be the first to tell you, success has not been easy."

Miss Antonia Leatherwood had ridden in from the hamlet of Laurel Trace, and after introductions, she announced that her back ached and her head hurt from the unusually bright sunlight that day. She appeared both optimistic and tired. I liked her forthright attitude at once.

We were seated in the former home of Colonel McDowell, a fine brick edifice recently purchased by the Garretts of St. Louis. The lady of the house had welcomed us graciously and, with apologies, excused herself to take a previously planned mid-afternoon excursion. Miss Leatherwood was a friend of Mrs. Garrett and would be staying in their home for a few days.

After accepting tea and a large slice of pound cake from the ornate silver serving plate, she responded to Miss Fairfield's remark. "Success, ah, no, I don't claim that." She bit into her cake with unapologetic enthusiasm. "My work with the women is better likened to a slow trickle after a frozen snow melts. Slow."

"I would like your appraisal, Miss Leatherwood, of what I, with Lila at my side, might do to aid the women in Jackson County," I said. "I understand that you are involved with a movement to help women help themselves. Beyond that I am ignorant. Please tell me about your work. Be assured I am here to learn from you."

Her fingers hovered above another slice of cake and as she hesitated, I added, "Whatever you say will remain with me unless you wish me to tell of your success, uh, your situation."

"You see my weakness for sweets." She brushed a crumb from her bosom.

I thought perhaps she was giving herself a moment to think of how to begin.

"The problem is twofold, as I see it, Mrs. Boylett." She placed her cup gently on its saucer. "First, the skills that sustained pioneer families are no longer routinely learned by most young women. Cloth can now be bought more cheaply than made, provided, of course, you have an income. And these days one may or may not find a loom for weaving in the mountain cabins and farmhouses. Sheep are not abundant, so finding wool is not easy." She looked at us. "Do you weave?"

"I did not learn at my mother's knee," I said. "In fact, I cannot claim expertness with any so-called women's work though, of course, I sew and do needlework. However, my employer in Charlotte saw to it that I learned to weave though I know scarce beyond the basics."

"I cannot weave," Lila said. "But I could learn. It's in my Irish blood, isn't it?"

"I don't weave," Claudia said. "but I was required to learn needlepoint and cross stitch at an early age! How we girls sat over our samplers, how I pricked my fingers. On my sampler, framed in our upstairs bedroom, I fancy I can see little specks of blood!" She smiled. "And you used to do the same, didn't you, Aunt?"

Miss Fairfield placed a hand on her niece's arm and spoke gently. "It was expected and undoubtedly instilled a certain discipline among the young."

For some moments we appeared united in a common understanding of our womanhood, regardless of wealth, influence, or geography. When Miss Fairfield stirred, Miss Leatherwood returned us to the present.

"In the North or the South, it was the same," Miss Leatherwood said. "If looms and spinning wheels are made available, I believe some women, with encouragement and instruction, would again take up those skills. That has been the case in Laurel Trace." She rubbed her hands together. "The second problem is more difficult to address. Whatever the women make must get to buyers. Those buyers are not here. I dare say not many local families with the means to do so would choose handmade items over store-bought. Do you agree, Miss Fairfield?"

Miss Fairfield nodded, and Claudia said, "You saw the Murano glass at the home of Mrs. Jones-Abley, Sarranda. It is certainly far more prized than local pottery."

"Brought back by that nephew from his Grand Tour." Her aunt glanced at the one well-furnished room not yet disturbed by extensive renovation. "And you can see the fine taste exhibited here."

Miss Leatherwood leaned back. "I found when I came here that the town girls, those that need employment, have no interest in working with their hands beyond service in the hotels and homes of the more well-to-do." She glanced at the Fairfields but went on, "And the mountain women are isolated, too often, both from neighbors and from villages. The state of transport to outside markets and the lack of centers where women could work together militate against much profitability at this time."

"Is it too soon after the war?" I asked. "Do you find people weary?"

"A good word. Weary, yes. Simply surviving is exhausting. Children die before a doctor can reach them. Often the law is far away and, more often, not called for feuds or shootings. Such assistance as can be given seems almost an empty, futile gesture. As the children of our soldiers grow up, perhaps there will be a renewal, a vitality." She closed her eyes. Lila glanced at me as if to ask: will we go on?

"I have to believe something can be done," I said. "I understand what you are saying. But futile? That is a strong indictment."

"As both the land and the people recover—and indeed they shall—things will get better," Claudia said. "We are seeing change here constantly."

"Yes," Miss Leatherwood said, "but I shall not be here to see it. I have been summoned home, just this week."

"What? My dear Antonia," Miss Fairfield exclaimed, "we did not know."

The woman issued a wan smile. "Nor did I. In a few days I shall travel north with the Garretts. Then I will be sent to a western territory. Just where I have not yet been told."

"Have your superiors decided that our southern mountains are not worthy of further effort?" Where my bitter words came from I vow I do not know.

"Why, Mrs. Boylett, how can you know that? Such a judgment is surely premature." Miss Fairfield's tone was indignant. "How can you presume such an attitude? Say such a thing?"

Clearly I had offended her view of Miss Leatherwood's sorority's work. I flushed at her rebuke and, indeed, at my own insolence. I put my fingers to my hot cheek, dismayed. When I began an apology, Miss Leatherwood held up her hand.

"Let us not argue, ladies. I must be honest. What Mrs. Boylett expressed was, indeed, my first thought, as well. However, I can't say with any certainty why I have been recalled and thus will speak no more about it." She looked at me. "I will escort you tomorrow to visit some of the women in the community I have dealt with—and more, I wish you all success—however you continue."

"Didn't Mrs. Garret offer us the run of her home, Antonia? Will you ring for some sherry, perhaps?" Miss Fairfield spoke as if reprimanding a child. "Your news is a shock."

"Of course." Miss Leatherwood rang a silver bell and, when a woman appeared, wiping her hands on a white apron, she requested sherry and a pitcher of cool cider.

Thinking that to refuse would offend but that sherry would not help me mind my tongue, I sipped with care. I did not want to become accustomed to the drink. Once we left Asheville, I did not expect to be served sherry. I remembered Rankin's brew of sweet brandy that soothed Grandda's throat on many an occasion. I said, with a slight smile, "My grandda's special brandy would 'warm the cockles of your heart.'"

"This is warming, too, isn't it?" Miss Leatherwood said. "I've been offered moonshine, white lightning, some call it, but have not had the courage to try it."

"You should take a flask with you for the West. It is good medicine."

"Good for cleaning cuts, isn't it?" Lila murmured, and we veered to a discussion of herbal and liquid remedies for ailments and wounds. Lila told me later that, though she'd cleaned her father's abrasions with his drink, she was thinking of wagon trains and red Indians on the Plains.

Miss Leatherwood soon excused herself to rest. Jessie drove me to meet a man who arranged to have our trunk and cases of books, clothing, and various necessities sent to Frady's store in Greene's Valley. He rubbed his bearded cheek. "Can't say for certain, ma'am, when it'll get there. Depends on the weather and Old Man Troop's hosses and what else he's taking that way. Might be four or five days."

At the post office, with some trepidation, I mailed a letter to my son, Fredrick, telling him that I hoped to see him and that we needed a place to stay. I didn't say I hoped that the cabin was unoccupied or what I dreaded—that he would not want to see me. I had left him over six years ago. He was no longer a boy.

The following morning the Fairfields were committed to a tea and a rehearsal of a reading to benefit the new library; they could not accompany us to Laurel Trace where Miss Leatherwood had established a "sort of community center" among the womenfolk. We expected a journey of at least two hours, so I felt they were happy to be obliged to stay in town. Miss Leatherwood came in for a quick cup of tea. She would return to Asheville to prepare for her trip north. She'd been promised a ride back with a wagon of penned turkeys.

"Mr. Garrett has generously given my horse to the family who boarded me out there. And," she said, "my hosts continue to consider me 'a dainty lady,' who should not ride alone." She frowned at the horses' equipage. "I shouldn't think it'll be sidesaddle for me in the West."

Waving farewell, the Fairfields retreated indoors. "I can't see them ladies on these horses, can you?" Lila said.

I had to agree. We thanked the man who had brought the horses, ours donated by the local stockyard after some persuasion by Mr. Garrett. Within half an hour we were well beyond the town, adjusting to the gaits of our horses and not talking. Our animals were old and tame enough, but when they picked their way along a particularly rocky lane, we shifted uncomfortably in our sidesaddles.

Some time later, Miss Leatherwood said, "We are taking the shortcut rather than the wagon road. The drovers' road is often quite busy. I thought you'd enjoy the peacefulness of this route." As we ambled along, I considered the ride a preparation for what lay ahead, and I breathed deeply, enjoying the quiet of the countryside. Several times on the narrow trail we dismounted and walked alongside our horses. The quiet was broken only by crows cawing, other birds twittering in the trees and bushes, an occasional snorting of our horses or the bawling of a mournful cow. Though the autumn air was cool, the sunlight warmed us, and we soon wrapped our cloaks into bundles and tied them to our saddles.

When we left the shade of pine trees for an open valley, I could not help myself. I hummed a tune I'd heard in Charlotte and then burst into song. "My life flows on in endless song: / Above earth's lamentations, / I hear the sweet, tho' far-off hymn / That hails a new creation....How can I keep from singing?" The song sprang forth from the sheer joy of being in the outdoors. And in the open landscape I did not croak or creak as I thought I did indoors.

Miss Leatherwood looked back and, behind me, Lila giggled. "I forgot some of the words," I said. "And, pray, do not condemn my slaughtering the tune!"

We halted and I laughed aloud. When had I last done that? Twirling around, I gestured widely at the mountains, "How can I keep from singing?"

"Yes," Miss Leatherwood said. "I know some of the words. And your, uh, alto, does the song some justice." She hummed softly and then sang, "No storm can shake my inmost calm, / While to that refuge clinging...I lift my eyes; the cloud grows thin; / I see the blue above it...How can I keep from singing?"

"Is it a new song?" Lila asked. "I do not know it."

"I heard it from some Quakers," I said. "I haven't seen it written down."

"How can I keep from singing?" Lila said. "I want to learn it."

"In another quarter hour we shall be there." Miss Leatherwood pointed ahead. "The path is smooth if we keep to the side of the fields. Let us sing as we go." The stubble was the remains of a stand of sorghum cane; perhaps we would see molasses being made. And be offered some.

Soon we intersected a well-rutted road and then came into a clearing. I heard the buzz of a sawmill and knew there must be water power nearby. The thunk-thunk of a wheel turning brought sudden tears to my eyes. I looked for a creek and saw a line of trees, including still-green willows to the left. The mill would be up that way. I dearly missed the old mill, Grandda's mill, the mill I had learned to run, of necessity, during the war. My horse stumbled and I gave my attention to staying on in a somewhat ladylike manner. Still my ears were attuned to the rumble of the mill, though the sawing of logs had stopped.

Miss Leatherwood rode to a church house just beyond the center of the settlement, and at once three women came down the steps and held her hands as she dismounted. Lila slid down and helped me ease off Old Josie, as the man had called my mare. I wanted to rub my backside but rather than embarrassing my hostess, I stretched instead. Lila, undaunted by the horses, took the reins of all three, awaiting instructions from Miss Leatherwood.

"Let Ellie take the animals," one woman said, and the younger one stepped up, spoke shyly to Lila, and led the horses toward a hitching post.

Six or seven cabins sat beside the road before it curved and wound up the mountainside. On one porch, a man had one leg propped straight against the pole across the front, the other missing. He ignored us entirely, whittling with concentration. Three children who seemed under age six played without a sound in their front yard, swept clean. They looked at us with some curiosity and then returned to their play, picking up and rearranging small sticks and stones.

"Come on in and warm by the fire," one woman said. "We got us a potbelly stove in here."

Miss Leatherwood introduced us to Britta Mae, Elizabeth, and Ellie, and while we warmed our hands at the stove more from politeness than need they offered brief comments about themselves.

Britta Mae was a widow with six grandchildren. "He come home from that Ohio prison and died not two years later. Consumption. Corrupted lungs," she said. "He didn't live to see a new corn patch come up."

Elizabeth's husband, a few years older than she, was currently "laid up with stomach troubles." She half-smiled. "Troubles brought on by Mr. Drink. Sometimes he cries in his sleep, fights them battles all over agin. I just let him be." I thought of Carly, Adelaide's young brother, who also sought the friendship of Mr. Drink.

Ellie, perhaps in her mid-thirties and obviously the youngest, was recently married. "We tied the knot just last year. Alston, he's a good man, but not from around here—"

"And," Britta Mae interrupted with a grin, "a mite young and still learning."

Ellie tossed her a look of amusement. "He come up from South Carolina to bring some stock, stayed to help his uncle with the mill and lumbering. He's twenty-three, Mrs. Boylett. They're just jealous." Good natured exclamations followed with a touch of ribaldry mixed in. Lila and I listened and chuckled.

Then, in a serious mood, Miss Leatherwood told them why we were there and that we would be going toward Webster later. "I confess," she said, "I know little of what lies west of Asheville. It all seems closed in by those mountains." I thought of those mountains as my home, and I longed to head toward them.

"I'd like to see what you're doing," I said to the women.

With both pride and reticence about their efforts, they led us to the small room at the back of the church where they and four or five other women met "pretty regular" to weave and sew. "God willing and the creeks don't rise," Ellie said, "we come together two days a week. Stay as long as we can. Luckily none of us have children at home—right now." She glanced at the floor.

"She's expecting, is this one," supplied Britta Mae.

"And proud of it," added Elizabeth. "'Tis only natural, but she tried to keep it from us!"

"The pride," said Britta Mae. "Not the fact. When she rushed out the back door during that last pouring rain, we knowed."

We congratulated Ellie, who ran her fingers through her long hair, already faintly streaked with gray. "I was engaged before the war. Markham died too young, somewhere in Pennsylvania. I never thought to marry after that, but Alston, he come up from South Carolina. Well, I took one look at him and that was that."

"The poor boy didn't have a chance," Britta Mae said.

"Let's look at what you've done here." Miss Leatherwood walked to the unfinished coverlet on the loom. I had learned weaving on a six-harness loom, simpler and smaller than the heavy and complicated device we stood around. I didn't recognize the beautiful and intricate pattern.

"This old pattern calls for an eight-harness loom, and we were fortunate to find one in Elizabeth's granny's barn." Miss Leatherwood ran her hand along the edge of the loom. "How it survived is a mystery but here it is. We cleaned it up and Elizabeth figured out how it worked." My heart sank a notch. Should a loom materialize, I dearly hoped to find someone else to teach the skill.

I must have looked uneasy because Elizabeth spoke, "It come so natural to me. I guess I remembered from seeing Granny work it when I was six or seven." She held up her long fingers. "She died long ere I married, and the old barn just set there all these years, too far back to be burned by either side. The loom was 'bout buried under years of spider webs and cobwebs."

"And three copperheads close by." Britta Mae shivered. "Remember when we started to move it and them snakes slivered around."

"Good thing they was hibernatin' and not too lively," Elizabeth said. She fingered a basket of yarn. "This wool is from the Davis family sheep. We dyed all this ourselves."

"Walnut hulls," I murmured. "And this darkish yellow shade?"

"Poplar leaves and willow, mixed," Ellie responded. "I'm the dyer!" She told us her techniques for achieving the various colors. Lila seemed entranced.

For well over an hour, we wandered around the room, handling ball winders and spindles, watching Elizabeth demonstrate her dexterity with the loom, listening as the women talked of the warp of the fabric, the coverlets and small floor rugs that sold best, the fun of gathering leaves, roots, and bark for the dyes, the tedium of cooking, stirring, straining, and then the joy of seeing a piece come off the loom, and a certain sorrow at parting with it.

"But," Britta Mae said, "we're gittin' used to givin' up the pieces. This winter we'll be in here a-workin' away for the spring sales."

"That's when we can get our work to Asheville," Ellie said. "Don't we like to see the men coming back with sugar and shoes and such!"

The three women were obviously good friends. And by the time we went on our way to spend the evening with Britta Mae, they chatted with us as if we'd known them for months. I prevailed upon Britta Mae to walk with me to the mill up the branch. The tiny building had only one run of stones, and, she said, was more useful generally now for sawmilling than for grinding corn. She waited while I looked at the flume, the small overshot wheel, and the stones. When Britta Mae noticed my long face, I confessed, "I long to work my grandfather's mill." Dusk overtook us and we returned to her cabin where Lila had seen to our horses.

Our overnight visit was a success if judged by friendship and a good hot supper of pickled beans, stewed potatoes, and cornbread, a breakfast of biscuits and fried eggs, with the sleep of the weary in between. Before sunup, in Britta Mae's yard, two other women came to wish Miss Leatherwood a farewell and to see us. The women presented her with a lovely scarf from their loom. A sense of loss showed in their teary eyes. With our gratitude and good wishes, we saw Miss Leatherwood off on the turkey-wagon. "That's one woman will be missed, she will," Lila said.

"Ye might can use these," Ellie said as we prepared to mount. Among them the women had bundled up apples, a jar of honey, a jar of molasses, a piece of fatback, and a small mold of butter for us. "All of it will keep a few days," Britta Mae assured us, arranging the sack over my saddle horn. "Ye'll be taking a fair road most of the way, according to Alston. Good luck to you both." The little group watched us depart, and I turned to see them heading for the church house.

Riding with the sun on our backs, I pondered on the women's work; they readily confessed the problem of getting their goods to market. Even though very little cash passed into their hands over the months, as one they declared they liked what they were doing, what Miss Leatherwood had inspired them to do.

We came by the light of the full moon to the edge of Webster and found the home of the Misses Lynch. They awaited us, having been told by a horseman who passed us by that we would be arriving. Saddle-sore and exhausted, we almost fell into their arms, and they at once declared we must call them Agnes and Rose.

They prepared a bath for us in their kitchen and welcome it was to my aching limbs. "Plenty of water," Agnes said to me, "good and hot. Take your time soaking while we give this young one some milk and pie."

They insisted I also needed warm milk and apple pie, and while we waited for Lila, Rose brought me a copy of *Scribner's Monthly*, the magazine Mrs. Whitney had shown me years earlier, saying, "This is about your county seat." I picked it up and read to Lila: "*In the valleys we saw the laurel and the dwarf rosebay, the passion flower and the Turk's cap lily, and on the mountain sides the poplar or tulip tree, the hickory, ash, black and white walnut, the holly, the chincapin, the alder, and the chestnut in profusion. Webster is a little street of wooden houses, which seems mutely protesting against being pushed off into a ravine. For miles around the country is grand and imposing...As we reposed on the porch in the evening, sunset came with a great deal of glory....*"

"Alas, you missed the sunset today." Agnes smiled. "The writer stayed only a short time. She had a poetic eye, did she not? Now we boast of a population of a hundred or more."

Refreshed and clean of saddle-dust, we told that evening of our Asheville and Laurel Trace visits. We retired early, slept long and well, and left after a hearty breakfast, promising to visit once we were settled. Our destination was the farm that my son Fredrick loved and worked and had been made heir to, with the death of Old Man Mack.

When Lila and I approached the farm, reluctance mixed with apprehension overtook me. How would Fredrick greet me? Call me "Mother" or claim me as such? Had he married? Had he received my letter that gave two or three possible dates for our arrival? Lila rode with a dejected slump to her shoulders. We'd had no word from her mother. I assured her that the mail was unreliable and repeated the adage, "No news is good news," but she had apparently sunk into homesickness.

A shaggy collie announced our arrival and my son strode toward us. I saw the flash of recognition, the smile of son-ship on Fredrick's face, but when he reached our horses, his tone was friendly but distant.

"Hello, Mother." He grasped me by the waist and set me down in front of him, and stepped back. No welcoming hug.

"Fredrick," I said, "you're all grown up now. The farm agrees with you." Indeed, he looked the very essence of the well-fed farm boy, not chunky but solid. Healthy, tan, his sandy hair cut neatly, his hands clean, his shirt ironed. I thought to embrace him, but when the farmhouse door opened, he turned immediately at the sound.

"They're here," he called out and took a couple of steps toward Mrs. Mack.

Our introductions were hurried. Mrs. Mack's attention was on the hillside, a frown of distress on her face.

"Right now? Is it her time?" Fredrick said. We turned toward the distinct bawling of a cow some distance beyond the barn.

"I'm afraid so. I've just come from there, was on my way to get you when—"

"Is the cow calving?" I interrupted.

"Yes," she said. "It's old SaryJane. She's always been a troubled one and she's on up in years."

"Don't let us keep you, Fredrick," I said. He looked from us toward the bawling of the cow, twisting his hat in his hands, boyishly indecisive. "We don't have time to visit and must not keep you from the cow. We want to ride on if—"

"The cabin's empty, and you're welcome to it," he said. "The renters have been gone two months or more. You'll pass by the Reverend Blanchard's church."

"Thank you."

"Gotta hurry, sorry." He stuck his hat back on and rushed off.

"I'll be there in a minute," Mrs. Mack said. "There's no one else here today to help." Moving toward the sounds of a difficult birthing, she said over her shoulder, "Old SaryJane was Mr. Mack's pet, you might say. We wouldn't want to lose her."

Our encounter in the front yard of the farmhouse lasted less than five minutes. Lila had murmured only a greeting and a goodbye, and we turned Josie and Belle toward the home of the Reverend and Mrs. Blanchard. Susanna's cousin was to let him know we were coming.

CHAPTER TEN

Lila had a lovely singing voice, a natural soprano, but not until she joined Reverend Blanchard's congregation in singing "Amazing Grace" did I see how profoundly her voice affected the listeners. Maybe it was the natural lilting remnant of her Irish parentage, maybe her youth. For a moment, her fellow singers hesitated as they listened; then the minister's God-invoking bass called them back to an inspiring rendition of the celebrated hymn.

One head seemed glued in Lila's direction; the head belonged to my son Fredrick. I saw that one woman watched him with a face closed in anger and the girl at her side with dismay. Fredrick hardly blinked, and, when the final note sounded, he stood as if rooted to the floor until Mrs. Mack patted his arm with what seemed affection and understanding. He took his seat. A tremor of jealously shook me. She loved him as she would a birth son and he, without hesitation, squeezed her age-spotted hand. It was a noble thing I'd done, I told myself yet again, leaving him to a couple who needed him, who wanted him, who could offer him security, the security of land to plow, cows to milk, fields to harvest, a warm home of planed boards and brick chimneys.

Fredrick was bound to the farmland as I was not. Even as a boy, he'd sometimes studied the garden rows as a scholar might study lines on pages or a miner seek a glint of gold. My garden and cornfield, potato patch and beans rows had sustained us, but I felt no such closeness for the soil. My love was ever the mill site, the pond and sluiceway, the millstones, the buckets of the wheel. I liked the chains and pulleys, the hopper, the gears, the simple mechanism that produced meal from corn. Fredrick's spirit was bound to the first step: creating—sowing, hoeing, harvesting; mine to transforming the harvest by sifting and grinding; Jessie's and my mother's to the final step: the cooking and the feeding. I smiled at my imagination and turned my attention to the Reverend Julius Jefferson Blanchard's words.

He spoke quietly, his voice controlled and inviting. He asked us to live in a spirit of forgiveness and understanding, to "put aside our hatreds and our envies, our outrage and spite." Those around me listened intently but one man's mouth twitched at the minister's charge to forgive; the woman beside him, with apprehension, put her hand on his arm, willing him to relax. The minister continued: "It is hard, my brethren, to forgive when you cannot forget the horrors, the degradation, the killing and the ruining of our people and land—and," he paused, "their people and, to a lesser degree their land. Hard but not impossible." His gaze swept over us. "I do not ask you to forget, for to forget is to risk repetition, for our sons and grandsons, our children yet unborn. No, we cannot forget but we can forgive our enemies, as our Lord, asked us to do. We can start from where we are—"

A man behind me muttered, "Defeated and lost. Ruint."

Mr. Blanchard apparently did not hear the man, but he paused for a breath. "We can begin now. Now is what we have, now, not then. Not even are we promised tomorrow. Now is the time, the fullness of time. Let us use our bodies and spirit to rebuild. Let us live to forgive and live responsible for what is ahead and, my brethren, let us pray."

After the service we shook hands with the Reverend Blanchard and stood to the side of the rough clearing in which he'd built his framed church. "He seems a kind man," Lila said.

"Very kind, indeed, and so is his wife, to invite us to dinner."

"Do they know I'm Catholic?" Lila asked. "Does it matter?"

"I think not, to both questions." I regarded her with a question of my own. "Does it bother you, Lila, that you find no church here, no priest?"

She had never mentioned the need for her church, for a confessor, and I did not intend to pry. She said nothing, watching with interest the people shaking the minister's hand and walking on toward their wagons or down the road. Fredrick came out the door and looked around before putting on his hat. He turned to give Mrs. Mack a hand down the three steps. A most considerate son. His eyes sought mine, or Lila's. I wasn't sure. At any rate he guided Mrs. Mack in our direction.

"Hello, Fredrick, Mrs. Mack," I said.

"I didn't know you would be at the service," Fredrick said.

"Nor did we," I said. "We met the Blanchards late yesterday. We slept in their old cabin, and they invited us to attend and to take dinner after the service."

"It's good to see you again, Mrs. Boylett." Mrs. Mack took my hand. "We were not at our best when you stopped by the farm."

"I hope the cow is fine and the calf survived." I said.

"Yes, thanks to Fred." Her voice quivered slightly. To her he was Fred. "He saved her and we got a baby bull." She repeated her words of the day before, "He's good with the animals."

Fredrick blushed at her compliment. Lila stood quietly by my side. "Lila's from Massachusetts," I said. He removed his hat and nodded; she ducked her head in acknowledgment. His tanned checks turned redder. Lila lifted her eyes and a small smile lit her face.

"Will you be staying now you're back?" Mrs. Mack asked. "Does it seem much changed to you around here?"

"My plans are not yet definite. I hope it has not changed too much for me to feel at home."

At that moment the Blanchards came up to us and invited Fredrick and Mrs. Mack to dinner. Both declined and she said, "We must get home. We have a new calf."

Fred shook Mr. Blanchard's hand again. "Good sermon, sir."

"Let us hope," his wife said, shifting the baby on her hip, "that some of those present take it to heart." After an uncomfortable silence, she looked around. "I will gather the children."

"Perhaps you will call on us, Mrs. Boylett, Lila," Mrs. Mack said.

"When we are settled, thank you," I said and Lila smiled. Fredrick muttered a goodbye. I walked a few feet with them, and Fredrick told me a little about the cabin's renters.

"A fine young man," the Reverend Blanchard said when I rejoined them. "They live a far piece from here, as you know. But they're coming more often to our service. Their preacher has taken leave, left, in fact, for other parts." He surveyed the dispersing crowd. "That's why we had a full house today. Did you like our church, Miss?"

"It's different. Unlike what I was accustomed to," Lila said. "We weren't regular to church."

"Indeed," he said. Good manners likely kept him from further questions as did the return of his wife and children. We walked toward their home, a short distance from the church. I would tell Lila that Zack's family was Catholic though he, with his marriage proposal, promised "immersion" and attended our church.

Mrs. Blanchard declined any help and asked us to wait until she put dinner on the table. "It's cooked, only needs a bit of warming, and the table's set." She beckoned the children to help her and we admired the spacious yard and garden to the side of the house. Beyond were pastures and fields. It was so like my grandda's place before the war: well kept by industrious hands. The yard was swept clean, the lilac bushes and the boxwoods trimmed. The fencing, lacking not a single rail, stood firm and proud. Mrs. Blanchard's chickens were nowhere in sight, shut up perhaps on the Sabbath. High on the hillside behind the house a cow grazed alongside a mule and two horses. Though in no way showy, it was an enviable home place.

Lila and I sat in the two straight chairs on the porch and within minutes an elderly woman joined us. Mrs. Blanchard stuck her head out the door. "My mother-in-law, Elissa Blanchard. She doesn't hear at all, but if you look directly at her and speak slowly she may read your lips."

The older woman sank into the rocking chair. How glad I was that I had not sat there. "Sarranda Boylett and Lila McNeely," I said.

"Good day to you both," she said.

In our one-sided conversation, I answered her questions slowly. I was born in the valley; I lost my husband in a Yankee prison camp. I had moved away. I was back. "I am here to help however I can, with the backing of ladies up north."

"Yankee women?"

"Yes. Good churchgoing women who want to help their southern sisters, so to speak."

The woman may not have caught all my words, but just as Mrs. Blanchard stepped out to announce dinner, she murmured, "Southern sisters," as if the concept were strange to her.

Lila jumped to her feet and offered her hand. Elissa Blanchard took it and rose unsteadily. Her daughter-in-law moved toward her, but Lila said, "Let me help the granny to the table." The old woman leaned on her arm. Her snuff-stained lips curved into a smile and I wondered just how deaf she was.

The warm biscuits and the stewed chicken and dumplings sent up an inviting aroma. The baby gurgled in a cradle near the fire. Three older children sat around the big table with us. Two younger ones sat on the floor with a bench serving as their table. We bowed our heads for the grace, surprisingly brief. Mrs. Blanchard served her mother-in-law and her husband and then handed the dishes around. The children ate silently and willingly, sopping their biscuits in the stew. One girl, perhaps six, raised a hand for another biscuit, but at her mother's frown lowered the hand. Our meal was taken in silence except for a few "pass me, please" requests. When Mrs. Blanchard replenished our coffee and sliced the blackberry cake, the minister leaned back and asked me our plans for the coming months.

"You've come in what might be the last of our good fall weather," he said. "Greene's Valley? That's where you're from?"

"Yes, I have a cabin there, that is, Fredrick does. The rats and snakes may have claimed it since his tenants left." Lila looked startled, and again a faint movement of the old woman's lips seemed to indicate she understood my words though I had spoken directly to her son. I was uncertain whether he knew I was Fredrick's mother but, of course, he did.

"The boy'll see to it. You're welcome to stay awhile with us if you need. In our home, not the old cabin."

Here the younger children's heads came up, paying attention, their faces blank. How often, I wondered, did they give up a bed for their father's guests? "That is very kind of you," I said. "We're expected tonight at the home of Mrs. Theodore Burton."

Mrs. Blanchard nodded. "She is some miles from here by the road. A, uh, kind woman, we're told, though not churched."

"Kindness is not for the churched only," Mr. Blanchard went to pick up the fretful baby. "Hannah Burton lost her son and husband. Now she does not venture far beyond her cabin."

"Not unusual, surely."

"I'm surprised your acquaintances didn't warn you," Mrs. Blanchard said. "She's been known to greet visitors with her husband's rifle, the one his captain delivered to her on his way home."

Lila said, "Oh, she does know we're coming, doesn't she, Sarranda?"

"Indeed, if our message arrived. Don't worry, Lila. No doubt she expects us." Privately I wasn't so sure of the reliability of the farmer in Webster who assured us that he lived within two miles of her place and would go directly there. The Lynches had deemed him trustworthy, saying they knew of Mrs. Burton "by reputation only." I had not asked what they meant.

At Lila's questioning glance, I said, "We've only to 'hallo' from the clearing. She will not shoot two harmless women without cause. Not that you are entirely harmless."

Mrs. Blanchard's eyebrows shot up. "Does this young lady also shoot?"

My story of Lila's encounter at the train depot was met with giggles from the children and a hearty snort from their father. "Oh dear," Mrs. Blanchard said, "Some of our young men these days."

I sipped my coffee. "No harm done. As long as there are men such as the man with a knife."

"But there may not always be so." Mrs. Blanchard looked worried. "Can we not send O.William with them?"

"He is promised to the Youngs tomorrow and he could not travel there and back easily tonight." Mr. Blanchard looked at the boy. "Their gelding needs to be shod, and O.William is a fine hand at the job. He is promised, I'm afraid."

The young man said not a word. He flushed, asked to be excused, and was out the back door quickly. His mother said, "O.William is shy around girls but a wonder with horses."

"And I had thought to make a preacher of him." Mr. Blanchard spread his hands as if in resignation. A look from his wife indicated this was not a new topic of conversation.

"He's young, yet. Do not lose hope," she said.

As of one accord the children jumped to their feet, and the young girl grabbed the boy's hand; she wiped a bit of dumpling from his face. "I'll clean him up, Ma," she said, dragging him toward the back porch wash basin.

When we thanked our host and said goodbye to the children, lined up in order of age, O.William brought our horses to us. They had been brushed and their hooves cleaned. The boy handed me up and reddened as he held his hands for Lila to step into.

Still a bit awkward about mounting, she put a hand to his shoulder, at which he blushed even more. I caught his mother's smile and ignored the boy. He was thirteen or fourteen, too young for Lila.

I was reminded that Fredrick, on the other hand, was of marriageable age and beyond. And that girl at church had fancied him. I could tell. A single man with prospects was certainly a community commodity. I wondered why he had not married, but it was not my place to worry about his status. With directions from Mr. Blanchard and a bag of apples and biscuits loaded with ham, we set off in mid-afternoon.

"You should be there by early dark, at the latest," the minister said. "Don't miss the fork over the creek beyond the burned barn on past the old apple orchard. Nothing past there for miles."

"'Cept a pack of wild dogs or wolves, depending on who's telling it," added Mrs. Blanchard.

Seeing Lila's mouth open, Mrs. Blanchard said, "It may be a rumor the woman herself started—"

"To escape the botheration of visitors," Mr. Blanchard said. "Go in peace."

Almost three hours later, we heard the cackle and squawk of guinea hens before we left the darkening woods and came into the clearing of the Burton place. Their noise would have raised the dead or, at least, the drunk.

"Announcing our arrival," I said. The guineas scattered as we rode closer.

"Noisy fowl," Lila said.

"But helpful to a lone woman way out here."

We halted and I shouted, "Hello. Hello, Mrs. Burton."

After a few minutes, a tiny woman appeared in the cabin's doorway. She looked so much like my grandmother, a wizened, dried-apple kind of woman, that I shook my head, thinking a mirage. I recognized the sag of her apron pocket: a can of snuff and a sharp pocket knife. She was the distant cousin of one of the Asheville ladies and, though generally unwelcoming to passersby and Yankees, she had agreed to put us up. From her place, it would be an easy ride to my valley. We nudged our horses, advanced slowly, and reined in at three boxwoods before the small cabin. When Mrs. Burton stepped onto the porch she propped a rifle behind her, inside the doorway. The gun was a few inches taller than she.

Before dismounting, I introduced Lila and myself. She indicated we should tie the horses to a lone tree a few feet from her door.

"Come in and set a spell," she said. "I been looking fer you this day."

"The Blanchards were very hospitable," I said. "We ate a large dinner."

"Had supper?"

"Yes, we ate what Mrs. Blanchard furnished us, not knowing when we'd get here." I rubbed my backside and was rewarded with a bare hint of a smile.

"Ye can take your belongings there." She pointed Lila to the bed in the corner. The floor was wide planks, worn smooth. Two boards looked newer and rougher and a strip of bare earth showed where one board had been.

"Thank you," I said. The one room was windowless and dark. My eyes adjusted to the meager light coming in from the open door and the small fire. Strings of beans and dried apples hung in the corner near the chimney. Our hostess stood on tiptoe to hang her firearm over the mantel.

"I sleep up there." She indicated a set of slanting steps at the far end of the room. Her quilting frames had been pulled up with ropes to the overhead beams and I saw that a small portion of a ceiling must be her sleeping loft. "I kin still get up there and while I still kin I will."

"We don't want to impose, Mrs. Burton." I hesitated, not intending to contradict her or have her assume I didn't believe what she'd said. The bed looked inviting; the quilt pattern was The Little Dutch Girl and the pillows were fluffy with goose feathers.

"It's company bed now," she said, "not that I get much of that. Big enough fer the both of you. I expect they told you I'us married once. He didn't come back from the war." Her voice turned sharp. "You might as well hear it from me if ye ain't heard it already. He fit fer the Union side. Some people around here ain't forgot that. One of the Keever boys said he seen him out in Texas somewheres a few years back. Don't surprise me. Me and young Ted on one side. Him on the other. We parted that way, me mad as a hornet and him set on what he thought right."

She poked the fire. "I'm over him, I reckon, and that's all I'm saying about that." I thought Mrs. Burton was glad to say what she said, that some anger at her insensitive neighbors lingered, and she could speak to strangers about it.

"I got a pot of coffee keeping hot." She handed me a mug. "Some cornbread and milk if you're hungry. I don't keep sweets, not since my bee gums was destroyed years back. Can't abide store-bought sugar, and honey's hard to come by."

"Coffee sounds good to me." The pot hung from a spike that had been driven into the fireplace and supported by a tripod; the coffee was strong and hot. A skillet at the side of the fire held a cake of cornbread. "Lila?"

She was inspecting the beans hanging in the corner and didn't immediately answer. Mrs. Burton said, "The youngster looks like she needs more nourishment. I'll get the milk from the spring."

"Let me go for it," Lila said. "I like cornbread."

We did not speak much while we ate. Mrs. Burton said, "I'm runnin' low on salt and the bread's not worth feedin' to the chickens. And you need not say otherwise." Lila declared again that she had taken a liking to cornbread and ate two big slices with her buttermilk.

Later we sat close to the fireplace with its small blaze. "I seen you looking at my floorboards. My husband, to his credit, seen to it we had us a good floor with planed boards. I prized up three of 'em to burn last winter when the snow come up over my waist. Old man Watson put me in two new boards. He died before he got the other one done. His youngest boy promised to do it," Mrs. Burton said. "He'll git to it, I reckon. But already he's casting his eye on leaving these parts, and him not but thirteen."

"Can I cut you some wood?" Lila said.

"Law, no, child. It's too dark fer ye to see now. We'll make do the night." Indeed, though the fire was small, so was the cabin and soon we'd be in bed. I'd slept in much colder quarters and so, I surmised, had Lila. Her eyes were drooping and in a few moments she went to the outhouse and then said goodnight. The ropes of the bed creaked as she snuggled in.

Mrs. Burton stirred the embers and placed a stick of green wood at the back to keep the fire going all night without much of a flame. She turned to me with some questions that had been smoldering during our repast.

"Yer not one of them Yankees. I heard you're one of us, but," she surveyed my serviceable dress and boots, "but ye be a bit different, I say. Not a preacher woman, are you? I don't hold with women a-preachin' the Lord's gospel." She sipped her coffee. "No, ye didn't say a blessing over the supper. And ye don't strike me as just a-ridin' around looking fer a man to marry. Not too many eligibles left in these parts."

When I didn't answer, she said, "Spit it out. What?"

"I'm from Greene's Valley. My grandfather had the mill there, lost it during the war. Now it's in the hands of northern businessmen—"

"Carpetbaggers. They know aught about running a mill."

"I long to see the mill," I said, "but I went North at the behest of a group of women who want to help us, help our mountain people."

"Help how? What can a batch of women do—up there?" Her curiosity was edged with hostility.

"We need teachers for our children," I said, "but I am not trained as a teacher. I hope to find some way to help the women help themselves and their families. Some women in Massachusetts trust me to find a way to—" I stumbled in the face of her direct stare. "To do something, train women, perhaps in some craft or skill. Something."

I stared at the flickering flames, flaring up, dying depending on the wind coming down the chimney. My hopes were like that: flickering, flaring, rising, fading. I had hardly started my mission; how could I be so uncertain? Or how could I have been so naïve? I knew this county and felt at a loss. Yet young women of the North who knew nothing of mountain ways had ventured into these parts—small wonder that only a few stayed and those who did could claim small success. Still they were dedicated and brave, perhaps more so for their unfamiliarity with the people and the land.

"Won't be easy." Mrs. Burton lifted her spit can to her mouth, covering her lips with her hand.

"No. Tell me, Mrs. Burton, what would you do to help?"

"Give some funds, a hearty body and fewer years on this frame of mine?" A smile creased her wrinkled face.

"I don't want to preach or teach but I do want women to come to see that they—and I don't mean to offend—must not depend entirely on their men folk."

"There's naught work for men around here 'cept working for them that's come down. Laying rock, building houses or stores, and making moonshine."

"Men's work," I agreed. "Yet during the war—"

"Didn't see no women a-laying rock or tending stills," she said. "Not that we'd know about the 'shine."

"Over beyond Asheville, some women are making quilts and coverlets, baskets, weaving..." I trailed off. "That small group, though, can get their goods to Asheville, even to cities on the train. I don't know if that's possible here."

"We got the train a-comin' sometime, we hear," she said. "You think women will be glad to make their own money—if it's possible? And their men'll be glad to have them do it?"

A shrewd question. "I know my mother was glad to have her egg money, to be able to barter on her own. I know, too, that my few acres could not produce enough to sell, had there been buyers. And, I confess, the question of men taking to their womenfolk having even a tad of income—well, I don't know." I gazed at the fire. "What do you think?"

"Depends on the man, I'd reckon. My man, now, he'd a-took a broomstick to me if I'd tried to work anywhere but in this here cabin and the fields."

"Oh, did he ever hit you?" My question was presumptuous, but she answered without hesitation.

"Never did. Didn't give him cause to. Once when he'd been a-drinking, he raised his fist to me. I stepped right up to him, surprised him. I told him, 'Hit me hard, Dore,' his name was Theodore, 'and kill me 'cause if I get up from the floor you've hit your last lick. I'll kill you.'" She spit again and wiped her lips. "I'll never forget the look on his face. Guess he weren't too drunk to take in my meaning. He never raised a hand to me again and we never spoke of it."

"Times have changed," I said. "The war left too few able-bodied men, and women can't depend on some of them that's here. Some never could, in truth, I suppose. My pa went to seek his fortune in the West, died in California." The ache of my little-girl self surfaced briefly. "But we had my grandfather and managed, until the war." I lifted my head. "I can do something here. I will do something here."

Perhaps the weeks in the North forced the next thought into words. "This is my home. I won't leave it again."

Mrs. Burton pushed to her feet. "The wind's rising. You go ahead with your business." She waved toward the outdoors. "Take the lamp if ye need it. I'll see to the fire."

"The moon's full," I said. "I won't need it."

"Then I'll blow it out. I can see in the dark better than any old painter."

The next morning when I woke to the rooster's crow, Lila stood at the table, trying her hand at making biscuits. Mrs. Burton was fussing and instructing like a grandmother. Dressing quickly I brushed my hair and twisted it into its customary roll at my neck, went to the outhouse and to wash and joined them just as Lila carefully placed the skillet in the ashes, following directions to put the lid on.

"She'll learn," Mrs. Burton announced. "Make some man a good wife."

Lila said, "I told her I'm not looking for a man yet. But she won't believe me." At my raised eyebrows, she smiled. I remembered Fredrick's gaze only yesterday and, I think, so did she.

I had slept so well and so deeply that I had not heard Lila get up early. She had washed her stockings and undergarments and hung them on a line strung across the room in front of the fireplace. At my glance, she said, "Mrs. Burton gave me permission, didn't she? If they're not dry, we can take them damp."

"The girl's a smart 'un. She's up long before my old Shoofly crowed out there."

Lila made the bed and went out to see to our horses. I watched while the old woman prepared our breakfast. In a few minutes, she laid two fried eggs on my plate and two on Lila's, took the biscuits from the fireplace, and set a crock of blackberry jelly before us. She apologized for the lack of meat. "Won't be long before hog killing time and I'll be eating fresh sausage," she said. "I'll go along to Watsons and help out. I always had a hog till the last year. It got out and, lickety-split, that's the last I seen of it. Heard it was caught way over the mountain—or at least somebody caught a hog over there. My neighbors'll give me a portion for helping out."

"Keeping a hog would be a lot of trouble," I said. She would not have a lot of leftovers to slop a hog and bending over to pick plantain would be hard.

"My chickens are 'bout all I can manage these days." She grinned. "I hope the preacher don't feel the need to come a-calling anytime soon."

At Lila's puzzled look I said, "Preachers expect fried chicken."

"But—?"

"He'd be a-coming a long way, but I 'spect he won't come, chicken or no. Till the final call, that is, when I'm all laid out."

She put another biscuit on Lila's plate. "Don't fret about my henhouse, child," she said. "I do like to see a good eater." She herself did not have an egg. Likely we had enjoyed her company eggs.

As we expressed our appreciation for her hospitality and settled into our saddles, Mrs. Burton held up a hand and scurried back into the cabin. Returning, she handed Lila a bundle in a yellowed pillowcase. "These here quilt scraps I was a-savin' to make a double wedding ring quilt for my boy's wife. He didn't come back, and she went and married a Bledsoe in the next county." She spit into the dirt. "Before we even got the fatal word about him. I didn't have it in my heart to give'em to her. Ye'll have time on your hands this winter. I put the pattern in there."

"Oh, thank you, Mrs. Burton." Lila beamed. "I'll learn to make little stitches like you're supposed to. And I'll show you the quilt next time I see you."

"Law, child," she said. To me she handed a knitted cap. "This'll keep your ears warm," she said. "'Twas meant it for my boy. I've kept it all these years. You wear it in good health and good fortune."

I wanted to leap off Josie and hug her, but she waved us on even as I was thanking her.

Lila rode up next to me with a question. "I heard what she said last night. What is she having painted?"

I don't think my explanation that "painters" were panthers was reassuring.

PART THREE

CHAPTER ELEVEN

We ambled along in the crisp air, leaves crunching under our horses' hooves, disturbed only by an occasional snort from a horse, call of a bird, or a rustle of a squirrel skittering through the underbrush at the trail's edge. We rode single file and silently. We saw only two other persons: an old man leaning heavily on a cane and a barefoot boy, maybe ten years of age. They stepped aside, and when we asked where they were headed, the man pointed down the trail. "Yonder." The boy carried a tow sack that looked to be full of cabbages.

"Not very friendly, are they?" Lila said. "Wonder where they're going."

"Whatever their destination, yonder's a long walk." I smiled. "Maybe they'll stop at Mrs. Burton's."

Soon, I began to recognize familiar sights: two willow trees whose trunks rubbed against each other like lovers—older lovers by now—and then the gray rock cliff. It had seemed so big when I was a child. It came straight down from the hillside, lichen splattered on it like paint, a spring of clear water pooled beneath it. A bullfrog's croak and splash startled Josie and me. I reined her in.

We slid to the ground. Lila took our biscuits from a sack, and we cupped our hands in the cold water and drank. "My cabin's not far from here. I wonder how it looks."

"It's been lived in?" Lila was picking up buckeyes, with a question in her eyes.

"Not edible," I said. "But put one in your pocket for luck." I rinsed my hands. "The last renters headed out for Missouri this spring, Fredrick told me. Two Mormon families used to live over Salter's Ridge not three miles away. They went out West, and the men returned for their nieces and nephews and cousins. They preached around here when the regular church's minister allowed. They converted the tenants."

I rolled my shoulders to unkink the tight muscles. In time I would get used to riding Josie, but now, I felt creaky as a rusted hinge. I went on, "The renters had a sick child and weren't doing so well. They were easily converted and set off with the Mormons. For the best, Fredrick thought."

I knew little of the Mormon faith, only that one of its chief doctrines was caring for its own, a tenet bound to appeal to unfortunate families that saw small hope of thriving as long as they stayed here.

"I've never heard of them, have I?" Lila said. "I'm woefully ignorant."

Not mentioning what I had heard about their marriage practices, I told her, "They're establishing themselves in Missouri and farther west, in Utah."

Thoughts of the cabin I had deliberately kept from intruding. It was not a showplace when we lived there and was surely less so now. I must think ahead, not back, not open the wounds of Joey's death, of the news of Zack's death, of Larsen's leaving and Fredrick's turning hostile, not recall my one splendid night. *Such memories hinder. Best consign them to the rag bin.*

Thus I was unprepared for the cabin when I saw it, coming upon it almost unawares, thinking the trail would widen. I remembered a decent wagon road from Frady's store, but we had bypassed that route to take a shorter, rough trail. This trail narrowed, almost choked off by the twisting growths of rhododendron. We slid off Josie and Belle and led them through the close pathway. Obviously not many people passed this way.

The structure stood small and forlorn. One end of the front porch sagged; the log that had long held up one corner had been replaced with a rock. Some shingles had blown off the roof. Bigger than Mrs. Burton's, the cabin had two windows, but it was no larger than the Garretts' parlor. Yet I, three boys and a husband had managed in the small space. True, Zack had been mostly absent when the boys were born and afterwards. I spotted at once my rosebush, straggly, its leaves eaten away, bare of any trace of color. Tears blurred my eyes. On our wedding day, Zack had slipped the rosebush into our wagon and surprised me with it the next morning at the cabin, the only gift he could offer—and it likely stolen from his neighbor. Wedding Pink I'd named it.

Fredrick had promised to look after it, and maybe he had, the best he could. Of course, I had not expected him to ride all the way over to the cabin just to check on the rose bush. Undoubtedly, though, I had expected too much. Walking closer, however, I saw the dirt loose around the bush. He had must have come over when he knew I was returning. I stood back and regarded the desolate sturdiness of the place.

In this cabin I had grown up; seen my father depart for California gold, seen my brothers leave and, in their own way, return from the war—one wounded beyond the visible loss of an eye and an arm, the other filled with a false bravado encouraged by a plantation-born wife; seen my mother fade into indifference. Here I had come as an ignorant bride, birthed my sons, lost my husband and little boy to death, and my older boys to the West and the land—to hope and security.

My second life began with my years with Mrs. Whitney. Like the sunlight breaking through the mist, a dawning spread through me: this defeated and recovering land claimed me. I wanted nothing more than to stay here, at whatever the cost. Had I returned under false pretensions? Was helping others my first obligation? Was I capable of changing the lives of women or at least getting them to see they could improve their lot? I had a box of books to be made available for schooling. Returning with small funds and good intentions, I must do something; my sponsors would expect reports—of failure or success.

The time was ripe for change. The war had already changed much. It had left large areas blank, economically and otherwise. Something would fill in those blanks. Nature abhors a vacuum, so I'd heard a lecturer say. It seemed true enough. In Asheville I saw the opportunities for commerce, the chance for improving both one's own condition and the community's. Men with money, energy, and vision were finding "The Land of the Sky" fertile ground. The mountains to the west could not long go untouched with the railway coming. Rumors of lumber companies seeking the virgin forests already abounded, and camps and hotels were sure to be built. Even if we who had grown up here could not initially provide the financial means for growth, we, women along with men, should have the skills and education necessary to prosper. I patted Josie's neck and returned to the present moment.

The log cabin surely struck Lila as a poor habitation—at least, in relation to the homes she'd served in. I looked around with some dismay, but Lila needed no instruction. We found clean rags neatly stacked on the mantel and an old broom in the corner. "Thank our lucky stars," I said, "the renters left us a broom."

Lila swiped down arcs of webs and, standing as far away as possible, with dress held above her ankles, she crushed lethargic, fat spiders. I dispatched dust, cobwebs, wasp nests and mud dauber cells.

"I'll see about the spring," I said. "It may need to be cleaned out." Somehow, it seemed my duty to see to our water supply, and the spring surprised me, pleasantly. When I scooped out a few handfuls of wet leaves, the water soon cleared. A couple of spring lizards darted to the bottom, seeking a thin layer of mud. I cupped my hands for a sip of cold water and it did not disappoint. I collected a pail and took Lila a cup. We drank greedily, as Grandda once said, like "thirsty monks."

"The best water I've had since," Lila smacked her lips, "since we stopped at the cliff. Was that just an hour ago?"

We didn't wait for water to heat. She wiped the table of its grime and wiped again to show its walnut grain that no shine would ever brighten. Solid and sturdy even now, it did not wobble under Lila's swift and sure attacks.

I dragged the musty-smelling corn shuck mattress outside and shook it, thankful that the air was dry and crisp. Not a bedbug in sight. The covering was in need of a good wash, but that would have to wait. Thank goodness the former renters had left it behind, even if they had not replenished the shucks this or last season. Alas, the bedding in the loft was ratty, to say the least. Mice had chewed holes in the filthy, thin pillow cover and feathers floated on the floor like fossilized snowflakes. Lila swept them up into a sack. They smelled so awful we took them outside.

"The wind will carry them away, it will," she said, "if we let them go." We reconsidered and left the feathers on the porch for the night, hoping they would smell better on the morrow.

"We'll keep them," I said, "until we find others or you can't stand them." Later that night, carrying a quilt, Lila insisted on sleeping "up the steps," as she called the small loft. She did not say that she could scoot up the ladder more easily than I, and I did not quarrel with her assessment.

Thanks to my son, we were not dependent on the hospitality of others for a roof over our heads. We had some dried beans, lard, cornmeal, and eggs from the Lynches. Soon I would visit the community's store. I had written to kind Mrs. Frady, she who put me in touch with Mrs. Whitney those years ago. Old Mr. Frady had since died of dropsy, but his wife still kept the post office/store.

By dusk, when I had knocked two squirrel nests and the dried skeletons of birds from the chimney and poked and prodded to see that it was clear of animals, dead or alive, we were more than ready to rest. I laid a fire and sent up a silent plea for the chimney to draw as properly as it ever did—and that was not perfect. My mother had shrugged and said, "Once a poor chimley, always a poor chimley."

I had lived with a poor-drawing chimney and could again. I mixed water and cornmeal with a bit of salt, and dropped the fritters into a dab of sizzling lard. Once I took them off the flat skillet, I cracked us each an egg in the hot grease. We ate the thin and tasty fritters with our fingers, grinning, wiping our hands on a single towel. Lila handed forks for the eggs. Hunger sated, we sighed in weary satisfaction.

While Lila cleaned the pan, utensils and plates with sand, I reflected again on how grateful I was for her company, how fortunate that circumstances placed us together. She was anything but talkative and that trait I appreciated, but she had a retort or a giggle if called for. I supposed her occasional pensive air meant she fretted about her mother or siblings or was homesick. Certainly she did not complain or whine. She watched and learned, was appropriately respectful of her elders, and had won Mrs. Burton's heart. Mine would have been a lonely return without her.

"Thank you, Lila, for all you've done today. The cabin is livable, is it not?" In the days ahead we would scrub and clean more thoroughly. Other tasks had to be done for the coming months: the chimney checked and rechinked, if needed, the roof shakes replaced, and wood cut. The renters had left only a small stack of wood outside.

"'Tis a grand adventure, it is, Sarranda. It feels like I'm in a new country." Her words were cheerful but her eyes were sad.

"What is it?"

"I wonder... nothing," she said.

"Are you in pain? Tired?"

"I was thinking about me mam and the young ones," Lila said, "and everything back home." She brushed a cobweb from her hair, seeming suddenly very young and vulnerable to life's hardships. "'Tis too soon for a letter, I know."

The Fairfields had promised to send on any letters. "You're sure to hear in a week or two." I poked at the fire and smiled. "We don't have the Pony Express here."

In the next few days, we scurried around, preparing for cold weather. We ventured almost half a mile from the cabin to scrounge for firewood and, at first, we dragged the limbs we found back to our chopping block. Lila looked with interest at our horses, thinking to use Josie as a work horse. But Josie sidestepped, refused to bulge, and had the audacity to bare her yellow teeth. At her lack of cooperation, Lila tossed her head and came up with another idea. Laying a rope on the ground, we piled several tree limbs and brush together on it and tied up the bundle. We pulled together, hard and sweaty work, soon mastering securing the knot and "heave-ho-ing" as a team. We burst out in laughter when Josie and Belle turned their inquisitive eyes toward us and resumed their nibbling at non-existent grass.

As we walked in the woods, we were like eager school girls on an outing. I taught Lila to recognize poison ivy and to look for pine knots. "What's a pine knot?" she said.

I picked out what appeared to be a rotten log and showed her the resin inside. "It's perfect for getting a fire going," I said. "I'll show you tonight." Looking for the intriguing rich pine gave Lila renewed energy and she called out each time she found a specimen or thought she did. Two hours later, we secured the accumulated wood, wrapped the ropes around our hands, and pulled our heat source back to the cabin.

Chopping sufficient wood for cooking and for the winter was necessary and required sheer physical labor, and it had been years since I'd handled an axe. Though we took turns in spite of Lila's insistence that she do it all, our palms blistered quickly. We tied rags around our hands and chopped a few hours each morning. The second day I pulled on my gloves over my bandaged hands.

"Oh, Sarranda," Lila groaned. "Those are fine gloves, they are. The fine leather will be ruined."

"So it will, but I'm not going anywhere that requires fine leather, am I?" I was beginning to sound like Lila. I winced as I tugged on a glove. "I prefer skin on my hands."

The dew was not yet dry when we tackled the good-sized tree trunks we'd dragged home. We established a routine, one chopping while the other brought the limbs to be cut and stacked the pieces. Then we straightened up, rubbed our backs, checked our hands, and changed jobs. When we ceased our work, she grinned and mimicked my tone. "We should thank our lucky stars they left a sharp axe for us." She grew fond of "thanking our lucky stars."

After three days, I reckoned we could stop chopping and hauling and consider our next move. Not a soul had come by to see what was happening. Surely anyone going to or from the mill would hear our axes and wonder. It was not that far away. Mrs. Burton had said Yankees owned it. No one else had mentioned it—but who in Asheville or Webster would?

Years ago, on several nights I had crept from my cabin through the darkness to sit at the mill. After Fredrick told me he wanted to be adopted by the Macks, I'd opened the water gate and set the wheel to turning in my despair and futile fury. Thus was birthed a ghost at the mill. In no time, the tale started: my grandfather, old Josiah Shadrack Greene, unhappy with the fate of the mill, had released the water to turn the wheel.

I frowned at the memory of that bitter night. Perhaps the word had circulated at the mill that two women were in the Boylett cabin, and no man wanted to show up who might feel obligated to help put things in order.

At any rate, we lowered ourselves to the floor in front of a meager fire after yet another supper of cornbread and pinto beans. Fortunately (another "Thank our lucky stars" from Lila), we had found a bushel of black walnuts in the barn, dry and ready to be cracked. A heavy slab of oak to keep varmints out covered the basket and we were careful to replace it when we took an apron full.

"Cracking walnuts is a skill one doesn't forget." I demonstrated as if I'd been cracking walnuts every day for the past few years. We each laid a flat rock on the hearth, positioned a walnut, and with another rock had a fine time cracking them, making a game of it: who could hit the walnuts with just the right force and judgment so as to pick out the bigger pieces. After misjudging a lick and nursing a sore thumb, Lila learned quickly. When she hit the thumb again, I said, "Bless your heart. Be careful." And into my head popped a riddle my Grandda riddled me when I was around eight years old.

"There was a little green house,
And in the little green house,
There was a little brown house,
And in the little brown house,
There was a little yellow house,
And in the little yellow house,
There was a little white house,
And in the little white house,
There was a little heart."

"Sorry, say it again, will you? A little green house?" Lila looked at her bruised thumb and, with some amazement, at me.

Realizing she had not seen the walnuts in their green hulls, I repeated the riddle, held up a perfect walnut half and dropped it in my mouth.

"B'gorry!" She picked up a piece from her stash and with exaggerated motion, put it in her mouth, swallowed, giggled—and got choked.

I pounded on her back hard until she gasped. "That little white house went down wrong," I said. The walnuts supplied us with merriment and supplemented our provisions. I wanted desperately to add salt to my handful of walnuts, but salt was best saved for bread and beans. After a few minutes I said, "Tomorrow we'll go down to Maude Frady's store."

We retired in good spirits, Lila reciting the walnut riddle, our blistered hands and her sore thumb notwithstanding.

CHAPTER TWELVE

The next day dawned cool and clear, the perfect late autumn day, and we walked to the store. "We can carry enough food back," I said. "And Josie and Belle couldn't really carry our trunks, if they're there."

"The horses look happy to stay home," Lila agreed.

Mrs. Frady had run the store and post office since her husband's death about five years earlier. We had not been close friends, but through her I learned of the post with Mrs. Whitney, and for that I was grateful. When the garment on which I'd sewn the buttons the Fradys gave me was so threadbare as to be immodest, I saved the buttons and they adorned my frock today.

After somewhat effusive greetings, Mrs. Frady stepped back and said, "I see you're still attached to them buttons, and right pretty they are on your brown dress."

"I'll keep transferring them, Mrs. Frady, until they crack with age," I declared.

"All these years, Sarranda Boylett, and you can call me Maude, surely. And who is this pretty lass?"

We were gratified that our trunk and cases had arrived and Maude promised delivery to the cabin as soon as the settlement's unofficial wagoner returned in a day or two. He was, Maude said, "Sleeping it off after a trip down Pickens way."

A note from Claudia and a letter from Adelaide gave us their best wishes but no real news. Lila had no letter from her mother, but she squared her shoulders and soon was gazing at the barrels of dried beans, crates of cabbage and onions, baskets of eggs, and a great wheel of orange cheese.

"Just delivered yesterday," Maude said of the cheese.

She gave us strong tea, beamed at Lila's enthusiasm for its taste, and put a plate of her molasses cookies before us. She told who had died, who had married, babies born, living or dying. She was not optimistic about the future of the community. "It's withering away," she said. "The folks renting your cabin weren't the only ones to leave for Missouri or Texas or somewhere. There's not been a school in four or five years, after the schoolmaster took off with a young woman no better than she ought to be. Nobody's looking to worry about book learning or a school, more's the pity, but it's not likely to change."

Maude frowned as if her tea were too bitter and added a last bit of news. "And I'm getting a feeling that the post office may not be here after I'm gone. It's too small to matter, I reckon."

"That'll surely be some years yet, if it does happen," I said. "Doesn't the government always go at a snail's pace?" I had noticed, though, that the shelves were not full. There were no bolts of fabric at all and the place was a bit dusty. "It must be hard to keep up with everything. Do you have any help?"

"Now, who would I trust?" She broke into a racking cough, a worrying cough that didn't want to let go. When she caught her breath, she continued, "The few girls around are saddled with babies and husbands." She paused. "More or less husbands, anyway. I tell you, I had no idea just how much work Mr. Frady did in here."

She must be well into her sixties, I thought, and wiry though she was, she seemed frail and tired. Her fingers were crooked and swollen with arthritis. She handled her cup of tea with caution, using both hands. "I've closed off the back room, just live in here and the kitchen." The back room had been added to the side of the store and had a separate doorway. She repeated, "Who would I trust?"

I looked at Lila; she looked at me; and we turned toward Mrs. Frady. "This one you can trust." I pointed at Lila.

The storekeeper stared at Lila, appraising her as if she were up for sale, a pony or a fine hen. "Can you read and do figuring? I see you're healthy and well spoken, even if you talk faster than I'm used to. But, then, we're getting used to some Yankee talk in these parts."

"Don't hold that against her." I realized I had been too quick to speak for Lila. "I may have spoken too soon. She may not want a job."

"Couldn't pay much, anyway, if anything," Mrs. Frady said. "Look around."

"I can do sums and I can read well enough," Lila said. "Not nearly as good as Miss Sarranda, but I've had some schooling." She said firmly, "I'm Irish—and American."

Maude chuckled. "And do you want a job or does Miss Sarranda want one for you?" She had noted the deferential title Lila bestowed on me. I thought we were finished with that.

When Lila hesitated, perhaps uncertain as to my attitude or her aptitude, I said, "Maude, you've told us about all the folks around here, but let me tell you why we are here."

The bell tinkled out front, signaling a customer, and she rose. "Have some more tea, then." She gestured toward the kettle and left us.

Lila whispered, "I could be a big help to her, couldn't I? I'm not good at long division but I can study on it." She pointed her finger at her chest. "Me, a storekeeper's assistant. I'd like to try."

Smiling, I poured more hot water in the teapot. "You could ride over on Belle. That is, if you're certain."

"I could walk, couldn't I?" Lila said in a low voice, "I like her."

Maude, returning, may have heard the words, for her eyes twinkled.

"Now, tell me," she commanded.

I summarized our situation and finished with, "Quite honestly, the good ladies may have been glad to see us go. We have sufficient funds for a few months, maybe longer if we get through the winter and can plant a garden and potato patch. Some corn." I took another cookie. "My friends in Bramford understand, I believe, my reluctance to work under the auspices of their church; others do not. I suppose I disappointed them, not being, uh, quite as God-fearing as they thought—or as definite in my commitment to further the church's growth or mission."

"You may be too hard-headed, Sarranda Boylett, to hunker under anybody's—" she grinned. "Anybody's umbrella. Independent you are." She handed the plate of cookies to Lila. "Is something wrong with these? Eat up, youngster."

Lila took two cookies. "I'm trying to mind my p's and q's." She had picked that expression up in Asheville and she looked happy at being able to use it.

We laughed. "Think about working here," Maude said.

"No need to think, ma'am. Just tell me when you'd want me and show me how to handle the till. I'd like it very much, wouldn't I?" Lila said and quickly amended, "I would."

"Then we must choose our provisions and be on our way," I said. "But first, Maude, please tell me about the mill, Grandda's mill. Is it operating?"

"Still going, still got its ghost, I reckon."

That ghost would always be around even if I confessed to birthing it—which I was not about to do. I smiled at the news.

"But I misspeak." Maude leaned back in her straight chair. A shaft of sunlight splashed across her forehead, revealing weariness and wrinkles.

"The mill shut down just a few days ago, about the time you got here. The owners, two brothers, generally don't come this way for their supplies. They head straight for Webster. So what I'm telling I heard from a Caney Creek boy and he'd been a-drinking when he told me. There was a bad accident. A boy got his arm awful mangled somehow. Old man Walker rode to the boy's house." Her eyes stayed closed as she spoke. "The pa come over with a shotgun and when he got to the mill, the boy was still a-laying there, bleeding bad. They got him to the doctor fast as they could once an owner showed up. The boy's pa went back later threatening to beat the living daylights out of the brothers."

She went on. "These Yankee brothers are the second owners since your cousin Lance sold out. The boy lost his arm, almost bled to death, with the men standing around useless as ditch water. And one owner's laid up for a few days, beat up, ain't filed no charges, though. Nobody knows when the mill'll open up."

"Oh no," I murmured. "I looked forward to going over to see it. I knew it had passed from my cousin's hands—"

"Been in these Yankee hands some months now," Maude said. She turned to Lila. "I know they're Americans, lass, but to me they're Yankees first." She dusted cookie crumbs from her apron. "Can you stand a crotchety old woman and her ways?"

Lila looked her straight in the eyes. "Yes." She touched Maude's hand as she might a grandmother's and instantly withdrew her fingers as if fearful of being too forward. The two of them would get along fine.

Maude said, "Your cousins are still around. Lance is up at the old home place." She referred to Grandda's house. "Earl's moved over across the ridge."

"I'll have to go calling," I said. "Sometime."

"I hear Lance's wife suffers from nervous prostration these days, so sooner's better than later," she said. "I'd get it over with if I was you."

"I'd rather go to the mill," I said. "Let's see what we need out front."

"Got a couple of hens I could part with." Maude pushed up from her chair.

I thought about keeping chickens through the winter: feeding them, breaking ice on their watering pans. They could keep the horses company in the barn, but even shut up in a makeshift stall some hungry fox or other varmint could pounce on them. I looked at Lila who shrugged. It was my decision.

"To be honest, Maude, for now they'd be more trouble than they're worth. In the spring, maybe. Thank you for the offer."

"Mr. Frady fixed up our henhouse right smart. I've not lost but one hen to critters in the night. The lass can take you an egg or two from here." She measured out salt and coffee into the small tins we'd brought and produced cloth bags for the flour and meal. "I made these pokes myself, especially for womenfolk who come in and can't carry a baby and twenty pounds both. They hold 'bout fifteen pounds." After filling our sacks, she held up a scoop of loose black tea.

I nodded. "I think we can indulge ourselves." Lila stood at the cheese, and I pointed to it. "And just a tad."

Two other customers stomped in. They were both big, broad-shouldered men whose presence shrank the store. Maude introduced us to them and them as the Massey brothers, Jam and Rim.

"Did I hear you correctly?" I asked. The men swept off their hats, to reveal heads totally bald on top, gray tufts falling below their ears. They bobbed their heads and stood grinning, hands behind their backs.

"You heard right, ma'am," one of them said. "Been Jam and Rim ever since our baby sister, long dead now, couldn't get out Hammond and Timothy. Since I was three going on four."

"And I was four going five. We almost forgot our real names by now," his brother said. "Guess they're over at Greeneville courthouse, but we joined up Jam and Rim and stuck together throughout."

"And," interjected Maude, "come back in one piece. Back to Tennessee. They moved here near two years ago."

"We're at the old Bronson place right far up the mountain." Jam turned toward the door. "We'll let you ladies finish your pickings. We'll be back when you're finished, ma'am." They ambled outside.

In a few minutes, we said goodbye to the brothers and hefted our sacks to our hips. Maude handed Lila a stubby pencil and some scraps of paper. "I've jotted down some prices and such, for items sold in bulk by the pound or peck," she said. "Our customers may not always know if our figures are right, but they'll expect you to be quick. And I'll expect you to be right."

Lila dropped the items into her pocket. "Thank you, Mrs. Frady. I'll study on these."

Our loads were not heavy when we started, but they grew heavier with the minutes and the miles. I was thinking of the mill standing idle, when Lila said, "That Jam and Rim, they're old, well, up in years. Did everybody down here join the army?"

"They look to be in their sixties, and signing on in their forties wouldn't have been unusual, not after all the young men had gone."

"Wonder if they're married?" Lila glanced sideways at me, and we halted for a rest. "I didn't see rings on their fingers."

"Don't look at me, you upstart," I said. "I'm not in the marrying notion." After a moment, I swung my tow sack and marched ahead. I confess that my thoughts went straight to the stranger-not-quite-a-stranger at the party. I'd never see him again, not expecting to return to the state of Massachusetts, but I was thankful he was alive and had all his limbs and wits about him. My heart had almost stopped when I'd heard his voice. His voice, his polished boots, the shape of his head and shoulders...

"Oww!" Lila's exclamation interrupted my dreaming. She stumbled forward, holding her sack wide. A large root protruding in the path had caught her unawares. Stepping quickly toward her, I grabbed the sack a moment before she thumped to the ground. She rubbed her hip, brushing a few leaves from her gown. "Lordy, that's got our eggs in it."

I set the sack down and looked inside. "No harm done to them." I helped her up. "Are you all right? You'll be sore tomorrow, but nothing's broken?

Not the eggs or a bone, but now you've a sore hip to go with your sore thumb."

"Daydreaming, I was." Her voice was rueful. She picked up her sack.

"Thinking of Jam or Rim?" My turn to tease. I lagged behind to be sure she was not limping.

"Wasting my time and just about losing our eggs," she retorted. "My mam was always telling me to stop dreaming and watch my step." She smiled. "I don't think she had this kind of stepping in mind."

"Many a young girl's rued the day she didn't listen to her mama." I was at once ashamed of my pious-preachy words.

"That I know, Sarranda. One time I went with a friend to that doctor's clinic, the one where they took Mr. Carly when he was so beat up."

She sounded disconsolate and lonely. A realization dawned. "Lila, were you fond of Adelaide's brother, Carlyle? Did he encourage you—did he—?"

"No, he never did. A perfect gentleman, wasn't he, the few times I saw him. Except when he was, uh, was not himself." She slowed and turned to face me. "And then he never even knowed, didn't even know, I was around. A gentleman he was."

"Is," I corrected. "He's very much alive, as far as we know, but Lila, you—"

Again she interrupted, somewhat harshly. "He never and I never let on. I didn't see him more'n two or three times, anyway. He's not for the likes of me. But he was always kind. I remember that."

Lila had not known many kind men or boys, I thought. Adelaide's brothers! Both of us smitten—to some extent and with some or no reason. Likely young Carlyle had no idea how she might have felt about him. He had been kind. Kindness could take many forms—words, attitudes, caresses, love given, even bed time. Perhaps it was a good thing she was far away from Bramford. Perhaps it was a good thing we both were.

"Yes," I said. "Remember that."

CHAPTER THIRTEEN

"I was restless in heart as Lila and I worked around the cabin the next day, a day of unrelenting drizzle. I couldn't put my mind on exactly what my next steps should be. Wishy-washy described my state of mind. We had not been here long enough to have accomplished anything thus far. But I felt that I must make a start, beyond settling in, before the winter might prevent our doing anything. I should visit the Blanchards again. Perhaps I could use their church though I could not possibly go that far each day and boarding with them or someone posed too many difficulties to ponder on. I wondered about the old schoolhouse; I could walk there and, if it was habitable, it might be a meeting place. More than wanting to think of church or schoolhouse, however, I yearned to see the mill.

Instead I mended, washed, and spread the garments on a line strung across the room. I heated some water but it was mostly a cold water wash they'd had. We needed an iron; maybe Maude had an extra one.

Occasionally Lila mumbled under her breath in concentration or frustration. She muttered, "What's a peck exactly?" but she wasn't asking me, for she soon said, "Oh, yes, I knew that." She was working on sums, dividing, subtracting, and figuring out amounts that a customer might need to know at the store. If a scoop of dried beans went for so many cents and two dozen eggs came to this much and a packet of buttons...and then subtract for the fresh duck eggs brought in—it was a chore but apparently she found it challenging enough. I heard a "yes," and a "right, thank you, sir," once in a while.

I didn't offer to help but that evening, seeing her serious face turn toward her scribbles, I said in a deep voice, "Now I want a half pound of eggs and three butter balls or did my wife say a pound of butter and three dozen eggs? And sliver off a tad of one of them cheeses and add this chew of tobacco—and what do I owe, Missy? I'm in a great hurry!"

"Oh, I'll get it right, Sarranda I will. Mrs. Frady'll have no doubt about me!" With a gleam of mischief in her eyes, she said, "Now, you tell me just how much does a sliver or a tad cost?"

Two days later, on a frosty morning, Lila walked to Frady's store and I set off for the mill. It might have been more reasonable to visit Cousin Lance first, but I was not in a reasonable frame of mind. I didn't feel like meeting relatives who weren't sorry to see me leave and who wouldn't be particularly happy to see me back. My head would send me to Cousin Lance's; my heart pointed me toward the mill. I could have ridden Josie but, like Mrs. Burton, as long as I could go on shank's mare, I would.

After the rain had ceased, a cold snap came through, chilling the air and bringing a heavy frost this day. Lila and I wore the thick coats our Bramford friends had given us but not our elegant muffs. I'd need my hands free. I carried a bucket, thinking to pick some persimmons. I knew there had been a few persimmon trees in the woods. I'd puckered my lips many times tasting the fruit before a proper frost.

Eager as I was to see the mill, uncertainty about how it would look caused me to dawdle, and I meandered rather than taking a straight route to my destination. I filled my bucket with persimmons before I heard the faint roar of the small waterfall far above the mill and then the stream's welcoming gurgle. I paused and sucked in my breath. This was no Eden, that I knew, but during my away-years I had dreamed of this place that Grandda loved and I loved. I had seen it so many times in my mind that I'd coated it with a sheen of unreality, like sugar water will glaze a cake. It could not live up to my vision. That realization stopped me at the far edge of the woods. Once I walked into the clearing, could I bear seeing anything less than my almost sacred place? I clutched the bucket's handle hard enough to hurt.

I marched with resolution through the young pines that struggled to survive under the canopy of oaks and poplars. I knew Old Blue, Lance's faithful hound and my friend, would be long dead, no longer guarding the building. However, another dog might be on a long chain close to the door, so I listened for a growl. I expected to see the tall spruce tree standing green and firm, like a Christmas tree unadorned by human hands. I stepped back in shock.

The tree lay toppled on its side; its massive root ball of dirt showed damp, tendril-like roots ripped from the earth. I walked around the fairly shallow hole, seeing evidence of ruined birds' nests among cones and branches. An earthy and resinous odor rose from the giant sprawled before me. Someone had attempted to chop off extending limbs, likely to clear the way for wagons. Embedded in the trunk was an axe, as if its owner had left in a hurry. Without thinking, I pulled the axe free and leaned it against the tree. Then, my hand at my throat, I stared at the tree, still green but dead, this fallen sentinel. At least it had been laid low by a natural force, not cut down by some misguided worker.

I raised my eyes toward the mill beyond.

The sight brought a smile to my face—simply because the mill was there. It had endured. I moved around the moist root ball, inches taller than I, to approach with a kind of reverence. I was five years old again, my granddad's "Queenie," riding my pony Stewart into the clearing above the mill. The mill had been a source of solace, of magic, another world to me—and that tug at my heart, swept over me again. Of course, I knew the practicalities of the mill's operation: its workings, its wheels, gears, cogs, hopper, its stones, all the hard work needed to keep it in repair. The life of a miller wasn't an easy one, but transforming corn into meal was, to me, purely satisfying; the task caught at my senses. I liked the powdery dust, the aromas both fresh and musty, the chaff, the smell of machinery oil, the mix of wood, iron and water.

Oblivious to all but the mill, I clasped my hands to my chest. The pail of persimmons hit my toe and they spilled. Above the door hung a new sign. Grandda's mill had not needed a sign. SANBORNE in dark blue letters on gray paint, the S and the B adorned with flourishes. The Sanborne brothers might be the owners, but it was Greene's mill to me.

The door was padlocked, a heavy chain pulled across it. No successor of Old Blue growled a warning or wagged a welcome. Where windows had never been, the rectangle openings were shuttered. On tiptoes, leaning across the small divide between building and bank, I pushed on a shutter but it was latched from inside. I walked around the lower side of the mill and peered down at the wheel. The stone foundation had been extended and a door had been installed to prevent entry from that level. The old wheel with its wooden buckets had been replaced as well, though to my eye, this wheel didn't seem to hang just right. In spite of the recent rain and weeks when the wheel hadn't turned, some meal dust remained visible in spots that rain wouldn't reach unless driven by a fierce wind.

Head down, irritated at my inability to get or see inside, I muttered several "Drats" to myself. Retracing my steps I saw what I'd missed before. Several feet from the doorway, a deep layer of dirt and hay had been scattered. I scraped my boot across it and revealed dark stains. Blood. This was where the mangled boy had been carried, where he lay bleeding a long time before being taken to the doctor. I shuddered and instinctively toed the hay back in place. Accidents were not uncommon at mill sites, I reminded myself; I should not judge hastily. In a fatal accident in the northwest part of the state a woman's dress became caught in the machinery and she was strangled; in another, a child slipped beneath the wheel and drowned. Accidents did happen. But in this case, through indifference or ignorance, medical help had been long delayed.

Now the Sanbornes might have difficulty finding willing employees or workers knowledgeable about the mill. They might consider the site jinxed. Mountain men who desperately needed jobs could be stubborn if they disliked or distrusted their employer. I looked around. When Cousin Lance first took over the mill, he had set up a coffee pot some distance from the mill, where customers could wait and drink coffee (or something stronger) without interfering with the grinding operation. I didn't see any evidence of a "refreshment spot"—not even a bench.

After walking around the mill again, soaking up its every aspect, I stooped to pick up the spilled persimmons and trudged homeward. I would surprise Lila with a new dish.

Before she arrived, I tried my hand at making a persimmon pudding—a trial and error attempt. My mother had never made it, but I had eaten it once at a church supper. I used cornmeal, a smidgen of flour, milk and water, sugar and butter, parsimoniously, to cover the stewed fruit.

Barely inside the door, Lila began telling me about her day. She'd had only four customers and they had been, she said, courteous and patient while she did her sums. In fact, two of them had lingered and bought more than they'd planned. "Mrs. Frady called me an asset," Lila declared. She fairly glowed, detailing transaction and conversations. "But they didn't talk much to me, directly," she said.

After hanging up her coat and scarf, she stepped to the hearth with curiosity. She lifted the heavy pot lid and sniffed the sweet aroma.

"Better let it cool a few minutes," I said. "Go on with your story."

She laid the table with dishes and forks. "Well, they listened right well, like they didn't know what I was saying."

I smiled. "Your Irish brogue, no doubt."

"Guess I'll be a stranger here for a while." She looked at the Dutch oven. "What is it?"

"Fruit from the forest, a gift of the gods," I said, naming it. I handed her one of the raw persimmons to sample. She puckered her lips at the first bite, swallowed, and with a tentative expression bit into the other two.

After our cornbread and milk, she ladled out portions of the pudding. I'd skimped too much on the sugar and butter and the result could only be called "edible," but it was a change. We sprinkled a dusting of sugar on it and Lila pronounced, "It's a bit like the Indian pudding our neighbor made once." We ate almost all of it, and, laying down her spoon, she said, "I like persimmons better in pudding than out."

"Honey would improve its disposition," I said.

I could not expect Lila to understand my deep attachment to the mill, but she listened intently and sympathized with my seeing a strange name above the door and being unable to enter the building. She knew that I had been responsible for the mill for a time during the war. She said, "Milling is man's work, isn't it? Hard work?" Then, shrewdly, "Something is on your mind. Are you thinking in that direction?"

"How can I be?" I returned.

She didn't ask my intentions and for the next two days we were content to put the cabin into better condition for the winter and to study the books and materials that a wagoner delivered. A letter from Adelaide told us she was adapting to a houseful of people and that Lila's mother was invaluable to the household and that her baby sister was fine. Her mother appended a single line: *I hope you are wele*.

"Me mam's not much for spelling," Lila said. "I'm happy she's situated in such a fine home."

When Lila prepared for another day of store work, I looked up from my coffee and my book. "Would you please ask Mrs. Frady about that extra backroom she has?" I'd been mulling over her "no school in sight" verdict. "It may be that we can use it for some teaching."

"Two little boys came with their pa the other day," Lila said. "So that's two might come. I'll ask."

When Lila left, I pondered starting a school. I could think at the same time I worked around the cabin, mixing clayey straw to chink some holes in the chimney and around the windows, shoring up some weak spots in the barn, scouting for more walnuts, for a bee gum (without success), lining the spring. And as I found flat rocks, I laid a path to the spring, mindful of the mud that would come with rain, snows, and thaws. I created quite a pile of kindling on the porch, always picking up twigs or small limbs that would be handy if the fire got low.

To my surprise at the end of October, I saw in the garden patch what had been there all along—half a row of turnips left un-dug by Fredrick's renters. The green tops had been laid low by the rain and covered by leaves that clung to them like sodden blankets; when I scraped away brown oak leaves, the purplish-white protrusions showed above ground. I found a hoe and soon had almost half a bushel of the tangy-bitter vegetable scrubbed and on the table. I didn't know if turnips could be dried. We had eaten them raw or boiled with a bit of streaked meat. When my brothers and I complained about the sometimes bitter taste, my mother reminded us, "They're good for you."

I washed some bedraggled leaves, put them and two companion turnips, sliced, on to boil, ready for our supper. The worst of the leaves would go to the horses. They wouldn't complain.

"Whew." Lila sniffed when she came in from the store. "Mrs. Frady sent me home early today. What's cooking? Another gift from the gods?"

"And the tenants," I said. "Turnips. Just look at them." Lila went to admire them.

"I remember me mam talking about carving up turnips in the old country—" She held up a turnip. "Pretty small to carve, they are. On Halloween, she said."

"Halloween!" I slapped my forehead. "So it is, this very day. Well, no bonfires and no witches around here, but we can eat fresh turnips."

I pushed the pot to one side. "I'm ready for some air. Let's go up to the old schoolhouse. It's early. We've been thinking we'd do it."

It seemed a longer trudge than when my brothers and I made the trek, but we found the site, overgrown. "Totally gone," I said. "We thought it would last forever. Be careful around those logs." All we needed was a snakebite on Halloween.

"Look here, Sarranda," Lila called. "Just look!"

With a stick she had pushed a sort of tent of logs aside and revealed a cache of slates, six or seven of them. We grinned at each other.

"Looks like they was hid here," Lila said.

"Maybe some children came to play at school after it closed." I held a slate up to the setting sun. "They can be cleaned up. This is the start of our school."

We fairly skipped back to our supper of turnips, pot likker, cornbread, and a chunk of pound cake Mrs. Frady had sent as our "treat."

The turnips were, indeed, bitter and I vowed to go in search of an old apple tree; if one still stood, some wizened apples might still cling to its branches. Adding an apple, even a soft one, would soften the turnips' taste.

"The word is getting around, Sarranda," Lila said, after we had washed up and had our feet toward the fire, I in the rocking chair, she on a quilt on the floor. "There could be three or four children come to the store for some learning. Mrs. Frady tells people we're here to help but we're not 'certificate' teachers. All the children she mentioned are under ten."

"I could teach the basics, reading and spelling, penmanship," I mused. "I'll simply teach as I was taught—without a paddle, of course. We have enough books to make a start. What do you think?" I had never envisioned teaching as something I wanted to do, but this small start would focus me and perhaps justify our Bramford friends' investment.

"You could talk about history and the continents and such," Lila said. "You're too modest. I can help them learn arithmetic. I'm getting good at sums and subtraction and figuring amounts." She yawned and stretched. "Mrs. Frady says I could do the teaching at the same time I'm working—when things are slow. She said she'd see to the discipline."

Lila grinned. "She said she'd just threaten no penny candy from her jar and no credit for the pa. I don't think she meant that last, though."

I shook my head. "She's a kind woman."

"She is. She says I'm like a daughter to her."

For an hour or so as darkness enveloped the cabin and owls hooted, we spoke of how and what we could do, and we began to make lists of lessons. Perhaps we could interest mothers or sisters or grandmothers in weaving or quilting sessions, but that would come when we were better known, if it came at all. With winter upon us, of course, book learning would be dependent on weather.

Thoughts of our tiny classroom filled my head for only a few minutes before I fell asleep. We awoke to a light snow. It created a magical scene around us—the naked trees now gauzy soft, the pines swathed, the sunlight sparkling, everything purity-clean.

"It's almost like an omen, isn't it, Sarranda?" We shivered on the porch and Lila reached for a few snowflakes that wandered toward the door. "I mean, it's like a sign that we're to go ahead—like a clean slate."

"Good word. I'm glad we found those slates."

I made a dash for the outhouse.

"I'll get our breakfast," I heard Lila call.

Later we walked, briskly and with purpose, to the store, carrying the cleaned slates. After a quick coffee, we cleared the backroom for schooling. The almost-bare room had some store stock, easily transferred. It was cold and we went to the front of the store to warm our hands throughout the morning. In the barn, Lila unearthed a long bench, practically buried under discarded chicken coops, crates, barrel staves, harnesses, and pieces of leather.

"Mr. Frady took just about anything in trade," Maude said. "If a square of leather or a bear trap without teeth was all the man had, he took it rather than shame him." She shoved aside spokeless wagon wheels. "Look here!" She held up a bottomless chair. "You can take this home with you. Can you cane?"

"No." I took the chair. "But we can use it, bottom or no."

"I could learn," Lila said.

Maude laughed. "I'll find some old rope or a board that you can fix it with."

The cold barn was empty of livestock except for an old donkey that brayed at us from a corner he claimed as his own. "The Owens supply me with milk," Maude said, her voice mournful. "I sure do miss Old Cleo."

As we searched for anything that could be used in a classroom and stirred up more and more dust, Amos laid his ears back and pranced out to his small fenced-in pasture. Maude stayed with me, exclaiming over various implements and odds and ends, remembering when it came into their possession; Lila was to attend to any customers who might wander in. Maude sneezed a quick half dozen times, wiped her eyes, and said, "Enough of that." Not one other sneeze ensued.

"These cobwebs are troublesome," I agreed. "But no rats is a blessing."

"Tom's the blessing," she said. "I could hire him out."

Maude filled me in on our potential pupils: the two least girls of Larna and Cletus Kirby, for sure. "You might not know them. They moved over from the Speedwell community after you left. Their ma's set her head on them learning to read, at least." She went on, "They farm some, and he farms up on the mountain." Her expression told me he did some bootlegging. "And might be that the Harmon boy, he's got a harelip, shows up. He's right smart but don't talk much. About nine, I'd guess."

She wiped a smear of dust from her forehead and looked with satisfaction at we'd done, throwing absolute junk into one pile that she said she'd burn "when the need arises," saving some jars of nails, and other items for our use or to give to or barter with anyone who wanted them. "They ain't many young'uns left right around here," she said. "Young folks are more leaving than staying and the ones staying..." She yanked at a lone bed slat and didn't finish. She preferred to stay silent rather than badmouth about her neighbors.

"I hope you'll be here a great many years yet," I said impulsively. She smiled and I knew we were now truly friends.

As if to prove it, she said, "Come and see what I've been doing for the past two or three years. I'm right proud of myself."

In her kitchen, she pulled back a curtain to reveal rows of cobalt blue jars, half gallons. She'd mastered the skill of canning with the new Mason jars. "Why, Maude," I said, "you should be proud. Look at those beans. They're beautiful." I ran my fingers over the raised letters on the glass in admiration.

"Greener than leatherbritches. Maybe better." Maude laughed. "But, you know, I love those things."

She picked up another jar. "I'll send this sausage home with you. Look at this. I use paraffin to seal it good." She unscrewed the lid to show the wax covering the sausage patties. "Take it with you. Sausage dresses up a biscuit." She placed the jar in Lila's hands and the girl gave her a quick hug.

I can't say our schoolmarming got off to a brilliant start. But start it did and then came a two-week hiatus. On our first day, four children showed up—three girls and the Harmon boy. The children allowed us to lead them into the schoolroom and sat like reluctant little wrens on the edge of the bench. We induced them to talk, finally, by sheer dint of asking questions beyond family or factual. Questions such as "how many brothers and sisters do you have" elicited shy or no responses, almost as if parents had told them not to "talk about us, none of their business."

A chance remark by Lila about encountering what looked like a white squirrel on the trail one day caused Sadie to burst out, "Oh, yes, Miss, they's some of them around." That led to rebuttals by the other girls, and even a reluctant "Yes'm" from Hendron Harmon when I asked if he'd seen such a creature. We treated the children with gentleness, trying to determine at what point to begin lessons. We decided: At the beginning with the alphabet, its sounds, its looks, numbers one through ten. The children repeated as we requested and held their slates with a ginger respect, balancing them on their knees.

At noon Mrs. Frady brought buttermilk and broken peppermint sticks, announcing to the quiet children, "Your treat for the day." For recess we let them try to pet the donkey, but Amos sneered and backed off, his ears laid back. In the afternoon Lila introduced them to addition, and we sent them home, each with a primer and some simple sums to do.

With cheese, buttermilk, and six eggs, we trudged to the cabin under a rapidly darkening sky. Before putting the kettle on, we donned our aprons to carry in firewood and spring water, and feed the horses. We talked very little and I nodded before the fire. "It smells like snow," I said, after my nightly excursion. "Real snow."

And snow it did, starting later that night and continuing, almost without letup, for three days. We did not see our pupils again until mid-November.

That snow set the pattern for the winter months. During a warm spell, when snow turned to slush, we'd make our way to the store and post office, getting a few provisions. Our pupils walked two or three miles unless someone with a wagon was coming toward Frady's; they arrived with a biscuit or piece of cornbread—and curiosity; they came with sniffles and heavy coughs, with runny noses and droopy expressions. We doctored them with hot teas and occasionally a warm compress or poultice for their chests. The children were joined by Pearl, the mother of Sadean, who was called Sadie, and Abecca. She sat quietly in a straight chair behind the children who had moved their bench closer to the pot-bellied stove Mrs. Frady traded for and Hendron's father had set up in the room. Generally we were less than warm but we soon forgot our chills and forged ahead.

I tried to engage Pearl in conversation while Lila was instructing the children, but like a terrapin upon hearing a strange noise, she drew back into her shell. I proceeded slowly, but got very little from her. She wanted her girls to get some schooling; she herself could sign her name but not read; she wouldn't have time to learn to weave, should we find the necessary equipment; and, no, she didn't know anyone who had a loom. Still, I fancied she was a bit perkier as she left with the children than when she first entered the backroom.

Lagging behind, the younger girl, Abecca, tugged at my sleeve and whispered, "Mama's speaking out the words in our primer like we do. We help her."

"Wonderful," I whispered back. "Better hurry up before they miss you."

"This teaching is hard work," Lila said, echoing my very thoughts, when we were sloshing through the muddy trail in December, our arms laden with necessaries from Maude. She put a coin in Lila's hand when business was good, but on this and most days she was unable to do so.

Instead she insisted on providing tea, molasses, lard, and she had looped a string of dried pumpkin over Lila's arm.

"'Tis more than my time deserves," Lila had protested.

"Christmas is on us," Maude said, "And you might be snowbound again. Take it, child, and this." She tucked some peppermint sticks in Lila's pocket.

CHAPTER FOURTEEN

Christmas came, with us snowbound again, from mid-December until after Old Christmas. We celebrated by watching the snow continue to fall, turning the black and white world into eye-threatening brilliance. "Whiter than snowcaps," Lila murmured. She could watch the snow fall for hours during the day while stitching or studying; and when the night wind blew from the north, she awoke with a dusting of snow that sifted through the cracks. The schoolmarm in her showed. "I hope our pupils are studying while they're home."

I had thought to get a packet of needles for Lila at Frady's, but the snows came and thus we had no gifts for each other, a fact that bothered me not at all. But I fretted that Lila found the time lonely or lacking festivity without her family. When I broached that subject, she said, "Ah, Sarranda, our Christmases were more skimpy than festive. My da liked to celebrate more than maybe, didn't he?" She gazed at the snow, "Yet, when I have my own house, I will have me a Christmas."

Early Christmas morning, I crept outside and dragged in from the barn the small pine tree I'd hacked down the day before when I was supposed to be tending to the horses. I propped it upright with the logs, close to the fire, dripping though it was, so that Lila saw it at once when she came down from her loft. I called out, "Christmas gift!" and explained that, gifts or no, we had always said it during my childhood. Her eyes lit up at the sight of the tree. As we ate fritters and molasses, she said, "We never had a tree. It's my first Christmas tree." I wished I had somehow adorned it.

After breakfast, I told her the old story of the animals kneeling on Christmas Eve to honor the birth of the baby Jesus, a story she was not familiar with, and she sang two Christmas carols. In the calm, quiet morning, each of us drifted off into our own reflections of family times—good and bad.

The best gift of the day—totally unexpected—was the sight of Fredrick. He came through the clearing on a sled pulled by two well-fed mules.

"My son," I gasped, and Lila jumped up. My eyes dampened. His dog perched atop a load of wood on the sled. Before Fredrick pulled the mules to a halt, Lila had straightened the books on the table and arranged the two chairs before the fire. He knocked the snow from his boots when he stepped to the door and told his dog to stay.

"Christmas gift!" he called, and I rushed to embrace him. He didn't pull back but neither did he prolong the moment. "Hello, Mother, hello, uh, Miss Lila." His gaze lingered on the plain little pine, lingered longer on Lila who stood red-cheeked by the fire.

She slipped a peppermint stick into his hand, murmuring, "Christmas gift."

He grinned. "Thank you."

Shifting from one foot to the other, Fredrick seemed ill at ease, not an unusual feeling, I suppose. This cabin had been his home for most of his early life, but his face didn't reflect happy memories. He had been cold, hungry, and angry here; he'd seen his baby brother die here, and his grandmother. He'd seen his father, his uncles, his brother, and finally his mother leave.

We offered him a leftover fritter and butter and hot tea, brewed in the enamel coffee pot only minutes before. "We're out of coffee now," I said. He accepted the tea, saying he'd eaten a big breakfast.

"Seems smaller than it used to." He looked around. "But it's got real windows now."

"Thank you for that, Fredrick. Remember those skins—"

He started to set his cup down and Lila reached for it. Their hands touched briefly and both drew back. Luckily Lila was quick to catch the empty cup before it crashed to the hearth. "Sorry," he said. "I'm clumsy as a big ox."

To ease the awkward moment I asked about Mrs. Mack's health, adding, "It's good of her to let you come here on Christmas Day. Does she have family close by?"

"No," he said. "We thought you might be running short of wood. That's why I brought the sled. And she sent you one of her apple stack cakes." He jumped up. "I'll get it and unload the wood."

"You can let your dog come in," Lila said, looking quickly at me.

I nodded. "No need for him to stay outside."

"Ponder's his name," Fredrick said.

Lila opened the door to admit the big collie; he at once nosed her hand and then lay down, his tail thumping a slow beat on the rough floor and his eyes tracking his owner's movements. I followed Fredrick and offered to help, but he put a heavy cake wrapped in dish towels in my hands and said, "You don't want to dirty your dress or coat, not on this day." He propped a foot on the sled and picked up an armful of wood. "She don't want the towels back, either, said you could never have too many dishrags."

"It's a most welcome Christmas gift," I said. "She is very kind."

After stacking the firewood neatly on the porch, he came in, blowing on his hands. Lila handed him a towel from the kitchen. She cut a huge chunk of the cake for him and poured another cup of tea. As we ate the moist cake, Lila grinned and said slyly, "This does beat persimmon pudding, it does."

"Indeed, it does. You might learn to make it," I returned. "I never could!"

Fredrick nodded with my assessment. He sat opposite me and directed his conversation to me, hardly looking at Lila.

Resourceful as ever, from beside my bed, she pulled a small halfway-caned stool that Maude had found behind the counter in her store. Over it she put the dishcloths from Mrs. Mack to make the broken caning more comfortable. I saw admiration on his face when we told Fredrick about the school; I did not mention the mill.

"It must be different for you down here, Miss Lila." He finally lifted his eyes and turned toward her. "Not like the city life up north."

"It's different," she said. "But don't go thinking it was all fun and easy there. I like being here and I will like it even more in the spring, won't I?"

"I heard you was from the ocean," he said. "I can't see it, myself, though I've looked at pictures of it."

"The ocean can be scary," Lila said. "The mountains make me feel safe." She bit her lip. "I don't mean bad things don't happen. I know from Sarranda that they can and have. But no big waves'll come crashing into our houses with the storms, will they?" She gave a great "whoosh" and swayed her arms to the right.

Fredrick laughed, the first time I'd heard him laugh in years, a hearty manly laugh. I chuckled and Lila giggled.

"Do that again, Lila," I said. "I didn't know you'd seen such waves."

"They came whooshing right up to the McBains' shanty, they did, when I was staying there when—" she soothed her apron. "When my mam was birthing the young one, the last babe that died."

Then as if defying those fears of the past she lifted her chin. "I've not liked the ocean waves since. The ocean's a mighty force, it is."

"I reckon you've seen a lot more of this world than I have," Fredrick said. "My brother's somewhere out West, least we think so." He faced me. "You heard from him?"

"Not in many years." I dared say no more. This was Christmas. If I thought about Larsen, spoke of him, I feared I would dissolve into a tearful mess. My misgivings and doubts were best saved for the dark nights when Lila slept and I lay awake, grateful for the one son living nearby, mourning the other, knowing not one person who might be able to tell me anything about him.

"Maybe he's a cowboy." Fredrick gazed at the floor, his hands limp at his knees. "He loved horses."

Lila poured another cup of tea for me. "Don't fret, Sarranda. Surely you would know if something had happened to him."

She must have seen my barely contained tears, for she asked, "Shall I sing a Christmas song for us?" She caught Fredrick's eye and said firmly as if she were talking to the schoolchildren, "I know you have a good strong voice. Remember I heard you at church."

Fredrick looked mutinous or perhaps just shy, like he wanted to escape. His dog whimpered, as in sympathy.

"You'll both have to join in," she said. Fredrick shrugged. At first, we hummed softly, a serenade to the dog; he perked up his ears. But when Lila swept into "Hark the Herald Angels Sing" and Fredrick and I found our voices, Ponder joined with such a great howling that we broke into laughter before we finished. Emboldened, we raised our voices in Christmas spirit, my son's strong bass and Lila's sweet soprano resounding in the room. We stumbled over lost words but finished with "Joy to the World," not missing a syllable.

Lila and I were all smiles. Fredrick held out his hands. "Merry Christmas, Mother. I'm glad you're back." He nodded to Lila, took his coat and hat, and spoke to the collie. "Come on, Ponder. Time to get back. The cows don't know it's Christmas," and he was gone.

When not at the store school, as we called it, Lila pieced the quilt top and her stitches satisfied even her after a time. Reading, mending our garments, cleaning, and reviewing our few school books occupied us. I heard Lila occasionally repeating under her breath: "I do, you do, he does. I don't, you don't, he/ she/it doesn't."

My grandda bequeathed me two very different books: one of poetry, the other of mill matters. I often read aloud from the collection of poems to an attentive Lila. If I handed her the book she flipped always to Wordsworth or Byron, mouthing the words of her favorite poems while tracing them with her fingers.

She turned a deaf ear when I read from the other book, Oliver Evans' *The Young Millwright and Miller's Guide,* a work I had referred to far more than to the Bible. I guess it could be called the miller's bible. Evans' details interested me but not her.

"I'm not mechanical," she said once, looking up from Wordsworth's sonnets. "The words and drawings in that book don't make me see," she paused, "they don't make me feel things like this does: 'The winds that will be howling at all hours, / And are up-gathered now like sleeping flowers.' That's something, that is."

I returned to the book my grandfather gave me on his deathbed, the one his father had left to him. I had carried the volume with me away from and now back to my valley. From it I learned the mysteries and intricacies of running the grist mill and I pored over it again with a kind of poetic intensity. Though I didn't think of myself as "mechanical," the drawings of gears and cogs and shafts provided to me such pleasure and imagery as might be called poetic mechanics.

The mill had not reopened thus far, so we heard toward the end of January, and it was uncertain whether it would. One day when only three or four inches of snow lay on the ground, crunchy from being refrozen during the night, I set my mind to go and see again the state of the mill.

"Do you have cabin fever? Shall I go with you?" Lila stirred a pot of leather britches with anticipation, as happily as if it were lobster stew. She had been up early, breaking the ice on the bucket of water. She'd learned to set the water on the hearth, but had apparently forgotten to do so. The cabin was warm enough near the fire; she had laid out some books on the table.

"Mill fever, I suppose. I will go alone." I added tartly, "And I'll be careful." I might be older than her mother, but I didn't need to be reminded at every outing to mind my step and be careful.

"If you're not back by sundown, I'll come looking." Lila peered into the pot.

With the wind at my back, I set a brisk pace, so I was facing the fallen spruce before my fingers had numbed to match my toes. I felt like caressing the tree. I sheltered behind its root ball, blew on my hands, heard only the wind. The mill looked forsaken as a lost calf or a lost child. It needed attention. I took the handful of walnuts from my satchel, munched absently, thinking of the times I left the mill at day's end, bone-weary, dusty and white-haired, my hands calloused but my spirit high with the challenge, the knowledge that *this I could do. This mill I could manage.*

Leaving the protection of the fallen spruce, I approached the bank of the stream, Greene's Branch. Was it called something different now with the changes in land and mill ownership? I wondered if the branch had frozen over. A straggly row of dog-hobble, its leaves green and leathery-looking through the snow, bordered the bank, partially obscuring my vision. I edged closer. I heard a low "Woof. Woof."

Fool that I was, I stepped and turned at the same time. A shaggy dog bounded toward me, not growling, but fast and unexpected. Before I knew it I hit the ground. Sliding down the bank, scattering snow, into the water I went, feet first and feet only. My boots broke through the thinly iced-over sides of the stream. "Damnation!" I attempted to right myself. "Good Lordy Mercy!"

The dog, with more sense than I'd shown, stood braced on the bank, wagging its tail and panting. I had one hand behind me and one foot out of the water, ready to push up, when a man's voice startled me all over again.

"What the hell—what the dickens you doing down there, woman?"

Twisting awkwardly upward, one foot still in the cold water, my skirt in disarray, I instinctively put a hand to my heart. I breathed deeply and yelled back, "And who in Hazel's blazes are you, sir?" The brow of the bank preventing my seeing him.

My answer was not calculated to gain a helping hand—not that I wanted one. "Your big dog surprised me." I pushed myself upright and shook my clothing to straighten it. My feet slipped on the slick bank and I tripped over the hem of my skirt. I tottered forward, trying to hold my skirt above my boots, clutching first with one hand, then the other, at a clump of wiry grass and dog-hobble.

The man, heavy-set and heavily clothed, whistled to his dog. The creature rubbed against his leg, watched me, and emitted a faint "Woof." Starting down the bank, the man muttered, "Damn dog. Damn woman."

"No need." I ignored his extended hand. "I can make it." My dander was up—at myself, I admit, for presenting such a spectacle to this man. And at his glare when he stopped short.

"Suit yourself."

I kept my eyes low as I clambered up the bank, boots sloshing and my backside a mix of snow and mud. Somehow I felt he was grinning; more likely, he was still glaring. He stepped back, the dog attached to his side, and I heaved myself over the top of the bank and stood before him. His face was, in fact, composed into a neutral expression while I frowned, angry at my stupid falling and embarrassed at my most unladylike appearance. To give myself a moment to compose myself, I looked down at my poor gloves, worn thin by all the wood chopping and now messy-muddy. Unredeemable, I feared.

"I said it before and I repeat, what are you doing here?" He spoke slowly, carefully, controlling any emotion. He put his hand to his beard, a reddish-brown with some gray at the jaw line; one tooth had a gold cap and a small scar sliced his chin near his lower lip. At least he didn't tower over me, being only two or three inches taller.

"I've come—I've come to admire the mill." I pulled myself up to my full height.

"Admire the mill? Wanted to see where it happened, did you? In this snow, in this wind? Who are you? I've not seen you around here." His neutral expression turned bitter. He surveyed me, I thought, with a mix of contempt and curiosity. "Idiot woman to be out in this weather."

"Is the mill posted?" I tried to deflect his anger with a haughtiness unwarranted, straight though I stood. "I saw no signs. Forgive me if I've trespassed, but—"

"I'm John Sanborne. I own this mill, along with my brother. Ill-begotten property though it is." He kept his hands jammed in the pockets of what looked to be a most expensive coat, with its fur collar and cuffs. "Who are you? No lady, by the looks of you."

"No, I'm no lady," I snapped. "And you, sir, are surely a Yankee through and through."

"That I am, and proud enough of it." He bent down and rubbed his dog's ears. "No gentleman, either. Never got beyond sergeant in the Vermont Regulars. We passed through east Tennessee and liked the looks of the area."

He looked at me, I at him—at an impasse. Everything I could think of to say would appear hateful or resentful. *You liked the looks of the area, this beaten- down part of the country, the people desperate, and you've made the most of it. You and your kind. A little money and...*

"Can't you understand me? People around here look at me like I'm speaking a foreign language." His voice roughened. "Except cash," he said. "That they understand."

I understood him perfectly. "I take your meaning, sir. Your words and your actions." I pointed at the mill. "That mill, now signed Sanborne, once belonged to my grandfather. He built it and he owned it until his death." My turn to glare. "It was burned before then, by soldiers or not, on one side or the other."

"Some evidence of that fire remains. But we didn't buy it from the original owner. Another of us Yankees," he emphasized the word, "who didn't stay even two years had it from the owner's heir." He turned toward the old spruce. I shivered. The wind which had abated temporarily now whipped around us, sending a spray of snow to my face. "Of which you apparently weren't one," he finished.

"My cousin—" I wiped wet snow from my face, leaving a smear of mud.

"Let's get out of this blasted wind." He looked around. "Where's your horse? I'm surprised I didn't see it—before you went sliding down that bank like some fool kid."

We headed toward the spruce before I answered.

"I walked here, and I'll walk home. And it's past time I started." I sneezed and reached in my coat pocket for my handkerchief to blot my nose. I said, "I'm Sarranda Boylett."

"That name sounds familiar, somehow." He moved toward me and I stepped back, jabbing my shoulder on one of the sharp roots of the tree ball.

"I must go." On another, warmer day I wanted to talk with him, ask about the mill, but now, bedraggled and muddy, I was at a severe disadvantage.

"My mare is over there." He pointed to the left. "I'll get you home before you suffer from exposure."

"No," I protested. "I can't impose. I am fine. I'm used to walking." I sneezed twice more.

"Damn it, woman, Mrs. Whoever," he growled, "one accident on this property was bad enough. D'you think I want you froze to death out here? Damn locals would blame me." He looked at my wet boots. "You can't walk anywhere like that."

"I can and I will." My feet were numb and I stumbled, heading out of the clearing, pulling my scarf close, slitting my eyes to prevent the wind's whipping out tears.

He shrugged. "Come, Boomer," he said to his dog.

I didn't hear the horse's steps, but suddenly Boomer pressed against me and a neigh sounded at my shoulder.

"No damn argument, woman. I can't leave you out here." With one swift and rough yank, I was hoisted onto the saddle. Too surprised to do more than grunt, I grabbed the saddle horn.

"I, I..." My stutter ceased as I arranged my garments in a satisfactory manner. I appreciated that the man turned aside while I was so engaged. The horse pawed and snorted, her breath sending forth great plumes. A thin snow started falling again. Would it ever stop? Would I ever be warm again?

"Can you manage?" Mr. Sanborne held the reins to calm the horse. My feet did not reach the stirrups but I would hold on. I nodded. His voice impatient, his head low, searching the ground, he led the mare from the clearing. "I see how you came," he said. "Snow's not covered your tracks yet." Obviously he thought I was too stupid to remember how I got to the mill.

It was difficult to talk with him leading the horse, Boomer making excursions off the trail, the wind gusting, then dying, gusting again. I tried once. "This is an imposition. I can walk." Perhaps I could have. In fact, had he not intervened, I would have. But my waterlogged boots were heavy and my feet icy. He ignored me and looked back only when uncertain about a turning in the trail and I pointed the way. Hunched forward, he couldn't have been entirely warm in his greatcoat and fur-lined gloves, but he marched on with dogged persistence.

I had time to reflect on this Yankee owner's attitude, but I confess that the chill, my runny nose, my attempts to grasp the saddle horn with numb fingers, and my general discomfort kept me from rational or irrational contemplation.

"There it is," I managed, unnecessarily, when the cabin came into view. Blue smoke curled through the snowflakes. Judging from the smudged snow, Lila had been outside several times, likely wondering if she should come in search of me. Mr. Sanborne looped the reins around the porch post and Boomer sniffed near the steps. I hoped my feet would support me if I dropped to the ground, but I was lifted from the mare before I had the chance to find out. As I'd feared, my feet failed me and I dropped to my knees. I gritted my teeth.

Lila was out the door in a flash, leaving it open. I croaked, "I'm back. Don't let the warm air out," and she whirled and slammed the door. When my rescuer set me brusquely on my feet, I reached for Lila's arm. My "Thank you, sir," was hardly audible through my half-frozen lips.

"What in this world happened? Are you hurt? Can you walk? Hold on to me." Lila put her arm around my waist, asked questions, brushed snow from my coat, and supported me all at the same time.

"This is Mr. Sanborne," I said. Without letting go of me, Lila managed an awkward curtsey.

He removed his hat briefly and nodded when I said, "Lila is...."

"Your daughter should get you inside at once." He placed a foot in the stirrup and swung into the saddle. "Looks like more snow. Anything else I can do?"

"You were most kind to bring me back." I hobbled up the steps. "Nothing more, thank you." He deserved a hot drink by the fire, but perversely I did not wish to invite him in.

"Would you have coffee, sir?" At the door, Lila turned back to him. He had waited to be sure we were indoors before leaving.

"Thank you, no. You must see to her." From his horse, he said, "We're sure to meet again and I may avail myself of your offer, Miss, at a better time."

He turned the mare back the way we had come, pulling his collar close. I think I heard a final, "Damn woman."

"Yes, we will speak again," I said and sneezed.

"Let's get you out of these wet clothes," Lila said in a motherly tone. "Then you can tell me all about it."

CHAPTER FIFTEEN

The time had come: time to visit family, if my cousin and his brood could be so called; of course, Lance was family—third cousin twice removed, Mama had called him. At any rate, Cousin Earl had inherited Grandda's house and Lance the mill, but Cousin Lance had gained possession of the house. Maude didn't know the particulars. He had sold or lost the mill at some point. The details were ever vague. The men didn't think the womenfolk needed legal details, just the declaration of ownership.

Earl and his hateful wife Dicey had moved somewhere over the ridge. Again, Maude knew only that "they'd moved after their last boy run away." A streak of anger heated my face. With malice, if not downright glee, they'd lost no time in turning Mama, my boys, and me out of Grandda's place after his death. I could tolerate Cousin Lance's wife but not Earl's Dicey. She couldn't abide me and I didn't trust her as far as I could throw a possum. I wouldn't be visiting them.

To Cousin Lance's credit, the day I left, happy to see the last of me, I'm sure, he pressed a silver dollar in my hand and bade me farewell. He undoubtedly knew I was back, but I did not expect a warm welcome. He and Noralee would see it as my duty to visit them, not the other way around. Unspoken and tangled reasons, as far back as I could remember, engendered distrust and even active dislike on the part of my mother and this cousin. Family secrets stayed buried, but their roots sent up offshoots like weeds that could crowd out any "kinship feelings" for generations. Too late now to attempt to discover the cause and, quite honestly and though I should be ashamed, I had no special inclination to do so. Still, the residue of family ties lingered like ashes on a decade-cold hearth; regardless of how they got there, they could not be ignored. I had told Maude I would call when the weather permitted. Today it did.

I saddled Josie, with Lila standing by making sure all straps were properly buckled. Her Belle's head hung low. She said, "This one's sickly. Look how dispirited she is. She's hardly eaten anything. I'll ask Mrs. Frady what we can do."

"She does look droopy." I patted the animal's flank before mounting Josie.

"Look how well this works." I had altered my oldest dress so that instead of a skirt it now had two "legs" and when I swung into the saddle and settled it around me I had a suitable skirt. "No more awkward riding."

Lila studied my apparel and nodded her approval. "Let's do one for me." She handed me the spice cake Maude had made. "I hope all goes well with your visit, Sarranda. Careful of the cake."

"They won't shoot me or turn me away, but it'll be frosty weather over there."

Three hounds came rushing from under the porch when I rode into the clearing. I pulled Josie to a halt. The years had not been kind to Grandda's place. Several shakes had blown off the roof, and I could imagine pails must stay handy for the leaks when it rained. One corner of the porch swing, its chain pulled loose from the ceiling beam, touched the floor. A window in the second story was boarded up. It didn't look like a healthy house. When the front door was opened, it hung crooked on its leather hinges. The big woman who stood on the porch, hands on her wide hips, didn't look healthy either, or pleasant.

I nudged Josie through the dogs prancing around her legs, waiting, I suspected, for a command to set upon this stranger. "Sarranda Boylett," I called out. "How are you, Noralee?"

"Can't complain, except for the chilblains. They got my hands all swole up," she said. "Come in and set by the fire. You'll want to talk to Lance, I reckon. Git, dogs. Git back from out there."

I slid off my horse and the hounds slunk to the littered underside of the porch.

Noralee waited as I navigated the rickety steps to the porch, gave me a steady look, and preceded me into the house. The front room was smoky and stifling; a fire blazed in the massive fireplace. Beside it a girl sat nursing a baby. She made no attempt to cover herself when I approached. "That's Evelyn Louise, our next to youngest. You remember her," Noralee said. "Her and her man live here with us. The others have scattered hither and yon."

I handed her the spice cake, told her it was from Maude Frady. "She got the sorghum from somebody down toward Addie," I said. "It smells good enough to eat."

Noralee had always had a sweet tooth and an appreciative gleam appeared in her eye, though she managed a grudging, "We thank you." As I hung my cloak on a peg inside the doorway, she half-grinned. "I don't remember you being a wizard in the kitchen."

"I didn't make it," I responded, gratified, at least, by her grin. I smiled down at the plump baby, now unattached to a nipple. Its mother buttoned her dress and struggled to her feet.

"Go and fetch your daddy," Noralee said. "It's time for Roman's nap." She waved toward a straight chair and pulled the rocker her daughter had vacated closer to the fire. This was the hottest room I'd been in this winter; I wanted a breath of fresh air and mercifully got one when the back door opened. I heard heavy boots clomping on the floor.

"I'm a-chilling all the time," Noralee said. "Can't git warm no way."

"Hey, Cousin Sarranda," Lance said. "Finally come calling, have ye? Heard you was back in these parts, in the old cabin. Keeping warm, are ye?" He glanced at the fire. I couldn't tell whether he was being sincere or sarcastic, mocking me or this hot room.

"Not this warm," I said, evenly. "We stay busy, though. A young friend came with me. We're keeping a sort of school at the store."

He grunted. "Heard." He looked toward the sounds coming from the kitchen. "We got us a cook stove. Iron, it is. Noralee, though, she vows she likes that there oven in the ashes. Likes it more'n she used to, anyway."

I nodded. "Mrs. Frady has such a stove she traded for. We make do with the fireplace." I said to Noralee who sat rubbing her arms, "Don't you like the stove?"

"Takes some gittin' used to. And now we got to get in wood fer it and the fireplace, too. I guess you'll take some coffee with us? That Evelyn Louise is clanking around back there."

For a few minutes we talked about the weather, the crops, the absent son-in-law ("worthless as Confederate paper money" was Noralee's evaluation), and the general state of the valley ("a right sorry place to be these days" was Lance's evaluation). I gathered they knew pretty much what Lila and I were doing. In fact, just as Evelyn Louise set down coffee pot and cups, Lance said, "People's taking bets on how long ye'll be here. Most don't expect you to last out the winter, bad as it's been." He leaned against the edge of the chimney, ignoring its heat.

"People? We haven't had the company of many people." Aware I sounded snappish, I moderated my speech. "The snow has kept us indoors."

I sipped the weak coffee, letting the mug comfort my hands. Noralee sat, her face as neutral as a stopped clock, and Evelyn Louise, baby on her hip, disappeared after handing Lance his coffee. The silence did not overly disturb me; I'd known families to sit for hours, days, without words. Sometimes a comfortable silence, sometimes not. After a quick look at my cousin, I forced myself to stare into the flames. He did not seem the blustering, controlling man I remembered.

Lance had never been handsome but a manly roughness had been replaced with lax features, eyes that drifted from place to place like hummingbirds uncertain of a landing spot. His blondish hair was now yellowish-gray; his sparse beard tobacco-stained and untrimmed. "Spaggy," my mother would have called it. His clothes hung loosely on his concave frame, almost as if the man had departed, leaving a wasp of a figure, one that needed to be fleshed out.

After a few minutes, wanting to know about the mill, I asked instead, "What are you doing with yourself, cousin?"

"Ah, God, Sarranda, what do you know about living here these days? You come riding in on a fine horse and set up housekeeping like the queen of the walk!" He slurped loudly and glared at me. "You don't know nothing. You don't belong here." His harsh words were so filled with despair and anger that my teeth jittered on the rim of the mug.

"What are you talking about, Lance?" I sat forward in the chair and put the coffee mug on the floor. "I'm a Greene, born here, like you."

"Your grandpaw's favorite, I reckon you still think you are. Well, Old J.S.'s been gone and forgotten by now. Keep your tomfool questions to yourself." He jerked away from the fireplace and stomped from the room.

"He's not forgotten by me," I said to his back.

The kitchen door slammed on his words, "Damn coffee's weak as dishwater."

"See what you've done, Miss High and Mighty Boylett." Noralee's mouth was a tight line of spite.

"Exactly what have I done, Noralee?" I said. "I didn't even ask about the mill. Mine was a simple enough question."

"The mill! The mill. The very word grates on my nerves. It's gone from us now, gone from the family, gone from you, too." She heaved herself from the chair, looming over me. "You think he don't care? Well, he don't—that's what he says. He says he don't care. Good riddance, I say."

"But what—" I stood abruptly She was shaking, rubbing her arms, a fierceness in her stare not there before.

"He's got another business now, enough to keep us in food and," she almost cackled, "and in drink." She looked toward the kitchen. "Evelyn

Louise's the only one we've got at home, her and the baby, and that man of hers, sometimes here, sometimes not. Can't stand the sound of the baby, he says, be it cooing or crying. Can't stand much, that man,and he's all she's got."

I started to put my arms around her, something I never thought I'd do, but she stiffened when I touched her shoulder, turned and sat down. The chair creaked under her weight.

"Can I help in any way?"

"Help? No, we heard you come back here to help, whatever that means. I ain't fergot that you couldn't stay and help yourself. Had to go running off. No, we do all right, thank you, Mrs. Boylett. You see what you coming here has done to Lance. It's set him off like a rocket. He'll be gone a day or two—tending to his business. Then he'll come crawling back, proud of the money in his pocket, if he's still got any there. Can you help?" She flung a heavy arm out. "Look around. The house is falling to staves day by day, but does he see that? He's a lost man, and I blame that mill. That mill he lost. No, he didn't get a pretty penny for it, shrewd them fellers are, but he signed his name, didn't he? It's gone."

She hugged her arms to her sagging breasts, shivered, and hunched forward. Her face hardened. I went to get my cloak, picked up a ragged woolen blanket, and draped it over her shoulders. How could she be cold in this over-heated room? I knew not to offer to get a doctor for her. I couldn't tender any comfort and, truth be told, I wanted to know more about the mill.

As if she sensed my unspoken question, she almost hissed, "Some Yankee come to see him after you took off, offered him money, give him drink. I vow he pointed out all the failings at the mill and that's all I know. He brought a lawyer out with the papers. Lance didn't even go to town to turn it over to them. He, whatever his name was, couldn't run the place and he pretty soon sold it and moved on. It changed hands again and now two Yankee brothers has got it. Carpetbaggers. I call them all the spawn of the devil."

"Maw, you all right?" Evelyn Louise poked her head around the door, and the baby set to wailing. "You need your medicine?"

"In a minute, daughter, in a minute. Mrs. Boylett is leaving." She pulled the blanket tight around herself, her eyes on the kitchen door. "She looks after me. I look after her when her man's mean to the point of blows. Lance don't let nobody look after him. You didn't do him a favor coming over here, but we been expecting you."

"Of course I'd visit."

She looked around. "This'll always be old J.S.'s, I reckon, never properly ours." She held on to the back of the chair, her breath ragged. "I even thought we might offer you dinner when you come calling, but you see how it is."

We walked toward the door. "That cook stove in there." She waved toward the kitchen. "I'd been a-pestering Lance for one, since I seen that dang wishbook. Thought I just had to have it. They sent it in a wagon pulled by two big old oxen the day he signed them papers. They set it up, their men did. I didn't know what Lance done, why that stove'd been set up, till he come home two days later, some money in his pocket. The stove in there. And now him gone. You know what he's doing. I'm not telling what you don't already know." She stopped talking abruptly as if ashamed she'd said so much.

At the door I held out my hand, but she looked away. "We'll manage. I'd just as soon you hadn't come back to remind him of that mill."

"The baby's a beautiful boy," I said. "You have Roman. Tell Lance, well, tell him I'm sorry I disturbed you. Goodbye, Noralee."

She turned back to the door before I was in the saddle, but I heard her whisper, "Goodbye, Sarranda."

CHAPTER SIXTEEN

February limped along—snow, slush, mud, some days of pure cleansing sunlight. Midmonth brought a dark day for us. We went out to the barn to find Belle dead and cold. She looked as if she'd simply crumpled to the ground. A shock if not a surprise. She had almost stopped eating and had begun to stumble. Even the molasses-soaked hay Maude sent a few days before had not interested her. Lila burst into tears, and I consoled her as best I could, wondering how we'd bury the animal in ground frozen solid. We stared at the emaciated body and then both turned to pet Josie who stood with a kind of military stoicism.

"Let's go back in," I said after we dried our eyes. "And I'll tell you about my pony Stewart and meeting Zack."

My grandda gave me my pony when I was five and I loved that pony maybe too much. I lost her, Stewart, a female I insisted on calling a "boy's name," when I rode toward the mill when I was about fifteen. Stewart had simply lain down and died. I was crying like a baby when Zack came along the trail, dried my tears, and went to fetch a sled to pick up my dear pony. Less than a year later we married.

I finished my story and patted Lila's hand, hoping I had distracted her to some extent.

"That's sweet, Sarranda," Lila said. "It was a real love match, you and him."

"Not completely," I said. "But it was love right then and there." I stood and went for my coat. "I'll go see if Maude knows anyone who can take Belle away and bury her."

"Can't we do it?" She must have known it was a foolish question. Instantly she said, "I'll go with you."

"Josie can't carry both of us," I said, "but we can get there and back before dark by shank's mare if we hurry." We set off, aided by a strong wind at our backs.

As luck would have it, Jam and Rim, the brothers from Tennessee, were down off their mountain buying supplies. I smiled to remember that Hammond and Timothy had been Jam and Rim for over fifty years because of a baby sister's lisp. They were loading up their sled with flour, salt, and a large ham wrapped in a cloth. Glancing at me they rolled onto the sled two barrels packed with sacks of sugar, which I ignored through instinct and Lila through ignorance of why two men required so much sugar and so few groceries.

They stopped their work at once and doffed their hats. I left Lila to tell them of our plight while I went to see if Maude knew anyone who could help.

"Looks like the youngster has found your help right out there." Maude's laugh ended in a cough. We looked out the front door. "Those two can't resist a pretty lass."

They insisted that we ride on the sled while they walked and led the mules. When the rutted road was fairly smooth, we stood, clutching the ropes that bound the barrels to the sled's upright posts. As the going became rougher, we slid to the floor, leaned, and bumped against the barrels. Undignified and uncomfortable we were, but glad to be riding. Jam and Rim attempted some conversation at first, but the wind defeated them and we huddled in silence.

When snarling and guttural snaps, yaps, and a mean bark or howl broke the dusk's silence, Lila and I jolted upright as the mules shied first one way then the other. Her hand went to her mouth. We were almost within sight of the cabin.

"Goddamn, brother, it's wolves, ain't it?"

What the other answered was unfit for our ears. They pulled the spooked mules to a halt. They looked at us, their faces red—from exertion or embarrassment.

"Wolves or wild dogs, sounds like," Jam said. "We heard they was around."

"They must have scented dead horseflesh," Rim said. "Sounds like they've barely started, a-quarrelling as they are. Ain't got their fill yet."

Lila had stepped off the sled. Why, I am sure, she could not have said. "Stay right in this wagon," Jam ordered so harshly that Lila leapt back on.

"Josie!" she exclaimed. "We've got to—"

I grabbed her arm, thinking she was going to dash toward the sounds. "She's in that stall, remember. She's not out in the open."

"Whoa, you blasted creatures!" Jam handed the reins to Rim and pulled a shotgun from under some blankets. His deft handling of the gun was reassuring, and the sound of its being cocked meant business. "Got your pistol, brother?"

Rim nodded. He guided the reluctant mules a few feet closer to the barn and tied the reins securely to a maple. The men started forward, one moving to the right, the other to the left.

One brother muttered, "Remind you of that skirmish outside Gettysburg?"

"Damn right."

"If need be, scamper up that maple tree," I whispered. "Wolf nor dog can get up there."

Lila clutched my arm and I attempted a smile, weak as it was. "I'll be right behind you!" We gathered our skirts about us and eyed the tree, ready if need be. The two men stopped within ten or fifteen feet of the barn. The noise had abated somewhat as if the creatures had caught the scent of danger and were listening. Josie neighed and I heard her hooves hitting the side of the stall.

"She's alive!" Lila said. "She's alive." The mules pawed and snorted.

The men looked at the trees near the barn, surely wondering if they were close enough and they themselves could shinny up fast enough. There might be half a dozen creatures in there, and two weapons would be no match for so many. Three scrawny animals poked their heads out of the shadows, stiffened, growled and bared their yellow-red teeth. The boom of Jam's shotgun caught us and the mules unawares. We bumped into each other when the mules shied and jerked the sled forward. We fell to our knees and then scrambled to our feet to see what had transpired.

Two bloody hounds lay on the ground, one faceless, his legs jerking; the other writhing and whimpering. The third mangy, gray long-haired mongrel raced toward Jam and lunged at his legs. It fell at the report of Rim's pistol, its fangs hanging on for a long moment and then loosening from the fabric.

"Damn, brother," Jam yelled. "Good shot. You coulda shot my foot off." He looked at his torn pants leg where blood was already showing.

"Dogs," I whispered. "Not wolves." Lila's face was white as the snow on the hillside.

Rim motioned for his brother to check inside. I heard him say, "You got the shotgun." Jam reloaded his gun, cocked it, and walked with a slight limp toward the barn.

Rim strode over and kicked the moving animal in the throat. It twitched and lay still. He swiped his bloodied boot against the mound of snow we'd shoveled for the path to the outhouse. He crept forward, his pistol ready should an animal run out. A blast echoed from within, startling us again.

Jam emerged. He spit and grunted. "Two more won't see daylight agin. They was still eating, close together. Greedy hungry. Dead."

Both brothers entered the barn. I thought we should do something, so we patted the fretful, wild-eyed mules and then left them. We circled far around the dead dogs in the barnyard.

"You ladies stay outside," Rim said. "Not a pretty sight in there, but the other horse is safe, just plain spooked."

Jam spread his arms wide to prevent our entering. "Looks like they ain't rabid. Lucky that."

"I have to—" I intended to see Josie. She might have injured herself by kicking at the stall's boards.

"Josie must have been scared to death," I said. "She might be hurt."

"I'll bring her out in a minute." Rim held up his arm to stay my progress. Lila, at my side, clutched my arm. We stood stock still. Then we started shaking like leaves clinging to a tree in a wind.

"Brave, aren't we?" Lila's lips quivered.

"Thank the Lord we didn't come back alone," I said. "We don't even have a weapon." I thought for a moment. "But I doubt they would have attacked us—"

"'Less we'd gone to the barn, thinking they was hurting Josie," Lila said. "It was fearful, it was." She moistened her lips and tried to smile. "Guess we can thank our lucky stars."

The men came out, each dragging a mess of a dog, ripped apart by a shotgun at close range, their jaws and paws red with Belle's blood, bits of her flesh in their teeth. The brothers bent down to examine the carnage and I averted my eyes.

We had a pile of dead dogs outside and a dead, ravaged horse inside the barn. My knees weak as rain water, I stumbled toward the cabin. Lila caught up with me and we leaned on each other until we reached the edge of the porch. The brothers talked in low voices as they strode toward the sled, and Jam returned, noticeably limping.

"Rim'll unload the sled here on your porch and we'll take the blasted dogs off with us, get rid of them." He scratched his head. "We reckon we could take the horse now, too. If you're not particular about where it's buried."

"Or when," Jam said. "It could take a day or two till the ground thaws."

"You need that dog bite taken care of," I said. "We're not in a position to dictate the burying ground. We're forever in your debt. But you need to—"

"Go inside and stay inside. This ain't a sight to be rememberin' or dreamin' of. Go on. I'll bring t'other horse out."

He pulled a pair of rough gloves from his back pocket and joined Rim who led the mules to the porch. In short order they heaved the barrels onto the porch and headed back to the barn. Chilly as it was, with sundown on us, sweat plastered Jam's sparse hair to his neck.

When they tied Josie to the porch post, we saw that she was unharmed. We obeyed orders to "get inside where it's warm." They stood unmoving until we did so.

I stoked the fire and placed the kettle over it. After awhile, we heard them washing up in the cold water outside the back door. They came in, blowing on their hands. "We can take them off," Jam waved toward the barn, "but we can't make it back tonight. We better bring the supplies in here." He looked around the sparse room. "If you don't mind."

"Don't want to tempt other varmints," Rim added. At Lila's worrying glance, he said, "Not big'uns, Miss Lila. The bears are a-denning now. Mushrats and such could make a racket on the porch trying to get at the goods."

I touched Jam's elbow and turned him around. "I'm going to wash and dress that wound before you leave," I said firmly. "It won't take a minute. Sit in front of the fire."

Lila emptied warm water into a basin. Jam started to pull up his pants' leg, already stuck to his pale skin. He sucked in his breath when he tried to separate the bloodied twill from his hairy calf. His face grew red, even redder when Rim said, "He ain't used to females staring at—"

Jam slammed his hand against the back of his brother's leg, almost bringing him to his knees.

"Shut your trap," Jam advised.

"Here, this might help." Rim handed me a flask from his coat pocket and stalked from the cabin.

"It's him can't stand the sight of blood," Jam said.

I laid a sopping cloth over the fabric to separate it from skin, pushed the material up, and swabbed at the bloody calf. The bleeding started again. Jam gasped when I rubbed the alcohol in, before I lapped a chunk of flesh the size of a silver dollar back in place. He clamped his mouth shut. I considered attempting some stitches but thought not. The dog had torn away some flesh. Jam eyed the wound with interest and, I noticed, with gritted teeth.

After a moment, he said, "That stuff tastes better'n it feels." He grinned. "Don't mind if I have a sip, do you?" I handed him the flask and waited while he took a sip, then a larger one.

The door opened and Rim handed me a wad of spider webs. "We used these on some of the soldiers," he said. "Not a spider in there of any size." Of course, I'd heard spider webs stopped bleeding. I wasn't thinking. Handing the cloth to Lila with a gesture to continue wiping away the blood, I took the sticky webs and daubed them against the flesh, covering the entire wound. Quickly I applied more pressure for a minute or two.

Lila handed me one of Mrs. Mack's clean cloths and I wrapped it tightly around the wound, securing it with a safety pin. "That should stop the bleeding," I said. "But you should see a doctor if it gets infected, shows red streaks." I hated to even think it but I said, "Rabies?"

"We didn't see no frothing or foaming, and we looked right careful," Rim said. "Reckon they was just plain wild and mean."

"And hungry," Jam said. "Packs is always hungry." He started to stand but slumped for a moment. "Damn, uh, pardon, ladies. I got through the war with less hurt."

His brother offered a hand, but Jam shook his head and stood. Lila knelt and pulled his trouser leg, stiff with blood, down over the wound.

"Thank you kindly, Miss. You shoulda been on the battlefield, Miz Boylett. You got a gentle touch." Jam went to the door. "We'll put Josie back in the stall for you, and throw some leaves on the mess. We best get started with our cargo."

In a few minutes the men had bumped the barrels of sugar into the room and left us with the command, "Don't worry 'bout us."

We scrubbed our hands hard with lye soap and put the cloths to soak in cold water. We sat at the table for a long time before Lila roused herself.

"Mercy, Sarranda. Do you think that's all of the wild dogs?" When she placed buttermilk and leftover cornbread before us, we stared at it, ate a few bites, sipped at the milk, and pushed it all away.

"I'm sure that's the pack," I said, "and Josie is safe, as are we." I was too much aware, however, that we surely needed some means of defending ourselves, if not against wild dogs, from other predators. I put the thoughts from my head. This was not war time. Now, no bounty hunters or outliers lurked in the mountain coves. "Let's be thankful for the brothers who saw us home."

We went to the fireside. Lila shivered and tugged off her wet boots. She put them and her stockinged feet before the fire. Somehow neither of us wanted to talk about the experience; we stared at the fireplace, listening to what might have been the wind or the ghost of Belle rushing through the trees. I shivered and Lila seemed to come out of a trance.

She stretched. "They were brave, they were. I won't sleep a wink tonight," she said, words belied not three minutes later, after she went to the loft and her head hit the pillow.

Jam and Rim came back the next day for their supplies, but they did not appear at the store for at least two weeks. Mrs. Frady told us that Jam was taking care of his leg and that Rim had brought a doctor to see him over his protests. He was, she reported, almost ashamed of being bitten but laughed about the spider web application. He told a customer who told Mrs. Frady, "That Miz Boylett globbed that mess on like she'd been a-doing it for years."

The brothers' wild dogs exploit was the talk of the community; in a way, it opened the way for Lila and me. At the store, customers lingered to speak to Lila after she'd toted up purchases. The men wanted to hear all the details, but what we could remember didn't satisfy their curiosity: exactly what the dogs looked like, male or female, size, breed.

When they could not believe that we had scarcely noted the specifics, I said, "Jam and Rim rushed us to safety and it was getting dark." They then tried to identify the animals: "Old man Truitt's hound's been gone for months," or "Miz Mason's uncle lost a dog, old gray thing, for certain it was one of them." They spent hours cogitating on whose dogs, why dogs packed up together, and usually left with warnings to us to stay close and keep Josie inside.

Two women joined our classroom sessions in March, ostensibly to stay with their children rather than leave them to whatever we might be teaching. Larna Kirby and Ida June Mason were sisters. They sat quietly, both stitching baby clothes for Ida June's expected. When the children went outside to pester the donkey or chase each other, the women requested a tablet and pencil stub from Maude. They paid close attention and by the end of their first day they could print their names and the names of their children. Andrew, Thomasina and Cartagena belonged to Larna; Jefferson Pitney and Anna Beatrice belonged to Ida June. The seven new pupils crowded the room but neither we nor they minded. Our school was on its way.

I wrote to Adelaide and, after the usual remarks about our lives, I described our school:

We now have eleven students who attend as our changeable weather permits; two adult women are learning to write and possibly to read though they are shy about demonstrating their ability. It would not surprise me to have them one day simply read aloud, having practiced much beforehand without our knowledge. The children bring a sparse lunch or not, depending on family circumstances; we do not insist on sharing because it shames those who don't have. Mrs. Frady, however, always manages a sliver of cheese, a penny candy, or a piece of cake for everyone. She is a silent angel who hovers over us.

The former schoolhouse has totally "fallen to staves," only some logs remain. You asked what your circle could do, short of financial assistance, and I appreciate your honesty about the economic situation there. History tells us that after a war, a boom may come, and then a great falling off, especially in manufacturing. Lila and I are grateful for the monies you provided; we have spent small sums on supplies and on cord wood for the stove. If your ladies find extra scarves, mittens, gloves, even socks, the children could use those. For now, we are operating the school without any interference, but at some point an educator from the state system will be made aware of it and then perhaps a regular teacher will be sent to our community. The weather and poor roads keep us beyond the concern of government officials.

Now, dear friend, you must tell me how you are, you yourself. You must know that I am naturally curious about, shall I say, things in general, with you. Are you well? Susanna has written once and Mrs. Settles not at all!

In mid-March there was more trouble at the mill. At the store school, we found Maude Frady abed. A severe cough racked her body, but she insisted on telling us the news.

Lila held Maude's head and I put a glass of water to her lips. She could hardly get the words out between bouts of coughing. "One of them...Yankee brothers is dead. Shot...close range. The ...man who done it's gone...nobody knows where."

Her news shocked us. We gasped, having met one of the Yankees. Was the dead man the man who had brought me home or his brother? She could not say. The shooting was beyond troubling. It put the mill in danger of not reopening at all.

"No more talking," I said. "You must rest. We'll make chicken soup from those leftovers. Lila can look after the store should customers arrive."

Maude eased back onto the pillows. "Fewer and fewer of them," she said. She was right about customers. Her shelves were not fully stocked, partly because of the snows, partly because her finances didn't allow for extensive purchases, and partly because the community, never heavily populated, was less so now. For the next week of slushy weather and bitter winds, we arrived at the store each morning and stayed until mid-afternoon. The children came, we taught, we cared for Maude, we rearranged goods and dusted and swept. We fed the chickens and the donkey, gathered eggs, made cakes, had tea and little conversation.

Lila, developing into a real little storekeeper, said, "Let's cut one of these spice cakes for the customers." We did and they accepted the slices shyly, and lingered a bit, especially when we put on a big enamel pot of coffee and its aroma caught their attention.

However much they appreciated the coffee and cake, customers were close-mouthed about the trouble at the mill. We learned it was not John Sanborne, but his older brother who had been killed.

"The sheriff knows who done it. We all know, and he lit out from these parts, long gone. Heard they's a wanted sign posted over in Tennessee," Cletus Kirby opined.

Another man bit off a chew from his twist of tobacco. "He's got relatives down in Texas. But the sheriff don't need to know it. Good riddance, I say."

Jam and Rim were nowhere to be seen. When I asked, Cletus Kirby shrugged and said, "Guess they got business to attend to."

A harsh wind brought down tree limbs one night after we were almost literally blown home from the store school; it tore shingles from the roof and howled with such ferocity that we finally arose long before dawn. At daybreak we ventured out to survey the damage.

Tree limbs littered our yard and the sagging end of the porch had been knocked askew. "It could have been much worse," I said. "That end of the porch is just plain unlucky."

"Thank our lucky stars it wasn't the entire porch—or cabin," Lila said. "We can clear this up today." She pointed to the damage. "We need a big rock or stump to level that end."

"I hope the mill was as fortunate," I murmured. I wanted to go over to see, but we had our work cut out for us and after breakfast we set to it. Clever and fearless, Lila vowed that she could replace the roof shingles which we picked up around the clearing. By the middle of the afternoon, having constructed a makeshift ladder, she began fitting them into place. Like an anxious mother duck, I watched. We had picked up, hacked up, and stacked up the fallen limbs. I felt quite proud of our efforts. The air was chilly-dry, but perspiration moistened my face; Lila was surely warmer, being closer to the sun.

"I'm going in to start our supper," I called to Lila, "and put some fried pies on the griddle."

I had finished making the pies when I heard a loud "Hello" outside. I hurried to see who approached, hoping the yell hadn't startled Lila on the roof. But she was standing in the yard, undoubtedly pondering her next "fix-it" task. She shielded her eyes as the rider came closer.

I recognized the figure at once. Mr. John Sanborne. In some dismay at my dishevelment, I rinsed my floury hands, dashed a bit of water on my face, and wiped it dry with the dishtowel. As I came to the door, he dismounted and bowed slightly to Lila. He removed his fine hat and, stony-faced, greeted us. Boomer rushed to me as if I were a long-lost friend. I could not resist patting his head.

"I see the wind did some damage here, as well," Mr. Sanborne said.

"As well?" I questioned. "Have you been harmed? I mean, the mill?" I looked down, flustered at my heartless words.

Before I could amend my question and express condolences at the death of his brother, he spoke. "Pardon my forwardness, ma'am, but could we go inside? I'd like to speak with you and I do it better sitting."

"Of course," I replied, "but please overlook the state of the cabin. We didn't expect a visitor." My words were snippity rather than welcoming, but both Lila and I looked a fright from our day's work outdoors.

"Madam, I am not here," he took a deep breath, "for a pleasant visit, but on business." He draped the reins around the porch post. "With your permission, Mrs. Boylett."

I nodded. Lila rubbed the beautiful mare's neck. How I wished we could somehow acquire a horse for her. Josie had become used to me and did not want Lila as her rider. She showed her displeasure by backing away although she settled into her slow gait once Lila was in the saddle.

Inside, Lila drew the rocking chair toward the small fire. Although Mr. Sanborne had declared himself "no gentleman" at our first meeting, he did not take his seat until I did so. Lila excused herself to wash her hands and see to coffee.

"We heard about your brother's...your brother's death," I said. "But only some days afterwards." I felt unsettled under the man's hard, yet questioning gaze. "We are sorry for your loss." Lila murmured her sympathy.

"Yes. Thank you both," he replied. "He was my older brother. It was his choice to come down here. 'We can make something of ourselves,' he said. He wanted to own property, to be a businessman. Small chance of that back home." He leaned forward and the chair creaked under his movement. He frowned, either in apology or irritation. "Needs tightening," he said.

"Are you a carpenter?" Lila could not contain her natural curiosity.

"A woodworker, Miss, a cabinetmaker by trade. Not a businessman. Nor was my brother, Thomas. His name was Thomas Albert, named for the Prince Consort. We called him T.A." He warmed his hands toward the fire, studied his fingers.

"Will you pour coffee for Mr. Sanborne, Lila?" I stood up, took a folded cloth and removed the griddle from the fire to the hearth. "We are in need of refreshment. Will you try one of the apple pies?" I slid them onto a plate.

My words shook him from his reverie and he leaned back, with another creak. "Ah, coffee only. Thank you. I had my noon meal late today."

Lila poured coffee for us, strong from sitting warm for hours before I moved it to the middle of the fire. Mr. Sanborne suddenly seemed to realize that we were not eating and would not unless our guest joined us.

He offered a stiff smile. "The apples smell good."

"Perhaps you would like to share with me, sir? If you're not hungry." Lila jumped up and sliced one of the pies in half. She brought me a whole one, knowing my fondness for them, and handed a plate to Mr. Sanborne.

"Where is your brother buried?" I asked. "Perhaps you can tell us what happened, if it is not too painful. People are not talking about it, at least not to us."

"He's buried on that piece of land we bought, two miles from the mill. The old Messer place." He took a bit of the hot pie, chewed, and said, "Good."

"Sarranda made them," Lila was quick to say.

In three more bites the pie was gone. Lila finished hers and took his plate. In a moment she returned with both the plates, half a pie on each. "Thank you, Miss. This hits the spot. It's not quite the way we eat apple pie in Vermont."

"I know the Messer place," I said. Years ago, old Mr. Messer had come calling on me once my widow's status was determined by news of Zack's death, and in his own miserable way had proposed marriage, assuming I needed a man and knowing he needed a woman. I could imagine that he had left the farm in a slapdash state. He had died and the house was sold "for taxes," so I'd heard. I repeated, "I know the place."

Mr. Sanborne said, "A falling-down shack is what we bought, fools to believe what locals told us." His voice turned bitter. "At any rate, the closest church graveyard was where the boy was buried, the boy who died after the accident. I was given to understand that T.A. would not be welcome there."

He must know that our sympathies were with the family of the boy, whose name we never heard;

he was always simply the boy. But Mr. Sanborne had lost his brother, and the hurt on his face at the denial of the church's graveyard for his burial touched me. I looked down, feeling shame while understanding that a community could be so hard. I could not defend or explain, so I picked at my apple pie.

"Tell us, if you will." Lila touched his hand.

"The boy died of infection the doctor said, taking no credit for it. And you may know there's no mother in the home, no one who might have tended to the arm, the wound, after, after the amputation. T.A. and I went to the house, after T.A. halfway recovered from the beating—but the father turned us away with a gun." He looked up, eyes on the mantel. "Understandable, I guess. We sent a woman to help. She used to work for the doctor, old now but the best we could find. She was turned away as well. We assumed the boy was properly cared for and did no more."

He closed his eyes briefly before going on. "I think the father watched his boy weaken, and went out of his head maybe with grief and anger. And the boy died while he sat and watched. And drank."

He noticed our surprise. "You didn't hear that? He drank for days apparently, passed out, and when he came to, his boy was dead, already cold." He wiped his forehead. "Well, the fire had gone out. Naturally he was cold. The father snapped, I suppose, after the funeral. He went on with his drinking, drunk at the funeral, drunk ever after. He was weaving-drunk when he came on T.A. out walking. Killed him close up with a shotgun. I heard the blast, but he was gone when I got there, both of them gone. One to his grave, the other God knows where."

He seemed impervious to our murmurs of sympathy. Lila again touched his hand, stood to remove our plates, and refilled Mr. Sanborne's cup.

"I don't expect you to believe me, but I don't care if the man's ever caught or brought to trial," Mr. Sanborne said. "He won't be. The sheriff as good as said so. Let the man make a life for himself if he can, wherever he is."

"And you, sir? What will you do now?" I shifted in my chair.

"That brings me to my business, my reason for being here." He stood abruptly. "I need to find someone to help with the mill. For now I must get it up and running, to pay our bills. Truth be told, I'd like to see the last of the blasted mill but until I can see my way clear—" he broke off and fumbled in his pocket. He found a cigar and held it before him, returned it to his pocket. He held up his hand to me. "I won't have that cousin of yours back on the property. He's no good to me, if that's who you're thinking."

I wasn't thinking of Cousin Lance at all, but I lifted my chin, intending to speak with all the defiance at my command. I stood and faced him. At close to the same height, we stared at each other, less than three feet separating us. An ember dropped and Lila yelped. Startled, I half smiled. My concentration was broken.

"Cousin Lance is otherwise engaged now. And his wife is unhappy with her cook stove—"

"I had nothing to do with that," he said, his tone mild. We both sat down again. His chair creaked. "But this," he gestured to the rocker, "this I can fix."

"Did the mill suffer during the strong winds last night?" My mind raced to various serious possibilities. After a moment I added, "Surely you yourself have some experience with running the mill?"

"Not much. Not enough. The flume has broken away. Worse, the wheel loosened during the storm. More than a loose bolt, I think. When I saw it tilted this morning, I knew I had to find someone with more know-how than I possess. Before another storm." He picked up his hat from beside the chair. "I have heard that you—"

"Can we ride over at once?" I interrupted. "The wheel must not be lost. Another storm might tear it loose. Can we go now?"

I clutched the corner of the rocking chair, heard Lila's sharp intake of breath and saw Mr. Sanborne's surprise. I steadied myself. The mill could not be in irreparable condition. Surely not. Its owner would not be so sanguine if that were so.

"It is late, madam. The wind is rising." We all looked out where trees were swaying, but only slightly. "Tomorrow—"

"Yes, Sarranda." Lila's was the voice of reason, though she spoke respectfully. "We can both go tomorrow. Mrs. Frady won't need me. I can go with you."

I looked from one face to the other. They were right, of course. I bit my lip and nodded. Common sense told me not to appear too involved; this was a business arrangement. I did not want to seem overly concerned for someone else's business after all. I breathed deeply and glanced my thanks to Lila. I hoped she didn't think I needed a chaperone.

"Let us sit down," Mr. Sanborne said. "I know little of your experience. The men don't say much to my brother and me." He frowned and amended, "To me."

"I am the prodigal returned," I said. "But, tell me what you can about the mill." I lowered myself to the straight chair. He offered the rocker, but I didn't want to feel too comfortable in his presence. And, as the guest, he merited the best chair, even if it creaked.

"Let me finish about the accident." He held up a hand as if expecting an interruption. "T.A. was long in coming to the mill when the boy was hurt. It does no good to explain he suffers, suffered from terrible headaches, the result of a cannon exploding right next to him. That also left him almost completely deaf. He was asleep—not drunk—having taken strong pain medicine when the rider came with the news." He rubbed his hands together, shook his head slightly and went on.

"I was not home. The man didn't try too hard, that's my opinion, to rouse T.A. When he woke up over an hour later, he knew from the bloody boot mark on the floor that something had happened. He went to the mill at once. He sent for the doctor who was busy elsewhere. It was a foul-up from the beginning. People want to believe the worse." He coughed and swallowed hard. "You as well, I expect."

"Lila, some spring water," I said, and she jumped up.

"Thank you." He gulped the water. "That's all I'll say about the accident. Well, I blamed myself for leaving the mill and men unsupervised. Now the boy's dead. My brother's dead. I'll have to live with that the rest of my life. T.A. may have it easier."

It was my turn to touch his arm in sympathy. He was right; the story now circulating was the one that would prevail. It was easier for the men to blame a Yankee owner than themselves, easier to blame a doctor than their delay in sending for him. I believed him but Lila spoke first.

"I believe you," she said. "Don't we, Sarranda?"

"I didn't come for pity or sympathy." Mr. Sanborne's voice was rough with anger or bitterness. "But if we do business, you have to know the truth. T.A. was an honorable man."

Handing Lila the empty cup, he tried for a smile. "Honorable as a Yankee goes."

Lila held his hand a moment in understanding, and his smile almost worked.

"It's a terrible thing to happen at any mill." I hesitated, uncertain of how personal I could be, but I had to know. "Can you move on from both deaths?"

His lips tightened. "I have to."

I stirred the fire with the poker. "Then, how can I be of help?"

He shifted in the chair, another creak. "I know you ran the mill during the war and Mrs. Frady advised me to seek your advice. Frankly, I don't trust the men who were there at the accident. They didn't take orders easily from us, from outsiders."

I said, "From what I've heard of the men who worked there, they don't take orders easily from anyone."

"Will you look at the building tomorrow? I believe it can be put into working order again, but if too much expense is involved, well—" He spread his hands, palms up. "Vermont is looking better and better."

My heart sank. Another owner. Another failure. Passing from hand to hand, the mill was bound to deteriorate, if not become known as "jinxed." That couldn't happen. I would help. If I could.

He went to the door with our promise to be at the mill early and I shook his hand to seal the promise. Then we collapsed, I in the rocker, Lila in the straight chair.

A hard knock brought us to our feet. Mr. Sanborne opened the door, a hammer in his hand. "I never travel without my tools," he said. "Turn the blasted rocker upside down. This won't take long."

"Yes, sir." Lila did as told and a few minutes later he stood, righted the chair, and, without another word, departed—with our thanks.

"Oh, Sarranda," Lila said. "He's a right sorrowful man, isn't he?"

"A hard man." I stretched out my arms, rotated my shoulders, relaxing for the first time since Mr. Sanborne's arrival. "A hard man in a hard situation."

"But you can help, you can," Lila asserted. "Me, too. We'll take the fried pies for our noon meal."

I chuckled. "You're smitten, young lady."

CHAPTER SEVENTEEN

Control. Steady, I told myself as we neared the mill the following morning. It was cold but, thankfully, not a windy day. I was nervous, jittery, my heart fluttering like a hummingbird, when I thought of actually seeing the millstones, checking the hopper, studying the pulleys. But I walked with determination, my back straight, my head high. Steady as a well-oiled gear shaft, smooth as a well-balanced wheel. All my talking to myself seemed to revolve around mill mechanics. No wonder. My head was filled with the possibilities of entering the mill, filled with sheer pleasure in being invited in.

But I must be calm. I'd behave as if Mr. Sanborne's request for help were an ordinary occurrence, no more than asking a woman to sew on a button. I would show no shakiness, no uncertainty about what I could or could not do. The mill's problems might extend beyond my capabilities; I was not a seasoned miller. I'd done a lot of reading and milled for a few months during the war under adverse circumstances. I had Oliver Evans' book in my bag to refer to as needed. Stop it, I told myself. If I couldn't help, I would say so, I would...

A shout interrupted my reverie. I expected to see Mr. Sanborne, but it was Jam who had called. He and Rim waved. They and a cross-cut saw leaned against the spruce.

"Sanborne said we could have this durn thing if we'd get it outta the way," Rim said. "Be a job to, uh, dismantle it, you might say, but—"

"We're the neighborly sort," Jam finished. "Even if his Vermonters marched right through our farm back in sixty-three."

"Yeah, and I reckon we owe him—" His brother's elbow in his ribs cut short whatever Rim might have said. "Something," he finished. He pointed to the axe I'd pulled from the tree. "Some idiot left a perfectly good axe here," he said. "Guess it rightly belongs to the Yankee now."

Lila spoke up. "We haven't seen you around much since the dogs." She looked at the big men. "Are you all right?"

"Fit as a fiddle at a hoedown, Miss," Jam replied. "Just a little bitty scar. Not worth showing off. We've been sorta busy lately."

I assumed they'd been making or selling their corn product and asked no questions.

Lila plunged ahead. "Did you know Mr. Sanborne's brother was killed? And he couldn't even be buried at that church—where was it, Sarranda?"

"Heard." Jam gestured and Rim picked up the other end of the saw.

"And the boy's pa disappeared." Lila was turning into a regular gossip.

"Heard." Rim spat to the side, spat on his hands, adjusted the saw on the tree trunk and bent to begin pulling. Jam, face serious as the grave, winked at me.

The Massey brothers had helped the boy's father disappear. I knew it as well as I knew how to adjust the flow of water down the raceway. I'd tell Lila later not to ask about it.

The men looked up briefly when Mr. Sanborne rode into the clearing a few minutes later but did not halt their sawing. He nodded, dismounted, and unlocked the mill. He threw the chain to one side and directed a grin toward Lila.

"Guess you've heard of the ghost, young lady? Look carefully and you might see some ghost dust."

Lila giggled and peered inside, left and right, as if looking for ghost signs.

"Most mills gain a ghost at some time, Mr. Sanborne," I said.

He stepped aside so we could enter.

My eyes took in every detail; the interior was achingly familiar, every inch of it. Some new boards had been added, in addition to the shutters. I went at once to Grandda's initials on the half-rotten floorboard—still there: JSG. My chest tightened as if I'd been long slogging through slushy undergrowth.

Entering my cabin weeks before had been a coming home, but I stepped into the mill with a reverence reserved for a holy place, blessed by saints, pagan or Christian. I didn't want anyone to speak until I had satisfied my curiosity and stilled my heart. We were a silent trio for several minutes.

Mr. Sanborne strode around, very much the owner. Lila wandered with unabashed curiosity, occasionally touching a stone or a pulley, looking at the hopper, peering down into the wheel base.

After a quick turn around the room, Mr. Sanborne followed Lila, telling her the name of various items, without elaboration. I was grateful that he left me to do my own reviewing of the mill. The millstones, both the runner and the bedstone, needed attention. The land or flat area could use some roughing up, and the furrows should be deepened. I ran my hand over the stones. They could grind for awhile and turn out fairly coarse meal, but they needed to be "dressed." I wondered if anyone in the county was available and competent to do the job. I glanced up. The iron pick used for hammering at the stones lay in its usual place, above the door lintel.

Spilled grain indicated either carelessness in general or perhaps haste after the accident. A wooden shovel leaned against the wall. Rankin had shaped that shovel, fitted it to its handle, smiled when Grandda praised its smoothness.

The air held a damp odor of musty grain, tinged with mice droppings, cobwebs and spider webs, but overall the interior was airy.

I went to examine the wheel and saw that it had pulled loose from its shaft. Reattaching and balancing the wheel would take manpower but it could be done. The gears seemed in good order, and the pulleys unfrayed.

"Well," demanded Mr. Sanborne when I joined him, "can it run again? Without great expense? Can you do anything about it?" He slapped his palm with his gloves and waited for my answer.

I could get the mill running again—of that I was fairly sure—but I should err on the side of caution. This man would not brook my not living up to whatever I promised.

"It can be done," I said, "but with some expense and the help of at least two men, men strong enough to work with the wheel."

We walked over to the wheel well and I again studied it. Yes, it could be done, I could see to it. Mr. Sanborne's gaze shifted from the wheel to me and back to the wheel. He strode to the doorway to stare at Jam and Rim. The scowl on his face deepened; he hesitated for a moment before beckoning to them.

They took their time in finishing the cut, removing the saw, laying it aside. Mr. Sanborne rubbed his chin.

"These do?" He stepped aside as they entered the mill. "They strong enough for you?"

"What the hell?" one brother said and the other said at the same time, "We didn't contract for nothing but the—"

"I need at least two strong men," I interrupted, "if this wheel is to be set straight." I didn't give them a chance to do more than glance at it. "Can you help?"

"Help who?" Jam said.

"Help me get the mill going again."

The brothers scrutinized the wheel and me, looked at Mr. Sanborne and each other. "Give us a minute," Rim said. They clomped back outside, but I saw Rim grin at Lila.

They would help. They were deliberately being obtuse, to annoy Mr. Sanborne. I smiled and gazed at the wheel. A new, much longer bolt, one or two buckets repaired or replaced—it wouldn't be too difficult.

After some spitting and shaking of their heads, and a few words, the brothers returned and agreed:

aye, they were strong enough, aye, they could be available when I needed them. "With proper notice, o'course," Jam said.

"We'll get back to the tree," Jam said to Mr. Sanborne. "Miz. Boylett here can let you know what we're worth." With great grins they went back to the tree and sawed with renewed vigor.

"They don't like me," Mr. Sanborne said, "and good riddance. They're good workers, though."

"Yes," I agreed. I couldn't think of any other men available and trustworthy. The Massey brothers trusted me, plus they hadn't looked as if I were a crazy woman for thinking I could repair a mill problem.

Lila took out the book of poetry and settled on a bench to read. Mr. Sanborne sat on the steps, watched the Massey brothers, and smoked his cigar. I noted every crack and every leak, every rat dropping. Later I walked the raceway up to the small mill pond. Several places in the sluice could be easily repaired with some boards and tar. It could use a good scraping down at the sides, but it would do until warmer weather. The pond's surface shone with a thin sheen of ice.

Walking back, I remembered my brothers delight in snatching water snakes from the silt and chasing me with them. Once Grandda had grabbed Jim by his galluses and pulled him, snake in hand, toward me. "Look at it, Queenie," he said. "It's wiggling 'cause it's scared. It ain't poisonous." He took the snake from Jim and held it out toward me. I gazed a long time before reaching for it. Grandda smiled and winked at Jim. "Off you go, boy," he said, "and put that critter back. It ain't done you no harm." The boys didn't snake-chase me at the mill after that. I missed their tomfoolery, but I didn't tell Grandda. Once, I caught a little snake and ran toward Jim with it. It slithered out of my hand before I reached him.

While on the trail, I made mental lists of work to be done and the order in which to do it. Overlooking any details would mean more time and more money spent. I sat on a large rock and took a small notebook from my pocket and made my lists permanent and orderly. I felt quite satisfied and was smiling when, back at the mill, I joined Jam and Rim who were hunkered down, passing a jar between them. The spruce was in pieces.

At once, Rim tucked the moonshine in his pocket and started to rise. I waved him to stay put. Perhaps I frowned.

"We're finished here for today, ma'am," Rim said. "We'll come back fer the wood another time."

"I trust you won't be indulging around the machinery," I said. "Another accident would be the end of Greene's mill. I mean Sanborne's."

"Don't fret your head 'bout it. When you want us here?" They stood and brushed sawdust from their pants.

For a few minutes we talked business. I would see to obtaining supplies and equipment. They would bring their tools as needed. We would communicate through Mrs. Frady about a schedule. I stuck out my hand. "Thank you both."

They blinked, wiped their resinous hands on their overalls, and gripped my hand as they would any man offering work. We understood each other. I would be in charge. A challenge tinged with anxiety. *I would not fail. I dared not fail.*

Mr. Sanborne had joined Lila but had not taken the liberty of sitting beside her. He'd pulled over a wooden bucket for a stool.

"No, I can't claim it's a battle scar." He fingered the scar on his chin. "Of course, I don't claim it's not, either, young lady."

"How'd you get it, then?"

"Brother. T.A. let loose a piece of barbed wire and I walked right into it." He touched his jaw. "Well, he claimed I stumped my toe at the wrong minute. I claimed he should've held on to it. Broke my tooth at the same time."

"How old were you?" Lila was curious as a cat.

"Eleven. Old enough to know better."

"I could tell everybody it was a Confederate bullet done it." Lila smiled as I approached.

"Might make me more popular 'round here." He saw me. "Ready to close up?"

I nodded. "A few business matters."

He agreed, almost with indifference, to all I outlined and held out his hand. "Here's the key. Keep a record of expenses. I'm away for a few days."

That evening, Lila told me Mr. Sanborne was returning to Vermont to give the family the news of his brother's death. "He don't, I mean, he doesn't have much family but he couldn't bear to tell them in a letter."

"You like him, don't you?" I had washed my hair and was toweling it dry.

"I do." She put her elbows on the table and her chin in her hand, a faraway look in her eyes. "He's kind of like a papa ought to be, he is."

"He's old enough to be your father." I twisted the towel around my hair. "I hope he sees himself in that light."

Lila turned pink. "Oh, Sarranda. I don't think he sees me as anything at all."

"You take my meaning? Have you encouraged him?" My own face turned red at my bluntness. "It's none of my business, is it? As you've said, he's a good man—"

"A good man he may be but still not be the man for me." She giggled. "Did I just make a rhyme? I read 'Ode to a Skylark' to him. He liked it." For an instant I saw a woman's quick frown before she smiled. "Don't worry, Sarranda."

"That's the second time today someone's told me that." I threw the towel on the chair and picked up a comb. "Is there more tea?"

We did not speak of Mr. Sanborne again that evening. Lila was young, true, but older than I when I married. Though I felt a great responsibility for her, I could not dictate where her heart might lead her. That the man was a Yankee might appeal to her; his attention, his courtesy was surely pleasant.

Later as I tossed on my corn shuck mattress, I reminded myself that a Yankee had appealed to me, that I had no good advice to offer, based on my own behavior. I had not revealed myself to Adelaide's brother when I knew as sure as stars shine that it was he who had shared my bed and disappeared, almost like the mill ghost that had never been.

I was not one to counsel Lila. I must trust her.

CHAPTER EIGHTEEN

The next day, while Maude supervised the unloading of supplies from Webster and Lila listened to the children read, I told Pearl about my undertaking the repairs on the mill. "I'll have to find someone to dress the stones," I said. "I've seen it done and have a drawing but I have to find somebody—"

"Sarranda, Mrs. Boylett," Maude called from the front. "They's a man here says he knows you."

I jumped up, flustered as a wet hen in a nest of wet straw. Just last night I had gone to sleep thinking of Adelaide's brother, my one-time lover. Could my thoughts have brought him here? Of course not. It wasn't possible. I smoothed my hair, hurried to the door, and then slowed my steps.

Maude stood outside at the wagon, signing a paper for the driver. He tipped his hat and clucked to his mules. When the wagon moved on, a man stepped into my view. My heart plummeted. He looked somehow familiar, but he was not whom I had hoped or feared I'd see.

"I'm Sarranda Boylett, sir," I said, a question in my voice. "Who might you—"

"Didn't know your name, nor ye mine," the man said. Looking straight at me, he drew a knife from a sheath at his thigh and with a flick of his wrist hurled it into the side of the store. It quivered for a moment, before he sauntered over, pulled it from the wood, and wiped the blade on his sleeve.

"Goodness gracious!" Maude threw up her hands. "What in thunderation is going on?"

"Ah." I remembered. A smile on my face brought one to his. "At the train depot. The man with the knife."

"Thought that might help," he said. "I was coming through Addie the other day and heard about two females a-teaching up this way." He hoisted a box of goods that had been deposited on the porch to his shoulder and started inside. Maude picked up one of the sacks, as did I.

A few minutes later, Maude handed the man a cup of coffee. "I'm passing through, on my way somewhere," he told me. "I'm Noah Lowdermilk, Noah Wayne."

Maude went to the schoolroom to deliver cake for the children and returned, Lila at her side.

"Are you looking for work, Mr. Lowdermilk?" Maude said. "Have a piece of this here cake."

Apparently Maude had told Lila about the visitor. She dropped a small curtsey. "The knife man," she murmured. "Thank you again, sir."

"The boys are behaving right gentlemanly now." He took a whet rock from his pocket and ran the blade of the knife over it in smooth strokes. He grinned. "'Specially if I'm there when the train stops."

After our cake, Lila and I swept up some crumbs, dismissed the children, and discussed their progress. Pearl sent her girls on outside and lingered to straighten up the room. Meanwhile Noah made himself useful around the store. We heard hammering and chopping and Amos braying when the movement around the barn and henhouse annoyed him, but when I pulled on my cloak, I was surprised to see the man sitting by the stove, his boots off, his socks steaming as they dried.

Pearl drew me back into the classroom with a furtive air. "Miz Boylett, do you think...sometime could I...well, I'm right handy with an awl. My uncle was a carpenter, tanned leather, too." She hesitated, then blurted, "Could I try my hand at dressing them stones?"

She looked down, as if ashamed of her outburst. Her fingers plucked at her skirt.

"Why, yes." Her interest pleased me. "Of course, you can come over to the mill and I'll try to show you." When she lifted her chin and met my eyes, I went on, "I've done it but never got the hang of it, somehow. It's uncommonly picky."

We grinned and she said, "My girls, they call me uncommonly picky. I guess they don't mean the same thing, do they?"

"Not likely. But come and see." I glanced at Noah Lowdermilk who sat as easily by Maude's fire as if he had crawled around it as a babe.

"Is he homesteading?" Pearl muttered. "'Nother useless man taking up space?"

I believe she said it just loud enough for him to hear, but he didn't bat an eyelash, just sharpened his knife, testing it on a sliver of pine. She flounced by him without another word.

Maude had poured sweet milk and laid out more cake. Apparently she and Noah had reached some agreement, for his bag was stowed in the corner. She gestured for us to sit down. When Lila and I joined him, Noah sat straighter in the chair and put his brogans on.

"He's staying here a few days or weeks, helping out," Maude allowed. "Turns out he's Mr. Frady's second cousin once removed from down Marion way."

Her bright eyes showed that she liked the idea of having a man around, feeding him, bossing him. "I could use some help, ain't getting any younger. He'll put him a pallet down in the schoolroom and be up and gone before you or the young'uns git here."

"Miz Sarranda, I hear you'll be a-running the mill over on Greene's Branch. The news already reached my cousins in Addie." His eyes gleamed as if some light shone behind them—green as jade they were. I squirmed a bit under that forward gaze.

"She's been over there twice," Lila said. "The blacksmith sent that big bolt she needs, and Mr. Jam and Rim are set to come tomorrow to see about the wheel, even if it snows."

He stared at me while Maude explained the Massey brothers, and Lila told him all about the wild dogs.

"I bet ye ain't a-scared of nothing, are ye, Miz Sarranda?"

It would be rude to say I preferred he call me Mrs. Boylett, and I knew I feared failure, failure to rescue the mill in terms of operation and ownership but he didn't need to know that. "Not much, sir," I said. "Now we must be going."

Maude immediately went to find something for us. We seldom left empty-handed, though I told her we sometimes felt like what Grandda used to call "poor cousins from Yancey County." She didn't offer us the rest of the cake, but she scooped out a handful of dried beans that Lila tied up in her scarf.

"The driver delivered this from the post office since there was no other mail coming this way." Maude handed me a letter. I recognized Adelaide's handwriting and slipped the missive in my pocket to read later by the fire.

As I turned to leave, she spoke quietly. "You'll hear it from somebody, might as well be me. Pearl's man's gone. Turned out, he was married to some gal down in South Carolina, around Pickens, before he stopped in a few years back and settled with Pearl and had them two girls."

Surprised, I said, "When did he leave? She's not said a word about it."

"Right after Christmas, right after some man come looking for him and found him, after all these years. Wife's brother, we think." She finished measuring out pokes of dried beans, jerking the twine tight to tie them.

Noah Wayne Lowdermilk said, "I'll be over to the mill t'marra."

Walking home, after I told Lila about Pearl's interest in learning to dress the stones, I mused on her situation and on Noah's sudden appearance and what it might mean. Lila skipped along, positively joyful.

She grabbed my arm. "Why so deep in thought, Sarranda? Pearl will help, and now there's Mr. Lowdermilk. Why, it's like they're heaven-sent, it is."

I broke away with a laugh and shook some snow from a low-lying branch onto her head. "You're right," I said. "Two hands will definitely help, even if Pearl thinks Noah is another useless man."

"I guess she knows about such," Lila said. I wondered if Pearl's children had told Lila what Maude had told me. "Still, you can find work for him to do, can't you?"

"That I can." I mimicked drawing a knife and flipping it toward a target. "But it won't do for one of the brothers to upset him, will it? He'll have to keep that knife under control."

"I think he looked at you right strong, didn't he?"

"Seems you think that about every unmarried man around here—not that there are that many." I increased my pace and she hurried to walk beside me. I grinned. "I am not looking right strong at any man, now, am I?"

"Me either."

Both of us sighed.

Getting letters was a special occasion and we had ritualized the reading of them. After our chores and supper, we sat before the fire. Adelaide's letter was splotchy and strangely hurried:

I hope all is well with you both. It is not here. My brother has been suffering greatly from pulmonary problems, leaving him weak and disconsolate. Perhaps he has never recovered from the war experience. The doctors recommend strongly a change of climate and suggest he will not recover should he remain here. We leave tomorrow for North Carolina, first to Raleigh where we have friends, one of whom is a doctor specializing in this sort of disorder. If all goes well, we will stop in Charlotte to see dear Mrs. Whitney. We will then journey to Asheville where we understand there are excellent facilities. Much is uncertain now. Please know, Sarranda, we will be in touch when we know more. Hertha Settles tells me I am in a nervous state. Certainly weeks of nursing my brother have weakened my constitution so that I, too, am to take the waters in Warm Springs when we arrive. In haste, your friend.

"Oh, dear," Lila said. "It sounds terrible. Poor Carly, Mr. Carlyle."

Adelaide had not given her brother's name. Two of her brothers had "war experience." Surely, she referred to the younger brother, but I had to know.

"I must write to her at once."

"She does not give an address in Raleigh." Lila looked the envelope and its date. "They're probably already there."

"Then I must write to Mrs. Whitney. She will inform us as soon as she knows anything." I had to do something. Lila read the letter again, slowly.

"They're coming to Asheville," she said. "She knows where we are." She stopped as if she had spoken too freely.

"Yes. You are right, Lila." I stood and stretched my back. "You are a comfort, and the voice of reason. Her brother will have the best treatment available."

She held her hands before the fire. "Spring is a good time, it is, for them to come visiting."

"Asheville has a new sanitarium for the treatment of persons suffering from lung disease," I said. "Someone mentioned a physician from Baltimore. I will ask Mrs. Frady."

"She knows everything." Lila sounded reassured. "She'll know."

"That Mr. Lowdermilk is a worker isn't he?" Lila said. We were walking home from the day at the mill. Ahead of me, she pivoted with a grin. "We can thank our lucky stars."

"He takes direction," I replied. "He'll know the rudiments of milling soon. If he stays long enough."

"Oh, he'll stay."

"The man's a roamer, a comer and a goer," I told her. "He said himself he's on the way to somewhere."

"Didn't say where, though, did he? Maybe here."

I picked up a fallen branch for our fireplace, something we always did as we walked home. Lila came back to take it from me.

"Sorry. I stepped right by that big limb and didn't see it. I'll drag it. You go ahead."

I didn't protest. My hands were sore from the day's work, sore and rough. But my spirits were good. If left to my own devices and direction, I could have the mill operating within a month, even as we continued our teaching. If Mr. Sanborne stayed away, I was sure the work would go much faster.

The following day we went to the store school intending to deal with long division, but the children asked about the mill and I found myself explaining water power and the process of milling. None of them had visited the mill and we promised a trip there, weather permitting—after they'd mastered long division and the rudiments of measurements.

When snow started falling, we dismissed school so the children could get home for dinner. At the cabin we had kindling to chop and water to carry in.

The next morning, since only an inch of snow had arrived, we prepared to go instead to the mill, just to see it. Something would need attention. However, as we started out the door, a wagon pulled up with the Reverend Blanchard and his wife and children.

Our school work, the mill, thinking of my family and friends up north had not prevented my mulling over the minister's church and his beliefs. I could find no fault with his Universalist thinking, since I had never felt particularly fond of the emphasis on eternal damnation that stormed from the pulpits of many mountain preachers.

We welcomed the Blanchards with glad hearts and handshakes. Mrs. Blanchard handed the bundled-up baby to her husband and, placing a hand on a young girl's shoulder, said, "Rebecca Ruth."

The girl held out a fat kitten to Lila.

"She would bring her to you, Mrs. Boylett. The litter was large. This one's sure to be a good mouser."

Lila stepped forward and took the kitten. "Does it have a name? Are you sure you can bear to part with it?" The black and white kitten snuggled against her chest.

"Mouser," said the boy.

"Molly Mouser." Rebecca Ruth pointed to her brother. "He's Jeremy, for Jeremiah." She went on proudly, "And the baby's name is Matthew but we call him Baby."

Smiling, I acknowledged the introductions and thanked her. "We can use a good mouser. So far, Lila has had to use a broomstick."

The girl's eyes widened. Lila quickly said, "She's teasing you. I've never hit a mouse. I just scare them out the door with a broom."

"O. William had to stay behind and work," Mrs. Blanchard said. "And the other two, Michael and Evangeline, are with their cousins."

Within a few minutes we were inside, and the children gazed around with curiosity. Mrs. Blanchard placed a basket on the table. "We didn't know if we'd find you home," she said, "and so we packed for a picnic if need be. 'Tain't good manners, is it, to drop in with such a brood?"

The Reverend Blanchard stood warming his backside at the fire, keeping an eye on the youngsters. "It is only fair to tell you a great many chickens have found their way to our kitchen lately," he said. "She fried up two for our journey."

We made a fresh pot of coffee and chatted an hour before the fire. The children took Molly Mouser out to become acquainted with the barn and visit Josie. The Blanchards had heard, of course, about the wild dogs and our store school. Their older children attended school at Wilmot, where O. William was being tutored before being taken into a lawyer's office. As we talked, one or the other glanced toward the door. Then came the neighing of a horse and the footsteps of Rebecca and Jeremy running to greet another visitor.

Fredrick slid from his horse, tousled the heads of the children, handed the reins to Jeremy, and strode up the steps. He was flushed and took my hand for a moment, nodded to Lila, and greeted the Blanchards. Obviously it was he they had been awaiting.

The children followed Fredrick in and lingered near the stool he perched on. The room could barely contain the visitors. Their father motioned for the children to leave Fredrick alone and they dropped to the floor near his feet. He assured us all was well with him and with Mrs. Mack. He knew of the Blanchards' visit. "I thought it would be a good time to come calling, as well."

"Yes." I resisted my own childlike desire to scoot closer to him. "Christmas was a wonderful time for us and here it is almost three months later."

It was not meant as a reprimand, but Fredrick turned red. He glanced not at me, but at Lila. Mrs. Blanchard said, "The weather's not been the best for traveling, has it?"

"We may soon have company—oh, Sarranda," Lila stopped, then asked in a more subdued voice, "May I tell them?"

"Of course," I said. But she suddenly seemed tongue-tied, so I related Adelaide and her brother's plan to come to North Carolina, adding, "We expect to see them sometime this spring. Her brother is ill."

"And the mill?" Fredrick frowned. "I've heard you're working with the Yankee owner to reopen it."

"Yes," I said. "We would like to show you the progress we've made in only a few days. After dinner, would you have time?" Mr. Blanchard glanced at his wife.

"We can have an early meal," I said. The children looked toward their parents.

"We started out early." Mrs. Blanchard smiled. "These two are surely hungry."

Her husband nodded. "Seeing the mill would be a pleasure, but we cannot stay too long. There is a meeting at our home this evening."

Lila rose, as did Mrs. Blanchard who said, "Let us put the food on the table."

Her husband laid his hand on Fredrick's shoulder.

"Reverend Blanchard," Fredrick said.

The minister cleared his throat. "Fred here has come into our Universalist fellowship, Mrs. Boylett. He wanted us to tell you, or to be here, thinking perhaps you might not approve."

"Approve?" I held out my hand to my son. "He is of age. He does not need my—or another's—approval, certainly not in matters of faith."

"Thank you, Mother." Fredrick took my hand. "It's not that I, that I need your approval, but I wanted you to know and not, uh, mind. It was not a step I took lightly. I have read some...I have read Dr. Channing's writings and the Reverend and I have talked much."

"It was Dr. Channing who wrote that the end of religious instruction is to stir up the minds of the young, to help them look steadily with their own eyes, not blindly follow their elders." Mr. Blanchard beamed at his young convert. "I don't quote the great man exactly, of course. Fred has come to the house for discussions for some weeks now."

"I attend his church, with less reluctance than I have others," Fredrick said. "The teachings seem sound to me—and good."

"You may know, Mrs. Boylett," Mr. Blanchard said, "that our congregations have dwindled in the aftermath of the war. Some cannot forget that the Universalist roots are in the North, as indeed that is where I came to know its doctrine."

"In that prison." Mrs. Blanchard spread a cloth on the table. "Thank God for that."

"Fredrick," I said, "I have not been a spiritual guide for you. I must credit the Reverend Blanchard for helping you find your way." I turned to the minister. "I believe the movement was strong when our country was founded and was preached in our state long before the war?"

"You have indeed read the tracts I gave you," he responded.

"I find the attitude of Reverend Blanchard's church kinder, more forgiving," Fredrick broke in. "I can worship honestly and judge myself and others gently."

Tears came into my eyes. My son was a man, grounded and good. I had not released his hand and I now squeezed it hard and smiled.

"You're not becoming a preacher, are you?" Lila set down a plate and directed a questioning gaze toward Fredrick.

"Uh, no, Miss Lila. I'm a farmer, not a preacher."

"But interested—and learning all the time," the minister said.

Fredrick looked uncomfortable and ran his finger around his collar. "I'll go see to your horse, and mine. Want to come, Jeremy?" The boy jumped to his feet and followed him.

"He's good with the children," Mrs. Blanchard said. "A bit shy, I reckon."

Mr. Blanchard said, "He wanted you to know. Me, I'd like to see him follow the pulpit, not the plow, but sadly, I don't see our church increasing its influence."

"It's his belief that matters, isn't it, not the place or the numbers?" I looked at the man as if for forgiveness. "It was the right thing to do, to let him go to the Macks. These acres would never have made him a proper farm."

"Don't fret yourself about his leaving you, nor you leaving here. Everything in God's time and God's plan," Mr. Blanchard said. "It's a comfort to him that you don't object and that Mrs. Mack didn't either. But she says she's too old to change her church."

I wasn't as sure as he was about God's plan, but about Fredrick I felt better. I hoped he didn't feel I abandoned him. I could only show him that he was still my son, my shared son and that I was proud of him.

"Dinner's on the table, Julius," Mrs. Blanchard announced, and Rebecca Ruth went to fetch Fredrick and Jeremy. The children stood back respectfully waiting for their parents to pull the two chairs to the table. After grace, they took their plates and sat on the floor in front of the fire where they could watch baby Matthew on a quilt.

"I can get you another chair or two, if you want," Fredrick said, bringing in the stool. "Now you're going to have company."

We filled our plates with fried chicken, pickled beets from a jar, cold baked potatoes, and biscuits. Lila poured water for Rebecca and Jeremy and coffee for the grown ups.

"Sarranda made us a persimmon pudding in the fall," Lila told the children. "But now we don't have a pie or cake to offer."

"They're not used to sweets," Mrs. Blanchard said, and both children flashed big smiles, showing perfect teeth. "I tell them they need good teeth more than sweets."

After we ate, Mr. Blanchard pulled out his pocket watch. "We can go to the mill," he said, "or we can stay by the fire and discuss—"

"Don't tease the children, Julius," his wife said. "Theology can wait for a bad-weather day. You told them they'd get to see the mill. We should start, though." She moved toward her coat and we were soon on the way.

It was an easy trip to the mill since Fredrick placed a happy Jeremy before him on the saddle and Lila held Rebecca on her lap in the wagon. Mrs. Blanchard insisted I ride next to her husband, saying, "I'll be out of the wind back here with the baby, and you two can talk of churchly things."

The slight breeze did not prevent our discussing his church and his sorrow that it was losing ground. People seek a kind of certainty that he could not give them, he said. In this time of recovery they sought answers shouted, answers that spoke of behaving according to rigid rules or "be damned." He had realized, he said, that those who seek for salvation in the church liked simple solutions for a broken land. They liked lines drawn, punishments meted out. He went on, "They say 'the Just shall inherit the earth' and it goes unspoken that they think they are the Just."

He shook his head, as he pulled the horses to a halt in the snowy sawdust of the old spruce.

"I've said too much, Mrs. Boylett. Please do not think my faith is shaken. It is not, but I am, at heart, a rational man. I can see that the days of Universalism are waning, here at least, and I can go nowhere else. Your boy can make a difference in his lifetime in his own way, as I have. For this part of the state to survive, it needs men like him. And survive it will."

"Yes," I said, "and thrive, with the help of its men and its women." He assisted me and his wife from the wagon. "Let me show you the inside." I'm sure he detected a suppressed note of pride in my voice. Unlocking the door, I showed them the mill's workings and explained what had been done.

After a while, Fredrick, Lila and the children walked up to the mill pond. The children raced back to report that they'd seen an owl, two squirrels, and a big frog. Lila and Fredrick appeared to be ignoring each other without quite succeeding.

With expressions of good will, the Blanchards returned Lila and me to our cabin. Fredrick, looking morose, had gone his own way by horseback rather than extend his journey by returning with us. Perhaps Lila told him she was looking forward to seeing Carly. I would not ask or tease her about his obvious infatuation. At any rate, neither would welcome my interference. The relationship would flag or flourish on its own.

Two days later, the Massey brothers came with word that Maude was "right puny." Lila went at once to the store. I stayed behind to hack and hoe and ready the garden plot. Hoe in hand I surveyed the area, thinking of potatoes, turnips, greens, beets. We would need to put up a fence if our planting was to succeed. If we collected small branches, saplings, and vines we could weave a fence. A horse coming into the clearing startled me; the sight of Fredrick again so soon startled me even more. Instantly, as is a mother's wont, I suspected the worst: news of Larsen's death, a fire at the Mack's, Mrs. Mack's death.

"Don't look at me like I'm a bandito," Fredrick said, dismounting. "I come in peace."

Not bad news then. And my son had developed a sense of humor. I smiled and wiped my face with my apron.

"Let's sit over there." I pointed. "Coffee? Lila is not here."

"I came to see you, Ma." He laid his hat beside us on the log. "No coffee."

We did not look at each other. I realized that it had been years since we had been alone. The thought did not comfort me, and I wondered what Fredrick had on his mind.

He commented on the garden and his spring planting. I asked about Mrs. Mack and the farm and he answered. We were clearly dawdling. Then he grinned and asked if he should cultivate a moustache. "No," I responded, "not unless a prospective wife asked it of you."

"'Twas one of the church folks," he said. "That's not what I want to talk to you about."

"What is it, Fredrick?"

"I came to give you this, Ma." He took an envelope bulky with papers from his coat pocket. I recognized it, of course. Two tears erupted and slid down my cheeks. I dabbed at them with my apron.

"The papers, the deed to this land. But it's yours, Fredrick. Is there a problem? A legal problem? Have the cousins—?"

"Nothing like that. I want to give it back to you." He thrust the envelope in my hand. "I went to Webster and got it changed over, deeding it to you, straight and clear."

After I wiped my eyes, my voice shaky, I said "It was a gift to you." The papers lay surprisingly heavy in my hand. "Fredrick, have you thought this through? Twenty acres. Did the Reverend Blanchard have anything to do with this? Are you sure?"

"Sure, I'm sure. Reverend Blanchard knows. I told him." He tapped his chest. "This is your solid, sensible son, remember? Look around you, Ma. Does this land look like good farming ground? Even good pasture? Steep and barely cultivated beyond your garden?"

Before I could speak, he said, "Oh, I remember hoeing corn over yonder and clearing the new ground."

Our eyes went to the hills rising beyond the cabin. Saplings, pines, holly and walnut trees now studded the new ground. There was enough almost level land for a calving lot, for pigs, for another barn and there had been a cornfield partway up the hill.

"Well, it's certainly not rich bottom land," I agreed.

"Never will be unless some nature quirk diverts the Tuckasegee," he said. "A big earthquake or something. And good bottom land's more to my liking." Our chuckles relieved the awkwardness between us.

"No, I don't need it, and to be honest, I won't need it." When he stood, his horse swung its head toward him. "I thought when you left I might need these acres, you know, in case things didn't work out. A man of property I was, in case." He didn't have to say, "In case the Macks didn't want to keep me."

"But now," he said, "I think I just held it in trust for you. Or held it—in case you didn't come back here." Again, he surveyed the cabin, garden, barn, meager by comparison with the Mack farm. "I don't know if you can make a living on it, but it's yours again. Sell it if you want to."

A hint of the ruthless boy was in his words. These acres really meant little to him; I realized that returning the property to me was more important to him than possessing it.

Two more tears ran down my face and dampened my collar. "Son. Fredrick," I asked, "have you forgiven me for—" I don't know if I meant for not signing official adoption papers or for leaving him and the valley.

He took my hand to help me to my feet. "Looks like you're gonna need a good fence around this garden. I'll come over one day and help."

He dropped my hand and, talking of what and when to plant, we made the circuit around the garden patch and back to his horse.

With one foot in the stirrup, Fredrick said quietly, "I never missed this place, all these years. Never got attached to it, I reckon."

"Maybe you had to work too hard too early. I'm sorry it had to be that way," I said as he swung into the saddle.

He looked down, his eyes solemn. "Had to be," he said. "But, Ma, you thought me greedy and maybe I was. A boy I was then."

I touched his leg. "Thank you, Fredrick. Thank you for the deed. You're a man now, and what I thank you most for," I wiped my eyes, "I thank you for calling me Ma today."

"Ah, Ma," he said and turned toward his home.

CHAPTER NINETEEN

Lila did not seem unduly surprised when I told her I once again owned the land on which we lived. So nonchalant was she that I asked, "Did you know he was going to do it?"

"No, but Fredrick will do what is right."

That April—not totally unexpected since I had written a letter addressed simply to the North Carolina Board of Education in Raleigh—our store school had a visit from a Mr. Edward Phelps, Superintendent of Schools in the western region of the state. He stood quietly in the back of the room. I think the children sensed his presence, but they kept their eyes on their teacher. Lila faltered just a moment when he slipped in, but recovered and went on with the recitations of the states and their capitals. She set up a spelling bee and asked Pearl to give out the words from her list. Pearl had earlier proudly spelled out the words for us during the children's morning recess.

"Miss Pearl is in charge," Lila said after dividing the children into two groups to face off across her desk. "Mrs. Boylett and I have a visitor."

With an almost queenly air, she handed the list of words to Pearl and joined us in the store. A man of stern mien, Mr. Phelps catalogued the difficulties of finding teachers, finding buildings, finding funds for schools of any sort. However, he was optimistic that the next years would be much better. Ex-Governor Vance had advanced—here he hovered toward a smile—the cause of public education as rapidly as could be expected.

"The county can only be grateful, Mrs. Boylett and Miss Lila, for your generosity in starting this school. There are no—"

"We do not expect remuneration," I interrupted. I explained as best I could the hopes of Adelaide's circle, admitting, "We are not exactly fulfilling them, but neither of us had schooling that prepared us for our school-mistress role."

Our talk appeared mutually satisfying. He complimented Lila on her classroom deportment and she, in turn, praised my teaching abilities; he hoped that within a year or two schools would be established within a reasonable distance of Greene's Valley.

"Progress is slow now but we must look to the future. This decade will see education coming to the forefront. It is of vital importance," he said. "Four months of schooling is very little. But better than none." He stood, returned his hat to his head, shook our hands, and promised to return when our school year ended to examine our pupils. "That official end is, of course, at your discretion. However, if you send word, I will see that certificates of attendance and achievement are available."

He spoke warmly to Maude for helping make the school a reality. When he left, Maude sat down with a sigh. "If we was drinking ladies, I'd bring out the 'shine, but instead, let's tell the young'uns and I'll find something good to eat."

From her kitchen we heard her coughing for quite a spell. Just as Lila made to go see about her, she carried out a cake. "This apple stack cake I was a-saving for the Massey brothers will be just the thing."

We had an impromptu party with cake and milk. The spelling bee winner, Cartagena, got an extra slice and she handed a big bite to Hendron. When her brother Andy smirked, she said defiantly, "He come in second."

We noticed that the children looked at Pearl with a new respect and she shyly accepted our thanks. Lila told them, "Mr. Phelps may return to examine you and hand out achievement awards."

"What's 'jamined'?" asked Anna Beatrice in a subdued voice.

"It's like taking a test to see what you remember," Lila said.

"We've never been examined before," Pearl said. "But I don't doubt we'll be fine."

"Yes, you will," Maude declared stoutly. "Just think of all you've learned."

As we walked home, Lila burst out, "They're wonderful children, they are. They aren't nearly so shy now."

"You'll make a fine teacher, Lila," I said. "In time you might go to an academy and return a full-fledged school mistress." I knew that a summer school for teachers had opened in Chapel Hill a few years before. I vowed to ask Mrs. Whitney to find out about it in case Lila was interested. Maude Frady had called Lila "a natural-born teacher." A fitting description. Who knew what the future might hold for a bright girl like her?

"I ain't even finished a proper school myself, Sarranda. Small hope for me there." She sounded more optimistic than her words. "See," she said, "I forgot and 'ain't' came right out of my mouth."

"And you caught it." I laughed.

"I've got to catch it before it gets out, haven't I?" She picked up a stick and threw it, jaunty as a boy. "I think we can have our pupils ready to be 'jamined' when Mr. Phelps returns."

Mr. Sanborne rode into the mill's clearing sooner than expected, on a Saturday morning. Nevertheless, the mill was in working order; all the machinery had been cleaned, checked and oiled. Lila carried our mouser with us on each visit and soon rats and mice were, if not completely annihilated, discouraged from expecting permanent homes there.

With dramatic intensity and laughter, Lila, Pearl, and I had wielded broom, rake, axe, and shovel, sweeping every corner and banishing the very thought of a cobweb. We had tramped up to the head of the stream to determine what needed to be done to clear the trail. None of us expected or wanted a visitor, so grubby we looked.

Mr. Sanborne strode up the steps. He had seen me muddy and now he saw me dusty. He greeted us as though we were dressed for church, sweeping his hat from his head and executing what was close to a bow, yet it seemed a forced jollity.

"Ladies, a pleasure." He gazed around. "Should I remove my boots rather than mar the floor?"

Lila immediately took his outstretched hand. "Welcome back, Mr. Sanborne."

I added my welcome and said, "The trip could not have been pleasant."

He mumbled something. I introduced Pearl and her girls who sat on the floor with their backs to the millstones, memorizing all the words in their Blue Book spelling primer. They barely glanced up at him.

Lila said, "They're determined to win the next spelling bee."

Walking him around the structure, I pointed out all that had been done and answered his questions. He seemed pleased enough with our labors, yet something in his manner and voice told me he was not as excited about reopening the mill as I was. Surely we had not put the mill back into operating condition only to have it sold again; surely he had not, in the midst of grieving for his brother, taken the time to look for a buyer. A great unease seized my heart. I could not bear to see the mill in the hands of yet another northerner.

Outside, Mr. Sanborne pulled a wallet from his greatcoat, prepared to settle accounts. He did not question my accounting for the hours the Massey brothers, Noah Lowdermilk, and I had spent. He merely glanced at my written record. "Pearl helped occasionally," I said, "but she doesn't expect payment. She's learning how to pick the stones, calls herself an apprentice."

When he started to add another bill, I held up a protesting hand. "No, she feels she has not earned it. Not yet. She is a proud woman."

"Then add it to the school's fund," he said. "You must need supplies."

"I'm not too proud to take it for that." I smiled and tucked the money away.

"That girl's got something on her mind." Mr. Sanborne looked at Lila. "Whether it's school or not, I can't say."

That evening I asked, "Is something bothering you, Lila?" We sat at the table with our dishes washed and our books before us, the kerosene lamp between us. Supposedly she was studying the school books, but her gaze seemed directed inward rather than downward. "Mr. Sanborne thought you had something on your mind." She had assured me once that he was too old for her. Yet he had eyed her in some speculation. Had his comment meant he was aware of her, too aware perhaps? Should I again caution her?

Her words stopped my muddling thoughts. "Sarranda, I can't not tell you—even if—"

My heart plunged. I placed a hand on hers. "Has he, have you, are you...?"

She giggled. "Listen to you! What are you thinking? Me and him? No, not him." She held my gaze, her eyes bright with happiness or tears.

"It's Fredrick. He wants me to marry him. At least, I think that's what he meant. He's awfully shy, he is."

I sat back in my chair.

Lila said, "He asked me if I was interested in marrying, and I said what kind of question is that? I've not been asked these dozen times, have I?"

"When was this?"

"Up at the mill pond when the Blanchards came over. Sarranda, I really didn't know if he meant—well, marrying him or what. So I didn't say anything for a minute or two. Then that big old bullfrog jumped in the pond and the children came running to drag us over there." She sighed. "That put a stop to that."

We started laughing. I could imagine the big plop and the excitement of Jeremy and Rebecca and the frustration and confusion of Fredrick. He liked his life orderly, so I believed, and his proposal—for that's what it was and Lila surely knew it was—had been disrupted.

"Did he never speak again?"

"Walking back, one child or another or both was always tugging at us, but he said, just before we came to the mill, 'I meant, I mean, marrying me,' and that's as far as he got."

We wiped our teary eyes. After a moment, I became serious.

"He is steady, unlike his brother Larsen. Unlike his Uncle Jim. But marriage needs more than," I hesitated, "more than steady. Are you thinking about what he said?"

"I am, Sarranda, that is, if you approve. He's a fine figure and good. I'm thinking, but I won't know, will I, 'til he kisses me?" She closed her book. "I guess I'll know then."

She grabbed my hand. "I know I feel unsettled when he's around. My stomach flip-flops. I'm jittery. And I like to see him happy. He's serious, he is. Not a silly boy."

"He's old enough and beyond to be married." I smiled. "That girl in church had her eye on him, but it took a little Yankee girl to wake him up."

She pursed her lips in thought. She looked so very young, but most girls around here were mothers long before they were her age. Perhaps I should not have reminded her that single or married, mother and grandmother, here she'd be a Yankee always. But she wouldn't be a serving girl.

"It's none of my beeswax, but," I said, "if you'd stayed in Bramford, were you interested in Carly Bell?"

"Carly was...well, he was like a far-off star that kind of fell and needed...care. I guess I saw him as a hero. But look at me, Sarranda, and tell me he could ever see me as I am, as I've become. To him I was a silly girl from a poor Irish fishing family."

It seemed a good time to tell her. "There's Irish blood in Fredrick. Zack's family was Irish and Catholic. Zack converted after we met—or seemed to. His family moved away and we had no contact with them." Zack's face had dimmed in my mind. Our years together had been few and not always joyous ones. "Fredrick never knew Zack's parents. He takes after my grandda."

Lila's mouth formed a little "oh" at my revelation, followed by a faint frown.

"I don't think I'm much of a Catholic, am I?" Her voice held a tinge of melancholy, but then she smiled. "Father Finley didn't think so."

Looking across the flickering lamp, I realized that she had grown up since we left Bramford. She was a loyal friend, a good teacher, and she had a mind of her own whether she was thinking love, education, or religion.

I laid my hand on hers again. I more than approved of her for my Fredrick. I rejoiced. I told her so. Spontaneously we pushed our books aside and stood up, joined hands, and danced a little jig.

"Irish jig," she murmured.

CHAPTER TWENTY

Happiness one day. Sorrow the next.

Jam brought word: Maude Frady was very ill, at times out of her head. Rim was with her; the doctor had been sent for. Could we go to her at once? Without a thought, Lila grabbed Molly Mouser and we threw our cloaks around us, banked the fire, and were ready within minutes.

Jam had saddled Josie for me. He held the reins of his horse. "Here, Miss Lila, this old hoss'll carry us both and that little creature, too."

When Lila looked at the horse and then at his girth, he grinned and hoisted her into the saddle. He motioned me to go ahead, saying, "I'll walk. At Josie's rate, we'll be there right behind you."

Judging from Lila's face, if worry could be weighed, his poor horse carried a heavy load. As did my own. Maude had been coughing with great frequency in the last weeks. We put poultices on her chest when she allowed. We pressed her to rest, to drink hot Spicewood tea, to let Noah Lowdermilk do the heavy lifting and outdoor chores. I can't say she paid more than scant attention to us.

Maude was sleeping when we arrived. A worried Rim said, "I've give her some medicine in honey to lessen the coughing."

"Where's Noah?" I wondered aloud.

"Over at Pearl's," Rim said. "Over there most of the time, Maude says, helping out. Cutting wood and fixing the roof."

"Not roving too far." Lila gave me an "I told you so" look.

I shrugged. The brothers left us, saying they'd come by tomorrow. After looking in on Maude, we tidied up the store and the school room, kept the room warm, and prepared a light supper of eggs and biscuits. Lila slipped bits of food to Molly Mouser at her feet. The kitten often curled at the foot of Maude's bed.

We stayed with Maude for seven days, taking turns teaching the children and tending to our friend. Pearl washed the cloths we used to cool Maude's feverish face and did a dozen other tasks along the way. Noah helped the Masseys and stopped for brief visits. The doctor duly came and wore his calm face before his patient. Maude whispered when he put away his stethoscope. "The Lord's ready for me, I reckon, whether I am or not."

As we shivered on the porch, the doctor said, "Her chronic bronchitis has much worsened. Do what you're doing for her. I know you've got some 'Massey medicine.' It helps her to rest. The coughing's wearing her down. Pneumonia is possible." His last words were, "I've lost three this month."

Jam and Rim conveyed me home once and to the mill once, where Mr. Sanborne stood watching Noah that day do some carpentry work. He seemed less interested in the mill than in Noah's working on the hopper. Lila stayed with Maude and tended, as need be, to the store. School we dismissed after the third day. The children were disappointed at not being examined even though they were needed at home to help with preparing the garden and fields for planting. We promised them an Independence Day party and, when they reminded me shyly, I said, "Yes, a picnic at the mill."

When the doctor came once more, he said, "Best prepare yourselves. It's a matter of hours." He motioned me to the schoolroom. "Has Maude talked much about her family?"

I thought for a moment. "I know that her grandson, whom I met before I left the valley, went to fight Indians and was killed out there, a young soldier. Her daughter Alexandra died some years ago, I believe. I know naught of Alexandra's other children. Younger, they were." As I spoke, my mind went to my own son, Larsen. I did not want to think he lay in an unmarked grave on the Plains, but I had not heard from him in almost ten years.

The doctor's words recalled me to the present. "There was some unpleasantness," he said, "between James Frady and Alexandra's husband's family. I forget the details, if I ever knew them." He settled his hat on his thinning hair, pulled his coat collar up against the wind, and went on. "Her twins are with their father's family, growing up somewhere in Oklahoma Territory. When Mr. Frady attempted to get in touch before his death, his letter was returned as undeliverable."

"So there's no one," I said, "except maybe far distant cousins in Haywood, Noah, of course, and Mrs. Whitney. I have written to her."

"Mrs. Boylett, please make her comfortable. That is all you can do now."

"We will do that, sir. Lila stays with her constantly."

"And take good care of that young lady," he said. "She's looking a mite peaked."

Neighbors came and went, sitting up all night, tending to meals, the chickens and Amos, quiet and concerned. Noralee and others sent word and food. Three chickens were delivered from Mrs. Burton to help feed those who stayed. Maude was a "steady" in the community, as one woman put it. "She was always steady in times of trouble."

Her body weakened, her breathing came in gasps, and her hand gripped ours, but we were not prepared to let Maude go. We turned our faces so the tears did not fall on her papery fingers. Even though always two or three women were there to help, Lila could not be prevailed upon to rest for more than minutes at a time. She spooned chicken broth to Maude's indifferent lips, bathed her face, and sang softly hours into the night. Mornings I would find her slumped over the side of the bed, her hand on Maude's arm. I think when Lila was close Maude breathed less harshly.

Once her face brightened and, bending close, we heard, "I'm ready to see James on t'other side."

Lila awoke the seventh night to find Maude no longer breathing. Her sobbing alerted me and I went to comfort her. I laid coppers on Maude's eyes and dried my tears. A woman broke sage and rosemary from Maude's garden and laid them near her. Within an hour Pearl, Lila, and I had washed and dressed the tiny body in her best black "funeral dress." She had pointed it out soon after our arrival, whispering, "For my burial...lace," and touched her throat.

By nightfall, several men had dug the grave and hauled a coffin from New Webster. "She ordered it back last spring," Jam said. "The reverend's coming tomorrow."

The funeral day was overcast and chilly. Fredrick and Mrs. Mack arrived, Ponder sitting proudly behind them in the wagon. The Reverend Blanchard conducted her service, sent her to heaven, from inside the crowded store. Pearl stood beside Noah, her girls on his other side, their faces at times both curious and bewildered. Noah twisted his hat in his hand and said, "The sun don't intend to show its face this sad day."

The men prepared to shoulder the coffin for the short but steep climb to the family cemetery where the graves had been raked clean of debris. Mr. Blanchard motioned to Fredrick who stepped forward and mumbled, "Let us bow our heads." In a strong voice he led us in the Lord's Prayer. Lila squeezed my hand.

At the graveside, I glanced up to see Mrs. Mack looking at me with a slight smile. Fredrick was at her elbow but he gazed across the open grave to where Lila stood with me and the Massey brothers. His face was set in sadness, but a flash of yearning showed in his eyes when he lifted them after the final prayer. He picked up a shovel. He, Noah, Jam and Rim, filled the grave. "We'll get a stone," I murmured to Lila.

After most of the mourners departed, Rim put into words my worry about leaving the store unattended. "We don't want nobody drifting by and taking what he sees and needs, do we? We'll stay here a day or two."

"Better safe than sorry." Mrs. Blanchard nodded as her husband handed her up into their wagon. "A few trifling folks might take advantage."

"Folks in need," Mr. Blanchard said gently. "Let us go, Wife." He bowed slightly. "We promised to visit your cousin Lance. You know Noralee is ailing?"

"They darken no church door," Mrs. Blanchard said, "but they sent for a preacher."

Her words surprised me. I knew that Noralee was sickly but in my concern for Maude I had given little thought to her. Sending for a minister was more drastic in some households than sending for a doctor. I vowed to go see her as soon as I could.

In the mild April weather, Lila and I set to on our garden patch, working fiercely. We chopped weeds and cleared the ground, hoed to loosen the soil, burned the brush, laid out rows, and discussed what we would plant. We were tired and shabby-looking women at day's end. Both of us, I believe, wielded hoe and spade with an unspoken anger that Maude had been taken from us and from the community. We did not say so, of course; we had to make a garden. To sit and mourn would have shamed Maude's memory. "Don't waste these good days," she had sometimes said. She had carried on at the store and post office after losing her husband, her daughter, and apparently all her close kinfolks. We could do no less.

"You must eat, Lila," I said.

"And you, Sarranda," she returned.

With those words, after our two days in the dirt, we faced each other across the table and let silent tears flow down our cheeks. "I dearly want some of Mrs. Frady's spice cake," Lila said.

"Will you settle for milk and bread?" I poured glasses for us and crumbled pieces of warm cornbread into mine.

Before the fire, our mournfulness broken, we talked of all Maude did and meant to us. Then Lila shifted in her chair and said, "Is it right to be so sad and yet to be happy inside, Sarranda? Is it?"

"Ah." I looked up. "Has my son—has my son kissed you?"

"Aye, he did. After the funeral. You didn't miss us, did you? We wandered down the hillside to a little bench. Maude and I sat there once. He made a right proper proposal, like he'd rehearsed it, so proper it was." She smiled. "I took his face in my two hands and just kissed him good. And then he kissed me, even better." Her eyes sparkled. "He'll be over to talk to you."

She needed no further assurance of my pleasure in her love for Fredrick but I gave it anyway. They'd had no time for plans and she wouldn't leave me without help at the mill. "It will all work out," I said.

"I'm happy and awful sad at the same time. But I can't help it, can I?"

Soon we were ready for sleep and whatever the morrow would bring.

The morning brought Noah leading Maude's donkey. "Have the stubborn creature," he said and tossed the rope to me. "Me and Amos don't get along. He's done naught but stomp around these days. He'd bite me in a minute if I let him."

Lila, Molly Mouser at her heels, led Amos to join Josie. Noah took a cup of coffee before saying, "Got word yesterday you're to meet a Mr. Deitz today at the store."

"Mr. Deitz? Today?"

"Lawyer man. He's riding out today, after dinner, I reckon. To meet you and Miss Lila at Frady's. That's why I come by, besides bringing contrary Amos." He picked up our butcher knife, took out his whet rock, and began sharpening the blade.

"Pearl and me's ready to work at the mill, whenever you say, Miz Boylett. The pond needs some digging on and that hopper—I leveled it up but I could carpenter a better one." He ran his finger over the knife and laid it down.

"Thanks for that. I'll let you know about the mill. It depends on Mr. Sanborne." I squared my shoulders. "It all depends on him."

We hurried our noon meal and arrived at the store before mid-afternoon. Within an hour, during which we dusted, swept, arranged and generally moped around, a rider hailed us.

"Jake Dietz," he introduced himself, dismounted, and handed the reins to Rim. "Mrs. Zack Boylett and Miss Lila McNeely?"

At our nods, he removed his hat and took a leather case from the saddle horn. "Mrs. Frady called on me a month and more ago," he said, "to conduct the necessary business." He cleared his throat. "The business of dying."

We went inside, leaving the three men on the porch, their faces to the sun, lazing like lizards but undoubtedly curious as cats.

Mr. Dietz was a man of few words. Once settled at the kitchen table, he took a paper from the case and handed it to me. "Your copy. Read it at your leisure. I'll summarize. With some exceptions, Mrs. Frady, having no close kin she could locate or wish to acknowledge, left her entire property to you." He faced Lila. "You, Miss."

Lila's face went ashen and her shoulders slumped. I clutched her arm, fearing she would faint. Glancing at the paper in my hand, I saw that the lawyer spoke true.

He handed Lila another sheet of paper but she ignored it. "This short statement she gave to me on her last visit to my office. She looked on you as a granddaughter, Miss McNeely. The store and acreage are yours to do with as you wish, she specified, with the help of Mrs. Boylett."

He turned to me. "Her clothes, a few pieces of jewelry, a locket, I believe...it's all listed here. Any of the personal effects or furnishings you are to have or to dispose of as you choose, Mrs. Boylett." He smiled. "She joked that you definitely needed two things—feather pillows and her irons."

"She said one day my dress tail could use a good ironing." Lila dabbed at her eyes.

"She noted that Noah Lowdermilk should have her six Rhode Island Reds and the farm implements listed. 'The better to settle him down,' she said. The property itself is in Miss McNeely's name, with you, Mrs. Boylett, as a trustee until she comes of age."

He dipped a pen in the bottle of ink he produced from his sachel. "Mrs. Frady did not know your birth date, Miss, so I must ask that for official purposes before I register the will."

In a small dazed voice, Lila told him. "A year and a little more, then," he said. "Mrs. Boylett, if you have any questions, please do not hesitate to contact me. In Webster anyone can direct you to me."

A silence of two or three minutes ensued. The lawyer studied his papers, fingered his mustache, and waited. Lila appeared incapable of taking in her change of fortune or speaking of it. I, too, had been blindsided by the lawyer's words. I would have assumed a family member, however remote, to be the beneficiary of Maude's "estate."

"This is somewhat extraordinary, Mr. Dietz," I said. "Unexpected, certainly. But so, so like Maude." My voice broke. "I wonder, sir, whether in the months to come, years even, if there is any possibility of the will being contested? Any relatives, any question of undue influence? I—we would not want that."

Lila cast a frightened look at me, then at the lawyer.

"The will is perfectly drawn, witnessed, and signed. Whether she anticipated such a possibility or simply was friends with Judge Halston, she consulted him and he, indeed, witnessed her signing." He stood up. "It's ironclad legal. You need not worry, Mrs. Boylett. And you, Miss Lila, are a woman of property."

When we walked out with him, the men tipped their hats to the lawyer but otherwise barely shifted against the porch posts. I led Lila back inside. "We must tell them," I said. "Better to get it out straight and soon, don't you think?"

"Oh, Sarranda, I can't..."

I poured a cup of coffee to settle my thoughts, and one for her. With my handkerchief, I dried a tear that streaked down her cheek.

We sat in silence. She might have been thinking of the future. I thought of the past. Leaving in my newly-made muslin with the buttons from Frady's store had brought me back to my world, changed though it was and I was.

After a few minutes, we took coffee, some chunks of cheese and soda crackers to the men. They sipped, chewed, and waited.

"Maude's will was a shock," I started.

Noah said, "She told me and swore me to keep it secret." Seeing our surprise, he shrugged. "Well, I am a cousin-in-law of sorts and I can keep my mouth shut." He wiped cheese from his knife. "I'll pick up them Reds and take 'em over to Pearl's this evening. Good layers, they are. Eggs anytime you want 'em."

His words made it easier to relate the rest of the will. The brothers nodded and Rim said, "We'll do what we can to help out."

Lila spoke. "Mr. Lowdermilk, do you think Pearl would come over and stay here at the store for awhile?" She looked at me. "I want to help you at the mill. I won't leave you to yourself in the cabin."

"I'll ask her. Somebody ought to be here." Noah furrowed his brow. "But she'll want to be in on the mill working, too. She likes that rock pickin' better than knitting or sewing."

"What 'bout that Lance's girl?" Jam said. "Didn't think to tell you, Miz Boylett, but her man's been gone fer a week or two. Mean as a striped snake, he was. We heard Lance sent him packing at the end of a shotgun."

"But Noralee's not well," I protested. "She didn't even come to the funeral."

"She's took to her bed, and the baby's crying don't help." Jam held the peach pit he was carving on up to the light and blew invisible particles from it. He must have a string of those carved monkeys by now. "Lance and us don't get along too well, but he told us he's got some widder woman to come live with them. Don't know if she's kin. Don't think so."

"The girl might be glad to get out of that hot house," Rim said. Apparently the brothers had been in

Lance's excessively heated house on business if not friendship.

Lila and I exchanged glances. She had not met Evelyn Louise and I hardly knew her at all, but we could take a chance.

"Thank you," Lila said. "Please, would you send her down sometime, Mr. Rim?" He removed a toothpick before grinning. Lila could not bring herself to call the brothers their Christian names and had settled on Mr. Jam and Mr. Rim.

"If one of you'll come hold the tow sack while I catch them hens," Noah got to his feet, "I'll be a-going on."

If we had been numb with grief at Maude's death and funeral, we were, I think, both stupefied at the lawyer's announcements. We stayed at her place—and it would always be her place— that night, offering to feed the brothers, but they took themselves off to tend to their own affairs. I knew we should be doing something, but after wandering around, sorting some things, touching furniture and objects, we ate a cold supper and then fell asleep before the fire. I awoke with a crick in my neck long before dawn and saw that Lila had simply slept on the floor, her arms clutching a feather pillow. As I stretched my aching back, I thought that she was smart; the rocking chair was not meant for long sleeping. As the sun rose, Lila opened her eyes, befuddled.

We had to bestir ourselves, however, and tend to our business now that three locations needed our attention— the cabin, the store, which would remain the post office until we were otherwise informed, and the mill.

Evelyn Louise walked to the store two days later, her baby Roman in a sling strapped to her side and a rifle over her arm. The walk of several miles must have tired her, but her face was ruddy and she smiled, if a bit nervously, when she announced, "Here I am."

Lance had insisted she bring his old rifle, and she declared she would feel safe sleeping at the store.

Lila, with briskness and authority, demonstrated weighing, packing, making change, and keeping a record of purchases, and Evelyn Louise paid close attention. We saw that she was quite capable, if slow at first, in money matters. The two girls were about the same age, and after Lila held Roman in her arms while Evelyn Louise piled a meager amount of merchandise on the counter to total up, a certain restraint dropped and I could see a friendship beginning. I was glad Lila had a girl to talk to. Occasionally, as I collected and sorted Maude's garments, I heard a giggle from one or the other.

"He's not a-crying much down here," Evelyn Louise said of Roman the next day. She entrusted him to the big arms of the Masseys when they stopped by, and behind the counter she placed quilts in a bushel basket for his bed.

Jam handed Evelyn Louise a wild turkey, ready for beheading. "Miss Lila," he said, "I've got a swap for you, if you're willing to listen."

"What do you mean?"

"A man down yon side of the river's gotta old mare he'll part with, for your donkey and whatever else you can throw in. I've seen the horse and she'll do. Bigger than yours was, 'bout the same age, though. She's trained to the plow."

I joined the circle. "As Josie is not."

"Something else," Jam said, waiting until Evelyn Louise went behind the store to deal with the turkey. "That widder woman at Lance's just plain despises that cook stove of theirs. The stovepipe come apart t'other day and got soot all over the place. The widder wants the stove gone. Lance ain't no happy man. He's tired of them women nagging, threatening not to cook a-tall 'less it's gone."

He said, "We thought you could use it. Told him we'd take it off his hands."

"I'd really like to have it," I said, thinking out loud. "It would mean an extension on the cabin. What a blessing it would be—just think, a kitchen by itself."

Jam nodded. I grinned and clasped his arm. "Knowing Lance, he's not giving it to you."

"Fair exchange, Mrs. Boylett. His wife needs her medicine. He needs his."

Rim added, "Yup."

"I understand. Noah can build the extra room, I'm sure. But, will you two take all the cornmeal you need the rest of your lives in 'fair exchange' from me?"

Protest, they did, until Jam grunted and acquiesced. "Can we stipulate that some times it'll come in cornbread or fritters?"

"Anytime. You two go tell Lila, will you? I bet she'll promise some sweet cakes as well."

That evening, Lila hung one of Maude's quilts on the wall, something I had never thought to do. She sat with her chin in her hands at the table, staring at it, teary-eyed. "I didn't ever think Mrs. Frady..." She ducked her head and started again. "A kind soul, she was, like a granny ought to be. I miss her dearly. I didn't ever think she'd do what she done—did. I must write me mam." For whatever reason, she had not yet told her mother her news.

Trudging home from the mill, an idea had come to me. Now was the time to broach it. "It's too early to make big decisions, Lila," I said, "but do you think your mother would ever come down here, to live here? Perhaps even to see you married? Adelaide could surely find another cook."

"Wouldn't that be grand, Sarranda!" The girl's face lit up, tears banished. "But me da, he'd never... If he comes home, she might not leave him, hurtful as he's been."

"You can think about it." I looked at the crazy patchwork quilt. "That will keep the wind out."

"My head's a-swirl with all that's happening. Maude. Fredrick. Amos. The stove.The store. Fredrick. But at least, no school for awhile."

"No. Who knows when we may have a proper school? Let's go visit that donkey of yours."

Amos made the decision easy. He laid his ears back, brayed, and dared us to touch him. When he snapped his yellow teeth at Lila, she drew back. "Off you go, you ungrateful beast."

"He was a one-person creature," I said. "A horse will be much more useful."

"I can't see Amos liking the plow or the saddle," agreed Lila. And so within the week Sassafras, a large gray mare of gentle disposition, joined Josie who ignored the newcomer and nudged my arm for attention.

Lila took to the horse at once. After brushing her mane, she ran a curry comb along her flanks. "I'll call her Sassy," she said.

"A name totally unbefitting." I rubbed the animal's nose. "Docile as she is."

Rim set about showing Lila how to hook up the plow. After watching carefully, Lila said, "Looks like rigging a ship, it is. Only simpler and lower to the ground." She stood with hands on hips. At Rim's glance, she smiled. "Not that I've ever rigged a ship."

"You're a-making a fine mountain lass." Rim unhitched the plow. "You do it this time." He winked. "Hold this strap in your left hand. Don't let old Sassy get the big head. She might take off like a ship afore the wind."

"I must pen a letter or two, Rim, before you go." I left them to the intricacies of hitching and unhitching the plow he'd delivered from Maude's.

Lila muttered, "Drat. Where does that buckle go?"

Inside I reread part of the letter from Mrs. Whitney's daughter. Her mother's eyesight, she wrote, prevented her writing but we were in her prayers and thoughts.

Miss Bell and her brother are enroute to Asheville as I dictate this letter. She asked me to let you know: Carlyle will need some time to recover. They plan an extended stay in Warm Springs at the hotel there, where he will take the waters. She is most desirous to see you. Is it possible you might meet them in Asheville? She asks you to write to the Fairfields if you can do so. Her brother's health is her first concern, but not her only one. I will say no more. I await your letters.

With all, as Lila put it, a-swirl around us, Adelaide's possible visit had lingered far in the back of my mind. As did her brother. Both brothers. Perhaps I had been remiss that evening in Bramford in saying nothing; at the same time, back and forth my mind went, like a zizzer button on a string or Shakespeare's Dane. To do or not to do. I didn't.

Next time I will not be so girlish and foolish. I will...I will...I will tell him. I must. For my peace of mind. He could be only a remembrance. One I would not erase, but one I could stamp "closed" as if by a waxen seal. I was a woman long grown, who had lived without the company of a man since the war and who could continue to do so in my "later years." And yet, I must know—to free myself of memory's thrall. If the moment came, I would bare my soul to Adelaide and let go of the tenacious memory of the man's touch.

Dipping my pen into the inkwell, I wrote assuring Mrs. Whitney I would attempt an Asheville trip, weather and other circumstances permitting. I did want to see dear Adelaide again; I wondered what, besides her brother's health, her other concern might be.

With Evelyn Louise at Fradys, with Lila happy as a kitten one hour, singing and thinking of Fredrick, and mute and sad the next, remembering Maude, I gave my energies to the mill.

Noah or Pearl came each day; he worked doggedly, she enthusiastically. He stood and studied each problem long minutes, rubbing his hands together. I appreciated his steadiness and agreed he should work on the wooden gear teeth "fer practice in case one breaks afore I've carved one out." He clearly had an eye for detail and a desire for perfection in anything he put his knife to. Pearl also studied the stones. She brought a slate and drew a new pattern for the bed stone. Soon I dared relinquish my beloved Oliver Evans' book for her perusal, and she returned it each day, carefully wrapped in a towel. She said, "I mostly look at the pictures," but I suspected she was continuing to learn to read. She wanted to understand what she saw happening.

I inspected every beam and pulley, tested each stair tread and window ledge, replaced or repaired every nail, bolt, screw, and board that needed it. We could begin grinding soon. Around the edges of Maude's death, people had asked about when the mill would reopen and we promised soon.

Mr. Sanborne was an occasional visitor. When to Lila I described him as "grouchy," she corrected: "Moody." I wondered if he found the shack he'd shared with his brother lonely.

One day he gazed at the mill for some moments before he said, "Shall we sit over there?" He moved toward a log bench on which he'd spread a blanket. "We have some business to discuss."

I seated myself with some dread. My tenure at the mill might soon be over. Watching it being run by another, whether Sanborne or his employee, would cause me more anguish than I wanted to think on. I had berated myself in the past few days when thoughts of turning over the mill to him intruded, called myself silly and stupid—while deep in my heart I knew otherwise. If I had to forfeit the mill, of course, I would; but if he offered me any sort of work there, I feared I would forget my pride and take it.

"You have a...uh...a remarkable regard for this mill, do you not?" He fingered his scar.

"I do. I should hate to give it up."

He crossed his legs and knocked some dried mud from his boot. With the hum of Lila and Pearl's conversation beyond, I squinted at the mill and he stared into space. If he would not speak, having taken me from my work, I would have to break the ice on this millpond. "You know of the mill's ghost?"

"Indeed."

"Shall I tell you how it came to be?"

I was very aware of his attention and small changes of expression as I told him of my last night at the mill, before leaving the valley. Having bribed Old Blue with stolen meat, I had opened the sluice gate, disengaged the pulley so no damage would be done to the machinery, and had set the wheel to turning in a farewell gesture.

I looked him straight in the eye. "It was my way of saying, 'You have not seen the last of me. I am going but I will return.'"

I twisted my hands and shrugged. "I cannot really explain. I would guess Cousin Lance knows I was 'the ghost' or strongly suspects, but to say so would make him look foolish now. You're the second person I've told the ghost story to. Lila knows. She finds it only an entertaining adventure." I trailed off, my thoughts back on Old Blue and the creaking of the turning wheel somehow easing my despair.

"I thank you, then, Mrs. Boylett." He met my eyes briefly but looked away. Perhaps too much emotion showed in my face. "I consider it a gift. We will leave the mill its ghost.

"Now, I must ask you to wait some days or longer for payment due you and the others—I have paid for the materials, no debt there—I am forced to travel to Asheville to advertise, to find a buyer for the mill."

"No! Can you not wait? We can grind within days. The pond and sluiceway—"

"Mrs. Boylett, it grieves me to tell you this. More now that I understand your, uh, abiding affection for the place." His voice was hoarse. "But, as you must follow your bent, so must I confess that milling is not my—not the way I wish to occupy my time. This was my brother's dream. We pooled our resources, sold our pitiful acres to come here. But I will never be a miller."

"What would you be, sir?"

He held out his hands. "As I've said, woodworking is my trade. Cabinetry and fine furniture. I was apprenticed to a master joiner, expecting to become a partner in time. He had no sons. When the war came, he turned to making rifle stocks, wagon wheels—unhappily, I believe. He died just after the war ended. His daughters were quick to rid themselves of his business." He took some time lighting a cigar before he went on. "They offered me some of his tools and I bought what I could with my severance pay. The rest went on the auction block, sold for a pittance." Though the sun hardly cast a shadow, he shaded his eyes with his hand. "Folks, regular folks, were not buying much after the war."

Lila came toward us, looking concerned. She placed her hand on my shoulder. "What is it, Sarranda? Mr. Sanborne?"

"He seeks a buyer for the mill," I said. "Perhaps I will be a schoolmistress, after all."

Before we could sink too far into gloom, he abruptly bade us farewell, saying merely, "I should return within three days' time."

CHAPTER TWENTY-ONE

Back at the cabin, we heard wood being chopped. There was Fredrick, sweating as he swung the axe with perfect rhythm. He finished splitting the chunk and wiped his face. Lila almost fell off Sassy in her pleasure at seeing him and he beamed. Had I not been there, I'm sure they would have rushed into each other's arms. So I greeted Fredrick and, while they looked at each other, led our mounts to the barn. I stayed busy for several minutes and then went for a jar of cool water from the spring. They were speaking earnestly as I went by.

When I returned with the water and cups, they had walked a short distance away and I heard Lila's lilting voice and some lines from "How Can I Keep from Singing." At my footsteps, they came toward me, holding hands. I poured water and handed a cup to Fredrick.

Lila detached her hand from Fredrick's and embraced me with the fervor of a woman in love—and she was. Fredrick looked solemn and sheepish, proud and uncertain—a man in love. Standing before his mother.

"I'm so happy, Sarranda. We're settled to be married...oh, soon, or the fall. It all depends. I won't leave you to manage by yourself. We won't, will we, Fredrick?"

Lila words rushed like a spring freshet, tumbling into the future; she glanced at her betrothed and at me, in a pure flurry. I took her arm and we sat down on a log. "Dear, dear Lila," I said. "Already you are more than a friend, and soon you'll be my daughter. Nothing could make me happier."

That statement was not absolutely true. *The stranger* showing up and looking at me as Fredrick looked at Lila would surely make me happier. Thank goodness Lila could not read my mind, but she noticed my tiny hesitation.

I hurried on. "Don't worry about me. Our lives have been shifting so quickly lately that I don't know what's to happen next." I kissed her cheek and grasped my son's hand. "You will make her happy. I can see it."

"I'll try, Ma," he said. "I've not told, uh, Ma Mack yet." It was the first time I'd heard him call Mrs. Mack that; he was acknowledging all she was to him and letting me know. My boy was a man, his own man. Mine and hers. "Gotta go do the milking. I'll finish cutting wood for you later."

In the early dusk, Lila and I sat on the cabin's porch, both of us tired of the fireside of winter, embracing the chill at the end of April. We talked a little about the future: a wedding date, Maude's place, and the school year. I could teach if need be without a proper certificate. Lila could not quite believe she would be a landed young woman and a married woman. I wondered if she and Fredrick would make their home at the Mack farm or at Maude's place.

"Fredrick would like us to come to church and then to dinner on Sunday," Lila said. "Will it be hard for you?"

"Not so difficult as to make me miserable," I said. "I have no quarrel with Mrs. Mack. I could like her. Of course, we will go."

"I'll be getting two new mamas, won't I?" Lila's smile was shy. "Like Fredrick."

I patted her arm. "I will be just Sarranda."

The congregation at the Universalist meeting greeted us with pleasure. Lila's voice was a joy to hear and she stood proudly beside Fredrick, Mrs. Mack on his other side, and I next to her. I again marveled at the genuine power of the minister's sermon and its healing message. It was a long way, indeed, to come to church but well worth it.

At the Mack farm I luxuriated in the comfortable living room's well-cushioned chair, the aroma of fried ham and peach cobbler lulling my senses. Neither Mrs. Mack nor Fredrick appeared ill at ease as they showed us the house and outbuildings—a quick tour because we were hungry and wished to be home by darkness. Lila said, "I still think about the wild dogs that dark night. Sarranda's braver than me about coming into the clearing."

"Of course, dear," Mrs. Mack said. "Everything is ready for the table."

After an excellent meal, I saw how easily Lila helped with the clearing up and how easily Mrs. Mack accepted her help. They would be good for each other.

John Sanborne flung aside the reins of his horse, glared at the mill, and strode toward me. His lips were tight. Apparently his trip to Asheville had not been successful. But I refused to be downhearted. We had checked everything, done everything except actually grind. This was the big day.

"We are ready to grind," I told him. "But I was reluctant to open the sluice gate until you were here."

Several men and boys stood waiting. Their two wagons were piled with sacks of corn, theirs and their neighbors. They had come the day before and had slept in the wagons, building small fires for coffee, eating from a sack of biscuits and cornbread, whittling. The boys whistled, jostled each other, and spent a lot of time tossing their knives at lines drawn in the sawdust left from the big spruce. Noah had given one exhibition of his skill but then ignored their competition and requests for more demonstrations. Earlier they had meandered through the mill, up to the pond, looked for tadpoles and the big bullfrog. They slid their fingers over the newly dressed stones and peered at the gears and pullies. Pearl stayed nearby in case they had questions, but they were shy about asking a woman anything. Had Sanborne not shown up, the men would have stayed another day, sitting, whittling, and chewing. I was the fidgety one.

"We are ready," I repeated, a bit annoyed at his distracted frown. "We waited for you."

"Damn bankers, same North or South." He muttered an apology for his language. "Go ahead with it. We'll talk later." He turned toward the men and didn't see my thumbs up signal. Lila ran to open the sluice gate, a couple of the boys right behind her. In a few minutes the water poured down the raceway. My heart almost stopped as I listened for the wooden buckets to catch the surge, the wheel to groan and begin the steady rotating.

Somehow, I knew, I simply knew that the wheel would turn without an unbalanced thunk-thunk, the gears would engage, the stones would turn as they should, and all would be well. The men hastened to undo the sacks, readying them for the hopper. The sun was shining on a clean and orderly operation. When Lila reached us, we clasped hands with Pearl for a moment before going inside.

Mr. Sanborne, lounging against a wagon, fiddling with a cigar and looking angry, could resist no longer. He stalked over as Pearl poured the corn into the hopper. A big smile lit my face when the grain ran through a narrow wooden trough slanted to send it into the eye and thus onto the runner stone. We had left the wooden hoop off the stones; Pearl's daughters gazed at the millstones and at her with admiration. Even the boys watched quietly. Pearl's face glowed. I saw Noah pat her butt and saw, too, that she did not notice, so engrossed was she in the turning of her well-dressed stones. I listened intently to be sure the stones were properly adjusted and not touching. I held my breath, waiting. When the first handful of meal came through the chute, I spread my hands under it, rubbed it through my fingers. I nodded, straightened up and breathed again: almost perfect texture.

"Damn, she's done it," one of the men declared. Another grabbed and shook my hand. Their nods were high, if silent, praise.

Jam and Rim glanced at Mr. Sanborne, perhaps to see if he took offense at my getting the credit rather than the owner. He tipped his hat to me, watched a few minutes longer, and walked outside, taking a cigar from his pocket as he went.

Only after several bags of corn had been ground and declared satisfactory did I join Mr. Sanborne near the stump of the old spruce. I would have preferred to stay beside the stones, all my senses attuned to the sound and rhythm of the grinding, but business called.

"Lila and Pearl are taking the toll," I said. "Everything went like clockwork. Perhaps one minor adjustment to the pulleys, but that's easily cared for."

"I commend you, Mrs. Boylett." A slight smile twitched his lips. "You look a happy lady."

"Indeed, I am pleased with the mill and everybody's work." I waved to the departing wagon drivers. "They'll spread the word that Sanborne's Mill is open again."

"Sanborne's folly," he said. "My creditors are like hounds snarling at a possum up a tree, ready to pounce the minute it falls. They think they've got me in a bind."

"And, sir, do they?"

"Aye, pretty much. I can hold off for another month or two. Got a bank draft from a family friend back in Vermont to secure the mill 'til then, but, by all that's blessed, I will forfeit the blasted thing before I'll beg from him again."

"You'd do that? Give it up to the bankers? Lose it?" My hand went to my bosom. Perhaps because he was a man and a Yankee, I had expected him to prevail somehow against creditors and circumstance.

"Aye." He held out his hands. "I'm aching to do something with these hands. Not milling."

He threw his unlit cigar down and ground it to pieces with his boot. "I don't mean to whine, Mrs. Boylett, and I haven't meant to mislead you. You've worked hard—and who knows, the damn bankers may need a miller."

"No, they'd let the place fall down and sell the property," I said. To him, the mill was a financial liability; to me, it was hope resurrected—for me and for the valley.

"There has to be a way," I said. I wanted to enfold him in my arms as a mother would a bullied child; however, I could sympathize with his prickly-pride aloofness and kept my distance.

"Come for supper." The invitation burst from my lips before I thought about what that meal might be. "It's been a trying time for you, and you may need a drink." I grinned. "We can offer you tea or coffee or water."

"Why, thank you, Mrs. Boylett." He glanced up when Lila stopped next to him.

"We have much to tell you," she said. "Do come."

His face cleared. "I'll fetch Boomer, then, and come on over in two hours?"

He left in better spirits than when he arrived. But his news left me in worse.

Lila bustled around the fireplace and the table. Our pantry was practically bare, but one of the men had brought a chunk of ham to swap for grinding his corn, saying, "We got more meat than we got bread, if ye'll take this instead of the toll." With the ham and leftover hominy, she decided to fry fritters and eggs and heat the stewed apples from the evening before.

I was not much help, mostly agreeing with her menu, agreeing that Mr. Sanborne was a fine man, agreeing that he was doing his best. I laid my head against the chimney and closed my eyes. What to do? I could see the man's dilemma. A brother dead because of the mill was bad enough, and to live his life for his brother's dream would kill something of himself. Yet to lose his brother's dream through mismanagement or clever bankers would be devastating to his sense of honor. My thoughts went round and round.

"Sarranda," Lila's voice jarred me from my ruminations. "Wake up! He'll be here lickety split."

I had to smile. Another expression Lila had appropriated. At least, she didn't reprimand me for not helping her or not listening in the last few minutes.

"I'm thinking, dear Lila, I'm thinking—"

At the rap on the door, I jumped up, knocking the chair to the floor. "Dear me," I muttered. "Let him in, will you, while I wash up?" I hurried to the back porch, splashed water on my face, and scrubbed vigorously, partly to bring myself some relief from all my thinking.

Boomer settled at the fireside, and soon his paws twitched in some rabbit hunt. Mr. Sanborne carried a bag of apples. He laughed when his nose and Lila's wave directed him to the steaming apples ready for the table.

"We can never have too many apples, can we, Sarranda?" Her merry laughter was contagious. The evening suddenly promised to be pleasant.

"And this, ladies," Mr. Sanborne pulled from his coat pocket a small bottle. "I may be out of order bringing this. It's hard cider straight from Vermont."

He uncorked and held the bottle for Lila to sniff. "It smells awfully powerful, sir."

I thought he had brought the cider to aid him in forgetting his financial predicament or to improve upon what might be a somber evening. Taking the bottle, I said, "This will surely warm us after supper. Or would you prefer a bit now?"

"After is fine." He rubbed his hands and stood aside while Lila lifted the griddle from the fire. "Fine," he said again.

We ate with great appetites and little conversation. At one point Lila said, "Look." Molly Mouser approached Boomer, instantly awake and alert, with a delicate finesse, pausing to study him before moving closer. Molly curled next to his big paw and their eyes closed. Lila looked ready to cry. Lately her emotions were close to the surface—whether the situation called for giggles or tears. Perhaps she missed her mother and siblings. For sure, she was in love.

"Would that we human beings could be as accepting," Mr. Sanborne said.

"And as trusting," I agreed.

After we ate, I pushed the coffee pot to the center of the fire and we settled before the flames. Lila brought cups for us, announcing, "It will be only a few minutes till it's hot enough."

"Meanwhile?" Mr. Sanborne picked up the cider.

"Oh, Sarranda," Lila said. "Why not? Me dad let us have a taste now and again."

"Why not, indeed." I held out my cup. "Just a smidgen for me, however. I fear it will go to my head, and I want to keep a clear head."

"Isn't your head always clear, Mrs. Boylett?" Mr. Sanborne tipped a few tablespoons of cider into my cup and the same for Lila.

We sipped with caution, at least Lila and I did. "Warms my throat, it does," Lila murmured. We sighed with appreciation.

Mr. Sanborne raised his cup and reflected, "First time T.A. found our uncle's stash, we indulged, ten or so we were. T.A. turned the jug up for a great gulp, got choked and started coughing and spilled a goodly bit. Not to be outdone he drank some more and wobbled toward the house. I had my taste and followed him, just in time to see him keel over." He took a hearty swallow. "Uncle Bran was more upset about what he spilled than what we drank."

I described Rankin and Grandda's special peach brandy. I then turned to Lila, "Don't you have some news for Mr. Sanborne?"

With much blushing, she told him that she and Fredrick would marry. "I never in all the world expected to come down here to find...a farmer!" She sipped again. "I vowed I'd not marry a sailor boy, but a farmer boy—won't Mam be surprised?"

Mr. Sanborne expressed his best wishes and leaned over to lightly brush his fingers across her freckled cheeks. "I'm as proud as if I was your uncle," he said.

"Oh, would you be?" Lila twisted her hair around her fingers. "I don't have any uncles in this country."

"Every girl needs an uncle," I said. "Perhaps he'll give you away at the wedding."

"Delighted to be of use, Miss Lila," Mr. Sanborne said. "Uncle John, shall it be?"

She blushed again and glanced at me. I smiled my approval.

After some moments when I suppose we were all thinking of family, gone or to come, I roused myself and swallowed hard. "I've been thinking."

"So you said before supper, Sarranda." Lila giggled and a small hiccup escaped.

"And you need a clear head?" Mr. Sanborne said.

"I've been thinking, Mr. Sanborne, about the mill and your, ah, situation. I have a proposition to make you. I hope I am still thinking clearly."

"Huh?" he said. "Beg your pardon, ma'am." He sat up straighter, a gleam of humor or interest in his eyes. "A proposition?"

"A business deal," I said, somewhat sternly. "Hear me out."

He set his cup on the hearth. Lila picked up Molly who had wandered over and rubbed against her leg. I took a final sip of cider.

"I want to buy your mill. I have this cabin and twenty acres, free and clear. I will sell it if need be. To buy the mill." I held up my hand as they both opened their mouths to speak.

"I gave the land to Fredrick and he has returned it to me. It is, as he said, poor land for farming except right around the cabin, but it is land." I stopped to catch my breath. "And as Mr. Frady said, 'they ain't a-making no more of it.' Surely a buyer can be found. The Fairfields or Mrs. Whitney may know someone who has more money than need."

"A proposition, indeed!" Mr. Sanborne declared. As if he couldn't quite believe my words, he asked, "Selling your family land—you sure it's not the cider speaking?"

"It's my love of the mill talking." Turning, I saw Lila's stunned expression. "I was thinking while you were cooking. Thinking that yes, this is home, but the mill is more than home. I can't let it go into hands that won't care for it as I can."

"Well." Mr. Sanborne looked around. "Well spoken. But let me think. I would not have you ruined to save the mill—nor do I wish to ruin myself. Let me think." He poured another gurgle of cider, held the cup to his lips, but didn't sip from it.

"Are there hardwoods up your mountainside? Oak, chestnut, walnut?"

I nodded. A moment of panic surged through me—no land, no cabin. Adrift, cut loose from my acres? What had I done? What had I said, committed to? My head cleared. The moment was quickly over. I would have the mill. My real home.

Lila looked from me to him and back again. Mr. Sanborne rubbed his chin. In the ensuing silence, I heard Molly purring in Lila's lap, heard Boomer snort in his sleep, heard an owl screech beyond the barn, heard Josie and Sassy neigh, and heard the coffee begin to boil.

"Oh, let me get that before it spills over!" Lila jumped to her feet, grabbed a towel and removed the heavy pot. "I'll get clean cups," she said. And the spell was broken.

"Nay, use this one." Mr. Sanborne held out his cup. So did I. A few drops of cider wouldn't change the flavor of strong coffee.

Mr. Sanborne stared at the fire. "We may be able to work something out to our mutual benefit," he said. "A swap of sorts—the mill for your property. You know the mill is not paid for and has maybe two acres of land? I'd like to walk your property to see the possibilities for logging, possibly selling some timber."

My hand was shaking when Lila poured the coffee. It was possible. It could be. But I did not want to make a mistake, to do something stupid—even for the mill. I must think further.

I repeated, "A swap?"

"Yes, but more than just that. After we walk the lines and look at the timber, I suggest we go into Webster to see a land appraiser, a good lawyer, and perhaps the bank. Adjustments would have to be made, I should think, so that neither of us feels or is cheated."

He leaned forward, blew on his hot coffee, and took my free hand. "Believe me, Mrs. Boylett, I have no desire to be unfair. I would like to settle in these parts—in spite of T.A.'s death here. There's nothing for me now in Vermont. I crave a quiet life. A life I can control, and that does not include worrying about mill machinery and unhappy workers."

Lila put her arm around my shoulder, but she addressed Mr. Sanborne. "You want to work with wood. A cabinetmaker, you are."

His eyes darkened. "The war, it deafened T.A. Me, I saw the killing and maiming on both sides, was part of it. I did my duty, obeyed orders. We all did. Now I want to try to forget." He sipped his coffee, unaware that he clenched my hand.

When I tried to disengage my fingers, he loosened his grip. "Sorry," he said. "I didn't mean to say all that." He grimaced. "Maybe the cider's talking."

"Let us finish our coffee, Mr. Sanborne, and while the weather is with us, we will see the mountainside and go to Webster. We have business to undertake."

He rubbed the scar on his chin. "Shall I ride over tomorrow morning?"

"You will find me a worthy business adversary," I said lightly.

"Of that I am sure, madam." He stood. "Come, Boomer. Thank you, Miss Lila, for the meal. Thank you, Mrs. Boylett, for your, uh, your proposition."

CHAPTER TWENTY-TWO

With a roughly drawn map of the property my Grandda had deeded to my mother, fortunately among the papers Fredrick returned to me, Mr. Sanborne and I set out soon after dew-dry the next day. He produced a sturdy walking stick of rhododendron perfectly suited to my height, with a curved portion that fit my hand nicely. When I thanked him, he said, "One of mine. It's what I do in the evenings."

"It's beautiful," I said. I imagined him in the old Messer cabin, lonely, carving, creating art from wood. He must miss his brother and feel a solitary soul in an almost friendless community.

"We won't walk the outside property line, Mr. Sanborne. I suggest we zigzag through the woods." I pointed to the map. "You and a surveyor will want to come back," I said, "if we come to a satisfactory agreement."

"Of course," he agreed, "but do you think you could call me John? After all, Miss Lila will do so."

He strode on ahead. I called, "I will do that," adding with some perversity, "once we are beyond this business."

I almost thought of him as a friend. On this day, if this was my final walk through Greene property that was to be Sanborne land, if I sacrificed acres I had not walked over in years for the mill I could not let go, I would enjoy it. I spied a patch of trilliums and beyond some mayapples showing shy flowers. I laughed aloud, whacked at an innocent clump of apple-shrub that snared my skirt, and stumbled.

When he turned with a frown, I yelled, "I don't need any help." I didn't intend to be rescued once again. "Go on," I said, leaning for a moment on the walking stick. "I'm fine."

For a while, we walked side by side, and he stopped to look at the tall straight poplars, to consider the diameters of chestnuts and oaks. The land quickly became steep and I huffed up the slopes, to where he waited. He appeared more at home in my woods than I, commenting on the terrain and trees, identifying and indicating their use or value for furniture or timber sales. My fanciful notion was that the stands of trees were showing off to impress him and me. Maybe that's why I seemed to be smiling as we walked together. I stopped under one fine black walnut tree. I would come back this fall to gather the walnuts—if the trees were there.

"Would all the walnuts go?" The tree was already hanging with small green walnuts, and a pang of conscience swept through me.

"Walnut's good furniture wood," he said, "but no, there'd be selective cutting." He eyed me. "Actually, these woods could do with some thinning. I'd pick trees for my use and supervise the loggers—if we go ahead with our business." His tone implied we were both playing games.

Over three hours later when we trudged back to the cabin, I was bedraggled, sweaty, and scratched. Lila was rinsing bed linens. Clothes hung on the line. The remains of a fire smoldered under the big iron pot from which she immediately scooped up a pail of hot water.

"B'gorry, you look a fright, Sarranda. I'll put this on the back shelf for you. Did you get in a tangle with a bobcat?"

"A fight with some dog-hobble and contrary old raspberry briars," I said.

She considered Mr. Sanborne. "You don't look much better. I'll fix some dinner, soon as I hang this up. There's soup beans and cornbread still warm."

"Ah, lass, I hope Fred knows what a treasure he's getting. I'll congratulate him when next we meet. Here, I'll help." He grasped one end of the sheet she had begun to twist; they wrung it out and Lila pinned it to her clothes line. Then he sat down, wiped his face with a big handkerchief, and took out his cigar.

When Lila handed him a dipper of water, I heard him say, "Damn good stand of timber up there. But don't you tell that woman I said so." They chuckled.

As we ate, we settled on going to town the day after tomorrow. Mr. Sanborne left, and I admitted I needed a rest. "I can stay on my feet all day at the mill, but in the woods—whew," I said and mimicked gruffly, "Damn good stand of timber up there, though."

"Sarranda! You're a wicked one, you are. You lay down for a bit. We can go over to the mill before dark if you want."

"Or if I'm able."

"We'll take Josie and Sassy," Lila said. "Cover up with this quilt. You were pacing around during the night. I heard you."

"Yes, ma'am," I said meekly.

Lila woke me in mid-afternoon and we arrived at the mill while Pearl was still there, along with Jam and Rim. Pearl at once reported all was well. The wheel sat idle; there'd been only two customers so she'd been picking at the mill stone.

The Massey brothers pointed to the mill stone that had been long abandoned in the stream bed; at Pearl's direction they had managed to tie ropes around it and pull it up the bank. "I want to try a new pattern on it," she said, "if it's all right with you."

"Let me see your hands," I said, and she held them out. "You've been busy with that mill bill. Just look at your prickly skin." Minute bits of stone had imbedded themselves in her skin as she'd chipped away. "Put some salve on your hands and arms, Pearl."

I saw their shadows before I realized others were at the mill. When I turned, defensively, the shadows materialized as two young women. They looked vaguely familiar.

"Mrs. Boylett, don't you remember us? I'm Trudy and this here's Lizzie. We come to the mill way back when you was a-runnin' it during the war."

"We're the Russells," Lizzie said. "Well, I'm a Russell. Trudy, she went and jumped the gun on me and married that Obie Hayes."

"He died after five years," Trudy said. "Least we got us a house out of it." Her smile was not that of a grieving widow. She added, "And no babes."

"Guess she just wore him into the ground," Lizzie said. They giggled. "We don't miss him much, 'cept for the cuttin' and cartin' in wood, and we can do that."

"Ah, he was all right," Trudy said. "I was a right good wife from fourteen 'til twenty and now I ain't looking."

"We heard you was back and runnin' this mill for that Yankee man and we come to see if we could help."

"Pearl's showed us around," Trudy said, "but she got busy with that there stone." She waved toward the departing Masseys. "We helped pull that old millstone up the bank, and then they walked us up to the pond."

"That Rim is right nice, ain't he?" Lizzie said. "Stoutish."

"Well, goodness, girls," I said once I had a chance. "Now I remember you." I stood back and surveyed them. "You've fleshed out some, I see, and all grown up." They were sturdy, blond, and blue-eyed, with braids wound around her heads. Youthful Vikings in linsey-woolsey dresses. "How far away are you? Did you walk over? Let's sit down on the steps. This is Lila McNeely, from Massachusetts. Let me talk to Pearl a minute."

The three of them settled on the steps. I walked a few paces away, and Pearl said in a low voice, "They're mighty interested and strong as young fillies. Headstrong, too. That Lizzie's looking—and Rim better watch out. I think they need something to do to keep them outta trouble."

"Spoken like a settled woman," I said. "Could you work with them?"

"Think I could. If they get too feisty, I can show 'em the door." She grinned. "I'm good at that," she said, the only reference she made to her man's leaving or perhaps to Noah's arrival.

"We'll give them a try," I said. "If they suit, tell them we'll have to pay them in tolls at first."

Two days later, on Webster's main street I took time to admire the imposing brick courthouse and to buy Lila a blue ribbon in the general store; Mr. Sanborne waited outside, the very model of patience. We found the lawyer's office a few steps further down the street. Mr. Dietz opened the door, seated us before his desk, and offered coffee. "My mother's down the hall, making it as we speak. She likes to know what's happening in here."

Mr. Sanborne spoke, "Isn't your business confidential?"

"She's been brewing coffee and not saying a word about what goes on in this office, ever since my father died a few years back. Now, what can I do for you?"

Mr. Sanborne turned to me and I outlined the situation: I wanted the mill, he wanted my acreage, we wanted expert advice, legal and financial, and the name of a reputable surveyor. When I finished, Mr. Dietz tapped his pen on the blotter.

"She covered it all," Mr. Sanborne said, "except my lodging. I need to be close to the logging."

"I'll sleep at the mill if need be," I said. "Lila can—"

"Not so fast, Mrs. Boylett," Mr. Dietz cautioned. "No need for that, we'll hope. First things first." He moved a small table between our chairs. "Here's coffee. Thank you, Mother."

Within half an hour, in which I participated almost as if the land I was bargaining with had little to do with me so sure was I that the mill would be mine, we struck a deal, subject to a surveyor's report and other legal necessities and to a period ("Give me a week," Mr. Sanborne said.) of waiting until a timber company provided an estimate on the value of a certain amount of "timber footage" needed to pay off his debt on the mill.

The cabin was a stalling point. Obviously I would leave it if need be; obviously, Mr. Sanborne would not be so mean-spirited as to turn out a widow from her family home. Obviously we could not stay there together. He rubbed his scar while I studied the portrait of George Washington on the lawyer's wall. Apparently both of us wished to be conciliatory at this stage. We spoke at the same time.

"Lila and I can stay at the store with—"

"I can set up a camp—"

"Let me suggest a compromise," Mr. Dietz spoke over our words, his hands steepled beneath his chin. "The store belongs to Miss McNeely, but perhaps she would allow you, Mr. Sanborne, to stay there for the time being. I hear that Lance Greene's daughter is living there, and Lance'd shoot you in a minute if—um, the barn is vacant." He smiled at me. "Yes, I heard Amos is gone. The barn could suit during the warm months, at least. You, Mrs. Boylett, can continue in your cabin until—"

The lawyer leaned forward. "In fact, here is an option we have overlooked. Mr. Sanborne, you intend to sell the place you now own, the old Messer place, do you not?"

Mr. Sanborne grunted. "Have to for start-up expenses. And it's too far for me to supervise the logging."

"Let me put some figures to Obadiah Waller at the bank," Mr. Dietz said. "He may write off some or most of your debt in exchange for the Messer property. The, uh, the house is hardly habitable but the few acres...well, let's plan on seeing Obadiah before the end of the week. I'll ask the surveyor to look at both properties."

He jotted another note. "It may take some time. Banks don't rush." He looked very pleased with himself. "It's worth a try. Never known a banker to turn down a deal involving land. And Obadiah reckons land is more solid than money."

"You're the trustee for Miss Lila." Mr. Sanborne turned to me. "Would she agree? Rent to me?"

"Yes." I thought Lila would never accept reimbursement from her soon-to-be Uncle John. "It sounds a workable solution." With the mill debt-free and mine, I could have a cabin constructed on site. At once I saw it in my mind's eye: below the mill pond, to the right on a rise where a small corn patch had once flourished.

After Mr. Dietz verified our agreements and settled on a date to see the banker, we left his office. Light-hearted, I was almost swimmy-headed. In my first business transaction I felt I had acquitted myself well enough as, in fact, had my "adversary," who had proved decidedly easy to work with. If all went as expected, I would own Grandda's mill; Mr. Sanborne would own my acreage. For awhile, I would stay in the cabin; he would stay in Frady's, or rather, Lila's barn—and the future? Who could know? I would not worry.

A few steps from the town well, I was unaware that I was humming until a few words broke free: "How can I keep from singing...My life flows on in endless song; / Above earth's lamentation, / I hear the sweet, tho' far-off hymn / That hails a new creation."

"If I knew the song, I'd join you, Mrs. Boylett. That's a right pretty tune."

Instantly the words deserted me.

"Miss Rose and Miss Agnes Lynch invited me to have tea with them whenever I came to Webster," I said. "They live at the far end of this street, to the first left. Shall we have tea, John Sanborne?"

"Yes, indeed." He offered me his arm.

"Sarranda," I prompted. It was past time he used my given name.

He laughed. "Sarranda."

Arm in arm we strolled along in the sunshine, I humming a bit, he apparently thinking. After a few moments, he said. "Sawmill."

I stopped humming. "What?"

"You could rig up a sawmill," he said. "It could be another means of profiting from the mill. For both of us."

"Yes, indeed. The mill at Laurel Trace was sawing logs, and my grandfather spoke of sawmilling, but the war put a stop to that. There used to be a sawmill miles over the mountain, but it was, uh, destroyed." My excitement stopped me right in the street. "Yes, I'm sure we can set it up."

John laughed and steered me from a passing oxcart. We interrupted each other, talking of what we would need: costs, machinery, an experienced sawyer, all the possibilities. Talking rapidly, we walked rapidly. "Whew," I said, pressing John's arm to slow down our steps, "This level street is more to my liking than my woods, but I'm no young filly."

He obediently slowed his stride, and I pointed to the home of the Lynch sisters. A horseman on a sleek black mare trotted by and tipped his hat to us. Glancing up, I nodded. Then I whirled around to stare after the rider. I stumbled as I jerked away from John Sanborne. His arm instantly went around my waist and he steadied me against his solid body. Purely a gentlemanly act, yet a tremor ran through me, and I moved only an inch or two away. His natural protectiveness pleased me. I did not want to cling, but I fit quite nicely against him.

"What is it?" His question jarred me away from his side.

"I, I—the man looked familiar." Adelaide and Carly Bell might very well be in Asheville, but was I destined forever to see *the stranger* in every tall, dark man? In the past busy weeks, he had not visited my mind or dreams. As if penetrating a thin fog, this bright sunshine illuminated the truth—our lives were linked by a gossamery thread of memory, not the rope of reality.

"Never seen him or that fine horse around here."

I reattached my hand to John Sanborne's arm and, without a thought of the quality of my voice, surprised myself: "I hear the music ringing; / It finds an echo in my soul— / How can I keep from singing?"

Fortunately, the Lynch sisters were home and delighted to share their afternoon tea with us. They made a fuss over my companion, seating him in the large rocking chair so that the sunlight shafted by him and not into his eyes. He allowed the fluttery attention and said, "Not since my dear mother passed have I been so well tended to, ladies."

"Mrs. Boylett, you are positively radiant. The walk and sun have brought color to your cheeks." Agnes settled a cushion behind my back.

"I hardly recognized you," Rose allowed. "Only a few months ago, you left us in a weary state, travel pale you were."

"I am indeed a happy person—"

"She cannot keep from singing," Mr. Sanborne announced.

"Today," I tried to glare at him, but his impudent grin drew one from me, "today, we have started a business transaction sure to keep us both busy," I said. "But I shall keep mum until Mr. Dietz completes his work."

"Dear Mr. Dietz," Agnes said, "He and his mother are friends of long standing. We shan't question you, then."

"Though we are naturally curious," Rose said.

"This woman has been managing the mill, old J.S.Greene's mill, and she's got three or four women working for her, plus one at the store," John said. I smiled, grateful for his kindness in returning the mill to my grandfather's name. He sounded proud of me. Embarrassed and pleased, I said nothing.

"Isn't that what you had in mind, Mrs. Boylett?" Agnes asked. "I remember our conversation of some months ago. You and the lass told us why you came back here."

Rose patted my shoulder as she might a child who had fulfilled a promise. Strange, only at that congratulatory pat, did I realize that I had indeed accomplished a mission worthy of my return. They weren't weaving, sewing, or basket-making, but women in Greene's Valley were learning, doing, coming into their own—running a store, picking mill stones, teaching school.

I found myself smiling and tearing-up at the same time. The three looked at me in consternation. Tears rolled down my face, right into the corners of my mouth. Salt had never tasted so good. But I didn't intend to blubber or wallow in happiness. I was a strong and rational business woman. I straightened up and reached for my reticule. John Sanborne whipped out a handkerchief and handed it to me with a flourish.

"Lord, woman," he said, "this is not the first time I've had to provide for you!"

Drying my eyes I chuckled. The sisters tittered and looked at John. Soon I was chattering away, telling them about Lila, Pearl, Trudy, Lizzie, and Evelyn Louise at the store. John Sanborne threw in comments along the way about a few men helping out, and the afternoon sped by.

A "Hallo" came from the front porch. A Yankee and feminine voice. Surprised, Agnes pulled back the curtains. A buggy sat in the street, and we heard a knock.

"We're not expecting anyone," Rose headed for the front door.

"They said sometime this week or next." Agnes poked her head into the kitchen, gave instructions for more hot tea, and joined her sister in the hallway.

"It's Adelaide!" I jumped up. "Adelaide Bell."

She came in to embracing, handshaking, and introductions all the while divesting herself of a lovely cloak and hat. I noted that, though her outer garment was black, her dress was a moss-green. In a few minutes we were again seated and more tea was on its way.

"Sarranda, dear Sarranda, I did not expect to see you today. Your mountains have certainly agreed with you. You must tell me all. Your letter reached us in Asheville, and we thought to come on here. We intended to see you at Greene's Valley within a few days. My brother Carly is in the buggy. He preferred to wait until I said my hellos. The ride was tiring for him. We will stay at the inn—"

"Indeed, not!" Rose objected. "We have rooms prepared for you, upstairs. You must stay here." She laid a hand on Adelaide's shoulder as if to physically restrain her.

"We haven't had such excitement in months," Agnes decreed. "And you will find our beds most comfortable."

John Sanborne took his watch from his pocket, a none-too-subtle reminder that we were not staying the night in Webster. I clasped Adelaide's hands in mine. How glad I was to see her! I told her so. And to see that she was not wearing mourning black. I told her that, as well.

"We must be on our way," I said. "Please visit us as soon as you can. We have much to talk about and show you. I'll say hello to your brother on our way to the livery stable."

When the Lynches' niece brought fresh tea and gingerbread for Adelaide, we quickly made our farewells. At the buggy, John spoke to the driver and I peered inside the collapsible hood. A pale Carly slouched against the cushioned back. He opened his eyes and blinked. "I have seen you," he started.

"Hello, Carly." I introduced myself and offered my hand. "How are you?"

"The mountain air suits me," he said. "It's good to see you. Adelaide is looking forward to spending time with you."

For a few minutes he spoke of the sanitarium in Asheville and their stay in Warm Springs with its sulphureous waters and grand hotel. The time there had been good for Adelaide, he said; she had declared she could live there, so peaceful she found it. "And," he shrugged, "she thinks some place other than Bramford would be good for me. Perhaps she is right. Since that beating, our hometown has lost its appeal."

John Sanborne's hand at my elbow reminded me that the sun was disappearing beyond the Plott

Balsams and that we should depart. I repeated my invitation to visit and said goodbye to Carly.

The warm livery stable smelled of horses and hay, sweat and urine. I waited just inside the entrance while John went for our horses. The rider who had passed us on the street, his back to me, was apparently arranging for the stabling of his black mare. The stable boy led the mare away and returned to hand John the reins of our mounts.

John and the man came toward me, and through the dust of the late afternoon sunlight I faced *the stranger* I'd thought of through the years, remembered through the seasons, seen months before. Fortunately my heart didn't show and I schooled my face to reveal no emotion, as I had done when marauding bands of ruthless men showed up to threaten, steal, or worse during the war.

But my hand went instinctively to my shoulder, and he, like a mute echo, touched his upper left arm. I stood Indian-still and he stopped a few feet away. His hand massaged his arm. Whether he recognized or thought he knew the woman staring at him, I was unsure.

John held out Josie's reins toward me but my left hand was at my shoulder, the other at my heart. He looked from me to the stranger.

"You two know each other?" His voice sheared through my inertness and I grasped the saddle horn.

"Lavender," the man said, under his breath.

"Her name's Mrs. Boylett," John said as if he owned it.

I smiled at his brusqueness and the man smiled in amusement or arrogance.

"Sarranda Boylett," I said.

"And have we met? It seems so, but I have a poor memory for names."

"We met—we were at the same party, the Beckleys' home in Bramford, last fall."

Realizing that John's gaze shifting from one to the other of us was not friendly, I stepped back and bumped into Josie's flank. She snorted and, glad for her interruption, I grabbed her reins and led her outside. I felt John's scowl boring into my straight back. He followed and so did *the stranger*, stopping at my side.

"Addison Bell is my name, madam." He clamped a soft brown felt hat on his head. His face was somewhat gaunt, his mustache and sideburns trimmed, and his hair streaked with gray and longish, as I remembered it. I could not "renew" our acquaintance under these circumstances, with John Sanborne glaring at the mountains beyond me, and a cool wind rising from the North. "You are Adelaide's friend?"

"Yes, we were at the Lynch home when she and Carly arrived. Now we must start for the valley." I allowed John to assist me into the saddle before saying, "Will you perhaps escort them when they visit us?"

"Perhaps."

Neither his husky voice, polite and steady, nor his gray eyes indicated any memory of me. But then, I concluded from his behavior the night he knocked at my cabin and from Adelaide's reticence that he had been trained for more than ordinary soldiering. Trained to keep his expression neutral. He touched his hat and turned toward the other end of town. John mounted with a great huff and a jerk of his reins.

The ride back was long and silent. I had plenty of time to think. Flitting through my mind, however, were not thoughts, but images like stragglers from warring armies, uncertain, swarming, advancing, retreating. I remembered my need, the stranger's body awakening mine to the realization I was a woman worthy of a man's desire, giving and getting pleasure. Three children called me mother but no husband had treated me with such consummate skill and consideration. A practiced lover, *the stranger* left me feeling as if I were the only woman he had ever so touched. Yet I knew it was not so. If, deep in my heart, I hoped to repeat that night, it was hardly the stuff to live on. Now I had my son's regard, friends in the valley, the lawyer's respect, John's admiration, and especially the mill—my mill—to run. I could foresee possibilities for happiness attached not to one night in the past but to whatever I brought to the future.

It was dark when we halted at the crossroads where I had met John that morning. "I can go from here," I said. "Thank you for—"

"Damn it, woman, I'm not sending you on alone." He removed a lantern from his saddle bag and lit it, muttering to himself that he'd expected to be back before dark. Perhaps I should have apologized but I thought he enjoyed grousing about our delay.

"They know their way from here, but a light helps." He nudged his horse, and Josie fell in behind him.

His solicitous behavior warmed my heart. He couldn't see my face, but I said, sugar-sweetly, "Thank you, then. Lila will have a hot supper for us."

CHAPTER TWENTY-THREE

Lila greeted us like a mother hen gathering her wandering chicks under her wing. "Worried I was, wasn't I?" she said, "when you weren't back by dark. Them dogs." She shuddered, whether in real fright or exaggeration. "Supper's ready."

John smiled at her bustling around, taking charge.

Within minutes she dished up bear stew from the Masseys. "They'd cooked it before they brought it over," Lila said. "Not like lobster, they said. It's been over the fire for hours. It's to celebrate your dealings."

"Good and tender," John pronounced it.

I told Lila all about the lawyer's office, and our expressions told her we were pleased with the likely outcome. John, she said, could stay at the store as long as need be.

"This woman knows how to bargain, but we'll both benefit, provided the d—dang bankers don't give us trouble," he said.

"Don't puff me up with pride." His words brought a warm glow to my face and I changed the subject. "The big surprise was Adelaide and Carly showing up at the Lynch sisters."

After I told her of our brief visit, Sanborne shifted in his chair, grunted and fingered his scar. When he tapped the table with impatient fingers and stared at me, I knew he was not satisfied with my summary. I muttered, "Adelaide's other brother is in town. Escorting them, I suppose. He may very well come out when they visit."

Lila looked bewildered at my mutinous tone. John Sanborne frowned at his plate as if a look would wipe it clean.

"Have you met him, Sarranda? I never saw him at her home."

"I met him, briefly," I said. "In Bramford." I ignored John Sanborne, saying, "Adelaide will be wonderfully surprised to find you an engaged woman of property, Lila."

"No more than me," she said.

I stood and began collecting our dishes. "It's been a long day."

At once John rose, thanked Lila, and pulled on his coat with irritation, a shift in mood I could not interpret. I had enjoyed his company and surely our day was a successful one. I had not behaved improperly toward Carly or his brother. Why should he be angry at me?

At the door, I asked that question. He said merely, "Good night, Mrs. Boylett."

Two days later, Jam and Rim dropped by the mill to tell us they would deliver Adelaide and Carly the following day; their light, hired buggy, Rim said, was not a suitable vehicle for the rough road. They brought eggs from Pearl's hens, tea and coffee from the store, and butter bartered from one of their customers.

When Adelaide and Carly arrived, we were well prepared for their visit. I had made a molasses cake studded with black walnuts, a ham hock and bean soup simmered on the fire, and Lila's biscuits and cornbread sat warming to the side.

The gray day was damp and drizzly, but the brothers had rigged a canvas on their wagon to keep our visitors dry. The brothers took no notice of the light rain.

Jam and Rim each took a hand to help Adelaide alight and did the same for Carly.

"We'll go on over to the mill, Mrs. Boylett," Rim said. "Come back fer your company afore dark."

"My brother Add is coming behind us," Adelaide said, as we brushed cheeks. "He had business to attend to before leaving Webster."

It is time, and past time...I couldn't finish the thought in the bustle of settling our company inside and showing our accommodations. Dear Adelaide showed no surprise at the smallness of our cabin or scorn at its sparseness. She seemed quite at home, warming her hands at the fire, admiring the quilt on the wall and the holly boughs we had stuck in a crock beside the door. Lila wore the shawl Adelaide had given her and Adelaide's glance acknowledged it. Amid much exclaiming and laughter about the trip, the weather, the towns of Webster and Asheville, we had our mid-morning coffee. Then Adelaide caught us up on the ladies' circles. They had sent two women to a settlement school in Kentucky and felt that was the extent to which they could commit. "With the urging of Susanna and her father, they are doing more to feed and educate Bramford's own youngsters," Adelaide said. "And rightly so, don't you agree, Sarranda?"

"I do," I assured her. "We're grateful for their help, but we don't expect further assistance from them. I know that I did not suit their purposes, but so be it."

"Charity begins at home," Carly stated, "or wherever one best can work." He smiled at Lila who simply nodded.

"My mother always said, 'Sweep around your own front yard before you go raising dust in another's,'" I said, "but that might mean refusing to see the needs beyond your door."

"Tell us all," Adelaide commanded. "Your both seem comfortable and content." Her voice held a touch of envy. "You have found your way."

Soon Lila was showing them the quilt top she was piecing from Mrs. Burton's scraps, and I was telling them of the mill. We stopped to put dinner on the table, gratified that both Carly and Adelaide had good appetites. We were still seated at the table when we heard the squishy sounds of hooves in the mud.

Addison Bell called, "Hello. The Boylett place?"

Lila jumped to her feet and met him at the door. He hung his coat and hat on a peg on the porch and entered with a bow. "Mrs. Boylett, we meet again," he said. I introduced Lila who handed him a towel to dry his face and hands.

He declined food, but took a cup of coffee and remained standing by the fire while we finished our cake. His presence seemed to subdue our spirits somewhat. Adelaide and Carly were less lively, and I did not attempt to engage him in small talk. Indeed, I avoided his eyes and hoped that he was not surveying the cabin through his memory, not seeing me as the lavender-scented woman bedded at night and left before dawn. As if aware of our change of mood, Lila talked with enthusiasm about Greene's Valley.

"'Tis a wondrous country, it is," she said. "I don't believe I could be happy now near the ocean. If only me mam and the others could be here," she hesitated. "I'd be the happiest person, wouldn't I? I'm to marry soon." Blushing demurely she accepted their congratulations and was properly reticent about Fredrick's fine qualities. When she saw our smiles, she stuttered to a halt, and grinned. "I'm thanking me lucky stars, am I not, Sarranda?"

"He's surely thanking those same stars," Adelaide said and we laughed.

"I should like to hear more of the school, Miss McNeely." Carly held his hands palms up as if to receive a gift. "I am in need of a wondrous country."

"You could teach at the school!" Lila glanced at me. "Couldn't he, Sarranda, I mean if, if—"

"Indeed, if Greene's Valley gets a school," I said. "The need is certainly here, and Lila and I may not continue teaching once—" I spread my hands and finished, "Once she is married and I am a miller."

On Lila's face, I think I saw the same question that I wondered about. Married to Fredrick, could she continue teaching? Could she travel across the state for more education? Could or would Fredrick sanction that sort of freedom for his bride?

"I would have more education, wouldn't I, if it's possible," Lila said. "It may very well be." She said to Carly. "We would make a school teaching team, we could."

I squeezed her hand and Carly gave her a grateful grin. "So, it may be, Miss Lila. So it may be. As you said, it's a wondrous country."

"And if not here," Adelaide said, "We learned of an academy in Webster that has a fine reputation."

While the talk flowed on and I joined in as needed, I was always sensible of Addison Bell's tall figure near the fire. *Unfinished business.* I feared if I met his eyes I would ...what? I knew we must talk, privately.

"I need some air," I said. "Could I show you our horses, Mr. Bell?" I moved toward the peg where my cloak hung.

"And Molly Mouser," Lila instructed, blinking in surprise.

"Of course, Mrs. Boylett." Addison placed his empty cup on the mantel and pushed open the door for me.

We walked rapidly through the fine mist. Perhaps the outside air sufficiently cleared my head. I felt calm and detached.

In the stable, I saw he had removed two heavy saddlebags from his mare and slung them over Josie's half-door.

"Madam," Addison said, before I could formulate a single word, "Mrs. Boylett, you have me at a disadvantage, I fear."

"How so, Mr. Bell? What do you mean?" I had meant to confront him, but now I waited to hear what he made of our "acquaintance."

He studied me in the semi-darkness of the barn, drumming his fingers on one of the saddlebags. Rather than answer, he said, "I am commissioned to a post in the West, Indian territory. There is some difficulty—I must leave at once, having delayed longer than my superiors liked in order to see my sister and brother safely to North Carolina."

Leaving? At once? Either relief or anger—or both—weakened my legs and I grasped one of the logs. His words shouldn't be surprise. Hadn't Adelaide said of him, "He is always disappearing"?

"I see." I repeated like an idiot, "You leave today. For the West?"

"Forgive me if what I say seems outlandish, even inane," he said, "but there is something, something about you. I have twice been reminded of the scent of lavender when you are near." His eyes followed the kitten, nosing several feet away.

"Lavender is a common enough scent," I managed. I had never worn it again.

"Not to me. I will be blunt, Mrs. Boylett. Have we met before Bramford? I know it was you in the garden that evening. I sense a connection, yet I cannot recall another specific—"

I touched his upper arm and let out a breath. In that gentle touch, I let him go. Go, he would, in any case, but I could release him from my fantasy. I could free myself.

"We have indeed met, a fateful night. I sewed up this arm." My right hand still grasped the log while the fingers of my left lay lightly on his coat, so lightly I did not feel the flesh beneath. "Several stitches were required." I kept my voice as light as my touch. "And some liquid medicine to cleanse the wound."

"The wound was cleanly treated and adequately stitched, according the doctor." His eyes darkened. "I was down with a fever for days afterwards, somewhere near Jonesborough. When finally I reached...my camp, they said I was out of my head, mumbling nonsense though they caught the word 'lavender.' And I associate its scent with, well, with a pleasant time, but my memory of such a time has not surfaced."

He drew himself up in a severe military bearing. "So I must ask, if you will forgive the ungentlemanly question, was there more to the night? More than tending to a wound?"

"There was," I said.

He clamped his hand on mine. "I did not, surely I did not..."

"Please do not think badly of yourself." I removed my hand from the rail. "You did not force me." My voice was even and I met his eyes. *With the blinders off.* "Let us say the need was—was there for both of us. I tended to your need and you to mine."

I had never spoken so boldly to any man, but in his troubled eyes I saw that I must free him from any guilt he might feel for having taken advantage of a lonely woman. I said, blunt as a rusted axe, "You behaved as I would have you behave—and left me different than you found me."

"I don't know exactly what you mean, but I take you at your word," he said. "Somehow, I feel a, uh, a connection, felt it across a room, in the garden, in Webster, and here, but...maybe the fever and the hospital stench, the smell of cauterized flesh, and rotting limbs...maybe I lost something along the way." His military bearing loosened and he leaned for a moment against the log wall. He turned to pick up the saddle bags. "But I remember lavender."

"Adelaide knows nothing of our encounter," I said. "You remember but a scent. I am the keeper of that night—for me." Again I touched his arm. "And you are truly going away?"

"Yes, I must, to Apache land. I am not one to linger anywhere, to my sister's sorrow. My brother understands, I think, my inability to settle to a, well, to a settled life. Do you mind that I shall take my leave now of Carly and Adelaide." He offered a tentative smile. "I'm a coward at saying goodbye. Leave-takings are hard for me. I prefer to slip away."

Yes, I thought, that you do. This time you go with my knowledge and acceptance. "I shall send them out to you," I said.

"Thank you. Sarranda, if I may call you that." His stare did not unnerve me. Our night together might some day surface in his memory. Perhaps not. I would not know. "Thank you" he said, "for tending to my arm."

Walking from the dimness of the barn, I looked back at his silhouette. "Goodbye," I said, and more softly, so softly I don't expect he heard, "Thank you to tending to me."

As I returned to the cabin, the April rain softened and warmed my face.

When Adelaide and Carly sat again at our fireside, I believe she realized that something of consequence had transpired between their brother and me. She would not ask this day. Sometime I might tell her, but not now. While Lila answered Carly's questions about the school, she looked long and hard at me.

It was Lila who asked Adelaide, "Do you become accustomed to his leaving? To not knowing where or how your brother is?"

"He has ever been so," Adelaide said. "We cannot change him. The war made him even more a loner and we must leave him be."

"Even when we were children," Carly said, "one moment he'd be playing Red Rover Red Rover and the next he'd be gone." He shrugged. "Our brother Johnson tried to beat some sense into him when he left us unattended at the swimming hole, remember, Sister? It didn't work."

I listened to their childhood reminiscences with a calmness of spirit. Hearing Addison Bell's name did not bring a surge of longing or a flash of sensual memory. He was gone and I would likely never see him again. And I would not be seeking him in memory or dreams. He was gone and I was here, not unhappy that he rode west, not bereft.

I saw Adelaide give Carly a significant look at a lull in the conversation, and he at once said, "Ah, Miss Lila, will you show me your garden plot? I am encouraged to walk more than I do. Is it far to that mill?"

"Too far to go today," Lila replied. "But we can enjoy the April air. The rain has stopped."

I sensed my friend had news of a personal nature, but her composed face did not tell me whether it was good or bad. She bit her lip.

"Tell me, dear Adelaide, what of your Colonel Morris?"

"Oh, I have much to consider," she responded quickly. "Carly knows but a little, Addison naught. You are the only woman I feel I can confide in about this matter."

Her eyes glowed but her smile seemed wry, even cynical. If I had my secret, she surely had hers as well. "Whatever you tell me," I said, "you know I will not divulge."

"Colonel...Franklin Morris has told me of a wife. An Indian wife, as was the rumor. Last month, he was called away and upon his return, he revealed that she had died in a fearful smallpox epidemic, as had most of her family."

"I am sorry." I reached for her hand. "Then he is now free."

"Free? Yes. Perhaps. There was—there is a child, a girl, certainly his. She is four years old. For the time being she stays with the family of the commander at the fort. But that is only a temporary measure."

"And he, your colonel, cannot abandon her and cannot—"

"He has asked me to marry him, Sarranda."

"And have you accepted his proposal?"

"It is one reason we came here. Not the only, of course. Carly's health required it, but my uncertainty was a factor. I needed time away from Bramford."

I reflected for long moments before asking, "You are unsure of his motives or unsure of your love?"

"I have cared for him," she hesitated, "loved him for some time, but I do not wish to be married as a convenience for him."

"Adelaide, I have not met your Colonel Morris, but all you have said portrays him as an honorable man. Does he now strike you as less than that? As a man who would marry for convenience? Couldn't he have done that and no one the wiser all these years?" I stared into her eyes. "You must follow your heart."

"There is more, Sarranda. Franklin's family knows of his 'indiscretion,' so they deem it. His brother is arranging for the sale of the family mills. They are not very profitable now, at any rate. He proposes to buy Franklin's share before the sale, offering a pittance, I'm sure."

I stood and poured more strong coffee for us. If ever I have seen a conflicted face, it was hers. For a few minutes we sipped the hot coffee.

"He will be less prosperous," I ventured. "Does that bother you? Is it the child? I'm sure you can manage 'the slings and arrows' of Bramford gossip should you accept the colonel."

"Yes, I could do that, and there would be sufficient, if not ample, income. We could manage." She lifted her eyes to meet mine. "I am not beyond the years of child-bearing. Yonaki, that is her name, might not be our only child."

Her words revealed that she had made her decision, I realized, and surely so did she, for she hurried on, "However, Franklin's family is urging him to consider immigrating to Canada, perhaps Nova Scotia. Somewhere. They want him beyond the reproach of their community. And I believe he wishes to be beyond their condemnation. As I wish him to be."

With a settled air, she set the cup on the mantel. "Sarranda, this is the worst coffee I have tried to drink this week!"

We laughed together. "It is strong, indeed."

Carly and Lila opened the door as I said, "Somewhere could mean North or South, Adelaide." I hugged her. "You know, deep in your heart, what you must do. As do I, as did I."

At her inquisitive look, my attempt at a sisterly sternness faltered to a gentle smile.

With an animation lacking at the beginning of our talk, she said, "I knew I had only to speak with you to know my mind."

"Your heart," I whispered.

After Lila hung up her coat, she gestured toward the coffee pot. Adelaide and I shook our heads. "The Massey brothers will drink it." I said, "Their stomachs are cast iron."

As if we'd beckoned, we heard their wagon coming into the clearing and soon their heavy boots on the porch. Lila had the coffee poured for them as they entered.

"Brought more company," Rim announced. "Met up with him at the mill, a-studyin' on fixing up a saw mill, he said."

John Sanborne stood in the doorway, Boomer behind him. Both were damp. Boomer sent water droplets flying on the porch. John appeared distant and morose. He shook his head at Lila's offer of coffee.

There was much ado as the Bells bundled themselves up against the damp, and the Masseys downed their coffee. John and Boomer stood aside as we assured our friends of another visit and bade them goodbye. John had nothing much to say, merely that he was going to Webster for supplies. With a backward look, he touched his hat to us and assisted Adelaide into the wagon.

After we put the cabin to rights and settled down, Lila gave me a sly look. With a flourish, she picked up the volume of poetry, flipped through its worn pages, and read aloud: "My heart leapt up when I beheld—"

"You're misquoting that, young lady!" My face reddened like a fourteen-year old's.

Drawing herself up like proper schoolmarm, she shook her finger at me, eyes sparkling. "If your heart could have leapt right out at that man, that John Sanborne, it would have. 'Course, gentleman that he is, he pretended not to notice. But he noticed all right." She looked at the page and grinned. "A rainbow in the sky"...hmm...so let it be when I grow old or I will—Oops."

"Still misquoting! Show some respect for your future mother-in-law, if you please." Grinning right back at her, I picked up my worn Oliver Evans book. "I've got some reading to do on sawmills."

Two of my favorite grist mills in Western North Carolina, both lovingly restored by family members and both capable of grinding.

FRANCIS MILL (1887)
Owner: Tanna Timbes
Address: Hugh Massey Road, Waynesville, NC 28786
www.francismill.org

DELLINGER MILL (1867), with Apple House in background
Owner: Jack Dellinger
Address: Cane Creek Road, PO Box 1125, Bakersville, NC 28705
www.dellingermill.com

These books about mills and milling have been helpful:

Evans, Oliver. *Young Mill-Wright & Miller's Guide.* Originally published 1795, many reprints.

Zimiles, Martha and Murray. *Early American Mills.* New York: Bramhill House, 1973.

Kalman, Bobbie. *The Gristmill.* New York: Crabtree Publishing, 1990.

Macaulay, David. *Mill.* Boston: Houghton Mifflin, 1983.

Other works read and appreciated:

Barnett, Phyllis Inman. *At the Foot of Cold Mountain: Sunburst and the Universalists at Inman's Chapel.* Pigeon River Press, 2008.

Langley, Joan and Wright. *Yesterday's Asheville.* Miami: E. A. Seemann Publishing, 1975.